Sandfires

Tom Crothers

Dream Catcher
PUBLISHING

Copyright © 2010 Tom Crothers

First printing – November 2010

All rights reserved. No part of this publication may be reproduced or transmitted in any form or by any means – electronic or mechanical, including photocopying, recording or any information storage and retrieval system – without written permission from the Publisher, except by a reviewer who wishes to quote brief passages for inclusion in a review.

DreamCatcher Publishing acknowledges the support of the Province of New Brunswick.

CIP available from Library and Archives Canada Cataloguing In Publication program

Crothers, Tom, 1932-

Title: Sandfires / Tom Crothers

ISBN 978-0-9865278-2-1

Printed and Bound in Canada

Typesetter: Michel Plourde

Original Cover Artwork: Daphne Irving

Graphic Art: Cynthia Perry

Editors: Tara Finnigan and William Eifler

Please Note:
Sandfires is a work of fiction; therefore, any similarities to real persons living or dead is purely co-incidental.

55 Canterbury Street, Suite 112
Saint John, New Brunswick, Canada
E2L 2C6
Tel: 506-632-4008
Fax: 506-632-4009
dreamcatcherpub@nb.aibn.com
www.dreamcatcherpublishing.ca

Dedication:

I dedicate this work to the memory of Milton Acorn. Milton was a man who could take our measure without malice, whether on his Island or the planet, and grace us with insights in poetry.

...
Nowhere that plowcut worms heal themselves in red loam; spruces squat, skirts in sand or the stones of a river rattle its dark tunnel under the elms, is there a spot not measured by hands;
from "The Island" Milton Acorn, Canadian Poet

Acknowledgements:

I wish to thank the following people for their willingness to read the manuscript of Sandfires and to comment, critique and encourage: Angelo Rizacos, Betty Ponder, Warren O'Rourke, Rosalind M. Gill, the late Suzanne Wallis, Jenifer Erlendson and Conrad Beaubien. I'd also like to thank Tara Finnigan, Acquisitions Editor for DreamCatcher Publications, for her precise and insightful editing; and as always, my love and appreciation goes to my wife and editor, Bessie, whose involvement gives so much pleasure and help.

Praise for Sandfires

Jenifer Erlendson, DLIT:

"*Sandfires* is an excellent example of a truly Canadian novel. Not only does it entertain—with its mile-a-minute action—but it also educates the reader about our nation's not-so-distant past.

Tom Crothers is a good storyteller. His characters jump off the pages and refuse to leave the reader long after the covers of the novel are closed.

Sandfires is a novel with remarkable insight into the consequences of entrenched family secrets and intrigue. It pits the question of what is moral against what is right in a fast-changing post World War One, Canada. The characters struggle with conflicts and conceits that are recognizably modern, reminding us that although the costumes and props may change, the complicated nature and fallibility of humanity is eternal."

Rosalind Gill:

"This book is a page turner. The reader's attention… is maintained by all kinds of unexpected and intriguing twists and turns, as we watch the characters face the music of their own lives and of their own imperfect selves.

The storyline…is rich and intricate, and the uncompromisingly honest and deeply humanistic portrayal of the book's characters captivates the reader.

There is an integrity and unity in the writing that makes the Canadian context a breathing character in itself…The overall effect of *Sandfires* is the urgency of human compassion, of attempting to understand ourselves and to understand others."

PART ONE

One

Ice Storms and Deathbed Promises

Charles and Elizabeth Ewart were dying. They lay together, tallow faced and smothered in quilts, their room breathy and humid with sickness. Their bed had been pushed so close to the roaring fire it blistered the varnish on the bedposts. To aid their failing respiration, a brownish liquid in a large copper pot steamed out an unpleasant, sweet-smelling vapour; and on either side of the bed, two pails covered with cheesecloth stood ready to receive whatever manner of fluid might come from their sick bodies. A lamp stood on a pine table stained with rings of lamp oil, and the family Bible lay open at Psalms. When the wind outside found a chink in the wall, the flame flickered. For a month now, storms had dumped tons of snow on the Island and covered everything in a membrane of ice. It was said to be the worst winter in living memory.

Sarah, their eldest daughter quietly entered the room to check on them. The old man opened his eyes and said her name. The firmness of his voice surprised her.

"Yes Father?"

"Get Ruth up here, I need to talk to the two of you."

She left the room and shouted down, "Ruth! Get up here right away, Father wants us."

Ruth joined her at the top of the stairs.

"What do you think he wants, Sarah?" she whispered timidly.

"I don't know, but don't you dare act like a baby."

Ruth whimpered and Sara shook a warning into her, "I told you, now. Get a grip on yourself. C'mon."

They stood on either side of the bed. A lifetime of rough talk and threats from the old man made them anxious, and they still expected him to roar at them. Ruth bit her bottom lip to keep it from trembling. She wanted to weep but Sarah's glare forced her not to. Their Mother smiled encouragement at them. The Father's lips moved silently for a few seconds, and the girls strained forward to listen.

"Need to talk, but first Divine guidance."

They knelt, and reached over the counterpane clasping their parents' hands. Their outstretched arms formed a perfect transept across the bed. The fire was hot on Sarah's back, and she wished the ordeal would be over soon.

He started with, *Our Father who art in heaven*, and the girls joined in, careful not to get ahead of him when he paused to cough or catch his breath. He then went into an entreaty:

"Dear Lord, we thank Thee for Thy bounty. For the benefits Thou has bestowed upon us of past health and fortitude to face adversity. Keep these girls on the path of purity an' keep them dutiful daughters even while we are in death. Strengthen their women's weaknesses so that they may do Thy will. We are heartily ashamed of our sins and ask Thy forgiveness in the name of Thy Son, Jesus."

Sarah could feel the sweat glue her bodice to her back while the old man spluttered and spoke as best he could.

When at last finished, he whispered in a phlegmy voice, "Now dig the shit out of your ears an' listen careful. Mother and me is ready to meet our Maker. You know where everything is. You know what's to be done. But there's somethin' you have to promise us."

"Yes, father."

"Don't marry before Charlie, either of yous. Look after him and help him 'till he finds a wife. As God's your Maker, swear to us. And swear not to tell Charlie. He won't go for it."

Their mother struggled to speak.

"Please girls. Heed you Father. Don't marry before Charlie. Swear…."

"Oh Mother dear, we swear, we swear," Ruth cried, collapsing over the bed sobbing.

Sarah dug her nails into her hand and said, "We swear Mother an' Father. Ruth an' me will go now an' let you rest."

When they were back downstairs, Sarah looked at the clock and said, "The storm's worsenin'. Charlie should have been back in by now."

Sixty feet of storm separated the house from the barn, where their brother Charlie was sitting with a farrowing sow, a cantankerous old pig that had a habit of devouring her litter. Several of the little ones already born ran around her blindly searching for a tit. When one got too close to her snout, she snapped at it and Charlie quickly snatched it up out of harm's way and shoved it inside his shirt, then waited for another pig to be born. The sow's tail shot up and her hind legs stiffened as she strained to push out another one. Two tiny feet protruded instead of a head. He put in his fingers and thumb and got a grip on the small hind-legs. As he pulled, the piglets inside his shirt squirmed and nudged at his belly with their wet snouts. He pushed his hand further into the sow until he had a firm hold. Hurting, she raised her head to bite him; but with his free hand, he lightly rubbed her nipples soothing her while he pulled the piglet all the way out. At last the afterbirth came and she devoured it along with the salt-herring he had brought her. She settled, turned on her side and with a grunt let down her milk. The piglets now released from the warmth of Charlie's belly, struggled and vied to suck life from their mother.

He stretched and sighed.

"Well, you're good little pigs, nice an' pink, but some of you'll be crushed before the night's out. Yes, it'll be the greediest of you, wantin' too much, an' the weakest of you, too stunned to get out of her way. There's not a blessed thing I can do more. God's will be done."

A particularly forceful gust shook the entire barn, and he wondered if the roof might collapse before the night was out causing the animals to founder. He held up his lantern and saw frost glittering on the walls. The animals' breaths were cloudy from the cold, prompting him to fork fresh straw around them. The sow lay on her side grunting contentedly. Charlie pulled down his earflaps and buckled on his snowshoes. Earlier, he'd dug a trench through the snow across the yard from the house to the barn, but by now it would be drifted in.

As he opened the barn door the wind caught it with such ferocity, it pulled him headlong into a deep drift. His lantern sputtered out, and in the struggle to push the door shut again he lost a snowshoe. As the wind rose and fell, he could see nothing through the swirls of snow but a flickering of light from the house. The shovel he'd placed beside the door was buried, so using his other snowshoe he dug and pulled to make a track. Ice formed around his nostrils and eyelashes and snow filled his mouth; gobs of it balled on his woollen mittens, and melted snow trickled down his neck, soaking his shirt. At last he reached the house, exhausted. His trousers had frozen to his legs, and the chill was moving up through his body. *If I don't get in, I'll perish. Please God let Sarah an' Ruthie hear me,* he prayed.

"Sarah! Ruth!"

The wind snatched the words from his mouth. Then mustering all his strength, he banged on the door with the snowshoe.

Inside, Sarah stopped stirring a pot of soup.

"Did you hear that Ruth?"

"What Sarah?"

"That bangin'. Listen! Maybe it's Charlie. C'mon."

They managed to push the door open enough to see Charlie almost buried in snow. Grabbing him, they dragged him into the kitchen and pulled off his frozen boots, trousers and wet underwear. Sarah covered him with an Afghan and rubbed his legs pink while he soaked his feet in a basin of hot water and Epson salts. Outside the gale continued to howl and pile deepening drifts against the house.

Ruth stood snivelling. Sarah turned on her.

"You get upstairs and see to mother and father. I'll get a bowl of soup into him. And you'd better take up a stick or two of wood. Go on, hurry now."

She set bowl of the thick soup in front of Charlie.

"You get that into you."

He was still shivering and barely able to hold his spoon.

"What was things like over in the barn? Did the sow pig?"

"A good litter, Sarah, but there's tons of snow on the roof. I'm scared she might cave in."

Sarah put more wood in the stove, intensifying the heat, and Charlie by now had control of his spoon. He broke up chunks of bread and patted them into his soup.

"Yes, nice little pigs …."

"Sarah!" Ruth stood at the kitchen door crying. "Oh Sarah, Father's real low. He wants to talk to Charlie. What'll we do an' him with no trousers on?"

Sarah wiped her hands on her apron and scolded, "Stop bein' a baby for a start. Go an' get him down a dry pair an' a shirt."

"But Sarah, Father wants him now."

"Well for goodness sake girl, get the dry clothes anyway."

Ruth ran back up the stairs and flung the trousers and shirt down over the banister. Sarah gathered them up and said, "You put them on. Father wants to talk to you right away. You can finish your soup later. An' Charlie don't say anything about the barn roof."

"It's not my fault Sarah. It's the snow. I…"

"Now don't you worry, dear. Just go up an' see what he wants. Him and Mother's not good."

Charlie made his way up the dark stairs and stood a moment before entering. The old man lay with his eyes closed, but his mother's were open. Charlie smiled and touched her hand.

"Come round here," the old man said.

He walked over to his father's side of the bed.

"Charlie, with your Mother an' me gone there'll be only you to look after the land and the girls. Where would they go if you brought a new wife into the house? You've never been much of a man, or are likely to be one, so God knows what kind of a woman would latch onto you. There'd be strife—far better if you seen them married off first. Your mother and me would go to our Maker content if you promised us not to marry before them."

Charlie shifted feet and mumbled, "I won't marry."

"Charlie dear," his mother said, her voice barely a whisper. "Don't tell Ruth an' Sarah, it would only upset them. Kiss me an' tell me you promise."

He leaned over and kissed her.

"Yes, mother, I promise."

Three days later, the old couple died within an hour of each other. Sarah saw them plucking the bed sheets and heard them raving. Knowing the end was near, she closed the door and stood still watching them, the light from the fire flickering over her. In a moment of clarity, her parents opened their eyes wide and turned their heads to each other. The old man's lips opened and closed in an attempt to speak, but it was more like a tremor of the lips. A weak cry came from her mother, "Ah my poor children, my poor children. Forgive us Father, forgive us…."

Sarah moved closer to them. She couldn't tell if they heard her or not when she said, "Yes, may God forgive you indeed. I'm glad you're carrying your shame to the grave, but go in peace Mother and Father, for nobody will ever learn about it from me."

Her Father's jaw opened widely, and a rattle came from his throat as his eyes turned glassy.

Charlie hauled the ticking and bedclothes out to the yard and torched them, leaving a black hole in the snow, while Sarah and Ruth washed their parent's bodies, dressed them in their Sunday best and placed them in the rough coffins he had made in the barn. Before nailing the lids down Charlie gave the remains a thick dusting of rat-poison and lime.

Each time he drove in a nail, Ruth flinched and clung tighter to Sarah. When the banging ceased, the parents' names were scrawled on the lids with a thick carpenter's pencil. Sisters and brother stood solemnly at the head of the coffins, and Sarah asked for God's blessing on the dead and the living.

They struggled with the coffins down the stairs and out the door. A splinter from the rough wood sliced deeply into Sarah's hand, but she managed to ignore it until both coffins were loaded onto the sleigh. They pulled their burden across the snow-filled yard to the icehouse where they struggled to lift their dead up onto the blocks of ice. Charlie climbed on top and dragged them into a dark corner. And there, Charles and Elizabeth Ewart remained frozen until spring.

Two

Others

There were other deaths in New Skye that winter. Jack Logan, feverish and ill, perished on the road while battling the driving snow and ice to get help for his sick wife, Betty. Heska Fenlon, wife of Freddy Fenlon, the Ewart's longtime hired man perished during a visit by the Reverend Mark Kerr. When Mark returned to the manse he found his baby boy dead in its mother's arms. Several days later, she too died.

Three

The Burial

Spring came bringing heavy rains. The frost left the earth allowing the people of New Skye to bring out their dead for burial. Horses stood patiently in the horse shed their wet flanks steaming. With barn smells still clinging to their wet clothes, people wearily entered the little church. Those who spoke did so in a whisper. As Mark Kerr took his place behind the pulpit, he seemed like an angel to Ruth Ewart; she closed her eyes and sent him secret messages of love.

Mark glanced over at the little organ half expecting to see his Mollie look up from her playing and give him one of her fleeting glances filled with promise and love. He had so relished his private intimacies with his Mollie; their wine-bibbing encounters when they lay beside each other naked for hours making love and talking sacrilege and dreams.

"Had I a private fortune," he used to tell her, "I would take you on long sea voyages to exotic places, dress you in exotic dresses, and bugger this shepherding."

She, in turn, put her hand over his mouth in a mock gesture of shock silencing his blasphemy, then laughingly, she covered him in kisses and caresses pleading with him to tell her more of what he would do if he were not a shepherd. The fact they had shared such passion and fun behind the closed doors of the manse added piquancy.

Now she was gone, lying in a crude wooden box with their baby beside her. Grief hung in him like a dead weight. He looked over his flock, took in their forlorn faces, pouchy and red from grief and work. The congregation grieved as much for his loss as they did their own. His very presence was an ennobling comfort to them, but he had nothing to give them.

Charlie, who sat staring into space, didn't hear Mark call his name. Sarah nudged him and whispered that it was time for him to sing. He stood and sang, "Abide with Me," *a cappella*, his beautiful voice filling the little church. When he finished, Sarah tugged at him to sit down again.

"Words fail me," Mark began. "Our grief is unspeakable. Everything I have to say is already crying within your own hearts. I can't add or take away anything. It is only the Lord who gives and takes away. What can we do but have faith that He has taken them to something better?"

He continued with a listlessness that came across to all as simple dignity; but in fact, he felt nothing but appalling emptiness. Mark Kerr's faith was not as firm as it appeared and sounded to others.

For the internment he led them out to the tiny graveyard. There, each family stood beside its freshly opened plot under dripping trees, waiting to put their dead into the ground. Mark barely looked as they lowered in Mollie and the baby. A couple of the elders watched him in case he didn't hold, but his face revealed nothing. One of them gently touched his arm.

"Reverend Kerr we're ready."

"The Lord is my shepherd, I shall not want…"

Gusts of wind carried his words out to the white-flecked sea; but the lost words didn't matter; all knew them by heart and mumbled them with him. The elders trudged from grave to grave dropping in the first shovelful of clay while Mark intoned, "Ashes to ashes, dust to dust."

When it came to Mollie, the shovel scraping against the gravel in the wet clay and the stones bouncing off her coffin were like blows to his flesh. Finally, the service ended. He left the dismal clusters of mourners and walked back into the church where the only sound was the rain beating on the roof. Gusts of wind dashed it against the windows taking him back to that first wet day in Edinburgh when he met Mollie. Now he was alone, the future a bleak abyss before him. He surreptitiously pulled a small bottle from his pocket and drained its contents.

Jesus smiled out at him from the windows—Jesus carrying the lost lamb home on his shoulder; Jesus walking on the waves taking a frightened and sinking Peter by the hand; Jesus holding up a lantern while he knocked on a closed door, but Mark was as indifferent as the glass Jesus was painted on.

"They're safe with *Him***,** now, aren't they?"

He turned to the voice not quite grasping what was said. Ruth Ewart stood behind him.

"Pardon?"

"I said they're safe with *Him*, now?"

"Yes."

"Oh, Reverend Kerr you were wonderful today, an inspiration to all of us. Your faith carried us through and you've been tested more than any of us."

Ever since Mollie's death, Ruth prayed that he would not leave the community. She promised God that if He kept Mark in New Skye, she would pledge herself to him. She fantasized taking him his meals, doing his washing and cleaning the manse. She even allowed herself the thought that perhaps she would bear him another son. At first she repressed this shameful idea, for hadn't she promised mother and father she would not marry before Charlie? Throughout the day she repeated to herself, *God's will be done,*

God's will be done. However, she knew exactly what God wanted, and the words of the prayer changed to, *I know Thy will. It will be done. I will bear him a son. The Lord's will*, she told herself *is greater even than my father's will.*

When alone she examined herself in the mirror and wished she was not so plain; but Ruth was not unattractive. She had a lissom figure, lovely light auburn hair and expressive hazel eyes. It was just that she concentrated on her "weak features." At Ruth's core, though, was a strong sensuality that terrified her. She avoided eye contact with men, because if one looked at her directly she felt her entire body blush.

It started the summer she was sixteen when she went to the backfields with Freddy Fenlon to garner scattered piles of hay that had fallen off the loads. He drove the horse and wagon towards a pile, and then both of them would fork it on. As she lay on the wagon letting her body go with its jiggling, she studied the back of Freddy's neck: the hairline wet with sweat, the corded muscles, and the fine tiny diamond network of wrinkles woven into his tanned skin. He was their hired man, and his daughter Janice her best friend. A warm, pleasant feeling suffused her—a feeling that intensified when Freddy turned round and stopped the world with his eyes. In that instant, he made contact with her secret feelings, and he was trapped in her moment of lust. She blushed. Freddy laughed and said, "There's a pile over there."

She jumped off the wagon and followed him, trying not to look at the backs of his strong legs. In silence she forked the loose hay.

"Ruth?"

She heard his voice but kept her eyes fixed on the meadow flowers entwined around the prongs of her hayfork.

"Ruth. You're a lovely little thing."

He touched her hair and cheek and took her hand.

"Here, come and sit down beside me. I want to tell you somethin'."

He was solicitous, fatherly, but she was still engulfed in the look that had passed between them. She wanted to run home, but curiosity and elation pumped by an overwhelming urge, prevented her. He put his arm around her; his voice was husky with lust.

"My God, child, do you know what I'm feeling right now? I'm overcome with you. You know what that means don't you, Ruthie?"

She could hardly catch her breath.

His hand around her shoulder moved down under her arm and lightly caressed the side of her breast. He kissed her cheek, moving his lips towards hers.

"Don't do that Freddy."

The warm tingling sensations along with a new feeling of power kept her from running. She squirmed out of his arm and turned her back to him; but what she really wanted was to lie back and feel his hot hands over her. Instead she could hear herself saying, "Freddy, we'd better hurry and finish the field, now. I have to help Mother with supper soon."

He inched forward, took her hand and placed it on his erect penis. Tiny beads of sweat lay along her upper lip. His grip tightened on her wrist. He leaned forward and flicked the top of her lip with the tip of his tongue. Power and fear coursed through her. She responded slightly; then as if jolted, she wrenched her wrist from his grip, leapt off the wagon and ran. Fear had won.

"Ruth, Ruth, wait, Ruth," he called. "I won't harm you, honest. Ruth wait!"

He caught up with her, held her and said, "Ruth, listen, I won't harm you."

She stopped struggling and said, "Let go then Freddy."

"Ruth, I couldn't help myself. Don't say anything to anybody now—not a word—people won't like you if you do—promise now?"

Confused, she still wanted to push herself against him; but instead, the fear drove her towards home. At the pump in the yard she splashed her burning face and hands, but the cool spring-water could not wash away the hot silken memory of his thing on her palm.

That night in their bedroom, she told Sarah about what happened; but Sarah was outraged more at her than at Freddy.

"Oh I'm ashamed, Ruth, ashamed," she cried. "You must ask God's pardon for leading Freddy on. Men are weak creatures, and when they get it into their heads we want them, they're like animals. They'll just rut and hate you for it, and you'll be ruined—ruined!"

She grabbed Ruth's hand and pressed it on the Bible

"Ask God's forgiveness, Ruthie."

"God forgive me," Ruth cried.

"Swear you'll never say a word of it to anyone."

"I swear, Sarah, honestly."

"Swear you'll stay out of Freddy's way, and never ever allow yourself to be alone with him."

Ruth in tears, cried, "I swear I'll stay out of Freddy's way an' never be alone in his company."

Through constant prayer she decided to commit her life to higher things. She deliberately distanced herself from men unless God told her they were noble of character. The Reverend Mark Kerr, in Ruth's eyes, was the essence of nobility of character. He was one who honoured his Lord and found favour. During the terrible time of the storms and sickness, the Lord rewarded him by giving him strength, comfort and dignity, which he gave to others. She adored him. Compared to him all other men were beasts.

While Ruth stood there in the silence of the little church looking at the light from the windows playing over Mark's distraught face, she prayed for a word from him; but at that moment, the door clattered opened and Sarah entered bringing in a gust of wind and rain.

Sarah stood for a moment, taking in the two silent figures of her sister and the minister. Then going forward, she nodded politely to Mark and said, "We're sorry for your loss, Reverend Kerr. If there is anything we can do for you, please let us know. Ruthie, dear, we must go home now. We have the runnin' of the farm to think about now that father is gone. "

Ruth followed her out of the church into the rain, praying that Mark would call them back, but he stood absolutely still and silent, staring vacantly at the windows of Jesus.

Four

Charlie Ewart

The Ewart farm was regarded as one of the best in the community, and it was widely believed the old man had left by quite a bit of money. Now that young Charlie Ewart had the awesome task of filling his father's shoes, mothers reminded their daughters that he might be worth a second look. He was short, well proportioned and strong with hazel eyes and auburn hair like Ruth's; but because his skin was so soft, he had what some might call a girl's face. Charlie was an outstanding singer, and every Christmas and Easter he sang his mother's favourite hymns "O Holy Night" and "Were You There When They Crucified My Lord?" Most other times, he sang to himself while he worked. He didn't talk or smile much, but when he did manage a smile, he showed good even teeth. Several girls flirted with him, but the only women Charlie felt comfortable with were his sisters and eventually Betty Logan, the neighbour whose husband had died in the storm.

The night Betty was close to death, Jack Logan battled a ferocious blizzard to seek help. By morning the storm had abated, and Sarah sent Charlie to find out what was going on in the community. When he made it to the top of the lane, he saw Jack's frozen body sticking out of a snowdrift. Jack had died curled up like a sleeping baby.

Charlie contemplated the body for a moment, trying to figure out the best way of getting it onto his hand-sled and tying it down. Satisfied the remains were safely secured, he tackled the fifty yards or so of deep snow to Jack's place. By the time he arrived, he was exhausted, but he mustered enough energy to untie the corpse and drag it into the icehouse. Next he went into the barn to check on the animals and throw them some feed; before leaving, he reached under one of the hens and got himself a warm fresh egg to suck.

When he was about to go back home, he noticed there was no smoke coming from the chimney of Jack's house and that front door was open. Snow had drifted into the hallway. Cautiously, he entered. The wood stove was almost out, and frost was forming on the walls and furniture and clouding the air. He thought he heard a moan coming from upstairs. His heart pounded and he felt a terrible pressure in his head. Old Feardy was present.

"Jesus lover of my soul help me! Mother don't let Feardy come," he cried, leaning for support against the banister.

Old Feardy first emerged on the day of Charlie's tenth birthday. He and his mother were in the parlour singing while she played the pump organ. He loved standing close to her feeling her warmth, but the moment was shattered when his father, dressed in a large black-rubber apron, rushed in and grabbed him by the shirt collar.

"Look woman," he yelled. "You've two daughters. Do you want him too? Well, forget it. He's mine."

Charlie wriggled free, but the old man caught him and held him hard by the neck. His mother ran to free him but was felled by a punch to the face. His father dragged him outside across the yard to the barn and pushed him against the wall. He breathed whiskey on him, and his rubber apron stank of old blood.

"I'm stickin' a pig an' I want you to see how it's done an' help out."

He pushed little Charlie ahead of him into the barn, then banged on the side of the pen. The pig ran to the far corner, lowered her head and grunted while following Old Charlie with her milky-blue eyes.

"Now, you watch boy. There's no use gettin' in there—that's trouble, see? So first you make a noose tied with a slipknot. Then you lean over the pen an' hold it in front of the snout an' she'll make a bite for it. But as soon as she opens her jaw, you pull it tight over her snout. Then watch the fun!"

Old Charlie snared the pig. She dug in her rear trotters, but the harder she pulled against the rope the tighter it dug into her snout. She strained back shaking her head vigorously from side to side and screeching horribly. When the rope was taut almost to breaking, Old Charlie quickly tied his end around a post. He jumped into the pen, pulled down another rope threaded through a pulley attached to a beam and tightly bound the hind legs, and then he hauled her up hind-feet first. Charlie put his hands over his ears to shut out the pig's squealing. His father picked up a sledgehammer and struck the animal a skull-cracking blow between the ears. The pig's eyes went glassy.

"There, that'll do ye for a while," he said to the stunned animal.

Freeing the noose from her snout, he hauled her higher until she hung perpendicular. Drops of dark blood dripped from her nostrils.

"You come in here, Charlie an' bring them two buckets with you—hurry now!" he shouted.

Charlie, sobbing, did as he was told.

"Stop your Goddamn snivellin' an' put that bucket under her here—you're making more racket than the pig. Do I have to hit you wi' the sledge too?" The old man roared at his joke. "Now you reach me that knife in that other bucket there—it's sharp so grab it by the handle or we'll be havin' fried fingers for breakfast. Now watch."

The old man stuck the sow's throat. But just as the steaming blood splashed into the bucket, a terrible thrashing came from further down the barn. He stood up sharply, his hands and arms covered in gore.

"Oh, my Christ!" he yelled, "I forgot to put the mare out. Now I bet she's slipped her foal! Come on, you!"

He pushed the boy towards the horse. Little Charlie saw the aborted foal in its translucent, embryonic sac. The mare's ears were pressed back almost flat and her eyes bulged white. She reared up and thrashed the stall with her hoofs, the afterbirth hanging from her.

"Goddamn it" the old man yelled at Charlie. "See! With all your damned little girlish nonsense and your Goddamned mother, we've lost the foal."

"Now I'm goin' in to clean the mare off," he said holding the boy tightly by the shoulders. "But before I do, I'll have to try an' hold her while you run in an' grab that foal an' pull it clear out of the stall. And you be right sharp about it too, or she'll kick the bejesus out of ya."

"Ah no, Dad! No!"

"You're goin' in! You get the foal out!" he yelled, pushing the boy into the stall.

The last thing Charlie heard was the awful banging of the hoofs. He came to in his mother's arms. She was gently wiping his face with a wet cloth. Sarah and Ruth were crying. Old Charlie stood looking down at him.

"You nearly got us killed, boy. Now that foal's lying out back. When your mother's finished mollycoddlin' ya, you'll take a shovel an' bury it."

When he was able to walk, Sarah went with him and helped bury the foal. But the terror didn't abate; and while in bed that night, it gripped every muscle in his small body and wouldn't let him breathe. Ruth found him threshing, his face purple. Eventually, the soft closeness of his mother settled him.

"Old Feardy's got a hold of you, Charlie my little dear. Now I know how to keep old Feardy away so's he can't get a hold of you."

"How?" Charlie sobbed.

"Well, first, Old Feardy doesn't like anything nice, and the thing he hates more than anything is nice hymn-singin'. He's afraid of hymns because he's afraid of Jesus. Jesus is always in nice hymn singin'. So the next time you feel Old Feardy comin' to get you, you sing a hymn, an' keep singin' 'til Old Feardy goes away."

She sang softly with Charlie joining in between sobs:
God sees the little sparrow fall,
It meets His tender view;
If God so loves the little birds,
I know He loves me too.

Eventually he drifted off to sleep. But from that day of the horse, Charlie often felt that the clouds in the sky were moving through his head, and worst of all, that Old Feardy was everywhere: in the trees, behind the shingles, and especially in the wood stove. Charlie seldom stopped singing. When he was alone he sang out loud, and when he was with others he sang in his head. Sometimes while singing in his head, new words came into the hymns and it was as if Jesus was singing back to him; but most of all, Charlie lived in dread of his father.

It wasn't that the old man didn't love him. He did, but it showed itself in harshness. The day little Charlie was born Old Charlie got down on his knees and thanked God for setting things right. Elizabeth had given him a son after two girls, now he truly had something to work and build for. But the boy cowered behind his mother and sisters when he came near him. Old Charlie remonstrated to his wife that it was sinful to be always yawlin' hymns with a boy when he should be with his father learning to do man's work.

When they went with a load somewhere, little Charlie had to be coaxed down from the wagon. A normal boy would jump down and pitch in trying to do too much. The neighbouring men ignored him instead of joking and teasing him as they did the other neighbour boys. One day up at the feed mill Old Charlie heard Myra Swanson saying, "He'd be better off home with his mother and sisters."

Everybody laughed until they noticed Old Charlie.

Shame of the son grew like a dark weed. His father talked with him, prayed with him, cajoled him, beat him and once in a fit of rage picked him up and threw him into a pile of wet pig manure, yelling, "A farmer's life's about breeding, birth, shit and slaughter! If the animals don't shit they're dead, an' if we don't slaughter them, we starve! So, we feed an' clean up after them and give thanks. That's why the Lord made us farmers an' you an' me's blessed to carry out His will. You see a mess, clean it up an' don't leave it till it is done! Understand? Clean up the mess an' don't leave it till it's done! What is it you have to do?"

"Clean up the mess an' don't leave it 'til it's done," Charlie repeated several times at the old man's wagging finger.

Now in the Logan's freezing hallway Old Feardy's presence was so strong, Charlie hummed, *He loves me too, He loves me too, I know he loves me too....*

Another moan came from upstairs, and he cautiously ventured up. Betty Logan was lying on the floor. The fire in the grate was almost ashes, and the windows were covered in thick leafy patterns of ice. The room was foul with sickness.

Breathless from exhaustion and fear, Charlie was in a dilemma as to what to do. His head was cloudy. He wanted to run home.

He half sung and talked about what he saw until the words of the hymn changed to, *He loves me too…Clean up the mess!*

He looked down at Betty soaked in vomit and excrement. Then struggling with her dead weight he managed to get her back onto the bed and heap the bedclothes on top of her. He went back downstairs and shovelled the snow out of the hallway. Eventually he could close the front door. There was a good pile of kindling and logs beside the stove and soon warmth flooded the house.

He prayed while he cranked the phone.

"Hello," Sarah yelled through hum and crackle.

Charlie managed to tell her about finding Jack and Betty.

"Is she still livin'?"

"Yes!" Charlie yelled, as the phone grew faint.

"We can't leave here to help you, Charlie. Find clean clothes an' change her. Try to get a cup of hot tea into her. Do what you can. God is with you Charlie. Heat…."

Sarah's voice faded away completely, leaving only the hum. Charlie put the kettle on and ferreted around until he found clean bedclothes and a nightdress. He lifted her down off the bed again and put her on the floor in front of the fire. After he had stripped the bed and threw on clean blankets, he took off her foul nightdress. Except for his mother, Charlie had never seen or touched a woman's body before. When he was fifteen he walked in on his mother one day as she was stripped to the waist washing herself. She covered her nipples with her hands and said, "There's nothin' to be ashamed of Charlie, and I fed you when you were a baby, but now you're big it's not proper to look at me. The only woman you should see without her clothes on might be your wife someday. Now you remember that."

He took in Betty's form but kept his eyes fixed on two velvety moles on her neck just at the collarbone. He washed her and dressed her in the clean nightdress, then lifted her back onto the bed again. She rallied a bit. As he was trying to get a cup of tea into her, she rambled on about Jack. Her raving was whispering soft at times and at others it rose to a wail. Charlie tried to drown it out by singing. Eventually, Sarah appeared. Looking around her, she saw the dirty clothes and the basin with the water Charlie had used to clean Betty.

"You go on back home now, Charlie. I'll stay the night with her."

As he was leaving, she said without looking at him, "I hope you had pure thoughts, Charlie."

Every day since he saved Betty's life, Charlie went over to take care of her barn work. He now had the gruesome job of breaking Jack's body so that it would fit into its crude coffin. Betty was sitting up in bed sipping a bowl of soup Sarah had brought her when she heard hammering coming from the yard.

"What's that bangin' Sarah? Is Jack back? He's always banging or hammering away at something. He just went into town to pick up something or other." Then lowering her voice she said as if in confidence, "You know I'm expectin' Sarah?"

Betty had always found it easier to deny bad things in her life; but now, in her sickness, reality and unreality flowed together. All through her chatter and smiling, she watched every move of those around her.

Sarah felt uneasy being with her. Betty's dishevelled hair and blotchy china-blue eyes staring out from her pale face disturbed her. She was sure Betty could turn on her in a minute.

"The hammerin's stopped, Sarah. I bet you one of these days he'll walk in here and surprise me with a lovely crib with a hood for the baby. There's nobody like Jack when he's nice. He's always surprising me with little things he makes."

How can I make her shut up her stupid babbling? Sarah asked herself. She made up her mind then and there it was time to tell her the truth.

"Betty, Jack's dead."

"Well, he'll be in soon, now. I'd ask you to stay for a cup of tea, Sarah dear, but I think he'll want to surprise me first with the crib, like. Would you mind takin' this bowl? I'll show the crib to your later, dear."

Sarah set the bowl down and took Betty firmly by the hands, "Now you listen to me, Betty Logan. Jack's dead an' you're *not* expectin'? You'd better face up to it like the rest of us. Our parents are dead along with others in the community."

"I don't know what you're sayin' Sarah. Don't you hear him hammerin'?"

"No. He's not coming back. He's lying out there in the icehouse, dead! There'll be no baby an' no crib."

Betty yelled and kicked off the bedclothes. Sarah tried to restrain her but she bit her wrist and ran screaming downstairs and out into the yard. The snow was gone except for a few dirty mounds lying in the shadows. A knifing wind pressed her nightdress into her body like a second skin. However, she was impervious to the cold as she ran towards the singing coming from the open door of the icehouse.

Charlie was swinging his sledgehammer at Jack's curled knees. Beside him lay the empty coffin. Betty leapt on him like a fiend, screeching, clinging and clawing. Sarah was behind her, pulling at her. As the three wrestled, Charlie's face was pressed tight against the face of the corpse until Betty collapsed, exhausted. When they got her back into the bedroom, Charlie was crying, his fingers over his eyes like a little boy.

"There now, Charlie, you shush your noise. Go and finish with Jack. I can manage her. Go on now."

Before the month was out, Betty had recovered her strength and most of her wits, but there were changes in Charlie. More and more, Jesus sang to him. At night, Sarah and Ruth heard him singing and crying himself to sleep. He grew more distant and took to sitting in the darkest corner of the kitchen.

Five

Sarah

Early in May, Charlie and Freddy Fenlon along with other hired help cut and planted potato sets on the Ewart land. Throughout an exceptionally hot June and July, they harvested the hay, and by August the grain was ripening to gold. Sarah and Ruth along with a couple of neighbour women fed the men at long makeshift tables that stretched from the kitchen to the parlour. To look at the health in their faces, burned brick red like the Island soil itself, one would never have guessed there had been so much sickness.

The general devastation of winter, however, had wrought irrevocable changes in the Ewarts. The death of Freddy's wife Heska, and that of her own parents, and the odd way Charlie had become, all took their toll on Sarah Ewart. She worried about Ruth who was drifting in and out of her own world; and if she didn't keep after her, Ruth would let herself go. Once, she saw her standing at the end of the house talking to herself, and another time while washing the dishes, she held a plate before her face and talked aloud to it. Sarah struggled to hold Ruth, Charlie and herself together as a family, and the future of the farm worried her.

She didn't like being so dependent on Freddy Fenlon who was taking on more responsibility and was making major decisions that Charlie should be making. It crossed her mind that Freddy might be trying to take over; yet, she knew Charlie would be lost without his help – they all would. She returned the favour by cleaning his house and washing his clothes. For the sake of propriety she always made sure he was out when she took his washing over. Before entering she'd call his name, and if he answered she'd leave the basket in the porch; but as the summer drew on, she thought of Freddy less and less as a hired man, and when she had his house to herself she rummaged through it.

Heska's cedar chest was a source of wonderment. What a shame Janice couldn't have made it hers, she thought, as she looked at a picture of Heska and Freddy holding Janice in her Christening robes. Janice Fenlon and Ruth were raised together. But when Janice was sixteen she went to live with an aunt in Boston. Her going away broke Heska's heart; and though nobody spoke of it except behind closed doors, it was generally understood she got in trouble. Community gossip pointed the finger at this or that man, and it was rumoured by some that Old Charlie Ewart had something to do with it. In any case, Janice never came home again.

Sarah fondled the items in the chest: beads and brooches, tortoise shell combs, a china doll with a cracked face and Janice's christening robe, bonnet and bootees. Everything smelled of cedar and lavender. She also unearthed a pair of brass armbands engraved, *Vulcan, Eater of Fire!* Curious, she examined the strange armbands, repeating aloud the inscription; then, losing interest just as quickly tossed them back and turned her attention again to Janice's baby things. She ran the satin ribbons of the bonnet gently between her finger and thumb and set the bootees on the palm of her left hand. But the true treasure of the chest was a silver hand mirror intricately worked in tiny rosebuds and filigree. From the time she was a young girl visiting the Fenlon's, she longed to touch it and trace the intricacies of its frame, but Heska wouldn't allow any of them to go near it, not even Janice.

"Don't touch it, my dears," she warned. "It's charmed and might do you harm."

The dire warning stayed with her. She played a game with it by leaning right into the box and pulling the lid down to rest on her back, shutting out as much light as she could. Her breath warmed the dark space, making the cedar-scent almost overpowering. Then raising her back ever so slowly she let the light filter in, and she watched her face emerge in the mirror. Always, she scrupulously avoided touching it. At times she would scold herself for acting like a silly girl, but the mirror obsessed her. It was then she indulged in a new habit. Freddy kept a stone jar of rum beside his bed. At first, she took a sip to settle herself, but as the pleasant warmth of the drink made everything more intimate, she was soon tippling.

At other times she was given to crying jags during which she talked to God about her worthlessness and about being brought into the world soiled with her parent's sin. It was during one of these bouts that Freddy came in and caught her sitting on the floor with the contents of the chest spread about her like a child spreads its toys. Dimly, through her tears, she perceived him standing there; then suddenly jolted out of her fantasy, she spilt the tumbler of rum over the christening robe. He towered over her, smiling, his stiff curly hair haloed by the light from the window.

"Oh, I'm so ashamed, Freddy, so ashamed."

She made to get up but stumbled. Freddy, realizing she was tipsy said, "There's nothing to be ashamed about. You're a wonderful strong woman, Sarah. All of us would be lost without you—especially me."

He tipped up her chin with his finger.

"A little drop of rum eases the pain. Isn't that why the Lord gave it to us? Weeping becomes you, Sarah, do you know that?"

She got up and tried to rush out, but he stopped her, holding her firmly by the shoulders.

"Sarah dear, settle yourself," he said gently stroking her hair. "Charlie's in the granary waitin' for me. Stay here til' after I'm gone. I'll never say anything. Anyway, I only came in to get this."

He picked up his rum jar and left. As she tuned into the sounds outside, she could hear Charlie singing.

Freddy was jubilant. On the way back to the granary he said to himself, my little place along with the Ewarts' place would make one God damn good farm. Ah sure, he concluded, they're almost one now except for the formalities. He took a swig of rum and offered the jar to Charlie. Charlie shook his head.

"Ah you don't know what you're missing Charlie boy. C'mon it'll give you a bit of stand-up, and you'll be less shy of the girls."

Freddy laughed at Charlie's red face; then taking another hefty swig, he thought more about Sarah up in his bedroom.

Six

Betty and Charlie

The Island had a superb summer. White barns gleamed in the honey warm sunshine; and the sea winds blowing over the dunes carried the scent of juniper berries inland. Oat and barley crops ripened to crisp gold, and the undulating meadows were petit-pointed with wild flowers of every hue: Queen Anne's Lace, Bachelor's Buttons, Dog Daisies, Buttercups and Honeysuckle. Great swathes of pink, purple and lavender lupines blossomed along the ditches; and the woods were carpeted with Star-Daisies and delicate Lady Slippers. In the recesses of the hedgerows, clusters of plump blackberries hung like dark jewels. The grazing cows seemed suspended in the wavy mirages of heat. In the afternoons they lay in the shade, twitching their ears and flicking flies with their tails. Sometimes, a hatch of manure flies swarmed, and then they stampeded over the pastures to blow them off their backs. The sea sparkled for miles out, and the strong salt air scoured and cleansed everything leaving no trace of the terrible winter sickness.

Betty Logan's physical health had fully returned, but her mind was still fragile, and she tended to drift into fantasy. She had accepted the fact that Jack was dead, but the fear he had instilled filled the emptiness of the house; and during moments when she let her mind drift, she fully expected to meet him coming out of the barn, or to stroll into the kitchen demanding his dinner.

Jack had gone to war and was decorated and commended by the King. When he came home the community feted him; and on Armistice Day, he led the special honour guard to the new soldiers' monument in Charlottetown. Everybody liked Jack, and the Conservatives had plans to groom and nominate him to run as a Member of the Provincial Legislative Assembly. To most, he was well mannered, quiet spoken and gentle; but the private Jack, shattered by the war, was given over to nightmares and bouts of moroseness. When he awoke, he screamed things like, "The rats are eatin' our eyes out! Or, my lungs is full of trench shit!"

He was a good-looking man, tanned and robust from working on the land, but every so often his face blanched and his eyes went opaque. In that state he was dangerous.

Betty had lived in fear of his outbursts. After times at the Hall, when they were saying friendly good nights to the neighbours, she'd watch for signs and pray that the friendliness would last, but if he would swill rum on the way home and swear abuse at the horse to speed up, she'd cower away from him. In the house he'd bang things around and yell, "What are you out to screw every man in the community?"

"What do you mean darlin'?"

"That Joe MacDonald was sniffin' at you all night like a mongrel."

"Aw don't say things like that Jack darlin' all he said was that he liked my dress."

"You were leadin'; him on. If I hadn't been there you'd be droppin' your drawers!"

He'd push her into a chair, making her sit still.

"Don't you move a muscle till I'm finished, d'ye hear?"

Then he'd pour on her a tirade of abuse.

When he went into town, she'd watch for him coming home. If he drove the wagon so fast up the lane that the dust rose in red clouds and the poor horse was in a lather, she knew there'd be trouble, and she'd hide in the parlour.

"Oh Betty," he'd call, softly.

She wouldn't answer. Then she'd hear him sneaking up the stairs and fling the bedroom door open.

"I'm down here Jack, darlin'," she'd call.

He'd come down, his face pale and perplexed.

"Where'd he go! Tell me now! Come clean!"

"Who Jack, who?"

That bastard you were screwin' in our bed while I was in town, that's who!"

"You're my only one Jack darlin'. There's nobody else an' there never has been."

"Liar! You flirt wi' everybody an' everybody knows it." When she sat with her head down, quiet, he'd become all reasonable, pleading almost, "Betty, come on, girl. I won't get mad at you. Just tell me the truth. It'll make us both feel better. Who is he?"

"I'll swear on the Bible Jack. You're my husband an' the only man in my life. Get the Bible."

Trembling, she relived how he'd fly into as rage and beat her. She still caressed her arm rubbing away bruises now long gone. She remembered how, full of remorse, he'd throw her on the bed and undress her sobbing all the while.

"I'm sorry, I'm sorry darling. You're so pretty how could any man not want you?"

She'd lie still through his futile attempts to make love to her, and as he'd move from tenderness to failure, he'd pummel her body accusing her all over again as he did so.

"You whore! You had your fill already. I hate you, you slut! No wonder I can't give it to you!"

Fear dictated her every move when Jack was alive; and much of her energy went into appearing and proving she was loyal and loving. At one point, she thought a baby would help matters between them; but he could not penetrate her long enough for her to conceive. Yet, she did long for a baby and fantasized giving birth to a son and nursing and bathing him. Tension and dread pushed her more and more from reality; and at times when alone, she enjoyed behaving like a little girl again. Even yet though Jack was dead, her fear of him was still alive.

The one bright spot in her life was Charlie Ewart. She watched for him coming up the lane to do her chores, and she was always there to thank him and wave goodbye when he had finished. Thoughts of Charlie increasingly replaced the unpleasantness of her life. She called him her sweet little Charlie and adored his silky auburn hair and lovely hazel eyes. The thought of his kindness when he saved her, and the sweetness of his singing and his shyness made her yearn to be with him; but just as she had thought there was more to Jack when she first met him, she was also under the illusion there was more to Charlie. To her he was her child angel.

One morning while he was working in the barn, Betty came in wearing a new dress.

"Charlie," she called to him. "Come up to the house when you're finished."

Thinking she needed help with something, he reluctantly complied. The smell of freshly baked bread and roast beef wafted from the kitchen. Betty called over her shoulder as she took a pie from the oven, "Come on in, Charlie, and sit down. I'll put out a bite of dinner for us."

He hesitated and looked back out to the yard as if ready to bolt.

"Come on now, Charlie," she coaxed. "Just you wash up at the sink there now. Everything's ready."

He mumbled something about Sarah having dinner waiting for him.

"Oh no, dear, I phoned Sarah an' told her you'd be eating here, an' she said that's fine with her."

She made an affectionate funny-face at him and gently urged

him to step in. While washing his hands he glanced anxiously at her and wished he was back home with Ruthie and Sarah sittin' in his own corner.

Betty set a plate before him heaped with beets, string beans, potatoes and roast beef covered in lovely thick gravy with big chunks of onions. She sat opposite with her own plate and beamed at him. He didn't move. She thought he was waiting for grace, so she said, "Do you want to ask the blessing, Charlie?"

When he didn't respond she said, "Okay I'll say it, dear. Bless us, Oh Father and this food, and we thank Thee for the gift of dear friends like Charlie here. Amen."

Charlie muttered, "Amen."

"Do you not like that dinner, Charlie?"

He nodded that he did. She smiled and lifted her knife and fork signalling him to do the same. He kept his eyes on the plate while he ate.

"Charlie?" He looked up from under his eyebrows for a second. "Charlie. I know everything you did for me the night you found Jack and brought him home. You're a wonderful, kind person, Charlie. And that day I attacked you - I was out of my head. Charlie, dear, there's nobody like you. I know you don't like talkin'. You don't need to talk. Lord knows I do enough for everybody. You take after your mother Charlie—got her gentleness. She'd be proud of what you done and of the way you help me out, now."

She stopped talking. Charlie had lowered his head further. Pathetic little noises came from him. She went round the table, held his head and stroked his hair making shushing noises. He rocked back and forth with quick little movements. She let him and then gently brought him to stillness, but he pressed his head tighter into her.

"Charlie, dear," she whispered. "You go out and bring me in a few sticks of wood for the stove, an' when you come back I'll have a nice piece of pie waitin' for you?"

She gently released herself from him, and he went out wiping his eyes with the back of his hands. In a moment he was back with the wood. While he ate his pie she watered her many plants around the kitchen window chattering away about this spider plant needin' cuttin' back, or that one gettin' too big for its britches. "Do you like plants, Charlie?" she asked.

Though Charlie had never thought about whether he liked plants or not, he gave a little nod and a smirk.

"Well come now, and I'll show you Granddaddy."

She led him through the living room, down the hall into the parlour. Sitting at the window in a brass pot was a huge fern, its fountain of fronds spilling downwards almost to the floor.

"Do you know how old he is, Charlie? Over a hundred years old! A whole line of grannies, all of them dead an' in their graves, kept him goin'. Oh he's come close to dyin' sometimes. Especially this winter when I was sick he nearly died. But thanks be to God, and you, Charlie dear, I was able to save him. Come here and look. When I was a little girl I used to put my face right close to him and stare down into him until I would imagine I was in the middle of a forest all lovely light green with the sun streamin' into it. It was just like in my story book."

She paused and smiled at him, then bit her lower lip and raised her eyebrows as if being naughty. Her big china-blue eyes grew large as she said, "I'll let you into a little secret Charlie. I've never stopped doin' that. Come and look in with me."

Charlie bent over and looked, but he couldn't see anything but fern fronds and soil.

"Isn't it lovely, Charlie? Now here's a secret. My mother told me that when Granddaddy dies the sand dunes along the north shore will catch fire and that'll be the end of the Island. Imagine!"

For an instant Old Feardy rose in him. Betty, noticing he was disturbed, put her arms around him. Her softness and warmth were so comforting he clung to her. His arms tightened and she pressed her pelvis against him. A rush of passion between them frightened her and she broke away.

"Charlie, darlin' I have to finish up the kitchen and no doubt you have lots to do at your place."

She didn't want him to leave abruptly; but she also didn't want things to go further, so she took his hand and lead him out. He stopped to look at a picture of Jack with three army friends arm-in-arm taken in France in front of a store that said *Vins et Spiriteaux*. One had a wine bottle up to his mouth pretending to drain it.

"I guess the dunes caught fire for them," she said.

She pressed her free hand to his cheek and pecked him on the other. He reached out and pressed her breast flat with the palm of his hand.

For Betty, what had taken place was an expression of pure love, mysterious almost; for Charlie, something he didn't understand had lightened his gloom for a moment, something he would turn to often as a plant will turn towards light.

When he arrived home, Freddy Fenlon was waiting for him in the yard. They strolled around to the back of the barn and sat on a pile of milled lumber seasoning in the sun. Two bluejays were tormenting a squirrel clinging to the bark of a tree, chittering angrily. Freddy rolled a cigarette, licked the paper and spat a string of tobacco off his lip.

He looked at Charlie and said, "There's a fellow up in Summerside with a couple of fox bitches in cub for sale. What do you say we go in together and buy them? Your father did okay with foxes. They're coming back again. You've already got the pens."

Freddy, knowing Charlie well enough not to rush him waited patiently for him to answer.

"What's he want?"

"Well he won't rob us. He's a second cousin of Heska's.

He called me up to give me a chance at them. But he needs word by the end of the week. It's dangerous to move them too close to havin' their pups."

Charlie looked worried. "I'll let you know."

Freddy knew it would be Sarah who would decide one way or the other.

"All right, then, Charlie, don't take too long or we'll miss the chance. I've some things to do up in the house," he said leaving.

Charlie remained sitting on the boards in the sunshine, humming to himself. He thought about Betty, and his hand moved down inside his trousers.

Seven

Foxes

Getting the foxes onto the Ewart place was part of a well thought-out plan. Freddy stood to make a lot of money so it was imperative that he persuade the Ewarts to go along with the idea. He poured a tumbler of rum and slumped down in his favourite chair to think. Thinking for Freddy meant allowing his mind to sniff around a problem like a scavenger searching for food and then letting it travel at will in free association of past and present. He recalled how his friend Jack Logan got him into rum runnin', and his first meeting with Jack's old army colonel, Walter Wittigar. Wittigar and some merchants and politicians very skilfully masterminded a smuggling operation that encompassed the entire eastern seaboard. The locals had a romantic view of the rum runnin' trade and saw it as putting one over on the Tax Collectors in Ottawa as well as bringing in a supply of cheap and illegal rum; but few had little idea that it formed a part of a criminal network that stretched far into the United States and mainland Canada.

Freddy and Jack first met the Colonel in the smoke-filled mess hall of the Armouries. The Colonel, a tall red headed man dressed in an immaculate white Panama suit, surveyed the room with hooded eyes. Usually, he was in the company of four men: Lionel Buell, Myra Swanson's cousin, two bodyguards and Hughes, a fat sycophantic little Englishman. When the Colonel was around, Lionel was seldom far away; and when they were in direct conversation, it was in brief whispers. Wittigar had brought the little Englishman back to Canada after the war to work as his general manager. He had myopic brown eyes that bulged like a Pekinese dog's. The Colonel always referred to him as "Mr. Hughes" and so did everyone else to his face; but behind his back, they called him "the Pup." The Pup assiduously made entries into a pocket notebook. When the Colonel asked for information, the notebook held the answer. From time to time he went back and forth between the Colonel and Lionel. He also made hand signals to the two silent bodyguards standing in the shadows. Everybody called them, Bubble and Squeak.

When Freddy and Jack Logan were motioned into the Colonel's presence, he said, without looking at either of them, "There's a shipment coming in at Georgetown. Be at the dock at about zero 2:30 hours. Blink your lights four times. Load up and drive over to Mullaly's potato shed for unloading."

He nodded to the Pup who gave Jack a roll of money and told him the rest was waiting for him when the delivery was made at Summerside.

At Georgetown, Freddy and Jack sat in the truck in the dark listening to the sea as it lapped under the dock. Eventually, they heard the soft put-put of a fishing boat.

"That'll be it," Jack said turning his lights on and off. Soon dark shapes were passing up cases of liquor and kegs of rum to the two men on the dock.

Freddy laughed to himself as he remembered that night. He and Jack had gone on many such adventures since then. Now that Jack was gone he had to deal with the Colonel himself. He eased himself out of his chair and refilled his tumbler. The room was now in dusk. He stood and raised his drink to the absent Jack.

"Here's to you Jack, my dearly departed friend, and all the money you've stashed away for us."

A week earlier, Colonel Wittigar had called Freddy into a meeting.

"The Georgetown wharf is no longer safe. The Mounties are sniffing around, and we're going to have to phase out Mullaly's side of the operation. We need another hiding place. Now the Ewart place where it backs onto the gut of the harbour on the North Shore is good. We can land stuff there and hide it till we find a way to move it later when the Mounties relax a bit."

"How can you do that?" Freddy had asked.

"Well, we'll set you up in the fox business."

"The fox business?"

"Yes. Know anything about fox farming?"

"I do."

"Well that's all right then. Now tell me, Fenlon, what does the bitch do when she's whelping and is disturbed?"

Freddy saw Lionel and the Pup exchanging glances and smiles. He didn't like any of them to start with, and the thought that they might be trying to make a fool of him riled him, but he decided to go along with it.

"Well everybody knows she'll eat her litter."

"Exactly. So we'll hide the stuff under the pens. And if the Mounties come sniffing around, you tell them that if they disturb the bitches they'll eat the litters and that they'd better be prepared to give you some papers saying they'll be responsible for loss of valuable stock."

"And just how am I going to manage all that, now?" Freddy asked, not hiding his contempt.

"You figure it out—damned good money in it for you. There's only those two women out there and little Charlie. I'm sure you can handle them can't you? But listen, don't get them on side, understand? You're the only one to know. Get in touch with me as soon as you've made arrangements."

Jack in his cups by now mimicked the Colonel, "Damned good money in it for you. Damn good money in it for you. Figure it out–Prick! Well, sir, that's exactly what Freddy'll do—figure it out. Freddy always figures things out an' that's why I've got all kinds of money that son-of-bitch Logan stashed away on his farm in an old ammo box. There must be hundreds in it an' when I figure out where it's hid, it'll be mine, too!"

Freddy sat back in his chair and thought about all the money and how he could get it. It came to him, *Betty Logan!* I bet she knows where it is? He thought. I'll pay her a visit. She's a lovely soft little woman in all the right places. She must be ready to jump at it by now.

He cupped his free hand around his genitals and raised his tumbler of rum and said aloud, "I'm here Betty my love, ready and willing to oblige like a good neighbour."

The sun was setting behind the trees, its deep redness making the black branches of the firs look like the masts of a burning schooner. Those areas of the land where the sun had left were rapidly darkening. The cows had settled themselves for the night. In the darkening room he still grappled with the problem of how to get the foxes onto the Ewarts' land. His mind took up its meandering monologue again.

Why should I have to go to them cap in hand? He thought angrily. What would the place be without me anyway? I've slaved on this land for years, and now it's in the hands of them three idiots, especially that Sarah. Sarah! Why didn't I think of her? She'll make it happen. When she started doin' my wash she would just drop it off in a bundle. But lately she been foldin' it an' puttin' it all nice and neat in the drawer. An' she's been makin' my bed, too, and pickin' up after me. Just like a little wife. I bet I know what's goin' though her head while she's drinkin' my rum and playin' with the stuff in the old chest. Jesus, the ugly bitch has feelin's for me.

That day Charlie an' me was movin' the bull to service the cow, an' the stupid bugger opened the pen door before I could get out of the way, an' the damn thing threw me, I could tell Sarah had a thing for me then from the way she washed my scrapes an' bruises. "Lie over on your stomach, Freddy. Can you manage a drink?" She said all soft like. She sure poured off a hefty one for herself too. The way she pulled my trousers over my ass then rested her hand all warm on the back of my thigh. Boy I was hurtin' some, but it didn't stop me gettin' a hard on. She was not only carin' for me but she was *showin' me she cared*.

If only she had a bit of meat on her like Ruthie, I'd go for it. How can two sisters look so different? Ruthie's all soft, but Sarah's stringy like an old hen. Old before her time—always was. Now she has them little hairs growin' on her chin. Oh well what the hell, what difference does it make as long as a fella has his eyes closed?

He cranked the Ewart's rings on the telephone. Sarah answered.

"Sarah? Freddy here. Come over I've something important here to show you."

"All right. Soon as I clear the supper table. I've a pie for you anyway."

Freddy lit the oil lamps and carried one upstairs to the bedroom. He went to the hope chest and studied the hand mirror. *Perfect*. Sarah's always goin' on about it. It come over with the old people from Skye. Heska made a big thing of it all right about it bein' a family heirloom an' all. She wanted the young one to have it, but she left an' I'll give the damn thing to Sarah. All this passing on stuff is women's foolishness, anyway. He closed the lid.

Her voice called from downstairs.

"Freddy? You there?"

"Up here, Sarah."

She hesitated at the bedroom door.

"Don't stand there, now, come on in."

The lamp Freddy had set on the floor cast her shadow, huge, up the wall as she moved across the room. He poured out two tumblers of rum. She demurred.

"I shouldn't, Freddy."

"Ah come on Sarah. Have a drink, now, an' then I'm goin' to tell you something very nice—something worth celebratin'."

She took the drink and felt it warming her. Freddy poured her another one.

"What is it you want Freddy?"

He opened the hope chest and took out the mirror.

"I want you to have it, Sarah dear," he said, handing it to her.

She recoiled.

"No Freddy. Heska wouldn't let us touch it–said it was charmed."

"Yes it is, powerful charmed. That's why it's right to give it to you."

She drank her rum, trying to ignore the mirror as it glinted in the amber light of the oil-lamp. He moved beside her, took her hand, and speaking very softly said, "It can only be passed on with the hand of love, and believe me Sarah this is the hand of love."

He closed her fingers gently over the handle and held them so she couldn't let go. She was shaking.

"Look, my darlin'. Look at us in it. You and me."

He put his cheek to hers. She saw his face turning. Their lips touched. Freddy knew he must be gentle. He felt her face hot as he brushed his lips over her flushed skin. She did not resist him. He explored her more daringly; and when her body lilted and undulated to his touch, he gently undressed her.

Sarah allowed her passion to overcome her fears and misgivings. Once she had decided to go all the way, she abandoned herself completely to him. It all came together with surprising ease. He did not expect such a passionate response. As he whispered his love for her, he knew she was his.

"I have to be goin' now Freddy," she said to him after he had made love to her again. As she moved to get out of bed he held her back.

"No not yet, dearest. Let's talk for a minute."

She relented and he caressed her.

"Sarah, I want you to marry me. The Reverend Kerr will do it when he comes back," he said.

She stiffened but he held her more firmly.

"Sarah, about tonight. I wanted to propose to you first, honest, but love made me so overcome with you, dear, I couldn't help myself.

To his surprise she answered, "It's a good thing you didn't for I would have turned you down and we wouldn't have done what we did. No Freddy, I can't marry you or anyone else. Though before God, in whose presence I have sinned this night, I tell you Freddy I would be your wife if I *could*."

The thought of losing his advantage angered him. He pushed her away from him, scowling.

"In God's name why not, woman?"

She was crying, holding her hands over her face. He was disgusted and annoyed but feigned tenderness.

"Come on, now, Sarah, what is it?"

"I made a sacred promise to Mother and Father never to marry before Charlie."

He swore to himself, but he was determined to play it out. Holding her more tightly, he said, "But what's to become of me then, Sarah? What's to become of us? I want you to be my wife more than anything—My God, I can't think of a thing more right. Especially now."

She freed herself from him. He attempted to hold her again, but she made him listen.

"Freddy, I'll be everything to you a wife should be except your wife in name. I can't marry you and with the way Charlie is now I don't think I ever can. May God forgive me, but I'll swear before Him to be faithful and devoted to you, to pledge my life to you body and soul. Will you do the same, Freddy?"

This is even better, Freddy thought. I would have married her, now I don't have to, but he was puzzled about what she said about Charlie.

"Charlie? What's wrong with Charlie?"

"There's changes in him. I think there's something not right about him these days. Oh, an' you're such a help to him Freddy. He'd be lost without you. We all would."

As far as Freddy was concerned, Charlie was the same gink he always was.

"Sarah, I'm heartbroken that I can't do the decent thing and marry you. As far as Charlie goes, I swear he's like a son to me."

"Let's swear on the Bible, Freddy, I'd feel better please Freddy?"

Ah what the hell, he thought and reached over for Heska's large Bible on the night table beside the bed. He set it across their bare thighs. The hard leather cover felt cold against her skin. He placed his hand upon it, and she placed hers on top of his. They swore undying and faithful love to each other, and Sarah was as happy as if she'd been married in a cathedral. Eyes brimming, she reached over for the mirror from the tangle of bedclothes and held it up.

"Freddy, kiss me in the mirror again."

Revulsion lay coiled in his stomach, but her heart was bursting with love as she saw his smiling face come into the mirror to kiss her.

Eight

Freddy's Pit

Word came to Freddy that the shipment was due in about ten days. He had to act fast and put pressure on the Ewarts, but he had to do it right. Sarah would back him–that he was sure of. While he and Charlie were loading barley for milling, he said, "Did you ask the girls about the foxes yet, Charlie?"

"I forgot."

"Well how about me loadin' the rest of the bags and you goin' in and asking them now?"

Charlie worked away without replying, but just as he was about to pick up another bag, Freddy put his boot on it.

"Charlie are you deaf or somethin'? Go on in and talk to the girls, now. It's important for me to know how it stands."

He waited and fretted for a minute before leaving to tell the girls about Freddy's suggestion. They didn't really understand the details, because he mainly went on about how he hated foxes. Ruth and Sarah remembered his nightmares and his terror of the pelts hanging to cure at the top of the stairs. Their father had dragged him screaming to the pens, threatening to take his belt and lift the skin off his back if he didn't get in and clean them out. The foxes' malevolent, beady eyes and sharp little teeth bared menacingly, and their furtive movements as they darted in and out of their wooden lairs frightened him, and their feral stink made his stomach heave.

"Maybe I should call Freddy in to tell us what he has in mind?" Sarah said.

Charlie moved to his usual chair in the corner.

"Now don't you worry about it Charlie. If Freddy has an idea it's more than likely a good one. Anyway we should at least listen to it, eh? I'll call him."

She patted his hand, but he pulled it back sharply to show his disapproval. Ruth took a chair over beside Charlie and sat close to him.

When Freddy came in, Sarah met Freddy's eyes and sent him a secret message of love and reassurance. He told them about the pair of bitches soon to whelp and that they stood to make a good bit of money.

"Freddy, the truth of the matter is Charlie hates foxes since he was a boy. You remember how he was when father had them? Charlie doesn't want them about the place."

This suited Freddy exactly, and with quiet magnanimity he outlined his proposal.

"Look now, here's what I'll do. You go half on the foxes and supply the pens and the feed, and I'll look after them. Charlie needn't have nothin' to do with them. He doesn't even need to see them. I'll move the pens to the other side of the woods at the back of the barn. When the pelts are ready for curing, I'll take them over to my house. What do you say Charlie boy?"

Charlie didn't say anything for awhile, and then he shrugged his shoulders.

"If it's all right with Ruthie and Sarah, I guess."

Sarah stood up and went over to Charlie. As she passed Freddy she surreptitiously pressed her hand affectionately into his back.

"Well I think it's good of Freddy. He's gettin' the raw end of the deal. All the work, isn't that right Ruthie?"

"As long as Charlie doesn't have to bother with them I suppose its O.K.," Ruth said not looking up. That afternoon Freddy phoned the Colonel and told him it was on and that he would dig the pit.

"Make sure you shore up the sides. We don't want the Goddamn stuff buried—it has to go in easy and out easy," the Colonel said.

"I think I can figure it out."

Wittigar didn't like the contempt in Freddy's voice.

"Just don't mess it up, Fenlon."

The foxes would be supplied free and the ownership papers made out in whatever way Freddy said. He was jubilant. In addition to getting the setup he wanted, he would pocket the Ewarts' share of the costs.

Besides wanting the Ewart place, Freddy's other ambition was to buy a hotel in Charlottetown or out at the North Shore. There was talk about how tourism was going to be big business on the Island someday, and the thought of getting in on the ground floor excited him. He fantasized owning an expensive car and mingling with rich men from the mainland and screwing their elegant women.

There'll be a fair bit of money at Jack's in the old ammo box, he told himself, an' that added to what I have an' gettin' might go a long way to makin' it happen. Well I guess it's soon time I visited the grievin' widow Logan.

Over the next few days, he dug a deep pit and shored it with split spruce trunks. Then he covered the top with the freshly milled planks, camouflaging them with chicken wire, soil and sod. When he finished, he got Charlie and they loaded the pens and carted them over to the new location. He noted with satisfaction that Charlie didn't have a clue that they were setting the pens over a pit.

Nine

The Stash

The day the liquor was expected to land, Freddy laid out his stash of money and counted it. He was delighted as he looked at the neat piles of different denominations. Because Sarah had taken to rearranging his house of late, he was concerned in case she found his money. He thought, why keep it in the house at all? I'll hide it in under the fox pens. Yeah that's a perfect place. All I need is for that snoopin' bitch to find it. He took one more admiring look at the pile. Not bad for a little orphaned brat from Nova Scotia. A kid can have the shit kicked out of him, but if he has brains an' guts nobody can keep him down an' Freddy Fenlon's got his fair share of both. He poured a tumbler of rum and raised the glass to himself then downed it. There's only one thing missin'–the money Betty Logan's hidin', not to mention that nice little bum of hers. He carefully gathered up the stash and put it into a canvas bag. Before making his way over to Betty's, he hid it in the pit.

When he walked into her kitchen she was at the sink washing freshly laid eggs. Startled by his entrance, she dropped one making a sticky mess over her shoe and the floor.

"I'd like it better if you'd wait to be invited in. What do you want, Freddy?" she snapped.

Freddy traced the shape of her body inside her clothes as she bent down to wipe up the egg.

"Sorry, Betty, I just came over to have a word with you that's all."

"All right then have it—I've a million things to do."

She knew he was looking at her and it bothered her. "I've company coming."

"Who? Little Charlie?"

"Say what you've come for and go, Freddy Fenlon."

He checked himself from mocking her with taunts about Jack threshing in his grave with jealousy. His purpose in coming was his share of Jack's stash.

"Betty, dear, I've come for my share of the money."

"Money? What money are you talkin' about?"

She realized there was a real seriousness in his visit. She eyed him and noticed he'd been drinking. It'll be better if I don't rile him, she told herself.

"Sit down, Freddy an' explain what you mean."

"As you know, Jack and me had dealin's. He kept the money in an old metal army box. I'm sure you know what I'm talking about. Half the money in it's mine an' I want it."

"Believe me Freddy, I've no idea what you're talkin' about. Jack never told me nothin' about a box or money."

Anxiety pushed upwards in her stomach like it did when Jack used to get going. Freddy settled himself at the table. He appeared relaxed and was smiling, but his stare accused her of lying. He stood abruptly pushing the chair noisily behind him.

"Then, Betty, you and me better go on a treasure hunt, for I'm not leavin' without it. Where'll we start?"

"Nowhere. You get out!"

She stared back at him, defiantly. Living with Jack had taught her that he could be worse if she showed she was afraid. To her surprise Freddy walked out of the kitchen into the porch. She thought he was leaving, but instead he slammed the porch door shut and bolted it. Then he grabbed her and shoved her into a chair.

"Will you decide where to start lookin' or will I?" he said leaning on the table with his big hairy fists. "Come on now Betty, save us both a lot of trouble."

"I'll call the Mounties, Freddy."

"Bugger the Mounties!" he said, grabbing her shoulder and pressing his large callused thumb hard under her collarbone. He pulled her to her feet, and said, "Now lead the way!"

She squirmed free and ran into the hallway, but he caught her by the hair and pulled her back. Needles of pain went through her as she felt her scalp lifting. To muffle her scream he put his hand over her mouth and pushed her to the floor.

"Now Betty, you settle down. I only want what belongs to me. I'll let you up when you come to your senses an' help me look for it."

He lay on top of her. His blue eyes were made brighter by the bloodshot from the rum, and the thick scar tissue at the side of his temple where he'd been burnt as a boy made him more menacing. His hand over her mouth tasted of sour nicotine and salt, and his breath stank. She couldn't breathe; but it was not his large hand squashing her lips against her teeth that stopped her breathing, it was utter terror.

As she squirmed, he could feel her softness and the bony ridge of her pubic bone, and the harder she struggled, the harder he pressed. *If I fight him he'll kill me,* she thought.

He felt her body go slack. The power he had over her stimulated him more; and the pleading in her eyes, he took as compliance. Cautiously, he removed his hand. She gasped for breath.

"Get off me, Freddy and I'll help you look for the box," she pleaded.

He tightened his grip on her wrists, and said, "That's better. How about a kiss first?"

Transferring her wrists to one hand, he began unbuttoning her blouse. Fear trickled in her nostrils like acid.

"Freddy, I'm not comfortable. Kiss me now and then we'll find the box and after make ourselves comfortable. Please Freddy, dear," she pleaded, not caring what she said as long as it would get him off her.

His tongue filled her mouth gagging her. Then mercifully his huge weight left her.

"Okay. Let's be friends and look first," he said pulling her to her feet.

"We'll start in the barn," she said, but he was too clever.

"No, the house."

She had seen the box he was looking for many times. Jack, though, would never tell her what was in it. So what, she thought, let Freddy have it and good riddance. The most logical place to start was the attic. Jack often rumbled around up there.

"The attic," she said. "We'll try the attic."

"Lead the way then, madam."

Freddy let her climb up the stairs ahead of him. He shut the attic door behind them. The tiny space was acrid with dust, mouse droppings, and the mustiness of old clothes. Years of accumulated bric-a-brac were stored in there. Dead flies littered the floor like spilt raisins. Ample light flooded in from a dormer window where a large, trapped bluebottle buzzed obscenely up and down the pane.

Finding the box was surprisingly easy. Freddy went immediately to a brick chimney that carried the stovepipe from the kitchen below. He searched behind it, and there was the steel box on the floor covered with old books. He pulled it out, his arm white with cobwebs. Rolls of bills of various denominations were all neatly laid side by side in layers.

"Look at that now, Betty. All them dollars packed neat like little cabbage-rolls. Take a gander at it woman. You an' me's gonna have some good times, eh?"

Betty had never seen so much money in her life. Jack had always cried poverty, and she had to beg him to give her even a few dollars at a time. Freddy turned to her.

"There now was it worth all that fuss? You should learn to trust old family friends."

He made her count the money with him. Then he stuffed as much of it as he could into his money belt and into a leather saddle pouch that was lying on the floor. The remaining bills, he tossed back in the ammo box.

"That's yours, left you by Jack. Now, what about you and me?" he said, exposing himself.

While Freddy had been searching behind the chimney, Betty fixed her eye on a small dagger Jack said he took from a dead German. She managed to conceal it in her skirt pocket, praying to God she wouldn't have to use it. But now that Freddy was moving on her, she gripped the handle.

"Take your clothes off sweetheart."

"Please, Freddy," she pleaded, "I don't want to. You got what you want, now please go."

"Not everything—you promised downstairs."

He reached for her and she stabbed his arm and rushed to get out, but the winter damp had warped the door, and it was stuck fast. When Freddy felt the blood flow down his arm, he yelled, lunged at her and punched her face. Then he ripped off her clothes and raped her. The blood running down his arm dripped on her.

As she lay whimpering, Freddy took a handful of bills from the box and scattered them over her like Fall leaves.

"There, you whore!" he shouted. "Now you listen. You'll tell nobody because if you do, Jack's goin' to be found out for what he was, a rum-runnin' crook an' they'll believe you were in it too. An' everybody'll think you led me on because they all think you're a cockteaser. They all know how you used to make Jack jealous by flirtin' at the times in the hall. An' I just might kill you."

He put the steel box under his arm and called back up the stairs, "I'll come and see you again, but I'll expect you to be more sociable next time."

Freddy was elated. He had the extra money, and he was convinced that once a woman had a taste of a strong man she'd want more.

Betty, her nose broken and her jaw badly bruised, went in and out of consciousness. It was well into the afternoon before she made it downstairs. Charlie was waiting in the kitchen for her. When he saw her bruised and swollen face and ripped clothes caked in blood he started whimpering.

"You go on home, now, Charlie."

But Charlie didn't move or say a word. Both of them sat quite still as the kitchen grew darker in the declining afternoon sun.

Sarah, meanwhile, was wondering why Charlie hadn't returned from Betty's to do his own chores. It was very unusual for him to be late, for you could set your clock by Charlie. She felt twinges of uneasiness. The cows needed milking and were bellowing in the barn.

"It's funny Charlie's not back yet, an' the cows bawlin' to be milked," Sarah said to Ruth who was chopping vegetables for supper. At that moment a bird attacking its reflection clattered against the kitchen window and fell, neck broken. The sudden violence of the impact startled them. Sarah untied her apron and said, "I'm goin' over to Betty's. You finish up supper, now."

The late afternoon sky was a conflagration of striated orange and red. Some of the houses far down the road to the east were showing a dull glimmer of lamplight in their windows, and the air had chilled a bit. By the time she reached Betty's yard the dusk had deepened and the barn bats were out swooping and diving for insects. There is no light in Betty's kitchen. Sarah's uneasiness sank to dread when she entered and saw the dark figures sitting very still at the table.

She lit the lamp, and she saw Betty's bruised face, and the ripped and bloodstained clothing barely covering her. Charlie looked the same as he always did except for his eyes. Their light seemed turned inwards. She took him by the elbow and led him outside.

"Charlie. Go home and attend to the chores. I'm goin' to stay here and talk to Betty. You go on, now."

He turned, and like an automaton walked into the darkness towards home. Sarah made a pot of tea and sat opposite Betty.

"You get that into you, girl, and then we'll get you cleaned up and you can tell me what happened and who did that. I know it wasn't Charlie."

"No, not Charlie. Freddy Fenlon."

Sarah gasped and her heart stopped in her throat.

"Freddy? Why? What for—what did he do?"

"He beat me an' he, he forced me, Sarah."

Sarah filled a large basin with warm water; and while Betty cleansed herself she went upstairs to look for a nightdress, all the while struggling for control. Her mind raced to find an excuse. Did Betty lead him on? Was he drunk? Surely to God he didn't break his sacred vow. If he did, that would make her no better than a whore. Whatever it was, she had to learn the truth. At one point her heart palpitated so wildly she sat on the stairs until it passed. When she returned, she said to Betty, "You lie down." Then covering her with a shawl she ordered, "Tell me every detail about what happened, Betty Logan."

Betty told her about Jack and Freddy's rum-running, and about the money, and what Freddy did to her. Sarah's heart broke as she listened, then rage took over and she ran in a fury from the house through the darkness towards home.

Ten

Freddy's Lot

On his way home after raping Betty, Freddy paid a visit to the empty fox pens. The liquor was due in later that night, so he unscrewed the front panel of the pens so that all they had to do was lift up the pit cover and put the stuff in. While there, he put the army ammunition box along with his other money into the canvas bag. He was about to put his money belt in too, but he decided to hold on to it. Never know when a fella's goin' to need some ready, he muttered to himself.

The knife Betty stabbed him with had nicked a vein, and he was still bleeding. When he got back up to his house he took off his blood-soaked shirt, ripped off a sleeve and tried to tie a tourniquet above the wound. Elation had left him; his eyeballs were scorching hot, and his guts felt like they were filled with metal filings. The throbbing that started in his arm was now strumming his entire body. In a limbo of numbness he drank more rum to kill the pain. Nothin' to worry about, he told himself. No bastard can beat or outsmart you Freddy boy. They couldn't do it when you was a kid–not my shit-kickin' old man, or even my old lady when she was soused to the gills, or later on with them Bible-thumpin' Christly Van Ezarts. Drowsy and weak, he lay back on the bed.

The four corner-panes of his window were made of red glass, and the afternoon sun cast a reddish glow and threw leafy shadows that flickered across the ceiling. He studied them, and exclaimed aloud, "Jesus look at that would you! It's like the flames on the ceilin'."

His heart beat in his throat as he tried to shut out the night his house burned down, but the smells, and the yells came alive again. He could even smell the sweat off Mrs. MacLeod, the neighbour woman, as she cradled him. He had passed out, but as he came to, he could hear the animals squealing as they were herded out of the barn. It too had caught fire, ignited by sparks showered upon it when the roof of the house collapsed. The red shadows across the ceiling were exactly the same red that scorched the sky and coloured the whole barnyard. He jumped up from Mrs. MacLeod's arms and ran staggering and stumbling towards the burning house, but a big man grabbed him.

Freddy yelled in his head what he yelled then.

"Lemme go, lemme go my brothers is in there!"

The man held him tighter and Mrs. Macleod gently shushed him.

"There, there, son. You can't go back in there. I'm sorry son but your family's all gone. We're takin' you into the hospital. You're burned and your head's cut open."

After a few days in hospital a policeman and a minister came in to see him. The policeman gave him a bag of sweets, and said, "Well Freddy. That's quite the bandage roun' your head. You look like you come from the trenches. The doctor said they stitched you up okay an' your burns'll get better soon. How are you feelin' yourself, now?"

Freddy didn't answer him.

"Freddy, the doctor said it was okay for us to talk to you. This man here is the Reverend McKenzie. He's goin' to find you a good home."

Freddy looked at the Reverend. He was a short fat man with a stern red face.

"Freddy," the policeman continued. "I has to make a report on the fire so it's very important that you tell me everything that happened. The Reverend McKenzie is goin' to witness what you say. Isn't that right Reverend?"

"Yes indeed, yes. But first let us pray."

The policeman grudgingly bowed his head, but Freddy remained as he was.

"Bow your head and close your eyes, Freddy," the minister said.

"I can't move my Christly head!"

The reverend was about to chastise him for being blasphemous, but instead cleared his throat and bowed his own head.

"Dear Lord, shower your tender mercy on this poor orphaned boy. Give clear passage to the souls of his parents and little brothers. Guide him O Lord in the ways of Thy statutes, In Christ's name we ask these things, Amen."

The policeman, impatient to get on with things, cut in before the minister might start talking or preaching.

"Freddy you're a real fine boy, a good soldier if ever I seen one. I want you to tell us just what started the fire an' how you knew about it, like."

Freddy liked the policeman but not the minister, so when he got his notebook out, Freddy directed his story to him.

"Me an' my little brothers was lyin' in bed. They'd cried themselves to sleep because of the fightin' an' screamin' goin' on all evenin'–between dad an' mom. We was nice an' warm an' I was nearly asleep too. I was lyin' lookin at the floor linoleum. The moon shinin' in the window was so bright I could see all the swirls in it. Then I noticed smoke comin' in the bottom of the door an' I could smell it, like wood an' straw burnin'. It drifted up an' curled up around the legs of the chair beside the bed and spread out under the seat. It was startin' to fill the room. I jumped outa bed, and flung open the door. When I did that the smoke come in in big thick clouds. It was choking me. I ran through the smoke to Mom an' Dad's room."

Freddy held up his bandaged hands.

"See? The door knob done that–it was red hot. The door an' the frame was all blisterin' an' the floor was in flames. So was round the window an' the bed. Dad an' Mom were just dark humpy shapes with the flames all over them. Then the flames started comin' after me too. They made a rush at me an' chased me down the stairs an' tried to lick me through the banisters.

"I run into the kitchen for water; but the flames was there too. They was all movin' down the wall an' across the ceilin'. The cupboards was burning an' all Moms preserves an' jam jars was broke. You should'a seen it all sizzlin' an' frothin' an' pourin' out of the cupboards from broke jars an pourin' down all over the floor. Strawberry jam an' pickles mixed up and burnin'. Stinkin'. Me an' my brothers was eatin' out the pots early–you know that sugary stuff that bubbles up when your Mom makes jam. Anyway Mom was letting us eat that earlier an' that 'minded me that Billy an' Donald was still up stairs. I tried to run back up to them, but the flames was burnin' the stairs, an' I couldn't get up. They didn't answer me when I called up. The windows started breakin' an' boy you shoulda seen the flames. They started to roar an' change an' brighten, like. The kerosene lamps exploded sendin' sprays of little flames like a bomb goin' off. Then all the little flames joined one another an' there was one big flame that was burnin' the whole house. I seen the front door open an' I run to her. Somethin' hit me but I kept on runnin' anyway 'til I was with Mrs. McLeod an' the horse an' pigs was all runnin' about the yard an' the barn was on fire."

"What do you think started it, Freddy?"

"The flames, mister."

When Freddy's burns and wounds were all healed, the Reverend MacKenzie came to the hospital again.

"Well, the Doctor said you're all better, boy, and you can go to your new home."

"What new home?"

"I've found you a good Christian home with a family called the Van Ezarts."

Although Freddy's family had been rough and brutal, caring and humour was been built into its fabric. When his dad wasn't drunk and roarin', he could send them into gales of laughter with jokes and tom-foolery, or else he and his little brothers would go fishin' with him and bring back a mess of trout that his Mom would fry up. Whatever warmth and love his old home had afforded was gone, and now he was even without his little brothers. The family he found himself orphaned into was far worse than his own had ever been.

The Van Ezarts were the direct opposite to the Fenlons. They all had white hair, flat milky-blue eyes and thin mouths that seldom smiled—a thin family of three with skin the colour of pale lemon. They seldom ate meat, the only exception being a boiled chicken on Sunday. Ezra Van Ezart decapitated it on Saturday night and hung it over a bucket to drain for blutwurst, which they served with cabbage for breakfast. The rest of the week the main meal alternated between boiled turnips, boiled potatoes, boiled eggs or cabbage and salt cod mixed with scrambled eggs.

Their furniture was essential and basic. Nothing was purchased that could be made. Mattresses and pillows were hand sewn flour bags stuffed with straw; sheets were improvised from bleached flour bags, and the bed frames themselves assembled from spiked-and-lashed-together poplar saplings and birch poles cut in the woods.

Between Bible reading and praying, which they did routinely morning, noon and night, they conversed little; and when they did it was to make moral pronouncements on themselves and on their neighbours. The Van Ezarts struggled against an all-pervasive sin that had fouled everything and everybody. Theirs was a world populated with demons from hell that turned every newborn into an earthly reprobate.

When Freddy came to them, they thanked God for the opportunity to "save" him. "Mother" Van Ezart, for that is what she insisted Freddy call her, scrupulously scrubbed everything and everybody. The entire house and even the barn exuded a mixture of carbolic acid, bleach and whitewash.

The night Freddy came she stripped him naked and threw his clothes into a caldron in the yard that boiled night and day, winter and summer. It later became one of his chores to fuel its fire and to keep it topped up with water. If the embers lowered so that the bubbles ceased, or if the water boiled below the crudely painted red line, Freddy would soon feel the sting of a thin birch rod biting into his legs. Always the whacking was accompanied by some moral aphorism from the Bible.

In preparation for Freddy's arrival, Father Van Ezart had already filled a galvanized steel bathtub with nearly scalding water. Mother shooed Freddy like a gosling. He cried and held his hands over his little boy's penis.

"You stop crayon'—You lucky, God brought you to this house. Now you stop or I give you something to cry for."

She gave emphasis to her threat by giving him a violent shake before lifting and plopping him into the tub. Freddy reacted to the scalding hot water with language he had used almost from birth.

"Ah jumpin' sufferin' Jesus, my fuckin' feet's melted!" he yelled.

Ezra Van Ezart plucked him from the tub and dumped him on the grass outside.

"On your knees," he said without raising his voice.

When he said "knees" he pushed Freddy down and held him in that position, his callused thumbs pressed hard into the scrawny little body just under the collarbone. The excruciating pain immobilized Freddy. It was a grip repeated so often he carried a bruise there most of the time he lived with the Van Ezarts. "Now ask God's forgiveness!"

"I don't know what you mean—ah you're hurtin' me!"

Freddy's face was forced hard into the grass and rubbed in it.

"Now listen you devil to what I telling you, and then you say same thing. Dear God—please forgive me for bad and sinful language. I will not take God's name in vain again. Now you say!"

Freddy repeated it through his sobs, "I will not take God's name in vain."

"I will not take God's name in vain again! Again you say it!"

"I will not take God's name in vain again."

"Now open your mouth."

Van Ezart's large soapy finger pushed itself rhythmically in and out of the boy's mouth until he gagged and vomited.

At last Freddy was dumped back into the tub. He ignored the pain of the hot water this time by concentrating on the salt taste of his blood as it trickled from his nose. He also barred his mind against the painful scouring by Mother Van Ezart with her homemade lye, ashes, and bacon-fat soap.

Until he ran away, Freddy had spent five years with the Van Ezarts. They had ground down everything in him except anger. The hope he would escape made him restless for the rest of his life. He grew inured to the slap, the birch, or the belt and developed a thick cushion of numbing hate that prevented them from breaking him. The lesson he learned best was that nothing mattered but getting out of a scrape. He schemed subtle schemes to get a moment's relief from the droning moralizing, the droning praying and the droning reading of the Bible. He waited and watched for an opportunity to repay the beatings and perversions perpetrated on him by a prurient Rupert Van Ezart, their fifteen-year-old son. Rupert would fondle him, and if he resisted, Rupert threatened to tell his parents that Freddy was sinful.

Vengeance came when mother Van Ezart caught Rupert masturbating in the hayloft. Freddy was high up on the pile when he heard her screams and slaps.

She then yelled down through the trap door, "Oh Ezra, come, come. We have shame here–sin and shame."

Freddy dropped nimbly out through the end hatch, and listened with sheer joy to Rubert's pain as his father beat him.

That night, at the table, Ezra stood behind the boy pressing his thumb into Rupert's collarbone and holding the large Bible above his head. Rupert squinched up his face in expectation of the Holy Book crashing down on him. Ezra, however, only droned the "lesson from the Lord" paraphrasing it to make it fit, "...and Onan schpilt his seed upon the ground and the Lord was sore displeased."

He indicated to Mother to serve, but added, pointing to the mortified Rupert, "We eat—you pray."

Throughout the grim meal, Rupert sat before his empty plate, his head bowed contritely begging God's forgiveness. After that, the tables were turned and Freddy became the blackmailer.

"If you come near me again. I'll run yellin' to your father and mother, and tell them everything and about what you do with my dick," Freddy told a hapless Rupert that night in bed. "And from now on you'd better do what I want or I'll tell them anyway."

Ezra Van Ezart stashed his money in various hiding places around the house. Freddy had wormed their whereabouts from Rupert. His chance to steal it came one day when Ezra and Rupert were off selling a load of hay and he was home alone with Mother. Before going, Ezra left instructions.

"Mother, there's a Robert Mackay comin' about half past twelve with a cow. Look at her good. She should be in calf. Give him twenty dollar. You Freddy, put her in the barn, gentle."

While Freddy and Mother were eating the noon meal she left the table and unbolted the pantry door. She's goin' to get the money, Freddy decided. When she came back, he noticed the bulge of her purse in her apron pocket. She studied him with her flat milky blue eyes, and then said, "You gettin' to be a good lookin' boy, Freddy. You glad I got to be your momma?"

She gave him a thin smile and tweaked his mouth between her finger and thumb.

"Yes," Freddy lied.

"I'm glad too."

He was uneasy and confused by the affection she was showing. At that point, Bob Mackay knocked on the porch door, and she went out to the yard with him to look at the cow. Freddy rushed into the pantry and found the cash hidden in a corn meal barrel. There was five hundred dollars in tens, fives and ones.

He heard Mother Van Ezart calling from the porch.

" Freddy, you help Mr. Mackay put the cow in."

In the barn, Freddy whispered to MacKay, "I'll give you two bucks if you take me to town and say nothin."

"Two bucks? You must be in some hurry, young fella."

"Mister wait for me at the foot of the lane."

He studied the urgency in Freddy's eyes. The neighbours around detested the Van Ezarts because they were foreigners and didn't fit in. Mackay laughed, "You want to get away from the Dutchies? Okay on you go then."

Freddy ran into the kitchen, and with feigned concern said, "Mother Van Ezart, I meant to tell you before I put the new cow in, but while you were out talkin' to Mr. MacKay I heard somethin' smashin' in the pantry."

"Oh you should have told me. Time wasted gives Satan a good chance,"

But as soon as she stepped through the door Freddy kicked her hard in the spine, sending her crashing into the cream and butter jars. He took a moment to mock and laugh derisively at the sprawling woman before banging the door shut on her and bolting it.

Eleven

Eater of Fire

In town, there was an Agricultural Exhibition. Freddy had never seen the like of the Midway. It was a kaleidoscopic world that turned in every direction on its own heady euphoria: hobby horses, circling mirrors, yellows, reds and blues all orbiting to bubbly organ music. The fire-eater, snake charmer, strongman, escape artist, bearded lady and their wildly painted booths captivated him. The smell of meat pies, sizzling sausages, candy apples, salt-water taffy and burnt sugar sticks famished him. He had never seen so many people laugh at once with such reckless abandonment. It startled him at first, but he was soon part of it, and his stolen treasure allowed him to savour whatever he wanted.

His favourite of all was the shooting gallery. The young man running it was only a few years older than himself.

"Fifteen shots for a nickel! Hit a shootin' star and get another five free! You here again, boy?" the carnie said, winking at him. "What's your name?"

"Freddy."

He had noticed Freddy was spending a lot of money. Too much money, he decided, for a kid in a homemade flour-bag shirt, oversized hand-me-down trousers held up with binder twine, and his hair shorn almost to the scalp. I bet the little bugger's a runaway thief.

"Well Freddy boy, this one's on the house!" he said handing him the gun. "You live near here?"

"Ah, used to," Freddy said with marked caution.

"Where's your folks?"

"They're dead."

"Geez, I'm sorry. Go on an' take a couple more shots, buddy."

Freddy, delighted, shot a few more stars out of the sky.

"Listen, how would you like a job with the show? Gimme five bucks an' I'll get you one. We're pullin' out tonight."

Freddy eagerly paid. Later he watered and fed horses, folded canvas and coiled ropes until, at last, the carnival rumbled on its way through the night. Happy, he rolled himself in a blanket and nestled in a pile of clean shavings and in moments he had fallen into a blissful slept.

He traveled with the carnival for several years. It was a harsh life, filled with bullies and cheats, but he soon learned to survive by becoming one himself. He acquired the stock and trade of the confidence trickster: knowledge of human frailty along with the right combination of charm and cajolery. He learned that when people desire something and that desire is embedded in naiveté or motivated by greed, they'll believe anything in order to fulfill it. He could beguile the innocent and the cynical alike.

Freddy grew especially close to Lord Vulcan the Fire Eater, known to everybody as Vulk. It was rumoured that Vulk was an Englishman of noble birth now reduced to a drunken carnival clown. He took a homosexual fancy to Freddy, but the most intimate he ever got was when Freddy put him to bed after he passed out. He regaled Freddy with talk about his beautiful mother.

"An angel, she was, Freddy, a beautiful angel. I believe when she died her soul passed into another baby girl. Sometimes while eating fire, I fancy I see her looking at me through the eyes of a young girl in the crowd, and I feel so terribly ashamed. Just a look you understand, a clean decent look of love that says, 'James, James, you are better than this'. Freddy, if you ever see a look like that in the eyes of a girl don't let her get away from you."

Vulk taught him how to eat fire, and when he was too drunk or sick to go on, Freddy stood in for him. One morning Freddy found him stiff and yellow with the backs of his legs and arms, purple: the fire-eater had died in his sleep. They took him to a church in a small Nova Scotia town. The vicar asked, "Why did you bring him here? Is he Anglican? He's baptized I guess?"

"How the hell would I know?" the carnival boss replied. "He's an Englishman. That's what yous fellas is isn't it?"

"Very well, but I'm afraid I cannot bury him in the consecrated ground of the churchyard."

"I don't give a damn, Pastor. How much'll do it?"

"It's entirely up to you. But usually the Church gets a minimum of two dollars."

Vulk was put in a grave outside the cemetery fence. The Carnival boss gave the Vicar two dollars, and the Vicar read appropriate verses from the Book of Common Prayer. For another dollar, the Sexton shovelled in the grave.

Freddy was sad. The Vulk had been the one man who had shown him kindness. After the funeral, he went through his thick leather portmanteau. There was a pair of red silk Turkish pants, a heavy brass chain necklace with a crescent moon attached, two brass armbands engraved with *Vulcan, The Eater of Fire!* Also there was a bottle of oily brown liquid for staining the skin. The rest consisted of a worn pair of once elegant boots, patched long underwear and a ripped silk dress shirt. There was also a sepia photograph in a silver frame of a pretty woman lovingly hugging a little boy against her stomach. Freddy became the new Lord Vulcan the Fire-Eater. It was when the Carnival traveled to Prince Edward Island he met Heska.

As part of the act, the Barker interrupted the show, shouting, "Ladies and Gentlemen, you have witnessed Vulcan take fire into his body and scourge his skin with flame. Yet the flame burneth not his flesh! Flesh, ladies and gentlemen, the same as you an' me. Yet, his defies fire!

"You saw with your own eyes he does not protect himself. Tonight, for the first and only time for you very lovely people of beautiful Prince Edward Island…." Here he paused, leaned forward as if sharing a confidence, and said, "You know, Lord Vulcan told me today that of all the places he has performed around the world this Island is the most beautiful he has ever seen. Well tonight I will ask Lord Vulcan to reveal his secret to us."

The Barker turned to Freddy, speaking gibberish. After a moment of dramatic concentration, Freddy made a deep bow of respect to the audience, and then answered back in gibberish.

"Yes, Ladies and Gentlemen, Vulcan will reveal his secret to us," the Barker confided. "You see them armbands?"

He made to touch them, but Freddy quickly pushed his hand away in a burst of outraged gibberish.

"Forgive me, Lord Vulcan. You see Ladies and Gentlemen if I'd touched them armbands my fingers would be burned to a cinder. Them armbands was handed down through his family in the wild mountains of Afghanistan. They're charmed and it's that charm that protects his flesh."

It was a stifling hot August evening, and the crowded tent was filled with the stench of oily smoke. At this point Freddy lit an exceptionally large torch. A ball of fire shot up and died into a cloud of thick black smoke adding further to the stink of the stale canvas, crushed grass and hot bodies.

"Vulcan will now thrust his hand in the midst of that flaming torch an' hold it there! If any of yous is faint hearted, leave, an' if yous ladies would like to leave, do so now!"

It was while holding his huge torch that Freddy noticed Heska. Her eyes met his. They were the prettiest eyes he had ever seen. He remembered Vulk's belief about his mother's soul living on in a young girl. Vulk might have been a boozer and a liar, but he was absolutely sincere in his advice to Freddy not to let go the girl with the right look in her eyes. Then, holding those pretty eyes in his gaze, Freddy slowly and dramatically brought his hand to the flame. Heska fainted.

The next day while walking around the farmer's stalls, he saw her again, selling eggs and butter. Before the day was out he managed to get himself a job in New Skye working at the harvest. The carnival left the Island, but Freddy stayed on and courted Heska.

As Freddy lay in the shadowed room reliving these events from his life, he fell into a shallow sleep. When he awoke his arm and head were still throbbing. He felt stupefied and was in a foul malicious mood. Just as he was raising himself off his bed, he noticed one of his old brass armbands lying behind the cedar chest, and said aloud, "Eater of fire! That's you all right Freddy boy. You eat fire an' they all can eat shit."

He tossed the armband back onto the floor again and watched it roll under the bed. With a start it occurred to him he might be late. The first load of stuff was due tonight, and he had to light a signal fire on the dunes. If they didn't see the fire they'd take the load somewhere else.

He gulped more rum and went downstairs. To his relief the clock told him he was still okay. That morning he had gone down to the shore and piled driftwood for the fire in a saddle of a dune. All he had to do was torch it.

He lit a couple of the living room lamps. His arm was stiff. No time to bother about that now, he thought, cursing Betty.

While out in the porch getting together a hurricane lantern and his oilskins, Sarah, like a demon, burst in. She flew at him screaming, "You pig–you dirty pig. You're not fit to be alive!"

Sarah's dark eyes were bulging. Freddy was taken aback. She flew at him channelling four red tracks down the side of his face with her nails. As she pummelled him, he reached out with his free arm and covered her face with his hand. The back of her head smashed against the wall. Blood dribbled down into her throat. She fell, and Freddy kicked her full in the stomach.

Ruth, on her way out to the barn to help Charlie, heard Sarah's yells. She rushed over and saw the struggling shapes inside the porch door, Freddy roaring. Ruth flew at him. He stopped kicking Sarah, grabbed Ruth by the hair and dragged her outside, and choked her till she blacked out. When he felt her go limp, he dropped her onto the grass.

As Ruth came to a moment later, she heard Freddy cursing into the night somewhere. Then she saw him emerge from the porch, carrying a lantern. Terrified, she lay very still with her eyes closed. The light hovered over her for a moment. Freddy mumbled something, and the light went away. Cautiously, she lifted her head to peek and saw his black shape carrying the lantern through the gate of the back pasture and down towards the shore. She waited until the swinging lantern disappeared before running to the barn to get Charlie.

"Charlie! Quick!" she yelled. "Sarah's hurt!"

They found her staggering around the yard. Charlie carried her home with Ruth running alongside, whimpering. After sipping a drink of water, Sarah became more coherent.

"He forced himself on poor Betty, an' gave her an awful beating," she sobbed.

Ruth told of how Freddy had choked her and showed them her neck ringed with bruises.

"Oh he was such a good friend and neighbour, an' now he's turned out to be no better than a beast. If you had a dog like that you'd shoot him. He's like an animal that's went back!"

Instantly, Charlie's mind drifted back to Pepper, his spry little border collie.

"You mean like poor little Pepper, Ruthie?"

"Yes Charlie, like poor little Pepper. Even a gentle little dog like Pepper has to be put down when he goes back."

Charlie remembered the day Freddie called him, "Charlie come with me, boy."

Freddy led him round to the back of the barn.

"See that?"

Dead hens lay here and there around the yard, and dying ones hid under bushes. They had been attacked. Freddy picked up one of mauled hens and showed it to little Charlie.

"See that, Charlie, look. Pepper done that."

There was a hole bitten into the hen's back. Charlie could see its gray lung inflating and deflating like a little bellows. Freddy promptly wrung the hen's neck.

"You have to shoot the dog, Charlie, he's went back. An' now he's had a taste of blood, he won't stop. The next thing he'll savage the rest of the stock and everybody else's. You know your father'll make you do it anyway."

Charlie studied the hen at his feet, gyrating feebly before it died. He looked at Freddy and shook his head.

"C'mon now, Charlie. You'd better do it. Go and get the gun."

When he came back with the gun, Freddy had Pepper tied up.

"Now Charlie, give it to him right between the ears on the back of the head an' he won't feel a thing."

As Charlie lifted the gun, his heart pounding, Pepper inched towards him on his belly, wagging his tail in hopeful pleading little wags.

"Do it Charlie—fast, now!"

He took aim but turned his head away at the moment he fingered the trigger. The bullet smashed into Pepper's spine. His hind legs splayed out behind. He looked up at Charlie, appealingly, as if merely begging a morsel of food.

"Charlie quick, again now."

He fired again, successfully. Pepper's tongue fell out of the side of his mouth and blood trickled from his nostrils. At that moment old Charlie came round the side of the barn to see what was going on. The dog, the dead hens, and little Charlie holding the gun gave him his answer.

"You're learnin' Charlie," he said, delighted. "You thought that miserable dog was your pet and you trusted him. But an animal's an animal an' it's like the Good Book says, *The wolf entereth the pen by the back door.* You did what you have to anytime a beast ravishes the flock, ya kill it. An' dogs when they go back is the worst–except maybe a man. But Charlie, I heard two shots. One should a' been enough. Ammunition isn't cheap you know."

As Charlie relived the day he shot Pepper he looked at his bruised sisters and he remembered the dead and dying hens. He thought of Betty, hurt and bloodied. Freddy had gone back, and Jesus told him he knew what he had to do.

"Where's Freddy at, Ruthie? Is he still in the house?"

"No, Charlie. He headed down the back pasture towards the shore—crazy, like a wild dog!"

Charlie said to the girls, "I'll go and finish up now."

In the tool shed he got his double-barrelled shotgun, loaded it and headed down towards the shore.

The night sky had clouded over the stars and there was the feel of rain in the air. Charlie heard the sea. That meant the tide was coming in and he should head for the dunes rather than the flats. As he got closer he smelt the spicy smell of burning wood. He could hear it crackle and saw the sparks flying up into the dark.

Cautiously, he crept over to the edge and saw the bonfire in a saddle halfway down. As he crouched there mesmerized by the leaping flames, Jesus sang a canticle about dune fires and Granddaddy fern being dead. The voice within him swelled up, forcing him to stand so that he could sing in fullness against the sea wind. As he sang, the lights of angels danced on the water. Freddy heard him and shouted, "Is that you Charlie?"

Charlie took in Freddy's dark shape behind the flames all wavy through the heat. He slithered down the slope until he was in front of the fire. The brightness lit up Freddy's eyes. He saw the gun in Charlie's hands.

"What's ya got that gun for, Charlie, boy?"

"You went back, Freddy, like Pepper. I have to shoot you. Remember? Once between the ears."

He lifted the gun and slid off the safety with his thumb. The flames glinted along the barrel.

"Aw Christ, Charlie! NO CHARLIE WAIT."

Freddy made a rush at him but was stopped by the blast, followed by the buckshot shredding his lower abdomen and thighs. Still alive, he writhed at the edge of the fire with one boot resting in the red-hot cinders. Charlie stood over him. Freddy was bubbling blood and moaning; his eyes were pleading and questioning.

"I'm sorry I missed your head, Freddy, an' have to use two shells—ammunition's not cheap you know."

He shot the top of Freddy's head away with the other shell. The body quivered a second or two before going slack. The sole of the boot lying in the coals was catching fire.

Far out to sea an ocean-going schooner had unloaded her cargo of liquor onto an assortment of fishing boats. These, in turn, were destined to rendezvous with dories at various places closer to shore. The two dories destined for Freddy had seen his signal fire and rowed in close enough for Freddy to see their lanterns bobbing like fireflies.

One of Colonel Wittigar's henchmen aboard one of the dories saw a second figure appear on the ridge of the dune. Only Freddy was supposed to be there.

"Hold still," he whispered.

Silently they lifted their oars from the water and watched the second figure join Freddy at the fire. The water carried Charlie's shots like thunder. The henchman who was watching through his telescope said to the others, "Holy Jesus! Little Charlie Ewart shot Fenlon."

After Charlie's shape disappeared into the darkness, the Colonel's man was dropped off further along the shore. He reconnoitred the area, and when he was sure no one else was around climbed down the dune to Freddy's body. The fire by now was mainly embers. Periodic gusts of sea wind fanned it to brightness, each flare-up casting a red glow over Freddy's corpse.

Later that night when Wittigar was told what happened, he said, "Why in the hell would little Charlie Ewart shoot Freddy Fenlon? He must have had some strong reason. Well it'll all come out in the wash. Listen up, now. In no way must this be connected with our business. Understood?"

He waited until those around him nodded in agreement.

"You say the foot and the leg are badly burned?"

"Right to the bone. But he got it in the gut and head."

"All right," the Colonel said. "A couple of you get over there. See if you can swipe a can of kerosene from Charlie's place. Douse the body. Build up the fire and throw Fenlon back onto it. Leave no footprints and no fingerprints on the can except the ones already there. Leave Charlie's kerosene by the fire an' get the hell out of there. Wait. There's four of us know. Make sure it stays at that. Right? Make it snappy."

Twelve

Prayers

Sarah and Ruth met Charlie at the kitchen door.

"We heard shootin' Charlie," Sarah started to say, but stopped when she saw the gun in his hand, "Oh, Charlie what happened?"

Ruth, biting her nails, stood terrified behind her.

"Poor Freddy. I had to put him down. Took two shots," Charlie said.

"Put that gun down and come into the house. You hush your noise, Ruthie, and put the kettle on."

In spite of her aching body and swollen cut lip, Sarah virtually pulled Charlie into the kitchen and made him sit down at the table.

"Tell us what happened."

"I have to go an' get a shovel now, Sarah, and bury him. He's all blood an' the foxes'll get him, an' the dune's afire an' Granddaddy's dead."

"Stop Charlie, stop! You're not makin' sense. Now listen, we're gonna have to pull ourselves together. We're going to get down on our knees to the Lord. Come on now."

Sarah was sure she was being punished for her sins, not only with Freddy, but for the deep stain of sin upon her family. Charlie and Ruth followed her into the parlour, and all three got on their knees on the rug beside the organ. Portraits of bearded Victorian men with their dour women looked down severely from its shelves and ornate crannies. As a little boy, Charlie loved the organ's pillars and carvings. He imagined that the souls of his departed relatives lived inside the organ, and when his mother played they were making the noises.

Sarah looked at a picture of her parents that had been cut out of a larger family picture. The two were about sixteen when it was taken, and the photographer had caught a certain look between them. The glass was cracked because the picture had been the focus of violent arguments between Old Charles and Elizabeth. He would fling it off the organ; but Elizabeth would stubbornly replace it again.

At sixteen Charles and Elizabeth Ewart were so passionately in love, they couldn't get enough of each other. Their bodies were helpless in their touching, and their lips could only speak with kissing. Elizabeth fell pregnant with Sarah. Anger and shame ran through the Ewarts like a molten river. At a family meeting it was decided to let them marry and to set them up with a farm on the other side of the Island.

Sarah learned about the shameful secret at a family reunion picnic when she was a girl of thirteen. She found herself talking to Aunt Leah, a woman in her dotage. The old lady was making scurrilous comments about various family members as they greeted and talked to one another. Sniggering, she said to Sarah, "How's Elizabeth and Charles gettin' on?"

"Who, Aunt Leah?"

"Your mother and father, child. You stupid?"

"They're doin' good, Aunt Leah."

"Them's closer than first cousins. You know what that means don't ya."

"No Aunt Leah."

"That means you might turn out to be queer in the head."

Sarah knew the old woman was trying to upset her, but as she made to move away, Aunt Leah grabbed her hand and pulled her closer.

"Guess who your grandfather give a baby to? His first cousin. He didn't marry her. Know why?"

"No," Sarah said. Now she was curious as well as angry.

"She was already married to another first cousin."

Aunt Leah snuffled and sniggered so much that a gob of mucus blew down her nose.

"Know who the baby was?"

"No."

"Your mother. Know who Elizabeth's half brother is?"

When Sarah didn't answer, Leah tugged her hand hard to make her pay attention.

"No. Who?"

"Your father. Now there's one for you to figure out."

Sarah was trembling and tried to hold back tears. At that moment a barn cat sat down in front of them to leisurely wash its face. The old lady pointed at it.

"Would you look at the wry neck on that cat. All our barn cats have wry necks because they're all first cousins an' brothers and sisters an' mothers an' sons. All the damn Ewarts have wry necks. You have one too, girl."

Sarah, not able to take any more, broke away and ran behind the house crying. The old lady hurled abuse at the cat. From that day on Sarah regarded herself as bad seed.

From her knees, on the parlour floor, she looked up at her parent's cracked picture, and then at a framed picture fashioned out of silver paper that said, *Bless Our Home*. She bowed her head and prayed fervently, "Dear Lord, please forgive us our sins. We have no one to turn to but to Thee Lord. Only Thee can help us now. Dear Jesus help us we're lost! Help Ruthie, Charlie and me. Our Father which art in heaven, hallowed be Thy name...."

They prayed until they were exhausted and drifted into sleep. A few tentative notes of birdsong cut through the silence, and the first light of dawn was casting a red glow over the sky. Sarah, stiff and sore, moved back into the kitchen filled with the terrible knowledge that Freddy was lying dead on the sand dune and that her brother had killed him.

"Charlie, you're not to go back down there, d'ye hear me?"

Charlie nodded.

"You go out and tend to the barn, now. Don't do everything—just what needs doin', an' come right back in."

On the way over he stopped to urinate. As he stood draining under the spreading dawn, Jesus sang a little verse Charlie had learned at school: Red sky at night, sailor's delight

Red sky at morning, Sailor's warning.

PART TWO

MARK KERR

Thirteen

Mark's Grief

When Mark Kerr lost Mollie and the baby he was faced with the task of telling her parents back in Edinburgh and his own parents in Montreal. He struggled to find words that would soften the blow but could find none. Mollie's mother, Margaret MacKinnon, had tried to dissuade them from getting married. The courtship was too short, and she was alarmed and saddened that Mollie was leaving home to go to a small island off the coast of Canada. Her parting words to Mark were *I know you'll take good care of my Mollie.*

Now those words wouldn't leave his head; her voice said them over and over–*I know you'll take good care of my Molly.* In the end he could do no more than telegraph the terrible facts: MOLLIE AND BOBBY DIED FROM INFLUENZA STOP LETTER FOLLOWING STOP LOVE MARK STOP.

A terse cable came back: WE HAVE NO WISH TO SEE YOU OR HEAR FROM YOU AGAIN STOP MARGARET MACKINNON STOP.

The MacKinnon's had lost two sons in the war leaving them only Mollie. When the baby came Mollie named him Robert James after her brothers. As she nursed him, she said, "Och, my wee Bobby-Jimmy we're all together again in you. What a miracle. What a miracle."

The curt answer from the MacKinnons was almost a final crush to his spirit. Ever since the funeral his grief had intensified to the point that he could barely muster enough strength to talk to people. He sat in the empty manse drinking. Death had shattered so much, but the extreme cruelty was the baby. He recalled seeing a sculpture wrought by Mollie's artist father of a woman giving birth atop a skull. Perhaps it was prophetic. Perhaps MacKinnon had been haunted by some tragic premonition of his sons' fate; a fate now fulfilled in the death of Mollie and the baby.

Mark cursed, wept and drank craving oblivion; and when short bouts of it did come, he awoke in worse pain than before. Grief paralyzed his mind, and he even stopped showing up at the church to conduct services. One evening a couple of the elders paid him a visit and were shocked to find him in the dark yelling obscenities at God.

"If you exist finish me? Strike me! A loving God? You're a blood-swollen bastard!"

When they lit the lamp and saw his stark eyes and white face, they knew he was broken. A group of ministers met and prayed with him, but Mark could find no solace in the resurrection and the life. He scowled at them while they prayed, then walked out in the middle of their fervent entreaties and took a swig of rum.

He hated Mollie for leaving him. He hated her presence in death. He wanted her expunged from his every waking thought; yet his grief spoke only one word, *Mollie*. The Presbytery members met and reached a consensus that he was too ill to stay, and they insisted he go home. Mark boarded the train for Montreal.

In his tiny bedroom compartment, he sipped whisky. It was dusk and he caught his reflection in the window looking back at him like a ghost. As the landscape skimmed by in the fading light, trees, telegraph poles, small rural churches, houses and cemeteries passed through the face in the window. The porter went by outside tapping on doors and calling out, "First call for dinner. First call."

The dusk had faded to black making his image in the window sharper.

He leaned his head against it, forehead to forehead and looked into his lifeless eyes while the wheels on the track mocked him—dead *Mollie, dead Mollie*. At last, exhausted, sleep consumed him.

When his mother saw him so pale and gaunt, his black hair now streaked with gray, she was appalled. She wept to his father, "Oh Sam, he's so broken...."

"With rest and care he'll come out of it in time, my dear. God's will be done," Sam replied, cutting her off.

Mark's father had been with the troops in the war and had seen trenches turned into abattoirs. He consoled and prayed with young men broken in body and spirit. The carnage and suffering had forced him to find a justifiable theology. In the end, he concluded that strength to keep going in the midst of such destruction came from God, and he found his credo in the Psalmist's words, *Yea though He slay me, I will believe.*

"Mark will pull through," he told his wife. "God has work for him to do, and, in that, he will find his solace and salvation."

But Mildred Kerr was not comforted. Ever since Sam had returned from the war he often drifted into moody silence, with eyes far away and full of pain. He would suddenly get out of bed and pace, or else go into his study and lock the door. She felt that if his faith was truly real he would not need to express it so often and so strongly. She wanted to question him, but some intuitive doubt kept her from doing so. She harboured deep misgivings about Sam's repeated optimism in the efficacy of the Lord's eternal plan, and when he applied this "optimism" to their broken son, the glibness of it angered her.

Mark, meanwhile, ate and spoke little. During the day he sat morosely in the garden watching his mother prune her rose bushes or grub around in the flowerbeds. She kept a surreptitious eye on him but refrained from showing how worried she was. Above all she avoided putting an extra strain on him by engaging him in trivial conversation. In his own good time he'll talk, she told herself. Mark, not wanting to hurt his parents further or to be offensive, restricted his drinking to his bedroom at night-time. But once, awakened by shrieks, they found him sitting up in bed, his eyes wide and stark. The room reeked of whisky. Sam, unable to stand the sight of him, went downstairs, leaving Mildred to soothe him back into sleep.

"It's alright Mark. Lie back, now, and close your eyes," she said, stroking his hair.

When she rejoined Sam, she said, "Sam dear, I don't want prayers or sermons, but I'm afraid if Mark doesn't get help he might lose his mind."

"Yes dear. I'll talk to him tomorrow and try to get him to see Philip Dixon."

Worry kept them both awake for the rest of the night. Sam had difficulty breathing, and a multitude of disordered thoughts stormed his mind. The next morning, Mildred took Mark a cup of coffee and sat on his bed while he sipped. He found it difficult to look at her.

"Your father would like to have a talk with you, Mark. Please go in to see him. A chat will do you both good."

He put on his dressing gown and went directly to the study. He was a little relieved when Sam wasn't there yet. The study hadn't changed much. The same stale pipe-tobacco smell, the same books, and the same old picture of the Last Supper, emphasizing a scowling Judas averting the Master's steady and knowing gaze, confronted Mark.

Once when he was a boy and was in the study to be chastised for some mischief or other, his father drew his attention to the picture and said, "Judas is sly and crafty. When a man cannot speak truth or think straight, he gets that very look, Mark." For emphasis, he tapped Judas with the stem of his pipe. "If you have nothing to hide you can look another man straight in the eye, just like the Master, there."

At that moment, Sam came in and cut through his thoughts. He took his seat behind the desk. Both men were uncomfortable.

"You had a bad night, Mark?"

Mark, absorbed, missed the comment.

"I'm sorry, father, what did you say?"

"I said, you had a bad night."

"Oh."

"Mother and I are in grief with you, Mark, but we're also very concerned about you. Shouldn't you be thinking of what's ahead for you?"

Mark didn't answer.

"You know as well as I that grief such as yours can take hold of a man and pull him down in the wrong direction."

"You're referring to my drinking, Father. I know how terrible last night must have been for both of you. I'm sorry."

"Ah me, well yes, of course that's part of it, but a complete negation of life and responsibility can lead to a collapse of the mind."

As he spoke he reached over and filled his pipe from the humidor. Mark still said nothing. As far as he was concerned, all that mattered was the obliteration of pain even if for only a few hours. Perhaps I should go away soon, he thought.

Sam studied him while he got his pipe going. Had he been a parishioner it would have been easier to talk of the Lord's unknown plan; instead he mumbled a paraphrase from scripture, "His way is not our way...."

He hoped Mark would end with, *and all we have to do is have faith*, much like reading a child's favourite story when you let the child finish the sentences. But instead Mark said, "I don't understand His way, Father. What's more, I don't believe there is a way, at all. I've no faith in that. I saw too many prayers go unanswered this winter–especially my own. Mollie and the baby are dead and I wish I were with them."

Sam's distress deepened. "Believe me, Mark, this too will pass. This cup of grief will be taken from you. He has work for you that will glorify both Him and you."

"How do you know that, Father? Did He tell you? He had work for Mollie—her music, her motherhood. Did He cut them down so that I could glorify Him? I'm afraid I've missed the point somewhere."

Sam sighed.

"Ah me, I just don't know, Mark. I'm without the answer you need. But I know you're on the wrong path, and I know, also, suffering can lead you to a clarity you've never known if you choose the right path."

Mark didn't want to hurt him but he said anyway, "Father, what you are saying is fine for those who want to believe it. That's the only way it will work. I simply don't believe all that nor do I want to."

Grasping for some sort of a hold, Sam countered, "Ah, but you said, 'It will work....'"

"And I also said that I don't choose for it to work!" he shouted.

Immediately he was shocked. He had never raised his voice to his father before. Sam paused. Then he went round the desk and said to him, "Mark, losing your faith is bad enough, but I'm afraid of you losing your mind. Please, son, don't slip from sanity. Will you talk with someone? Talk with someone I know?"

Mark misunderstood. Thinking his father wanted him to pray with him, he made to stand, but Sam, realizing he'd been misunderstood, said, "No, no. I mean a person."

"Who?"

"A man from the congregation, Philip Dixon. He's an alienist—a good man whose specialty is working with mental problems. Why not have a chat with him?"

"Let me think about it, Father. I will, seriously."

More bad nights ensued, and his mother decided to break the promise she had made to herself not to confront him. She sat beside him in the garden.

"Mark, your father and I are distraught. We lost Mollie and the baby and now we feel we are losing you."

She walked away from him and knelt down beside her herb garden. As she tended it, he could see her hand going up to her eyes. His father in the meantime had called Philip Dixon.

Fourteen

Turning Point

Mark found a note on his dresser table:
Dear Mark:
I had lunch with Dr. Philip Dixon today. He said you can call him anytime.
Here is his card,
Father

Mark thought about his parents. Both were aging, especially his father. Sam's hair was snowy white, and he had lost his old robustness. The only time it seemed to come back was when he was involved in the ecclesiastical debates and meetings having to do with a major ecumenical movement taking place in Canada. Mark mistakenly believed his father's enervation was a result of the death of Mollie and the baby.

His mother, who usually had the warmest of smiles, was markedly changed: her hair was streaked with gray, and at times, he thought she looked bitter and weary. The brightness had left her eyes. Out of concern for his parents, he decided to call Dixon.

That night Mark had a terrifying nightmare. In the dream he found himself walking up the narrow stairs of a dilapidated wooden building, its walls scabby with old red paint. As he climbed to the top, the walls moved closer together. It was stifling. His heart pounded. Suddenly he was behind the high railings of a narrow passageway; it was almost like a cage. He looked down on a room with a long oval table. A large, high, wing-backed chair stood at one end. Mark knew someone was sitting in the chair. He couldn't see him but felt his presence, and it terrified him. The chair turned slowly around; and Mark's fear mounted to such a pitch he surfaced from the dream, shouting. Instantly the dream left him and he was back in the reality of his bed, sucking for air like a dying fish and writhing in a tangle of sheets, soaked in sweat.

The horror of wakefulness was no less than the horror of the nightmare. When he closed his eyes, strange faces floated to him out of the blackness of his mind. Eventually he slipped into sleep, but in the morning the fear still lingered in him.

Fifteen

Philip Dixon

Philip Dixon greeted Mark, and after a few pleasantries said: "Well, Mark, I'm sorry you've been having such a rough time of it. How do you think I can help?"

"I really don't think you can. I'm here more to please my parents."

"Did they coerce you in any way?"

"No."

"So you are here out of compassion? Well that's a good place to start."

Mark felt a hook biting in. He drew back and said nothing. Philip appraised him.

"Mark, could you try to tell me a bit about how you feel?"

"I feel nothing and wish I could feel less."

Philip knew Mark was taking him in, so he left himself open to scrutiny. What Mark saw was a tall, slim man of about forty, dressed comfortably in a well-cut tweed suit and polished brown brogues. He had frank, gray-blue eyes and exuded excellent health. There were several disconcerting features, though: the lower half of his left ear was artificial; his cheek and neck were mainly scar tissue that disappeared down inside his shirt; and his left hand was artificial.

Philip smiled and said, "I see you've noticed my bits and pieces. The ear is wax, the hand is wood. The skin you see growing rather roughly on my face and neck is from my backside–the war. But you know, the Hun didn't do it, our fellows did. I was leading a reconnaissance patrol into no-man's land. While we were out, a replacement Commanding Officer had come in—should never have been sent back up—shell-shocked.

"Well, as we were heading back to the trench, one of the boys in my patrol kicked a trip wire—you know, one of those lines with tin cans tied to it? The new captain sent up a flare. He saw our shapes in it running towards the trench. Of course to him we were Germans—anybody out there he didn't know was a German. He ordered the men to open fire. The sergeant knew it was us and pleaded with him to rescind his order. He threatened to shoot the sergeant. A whole panic had already started. The Germans saw us in the flare and started shooting; and when they started, everything opened up. I was the only one left alive. When I came to at daybreak, I was covered with everybody else's blood, brains, and guts. It's a wonder somebody didn't finish me off to put me out of my misery. Later, that's what I wished.

"Now here's the part that's stranger than fiction. The captain was none other than my younger brother, who got shot by a 'stray' bullet. I never knew what happened until months later, because I, too, had gone off my head. My poor brother was reported killed in action and was posthumously awarded the Military Cross for valour."

Mark let out a spontaneous laugh and immediately felt embarrassed and confused. He put his head down.

"I'm truly sorry, Dr. Dixon. That was stupid."

Philip let him stew for a moment.

"That's all right, Mark, it's a joke—true nevertheless, but a tragic joke."

He poured him water from a carafe, but Mark's hands shook so, he could barely hold the glass.

"Listen Mark, if you truly want oblivion, increase your drinking by about four times. But it's a hell of a way to go—besides, while you're doing it you might do something you'll feel ashamed of."

"How do you know what I want, or don't want to do?"

"Well of course I don't know, but I suspect you don't either. What I do know is I'm looking at a man who's terrified, and that a natural antidote to fear is denial, seclusion, oblivion or aggression– you seem to have selected oblivion. But under it all is a very real desire to be rid of the fear."

Mark was angry.

"You assume a hell of a lot."

"Well, you tell me. Are you, or are you not experiencing very real terror?"

He didn't have the energy to argue, and rather than confront the issue he wanted to get up and leave. After a moment, however, he heard his voice speaking through the anger.

"Yes. I experience terror."

"Good. You have compassion for your parents and you have fear. Tell me about your fear."

To this point he had not consciously isolated the word "fear" from his state of being anymore than one would separate the word "air" from his immersion in it. His mind balked, then he mumbled, "I have no idea where to start."

"Start anywhere. It's all a labyrinth of subtle deception. So start anywhere."

Anger rose again and he shot back, "What makes you so cocksure, Doctor, you can intrude and lead me through my 'labyrinth of subtle deception' as you call it?"

"I've been through it and back, and I've taken many others through it and back."

Mark, even more angry, scowled.

"That's damned glib. Whatever's in me is personal. Mine! Not yours or anybody else's!"

"Yes and no, Mark. Your fear hides and disguises itself. Unless you confront it, it will consume you. C'mon Mark, give yourself a break. Just make a start."

Enervated, Mark looked at Philip for a moment, and then said, "I want to sleep, but I'm afraid to sleep, and yet I don't want to be awake."

Philip scribbled on a pad and handed it to him.

"Mark, you're run down. I want you to have a complete physical. See this doctor. His office will call you. In the meantime, I'm going to prescribe a mild sedative. Try to take a bit of a stroll every day—the park, the city, the campus—anywhere really. A dip in a pool isn't bad. Try to do with less whisky—better none at all, but don't push yourself too hard. I'll see you same time next week."

He stood, shook Mark's hand and led him through the door, rather abruptly, Mark thought.

After leaving Dixon's office, he strolled towards the McGill campus. The classes had ended for summer recess, and there weren't many students around.

How drastically my life has changed since I was a student here, he thought. Statues of past scholars and founders were still suspended in time among the same leafy trees and ivy-covered buildings. A new memorial erected to those killed in the war caught his attention. He studied the columns of freshly chiselled names, deeply cut and lined in red. Some of the names he knew—classmates who had left their books for guns. Most of them had been given the rank of lieutenant.

'Lt. Apsley, killed in action at Moines.' Old Curly Apsley, he thought, who used to sprint with such vigour; Snowy Johnstone who loved to get drunk and spout poetry; Harry Peterson who rivalled him for a girl and won. Then his eye stopped at Capt. Brian

Dixon, B.Sc., MM., killed in action at Dieppe. Philip's brother, the tragic joke.

Somewhere from the building behind, a rush of piano scales avalanched over him. He went in and saw a young girl of about eighteen totally absorbed in an energetic practice. Her hands attacked the keys, making her ringlets bounce vigorously. She looked up briefly, smiled at him, and then continued. Though she looked nothing like Mollie, her energy and playing brought Mollie alive in him. He reeled outside, leaned against the memorial wall and wept. He felt a light tap on his shoulder. It was the girl.

"Are you all right?"

Mark left without answering. After watching him walk quickly away in the direction of the university gates, she looked at the names of the dead for a moment, shrugged her shoulders and then returned to her practice.

He walked aimlessly until he found himself at the docks in the transatlantic departure shed. A liner was about to set sail, its passengers crowding the rails and waving to people on the dockside who had come down to see them off.

The ship's band was playing, "It's a Long Way to Tipperary." People sang along and threw paper streamers. It was as if the long ribbons of coloured paper were the last fragile link with loved ones. Mark stayed on until the large ship pulled away stern first from the dock and turned into the river. Its throaty horn bellowed a last farewell. He watched it sail away. The people still on deck waved and grew smaller with the widening gulf. He thought of Margaret MacKinnon's lone figure on the quayside the day he and Mollie sailed for Canada.

Margaret had journeyed down from Edinburgh to see them off. As a wedding present, the MacKinnons had bought them a stateroom. She spoke to the purser, "This is my lassie. She's on her honeymoon. Now here's five pounds and I want you to see to it that they are spoiled rotten."

He remembered how impressed they were with the opulence of the stateroom with its polished wainscoting, beautiful ornate bed and nickle-plated bathroom fixtures. A huge bouquet of roses along with a bottle of champagne and a box of chocolates sat on an elegant mahogany table. Mollie and her mother sat holding hands while Mark poured the champagne. They raised their glasses and sipped forlornly in silence until a steward tapped on the door announcing it was time for guests to leave. It was almost a relief for them to part. Margaret embraced Mark and whispered those despairing words, "I know you will take good care of my Mollie."

As the liner pulled from the dock, Mark and Mollie stood by the rail and waved to Margaret MacKinnon's lone, diminishing figure. After about an hour of watching the city lights on both sides of the Mersey River recede, Mollie shivered and said to him, "It's getting chilly, love, and I really don't like looking at the black water of the river. Why don't you take me to our bed?"

In their cabin, she said softly to him, "Let's turn our backs to each other and undress, then never turn our backs on each other again."

She stood naked, smiling self-consciously, her eyes deep with love. He took in the little mound of hair between her legs, the beautiful line of pelvic bone, her lovely thighs and small feet–feet so delicate, it seemed all her innocence was arrayed in them.

Slowly she opened her arms. He kissed her softly on the mouth. The feel of their skin was delicious. He lightly traced her lips, cheeks, neck, and breasts with his fingertips. Her soft hand covered his and gently directed him downward towards where her body folded into itself. The feel of her hair was electrifying, and the soft moistness of her, divine. He lifted her onto the bed and they rose and fell together, their limbs stretched and straining in erotic ecstasy. They fused and breathed as one, sharing the sweet taste of moist skin on lip and tongue. As they lay there floating and tingling, she whispered, "Now I truly belong to you, body and soul, for life."

She kissed him and held his head, stroking his thick black hair until he fell into a delicious slumber. Before the night ended they made love several times again. It was a journey of absolute joy. They could not bear to be out of arms reach of one another, and during a violent mid-Atlantic storm as the ship pitched and lurched on the high seas, Mollie conceived.

Another bellow from the ship now well on it's way up the St. Lawrence River brought him back to the empty present. It was turning to dusk when he walked along St. Lawrence Street towards town. The streetlights glowed like sick orbs in the half-light. A prostitute smiled and accosted him, inviting him into a squalid tavern. He ignored her but went into the bar anyway. She followed him, coaxing him.

"I can show you a nice good time. Buy me a drink an' I can tell you all the nice tricks up my sleeve."

He sat down at a little table and she joined him. She reached under the table and gently tried to caress his testicles.

"I'm sorry, but I don't need you. Please."

She persisted. The barman saw what was goin' on. He walked over.

"The man doesn't want you. So you take your *plait* out of here or I'll throw you out."

She left calling, "*Cochon! Merd*" followed by a string of obscenities.

As the evening wore on, dockers, sailors and more prostitutes crammed the bar, filling it with raucous talk, laughter and smoke. Suddenly the general babble shifted to a chorus of shouts and screams. Chairs and tables flew accompanied by broken glass.

A vicious fight had erupted between two drunken sailors. The police were called in and when they tried to separate them one of the cops received a savage kick. In a rage, the policeman lashed out with his baton at the sailor and caught him with a vicious sideswipe to the temple. The crack of wood on bone resounded above all other noise. The sailor fell and lay quite still, a puffy bruise welling on the side of his face. Blood gushed from his nose onto his white vest.

The bar was quiet while waiting for the sailor to move, but he remained still.

Mark staggered towards the felled sailor. The police shouted at him, "Stay back you!"

"Constable, please, I'm a Minister,"

"You're a fuckin' drunk!" The policeman said, giving him a hard punch to the stomach. "Now keep back, everybody. Get Back!"

Suddenly, the other sailor sprang to the attack, but the policeman managed to get him in a chokehold. The more the sailor struggled the more the policeman's hold tightened, and the sailor's face deepened from purple to black.

"Let him go! You're choking him to death," someone in the crowd shouted. But the policeman still held on until the struggling sailor finally lost consciousness. Meanwhile an ambulance and the police wagon arrived. Several more policemen came in and cleared out the bar, while the sailor who had been choked was handcuffed and dragged outside.

Mark, meanwhile, managed to stagger through the crowd out back to the toilet, a small square space with a plugged drain. The place stank of stagnant urine. He sank to his knees, retching, and when he tried to stand his legs failed him. A couple of beefy hands grabbed him. He was punched and dragged back out through the bar and thrown into the street. A large crowd had gathered around the door, laughing and jeering at him. A couple of prostitutes took him by the arms and led him away.

"Come sweetheart, we'll take care of you."

He came-to in an alleyway at the first light of dawn. His wallet was gone. After being sick several more times he made his way back up through the city until he finally reached home.

As he hung onto the door, banging on the knocker, the ground and the house floated slowly around him. When his mother appeared, he fell in the house covered with vomit and dirt. She put her arm around him and helped him upstairs to the bathroom where she stripped and bathed him. His father, distracted, watched helplessly from the top of the stairs.

When Mildred eventually returned to her own bedroom, Sam was sitting crouched over holding his chest. Alarmed, she wanted to phone the doctor, but he held onto her while insisting he was all right.

"It's just a spasm, Mildred dear. Sit close."

The next morning Mark could barely move. He had no memory of how he got robbed, or made it home from the bar. Sick and ashamed he stayed in bed for several days. Sam could not bring himself to talk to him. That was Mark's last bout of heavy drinking.

A week later he entered Philip's office.

"Glad to see you, Mark. How have you been?"

Mark told him about his experience at McGill and at the tavern. He also mentioned that he had not had a drink since.

"Good, good. Blackouts are serious stuff. Tell me, did she look like Mollie, the young pianist?"

"Not at all."

"What upset you then?"

To Mark it seemed obvious what had upset him.

"Well, I wasn't that upset. It was her playing and she was so young. I was overcome for a moment, that's all."

"Yes—a moment that stretched down to the transatlantic shed, then to a tavern in the red-light district, where you got drunk, beaten up, and robbed. The sailor died you know. It was in the papers."

The memory of the young sailor lying so still on that filthy floor was disturbingly vivid. After a moment he said, "It's everywhere, isn't it? It has the upper hand."

"What?"

"Death—chiselled on walls, newspapers, art—it flows through us."

"True." Philip agreed. "But then you're alive enough to make the observation, and the young pianist was alive enough to play."

"Yes, for a moment."

"True again, Mark. But it's a precious moment, because it's all we've got."

Mark grunted cynically, and said, "You sound like my father."

"And your mother? Do I sound like her too? Is there a difference between them?"

Mark was stumped. He was forced to admit there was a distinct difference between them. His father struggled to justify his existence; his mother justified nothing. He recalled one of his father's great sermons on St. Paul, *In Christ, Man is Fully Alive*, and concluded that his mother *is* fully alive, but his father just talks about it. He looked at Philip and said, "Yes, there is a difference."

Philip did not pursue the specifics of the difference. He knew that Mark had made an important distinction. Mark thought of the memorial wall at McGill. It was a monolith chiselled and carved with the names of the dead while just a few yards from it that young girl played with such vitality.

Both remained silent: Philip sitting on the edge of his desk, Mark on a soft leather chair. The only sound was a large wall-clock, its brass pendulum swinging back and forth ticking time away, and the odd squeak of leather as Mark shifted his weight on the chair. He hadn't taken much notice of Philip's office; but now, during this silence, he took it in. Its dark mahogany wainscoting, plum velvet curtains and soft leather chairs provided a comforting warmth. On the wall opposite was a painting of a young girl in varying hues of powder blue. She might have been a Madonna. Her eyes had a touching vulnerability.

Philip, noticing him studying the painting, said, "Mark, I would like you to tell me about your wife."

Pressure expanded in his chest.

"Try to relax, Mark. Take your time and tell me anything that comes to mind about her."

"She—ah, Mollie, played...so much of me is gone with her—so much."

"Yes, I'm sorry Mark. But when one takes so much away like that, it's a sure bet they've left you with a great deal. What about her family?"

Mark told him about the Mackinnons. It was somehow easier to talk about them. He told about the first time he visited the MacKinnon home for tea.

"They lived in Edinburgh in one of those large, granite, terrace houses. An elderly maid with hard eyes, and gray hair pulled back tightly in a bun showed me into the parlour. I don't know why I remember her except her whole presence seemed to say, 'You're not welcome in this house.' She always intimidated me like that.

"Alex MacKinnon was an artist–a professor at the university. The room had many pieces of art, but what caught my attention almost immediately was a bronze sculpture of a tiny woman giving birth on top of a skull. She was stretched fully backwards, her hair flowing down over the back of the skull. Her mouth was wide open as if screaming in her birth pangs. The baby's head was showing, and the skull grinned hideously like a medieval death head. It was powerful and shocking. Alex MacKinnon had done it in 1914 just before the war, or so the nameplate said.

"Above the mantelpiece was a large painting of two young lieutenants in a Scottish regiment wearing Glengarry caps. Their vibrancy was expressed in sunny colours and in their boyish smiles. They had their arms over each other's shoulders. I saw their eyes were the same as Mollie's, but in stark contrast to the life in the picture was a length of black crepe draped along the top of the frame. The signature on that, too, was MacKinnon."

Mark stopped talking. He pressed his head to his hands. Philip waited.

"As I stood there looking at that picture, I heard her voice saying 'Hello Mark.' It was Mollie."

He paused again and shook his head.

"What was she wearing?" Philip asked.

Marked looked at him as one might at a tormentor.

"She was wearing a cornflower blue dress with a pleated skirt that hung beautifully over her hips. A simple white collar, open at her throat, matched her white pumps. She looked like a very young girl who had suddenly matured to full womanhood. 'I see you were looking at the boys,' she said. 'Och, they never made it, poor wee laddies.'

"She said it casually with a feigned sort of objectivity that seemed to say death is death and there's nothing you or I can do about it. It was an attitude a person might assume who is trying to reduce the hurt and shock of death by being glib about it. 'Oh well, it's the same sad old story in thousands and thousands of homes,' she said. I told her that there weren't thousands of homes with pictures like that hanging in them.

"Whatever way I said it, it released her grief. She told me they were killed together at the Somme, and when the word came her parents collapsed into each other's arms.

"'One night, I heard appalling cries,' she said. 'And the next morning Mother locked the boy's doors. Then she went to her studio and painted day and night for I don't know how long. Father cannot bear to look at them.'

"It surprised me to learn that Margaret MacKinnon was the painter. In that moment Mollie touched my hand, hardly a touch at all, but I took it as some sort of a plea from her, and I put my arms around her. She clung to me until Margaret MacKinnon's voice broke us apart, welcoming me. I'll never forget the consternation in her mother's eyes.

"After tea, Mollie played the piano. She was brilliant and vigorous. Margaret asked her to go out to the studio and bring her father in to meet me. While Mollie was out of the room Margaret said, 'We've high hopes for her. Next year she goes to London to study at the Conservatory. Very few have that opportunity—especially girls. She is ever so precious to us—even more so now.'

"As she said it, her eyes rested for a moment on the picture of her sons. Mollie came in with her father. He was a tall man with such a weary face. I remember thinking that the power had gone out of him. He smelt of whiskey. With the briefest nod he mumbled something about being pleased to make my acquaintance, then he turned and walked out. Mrs. MacKinnon followed him and I could hear her scold him for not staying long enough for a cup of tea.'

"Was that the first time you met Mollie?"

"Shortly before that. I actually met her on the first day I arrived in Edinburgh at a welcome tea given by the Old Testament professor. It was a stodgy affair with the professor holding forth from the depth of a large overstuffed armchair that squeaked every time he moved. He was going on about his translation of the Psalms from Hebrew into Gaelic.

"Mollie was serving and I accidentally hit the plate she was holding and knocked a pile of buttered jam scones to the floor. When we knelt down under the table to pick up some that rolled under it, our eyes met. That was it. She was interested to know that I'd just arrived from Canada. About a week later her mother sent me the invitation to tea. Later Mollie told me, 'I pestered the life out of Mommy until she did so.'

"In the ensuing months, what the Mackinnon's feared most, I guess, happened. Mollie and I were deeply in love. A letter came calling me to the pastoral charge of New Skye, Prince Edward Island. I discussed it with her.

'It sounds divine,' she laughed. 'A wee island practically all to ourselves. Say 'yes' and we'll do wonders with it.'"

Philip didn't push him to talk any further, but after a pause, he asked, "Have you a picture of Mollie?"

Mark fumbled in his wallet and produced a small snapshot that Margaret MacKinnon had made them pose for on their wedding day as they were leaving the church. Mollie was laughing, standing tiptoe and brushing confetti out of Mark's hair while holding her spray of roses and baby's breath out to the side at arm's length.

"It hurt her very much that her father couldn't give her away. He was going to, but at the last minute he was too drunk. But there were no recriminations–the Mackinnons are not like that. Mollie just wept a little and said, 'Poor Daddy.'"

"She's very pretty–lovely, in fact," Philip commented as he handed back the picture.

Mark was having a difficult time.

"She was all they had left. If only I had known what was ahead. The MacKinnons have rejected me completely and in their own way have cut me off more from her."

He was profoundly overcome and could neither breathe, moan nor speak. As he writhed in the chair, Philip said, "Let it go Mark. Let it go, boy."

His face turned scarlet from the terrible tightness.

"Lie back! Take a breath!" Philip said and placed a hand on Mark's stomach and pushed. The trapped breath rushed out, and Mark let go a paroxysm of sobs. Philip gently brought him to a sitting position.

"Ah Mollie, it wasn't to be, wasn't to be."

Philip gently touched his arm and said, "Mark, I'm stepping out for a moment. Stay put and try to relax until I come back.

He continued weeping for a while, but his breathing was easier. As a child he hated to cry in front of people or give into emotions. He was embarrassed. When Philip came back carrying a coffee and biscuits, Mark found it difficult to look him in the eye.

"I'd like to talk to you for a little bit longer today even though you mightn't feel up to it."

Philip waited while Mark sipped his coffee.

"You mentioned to me that you were afraid to go to sleep. Are you experiencing bad nightmares?"

"Yes, constantly."

"Any recurring ones?"

"Yes, Doctor. We are all in the painting of her brothers. The baby is green. Not an ugly green, but limpid, living green like fresh grass–lush. He is exquisite—shining almost."

"Does the child terrify you?"

"No, not him, he fills me with a sense of peace. But the brothers upset me terribly. They keep saying, 'He's still in his mother's milk, you know.'"

"We won't go into that now, Mark, but I would like to hear of other nightmares—is there a recurring one apart from the child dreams?"

"Yes—the hanging on ones—"

"Tell me?"

"I am sitting on the incline of a steep roof. I'm digging in my toenails to keep me from sliding off into blackness below."

Philip persisted, "Is that the only recurring one?"

"Well no, but it has nothing to do with Mollie or anything."

"Tell me about it, please, Mark?"

Mark started slowly as if putting off describing the dream.

"A terrifying presence sitting in a chair. The walls have closed in. It's hard to breathe. My face is jammed up against railings forcing me to look down at the man in the chair. When the chair starts to turn slowly around so that I can see who in it I can't breathe at all. The mounting terror is too much and I wake up before the chair has turned completely around...."

Philip stood up abruptly.

"Well that's enough for today. Now, here's what I'd like you to do. Write down your dreams as well as whatever comes to mind. And Mark, don't let that baby go."

"Meaning?"

"Exactly what I said. Don't let him go. Think about this: love and self-revulsion are at war in you. Keep on with the strolling; the campus sounds good. You've expended a lot of energy today. Get some rest. You might feel the need of a drink, but take a sedative instead. Drink lots of water. Well then, same time next week unless you feel you're in crisis. If so, call me at once."

Again the Doctor practically pushed Mark out the door, closing it sharply behind him.

An unpleasant rush of anger suffused him, and it was only with effort he stopped himself from flinging open the shut door and screaming "I'd like to ask you a question or two Doctor One Eared Dixon!"

Instead, he went out into the bright sunshine, shaking and exhausted.

Sixteen

Myra Swanson

Mark was improving. He was sleeping and eating better, and was even opening and answering his mail. The letters were mainly from parishioners, letters of sympathy usually consisting of printed verses from the Bible along with a brief note. After he replied he seldom heard from them again. An exception was Ruth Ewart. The frequency and content of her letters caused him concern. She wrote as if they were a couple, and she talked about the preparations she was making for his return. In her latest letter she wrote, *Mark, my darling, I loved the things you said yesterday. Of course, I'd be honoured to bear you another son.*

He showed them to his mother.

"If I had read those by chance I might have assumed she was your lover. Why don't you show them to Philip Dixon."

"Did you answer them, Mark?" Philip asked after he read them.

"Of course not."

"Good. There might be a possibility the writer has a psychotic obsession and is delusional. They'll probably stop coming when her mind closes the physical distance between you, but by that time her condition will be obvious to others—if it isn't already. You might have a problem, though, if you decide to return. Will you go back again?"

Mark, thoughtful for a moment, said, "I suppose I'll have to address that soon because they're expecting me to, but I don't think I ever will."

It was true most of his parishioners were hoping to have him back as their minister, but a letter from the Synod of Prince Edward Island alerted him to the fact that he had enemies there too.

> Dear Reverend Kerr:
> We trust that God has increased your strength and comfort.
> It is with deepest regret we write to you in this time of your bereavement about a matter of extreme delicacy, but we feel constrained to do so.
> An accusation has been brought against you of conduct unbecoming a minister. Some members of your pastoral charge maintain that while actively engaged in ministry you indulged in the extreme partaking of alcoholic beverages.
> We, your brothers in Christ, do not accuse you, but we are forced to investigate the matter. We profoundly regret this. If there is any light you can shed on the matter, or if you wish to refute this charge, we request that you do so, forthwith.
> > Yours in Christ,
> > Hammond R. Rutherford, D.D.
> > Moderator, PEI Presbytery.
> > cc. Moderator General Assembly.

Mark answered immediately.

Dear Dr. Rutherford,
Thank you for your sympathy and concern. With regard to the accusations brought against me, I neither refute nor substantiate them.

Firstly, I found your letter somewhat vague, though I am treating it with the utmost seriousness. I am seeking legal advice. Secondly, I demand that my accusers be named, and the circumstances surrounding these accusations be fully revealed. If their complaint was in writing, perhaps you will be good enough to forward to me a notarized copy of the contents.
  Yours sincerely,
  Mark Kerr, BA, MA, M. Theol.
  cc. Moderator, General Assembly.

His father told him once that a minister should always bear in mind that he can't please everybody.

"If you take dissention so much to heart that it makes you unhappy or ill, you have a sick ministry. However, if the congregation rises up against you *en masse* that means you might be a Martin Luther in the making, or else it means you're simply preaching things that are irrelevant and unimportant."

After he thought about Rutherford's letter, he had no problem guessing that the complaint against him originated with Myra Swanson, and he knew that Hammond Rutherford would be only too glad to act on it.

Myra was the community tale-carrier. The local men referred to her as the 'manure spreader', and many of their wives felt she was well named. Nevertheless, she was seldom short of listeners or tellers. Mollie had once observed to Mark, "Myra's not stupid—just a bit twisted. And she gets most of her gossip from the men."

A single woman in her fifties, she ran the family business, a feed mill and a small general store. Her nephew, Myron, on whom she doted, and an indigent man everybody called Bud, did the crushing, bagging and shipping. Myra handled the business accounts; but if required to, she could heave and unload heavy bags of feed as easily as any man. She had bullish arms and shoulders, a short thick neck, and a close-cropped head of tight little black curls. Her skin was fresh and ruddy, and her bulging eyes the color of polished malachite.

Her store smelled of paraffin, malt and bran and was stocked with every conceivable item: needles, buttons, fishhooks, nails, iron files and larger tools such as hammers and saws. Cans of paint and boxes of food lined the walls. Clusters of pots and pans were tied to hooks in the ceiling; and shirts, dungarees and suits swung from the ceiling like hanged men. Every bit of space was used. She moved around with surprising grace and agility, and never knocked anything over with either her ample bosom or backside. A small room upstairs where she measured and fitted women for foundation garments and wedding dresses had a handwritten sign saying, LADIES ONLY.

She bantered shamelessly with the farmers who liked to "cabbage" a bit of extra time chatting in the intimacy of the small store. If a woman was "upstairs," they passed sly glances to each other and mumbled innuendoes. Each time Myra followed a woman for a "fittin'" she threw the men a knowing glance as if in some sexual conspiracy with them.

She knew everything about everybody: personal habits, favourite dishes, scandals, or potential scandals; and if there was something she did not know about a person, she could make it up with surprising accuracy.

Myra had a talent for saying something about someone without ever mentioning names or facts. No one was safe from her, yet everyone wanted to be allied to her. She was fun at parties and when they had "times" at the community hall, she could send them into "fits" with her fund of monologues such as "Bessie's Boil."

Her power lay in the fact that she knew just about everybody's financial situation. She gave credit and advances and held notes on many of the community farms. She knew who to court and who to threaten; and although she gossiped, she never talked or alluded to people's finances. On that subject she was closed as tightly as the huge iron safe that sat in her bedroom.

"Talking to Myra Swanson might be like scooping sludge off a mill pond," the men would say. "But when it comes to money deals, she's as tight as a bull's arse in fly time."

Everyone both in and out of town knew her cousin Lionel Buell, but few suspected that she was involved in Lionel's nefarious practices, and that her business was used as a conduit for rum-running money.

Lionel, a large, soft-spoken man was the bagman for the incumbent political party. He was toadied to because of his ability to grant political patronage. At election time he supervised the surreptitious but widespread distribution of liquor along with extra ballots to voters. Buell gave the impression of being wispy and soft, but he could be very dangerous if crossed. He and Myra were in the process of trying to secure one of the Island's first tractor dealerships.

When Mollie came to New Skye, Myra tried to ingratiate herself with her, but Mollie kept her distance. If she tried to warn the young minister's wife about "this one or that one," Mollie would divert the conversation to more general and safer subjects, but Myra persisted until and at last Mollie simply said, "Miss Swanson, I am not in the least interested in tale-carrying."

Incensed, Myra waited her chance to get revenge. Her opportunity came when a box from a Halifax merchant addressed to the manse was left at the store.

Mollie's mother had ordered a present of several bottles of wine and smoked salmon. Myra shook the box and heard the dull clinking of glass. With a curled index finger, she carefully enlarged a small tear in one of the corners enabling her to see the dark green ring of a bottle neck.

"Drink!"

"How's Myra today?" one of the men in the store asked her.

"Oh, well to tell you the truth now, I'm a bit concerned and shocked at something I found out."

The men moved a little closer.

"Come on now Myra, what on God's green earth could shock you, girl? I thought you seen, done and handled everything known to man, woman or beast?"

"No, serious now, I learned something that's really bothered me."

They all waited for her to continue. When she was sure she had their full attention she said, "What's the good of it all when them who should be settin' a good example to the rest of us don't know any better themselves?"

"My God, Myra, has that judge in Charlottetown been breaking the commandments again?"

"Especially the fourth?" another piped in. They all laughed because it was well known that a judge from town was carrying on with one of the women in the community.

"No, no, serious now. I'm not certain for sure, but I wouldn't be surprised there's drinkin' and goin's on in a place close to here where none of us would want it to be. The very last place for it. You know?"

The "you know" was accompanied with the faintest movement of her head in the direction of the manse. The men didn't want to hear any more. They liked the new minister and his wife. The next day Mark found an unsigned note in his mailbox.

Dear Rev Kerr,
Please be warned that someone is spreading shameful rumours that you are drinking heavy and committing other sins in the manse. Most of us don't believe it and know that she is always saying somethin' about somebody.
A warning from a friend

That Sunday, Marked called his sermon, *No Smoke Without Fire* and used as his text, James 3:5-6:

Even so, the tongue is a little member and boasteth great things. Behold how great a matter a little fire kindeleth! And so the tongue is a fire, in a world of iniquity.

As the sermon on the evil of gossip progressed, there was no doubt among the congregation that it was directed to Myra. Eyes turned surreptitiously towards her to see how she was taking it, but she sat impassive. Upon leaving church, however, she refused to shake the minister's hand.

Later, Mollie said, "Mark, I think you made a mistake today preaching against Myra. She just isn't worth it."

He laughed it off, then passionately embracing her, said, "The bed's waiting for us all nice and cosy. Let's spend a lustful afternoon before the parishioners start banging on the door. As the Lord said to the Pharisee, 'The Sabbath is made for man, not man for the Sabbath.'"

When Mollie had her baby, Myra sent a present of the cheapest flannel belly-binder; and when Mollie and the baby died, she expressed in the strongest terms to one of the elders that Mark should be encouraged to go away, "for his own good and that they should make a fresh start with a new minister."

Just before Mark left for Montreal, the Session of Elders put out the word in the community that they wanted two women to volunteer to clean the manse to make it ready for a temporary minister. Ruth Ewart and Myra Swanson volunteered, but each for very different personal reasons.

The Clerk told Mark, "The ladies will call on you, Reverend Kerr, to see if there's anything you'd like disposed of. Or to give you a hand with anything."

Ruth and Myra called at the manse on the day he was leaving. He dreaded the visit because it meant a discussion about what to do with Mollie's things. He'd had too many whiskies, and was in a who-gives-a-damn-anyway mood. Ruth gloried in the opportunity to serve in some way. For Myra it presented an opportunity to look around. When the women arrived he showed them into the parlour. Myra noted with satisfaction that he'd been drinking.

"I've packed my wife's personal effects and will take them with me. Her clothing, however, is upstairs. Please dispose of it as you wish."

He indicated he had no more to say and that they could go. Ruth struggled not to cry.

"Reverend Kerr will you pray with us?"

Without even answering he walked into the kitchen, poured himself a drink and stayed there until he heard them leave. The horrible emptiness of the house where he had known happiness for such a brief time filled him with further anguish.

Myra watched through her store window for him to leave. As soon as he climbed on the wagon and went over the hill towards town, she slipped back into the manse to look for evidence that would make her imagination a reality. She went through Mollie's lingerie, sniffing contemptuously and muttering, "Any woman that would put the likes of that on her body has the mind of a whore."

At last she found a bottle of champagne on top of the wardrobe that Mollie had hidden to celebrate the baby's first birthday.

"There must be more than this," she said to herself. "He was pickled this mornin'. Empties, empties. There must be empties."

Wild with frustration, she abandoned the search. On the way back she said to herself, maybe I'm lookin' in the wrong place. The cursed stuff may not be in the house at all.

Later, she returned and went out back and rooted around the old carriage shed. With her bullish arms she turned over the horsebox and emptied it of bits of harness, old blankets, shoes and traces; but all to no avail.

Her eye fell on a narrow wall ladder up into the loft. She climbed it with great difficulty, her large face beet red from exertion and her dress and hair covered in dust and cobwebs. Up there, she searched behind beams, and under old hay, but she turned up nothing. Failure to find anything only made her more determined.

Out in the yard, after looking behind bushes and turning over old cream cans, she decided there were only two places left—the outhouse and an old abandoned well. She tried the outhouse first. Flies rose in a buzzing cloud as she lifted up the seat cover. The stench from the deep pit filled her nostrils.

"Hmm, just like them not to know enough to lime their shit," she muttered aloud.

Lowering a lantern on a length of binder twine, she peered into the murky pit. Had she thought about it, the privy was an unlikely place to find empty bottles, for it was cleaned out regularly by the men of the congregation. But Myra, obsessed by her contempt for Mark, continued her quest. The light in the foul hole revealed nothing. Later, however, she would gleefully whisper the fact to others that Mark hadn't used the lime.

Just as she was about to look into an abandoned well, she saw Ruth Ewart walking mournfully around the house. I'll come back later when she's not here, she said to herself. She watched from the store window until she saw Ruth walking down the road towards her own place.

Myra went back to the abandoned well and lowered her lamp. As it passed down the mossy walls, a rat scurried into a hole in the clay. Then, triumphantly she saw the glint of numerous bottles lying in their secret place at the bottom of the dried-out well. Jubilant, she thanked God for rewarding her persistence.

The bottles did not belong to Mark but to his predecessor, the Reverend Dougald MacGreggor.

Old MacGreggor had ministered to the community for thirty odd years, the last fifteen of them as a widower. Although he preached regularly against "Satan's poison," he was taken with the drink himself, especially in his later years. The parishioners knew he "took a drop" but forgave him because his body was twisted and lame with the "rheumatic." As he grew aged and frail, some of the older men would discreetly leave him a bottle of moonshine inside the porch door. Dougald's drinking was regarded as something like a family secret in the community, and when he preached against the "poison," the wise in the pews understood that he was the object of his own fiery denouncements, and they viewed him as a kind of sacrificial lamb.

After her discovery, Myra paid a visit to Angus MacLeod, the fiercest temperance man on the Session of Elders. Angus, a crusty seventy-five year old, relished the idea of being thought of as a man of the Book and stern prayer. He vigorously opposed any newfangled ideas creeping into religion. Frequently, he had hectored Mark about his "soft sermons."

"Satan lurks, Reverend Kerr, and Satan must be routed. He's the foe, and you must gird your loins and lead us into battle. The Reverend MacGreggor, now, there was a Christian who could make you aware of depravity."

One time Mark preached on the humanity of Jesus and said that He was probably more concerned with love of this life than the afterlife. Angus was so incensed he called a special meeting of the Session to discuss "the Minister's heretical views."

Myra filled Angus with her findings of Mark's depravity and led him up to the bedroom.

"You have a gander in them dresser drawers, Gus, and I'll wait for you downstairs."

Angus had never seen fine lingerie up close. He rummaged through the silken items with his huge callused hands, then quickly slammed the drawer shut.

"Disgustin'! The sight of them almost burned my eyes," he told Myra.

"Now come to the well, Gus," she said.

As they passed the privy she nodded at it and said in a hushed voice, "They didn't even know enough to lime the hole."

Together, they lowered the lantern into the well. "There'll be more about this," Angus hissed after seeing the bottles.

The next day he went to see the Reverend Dr. Hammond Rutherford. Rutherford was a rotund little man with a neck lost in fat, and eyes set in soft puffy pouches beneath thick, black, wiry eyebrows. He perceived the world and humanity as being in various stages of decay and believed it his Christian duty to make everybody aware of it. An ardent opponent to change and especially to Church Union, he regarded men like Angus as bulwarks against those who would "decay the tradition" of Presbyterianism. "Social Gospellers—socialists and liberals," he often preached, "will lead the people on the primrose path to Hell!"

He called a meeting of his Pastoral Oversight Committee, a group made up of mainly anti-church unionists, and informed them of his meeting with Angus. After "prayerful consideration," they instructed Hammond to write to Mark and to the Moderator of the General Assembly in Montreal reporting the complaint about Mark's drinking. Their real motive, however, was to discourage Mark from coming back to the Island, but a letter from the Moderator of the General Assembly stated that the complaint was weak, and should be withdrawn.

Seventeen

The Bobby Rose

One hot Saturday morning while Mark's mother was pruning a rose bush, she stood and sighed deeply. Her face was flushed from the heat and exertion. Mark, alarmed, asked, "Are you okay Mother?"

"Oh, I'm fine, but it's so hot I don't think I'll do any more. Why don't you be a dear and fetch us a nice cool glass of juice?"

When they had settled themselves, she said, "I wonder if you would be up to doing something with me, dear? I think you might be strong enough, now."

"What, Mother?"

The ice in the jug clinked as he filled her glass.

"Well, I never saw my grandson, so I thought I'd like to plant a special rosebush for him. I have a friend, Arthur Pendleton, who is famous for his roses. Would you go out there with me and help me pick one?"

Mark's first impulse was to refuse, but Philip's words "Don't let that baby go," came back to him.

"Yes."

On the drive out she told him about Pendleton.

"He's a very special man and has become a good friend. He used to be head gardener of an old English estate—born into the job as they say. His wife died leaving him with a son and daughter to raise. When his boy was killed in the war he decided to bring his daughter to Canada and try to make a go of it on his own here. His roses have taken many top prizes; but not only does he cultivate roses, he paints them as well—brilliantly. Now he's becoming quite well known as an artist, too."

Arthur Pendleton, a large burly man with a pugilist's nose, thick iron-gray hair and large dark eyes was not in the least how Mark had pictured him; he looked more like a road labourer; yet, when he took Mark's hand in his great beefy fist, he held it with a surprising gentleness.

"I want a very special rosebush—one in bloom to transplant, Arthur. My baby grandson died this winter, and I want to dedicate it to his memory. He was Mark's baby."

Arthur nodded sympathetically.

"Well I do have one—a very special little hybrid. A rare little one, for it exudes almost as much scent by night as it does by day. Yes, that's the one for you to see. But I warn you. I don't know how long he'll bloom, though I've hopes that he will from early summer to late autumn. Come."

The walls of his house were hung with oil paintings of roses. Again, like the physical appearance of the artist they were a visual contradiction: the paint was thickly trowelled in blacks, deep reds, yellows and whites—almost sculpted onto the canvas. Yet, despite their rough texture the petals loomed like translucent skin.

"Now you go in here," Arthur said holding the door of a long solarium. "You'll see him down at the end on the right. Take your time. We'll have a cup of tea after."

The air in the solarium was fresh and perfumed from the several varieties of roses blooming in troughs of black loam. The special rose peeked out from dark green satin leaves. Its small size and lip-pink colour gave it an appealing fragility. It exuded innocence that one finds so appealing in a baby. Along side of it was a series of sketches with notes on its development.

"Exquisite, isn't it Mark?"

"Yes."

A young woman came in. She had large brown eyes set widely apart, full soft lips and a shock of thick black hair. It was not a pretty face but disconcertingly sensual.

Mildred greeted her, "Oh how do you do, Sally? Mark this is Sally Pendleton, Arthur's daughter. Sally, this is Mark, my son."

"How do you do, Mark?"

Mark took her proffered hand and smiled briefly.

"Well, all I have to do is bring the water to the teapot. So, when you are ready just come on back through."

Mark and his mother stood a few minutes more with the rose.

"This is the one. Right Mark?"

He showed his approval by lightly pressing her hand. When they sat down for tea, Mildred said, "The rose is perfect, Arthur."

"It would be a pleasure to let you have it, Mildred. However, until I've painted it and set some more slips, I can't let it go. It's a prototype, and we have to name and register it. Like to christen him, Mark?"

"Bobby."

"Right then. The Bobby Rose it is."

Sally poured tea from a large Brown Betty into shiny white teacups with little blue flowers; but for her father she filled a large army mug. As she held the tray in front of Mark, the silver sugar spoon was reflected as two little lights in her eyes. She, of course, was quite unaware of this but interpreted Mark's observation of the reflections as interest in her. She smiled, inviting him to take his cup of tea. Mark noticed her skin was the color of a very pale sherry.

"Mr. Pendleton, would it be possible to buy the painting of the rose?" Mark asked.

"Well, I seldom let a painting go except through an exhibition. Some paintings I think I'll never part with, but after a few months

I'm quite happy to see them go. However, let me think about it a bit. I haven't painted him yet. Perhaps you wouldn't even like it."

"The rose must mean a great deal to you," Sally said.

"Yes."

"We want to plant the rose in memory of Mark's baby boy who died this last winter," Mildred said.

This wasn't what Mark wanted. He didn't want to be engaged in a crossfire of inane expressions of sympathy, but Sally said almost off-handedly, "You made a good choice. It will please his mother."

"The baby's mother died too," Mildred said.

After a slight silence, Sally said, "At least, then, she was spared the dreadful grief of knowing she lost her son."

Arthur Pendleton stood up and Mark noticed an unpleasant look pass between Sally and her father. He turned to Mark and his mother and said, "Well Mrs. Kerr, Mark, I have to finish my tea on the job so to speak. You'll please excuse me, then? Nice to have met you Mark. See you soon again, Mildred."

He shook their hands warmly and smiled, but Mark sensed annoyance in him in the way he set his head and strode out of the room. Sally collected the tea things and disappeared. He noticed that her shoulders sloped at the same angle as her hips and that she did not move gracefully.

Eighteen

The Rev. Sam Kerr, DM

While Mark and his mother were visiting the Pendleton's, Sam Kerr walked down to his church to do a little more preparation for his Sunday service. He stopped writing to listen to the familiar creaks and knocks from the pipes echoing through the empty building. The sound intrigued him, and he often thought there might be a good sermon in it. As he lowered his head to continue writing, the study floated lightly around him. Pain jabbed his jaw and left arm. The dizziness subsided after a moment, but the pain persisted. He understood there was something serious going on, and it frightened him.

Sam fixed his eyes on the two volumes of *The Iliad* and *The Odyssey* given to him by a young Irish officer who had died from his wounds. With some effort he pulled *The Iliad* out of the bookshelf. It fell open, revealing a letter and a photograph of three nursing sisters. Another sliver of pain pulsed through him. Breathing was difficult.

Clutching both the letter and photo, Sam managed to make his way into the empty sanctuary. He stood illuminated by the great rose window high above the gallery. The hush of the place swallowed him up. Christ looked down from the chancel window.

"Have I betrayed you? I have betrayed Mildred and Mark and all the things I'm supposed to stand for. But you, dear Christ, the very best part of myself, have I betrayed you? If I have, I know I am forgiven."

Pain dug into his heart like nails, and suddenly he was nothing more than a dark shape on the floor, barely visible in the dying colours flowing down from the rose window.

The organist, who had come into the church for a practice session, turned on the chancel lights and saw Sam's body lying in the center aisle.

Mark and his mother had just arrived home when they received a call from the Clerk of Session.

"Mark, I am afraid I have bad news for you. Your father collapsed at the church. The organist found him. I'm on my way down there now."

"Have they taken him to hospital? Is he still there? What...."

"Mark, I'm sorry, he's gone. Please come over right away."

His father was dead. Mildred, sensing something, cried out, "What is it Mark? Is it Dad? Oh my good Lord! Oh no!"

"Yes, Mother."

He put his arms around her.

"What happened? Tell me Mark."

"He collapsed at the church."

When they arrived they were met by the police and a doctor.

"I'm Dr. Craig. Are you Mrs. Kerr? And you, sir? Are you his son? I'm sorry. He had a heart attack. It was very sudden. Perhaps you and I can have a chat, Reverend Kerr?"

Mark nodded.

"I'll wait for you in the vestry," his mother said.

While Mildred was alone in the vestry, the organist came in and handed her the photo and letter. He had found them lying under a pew and sensed they should be for her eyes only. After a quick perusal, she hastily shoved them into her handbag.

Nineteen

Burying and Surfacing

Mark talked with Philip Dixon about his father's death.

"I don't feel seriously affected. Am I becoming inured to death?"

"I doubt that, Mark. It's different when we lose a parent through natural causes. You have to be careful it doesn't sneak up on you and aggravate your depression."

"My mother needs me too much. She's grieving but her composure is remarkable. She has to cope with the dreadful prospect of facing the future alone; but not only that, there's the distressing business of vacating the Manse. I don't think there's a lot of money left. I lament the fact that I didn't know my father better; but to be truthful, the affection between us was never strong enough to fill the gap. Yes my father's death is dreadful, but to be honest, I'm more affected by my mother's plight. Am I callous?"

Philip took his time before answering.

"Your Father was a good man and he'll be missed. I'm glad you're strong enough to help your mother through this. I think sometime later you might have a stronger reaction to his death than you're having now, but I think you'll be able to deal with it."

Many clergy from different faiths attended Sam's funeral along with parishioners and a host of acquaintances. Mark relived that wet and stormy spring day when Mollie and the baby were buried. His mother, sensing this, put her arm through his and pressed him tightly to her. Her warmth comforted him, and his closeness comforted her.

The many ministers with their white collars and black umbrellas looked like a strange flock of birds attracted by the mounds of floral wreaths. An undertaker's assistant held an umbrella over Mark and his mother. Mark could smell his shaving lotion and mouth wash. A strange mix of smells, he thought, the man's toilet lotions, crushed grass, flowers and the wet clay from the open grave.

He saw Sally Pendleton and her father standing under a large oak tree. As the mourners slowly dispersed after the internment, Sally walked directly over to him and his mother and placed her gloved hand lightly on his arm. She and Arthur offered their condolences. Mildred invited them back to the manse.

It was crowded. She received mourners in the parlour while Mark moved around shaking hands and conversing with various small groups. Wet coats and umbrellas brought the dampness of the cemetery back to the house. When the Pendleton's arrived, Arthur took Mark aside and asked him about his mother's plans.

"Well, she has a month to vacate the manse. But to be honest we haven't had a chance to discuss what she might do. There's a lodge for minister's widows, but I can't see that being the right thing for Mother. The sad fact is that we were not very well prepared for this."

"Look, Mark, your mother has the green thumb, as they say. We're terribly busy at the nursery and need extra help. We've lots of room at the house. If she's interested we would be glad to have her."

"You mean give her a live-in job?"

"Yes, exactly. Sally and I agree she would be ideal."

"You could certainly put it to her in a few days," Mark said.

"Why don't you come out to the nursery first yourself? We'll discuss in more detail what we have in mind. If you think it would be a good thing, then perhaps you could talk it over with her. Let us know."

Twenty

New Possibilities

Mark was summoned to the General Assembly offices for a meeting. The Moderator, a tall man with a hawk nose and a deeply lined, unsmiling face came straight to the point.

"Mark, we have to make provisions for your mother. The Church will help relocate her. Have you anything in mind?"

"Not as yet."

"There are a few vacancies at the Lodge. We could start things moving in that direction. There's also the matter of your own future. The complaint brought against you has been dropped of course. It was politically motivated because of the oncoming Church Union. Are you still intending to proceed with a lawyer?"

"I don't see any need now, Dr. Malcolm."

"Mark are you free in your conscience?"

"Yes."

"Good. I'm hoping you'll go back to Prince Edward Island."

He could feel his palms sweat but let the Moderator continue.

"Church Union is just about a fact, but there is still a forceful opposition to it. Your father was tireless in his efforts–working on the steering committee and his inspirational sermons went a long way to persuade congregants that Union would be a good thing. We were hoping to have you as the man on the spot down there to help that along, to carry on your father's good work. How does that sit with you?"

"I'll think it over, but my immediate concern is to help my mother get settled." The Moderator stood up and held out his hand. "Of course, of course. Let me know as soon possible. Good day, Mark. Please convey my regards to your good mother."

After he left the General Assembly offices, he went straight out to the Pendleton's. Arthur was not home, but Sally met him and invited him in. She was wearing riding jodhpurs and a man's shirt open at the neck. When she sat down, she stretched out her shapely legs and looked sideways at him.

So self-possessed, Mark thought, sits like a man yet she's so thoroughly a woman. She knew Mark was appraising her and caught him looking at her open shirt. Neither of them spoke. She enjoyed his discomfort. Eventually he asked, "Do you expect your father back soon? I came on the business he mentioned."

She kept looking at him before answering, "Yes. In about an hour. Are you in a rush? Would you like some tea?"

"No thank you."

More silence.

"You can discuss it with me, but if you would rather speak with Father that's fine."

Now he was faced with the possibility of seeming impolite if he chose to wait for her father. Glad to break the deadlock, he said, "Yes, of course we can discuss it. Thank you, Sally."

"Come then."

He followed her upstairs, trying to avert his eyes from her backside encased in the tight jodhpurs. She led him into a bedroom. More paintings of roses adorned the walls. It was a bright room with a heavy mahogany bed.

"This would be your mother's room. She would have the run of the house, of course. It's a comfortable bed. Sit on it."

"No, no, that's fine thank you. It's a very nice room."

Placing her arms well behind her, she sat and pumped the mattress to show how firm it was and at the same time making Mark aware of how firm her breasts were as they strained against her shirt. She stood up and fixed him with her strange, wide-set eyes, and said, "Poor boy, you've been through a lot, haven't you?"

"Yes, I suppose so."

She took his hand. Hers was soft and warm.

"Come and I'll show you something of the work your mother would do."

She led him down the stairs again still holding him by the hand. He had no wish to let go. She led him out to the greenhouse where he and his mother had seen the Bobby Rose. The sun was streaming in, and the air was fragrant with scent.

"This is where we start our hybrids. It's like a laboratory. We would teach your mother our special techniques. Father feels that she would be just the right person. There aren't many he would trust to do this work. Oh, by the way, there's your little Bobby. He's doing very nicely, see?"

The little pink rose was now a spray of roses. Mark could not control the release of tension in his stomach. It came out almost like laughter, making him more desperate to control himself. She tightened her hold on his hand. He spluttered apologies, but she took no notice whatsoever and continued talking.

"Yes, he's painted now, too. I'll show you before you go. But first let's have a cup of tea. The kettle's always on the boil."

Back in the living room she gave his hand an extra squeeze before making the tea. He felt a sexual twinge. When she came back she said, "I think you should persuade your mother to accept Father's offer."

"Well, it's really up to her."

"What else would she do?"

"I don't know other than going into Knox Lodge."

She handed him his tea and said, "How could you possibly do such a thing? I've been there countless times with flowers. She would quickly grow old and wither in a place like that. Here, there's life."

As she was talking she walked over to a small framed picture sitting on the floor with its face to the wall.

"Now, I'll show you."

She turned holding up the picture of the Bobby Rose.

It was painted on an ebony smooth background that seemed to heighten the powerful simplicity of the little pale rose with its silken leaves. He was in a simple crystal vase with a spray of baby's breath around it. The light falling on the right side was made iridescent by a dewdrop on a petal and by the rim of the crystal. Unlike the other paintings in the house, it was done in egg tempera in the smooth style of the old Flemish masters.

The rose looked out at Mark with all the fragility and appeal of a baby. He gripped his hands tightly under the table.

"It is beautiful," he said, huskily. "It's more than just beautiful. The style is so different from the rest of your father's paintings."

She held the painting closer to him. "Look at the signature."

It was signed, Sally Pendleton.

Somewhere from the back, Arthur Pendleton's voice called out, "You there Sally?"

The impact was broken. He came in and seeing Mark, said, "Sorry I couldn't be here when you arrived. Has Sally explained things?"

Sally greeted her father with a kiss and stood beside him holding his arm. Mark took them in. They exuded vitality. He thought of Knox Lodge and of all those sad old women fading away in their staidness.

In all the places they had lived Mother made a garden bloom. Even where there was no garden, she miraculously created one out of whatever patch of soil was available. She expressed so much through her gardens. The loss of his baby she expressed, not in words, but in this special rose. He felt the Pendleton's were a gift from whatever compensatory force there was in life.

"Sally explained things very well," Mark said, nodding his thanks to her. She returned it with her deep look. "I think Mother would be wise to accept your offer."

"She certainly would be right for us."

Sally walked Mark to his car. The awkwardness and tenseness he had experienced earlier was gone. Before they parted, she said to him, "On Friday I am going on a little hike through some woods near here to look for specimens of particular ivy we want to cultivate. Would you like to join me?"

"Yes. Unless Mother needs me, or something else comes up that I must attend to."

"Of course. Let me know if you can make it. If you can, I'll prepare food for us. We'll make an afternoon of it."

"Thank you," he said, then added, "for everything."

She smiled and waved him a goodbye with just the slightest tickle of her fingers.

Twenty-one

Mildred

When Mark got home his mother was asleep in an armchair. The partially drawn drapes permitted just enough light to fall upon her sleeping face, exposing her weariness and grief. He covered her with a blanket. As he was doing so, a letter and a photograph fell from her lap. He quietly picked them up and placed them on the kitchen table while he made a pot of tea. As he studied the picture of the three army nurses he realized it had something to do with his father's war experiences. He unfolded the letter and read:

> Dearest Sam,
> I know we agreed not to contact each other again, and believe me, I do intend to stick to that, but as the coast of France grew more and more dim my yearning for you grew. I just couldn't let go of you. I'll send this to you at the chateau. If you are gone before it reaches you, I'm sure it will be forwarded. If not, perhaps it's for the best.
> Here is a photo of the three musketeers—poor Alice on the left was sent back to the Front and was killed. I have lost touch with Helen. So many of us have lost touch with friends in this awful war, not to mention you and me. I am losing touch with you, dearest Sam,

but not the love we shared.   Think of me from time to time. I will never forget you. The precious time we shared will not have been wasted. It lives yet within me, my heart.

Love always, Anna, XXX.

"You're home, Mark."

His mother had come into the kitchen. When she saw the photo and the letter she sighed and said, "Oh dear, I'd hoped you wouldn't see those."

Mark poured her a cup of tea. The dead may be free from their agonizing secrets, he thought, but not the living. A flash of boyhood memory came back from a time when they lived in a rural parish. He used to help one of the farmers. While ploughing one cold November day the shears turned over part of a human rib cage and vertebrae.

"Now, what nuisance do we have to deal with?" the farmer said. "Funny thing, Mark, but it doesn't matter what's in the soil, or how long it's been there, or how deep it's buried, it always works its way out to the top an' the livin' have to deal with it."

Now my mother and I are forced to share one of my father's secrets, Mark thought.

"He was holding those when he died," his mother said. "I knew he was quite different when he came back. Oh, to all appearances he was still the same old Sam, but there was a change."

She studied Mark for a moment, then putting her hand over his, said, "Poor darling, Mark, you have been through so much in such a short terrible time. I don't want to burden you. I thank God I have you as my child."

"You're never a burden mother. Please go on talking if you wish."

"I am afraid I may say things that will shock and distress you if I do."

They both sipped in silence.

"I know this may sound horrible to you, but you were very fortunate to have had your time with Mollie even though it was so short. You had something very few have—genuine passionate love. That's why your grief was so devastating. It was passionate grief. Your father and I never had that you know, that passion."

He felt his mother was taking him on a direction that was very new to him. To put things on a more level path, he said, "A boy never had a better home and parents."

"Yes, but the love came through you, Mark. You gave our being together reality. Besides that, your Father had the respect of those he served, and we took comfort in the fact that everything was in its right place. It never crossed his mind for a second to question anything as long as things were running smoothly. When he came back from the war I felt changes in him."

She leaned forward and tapped the letter and photo lying on the table. "No doubt these had a bearing."

"Finding them must have deeply troubled you."

To his surprise, she answered, "Yes, but not because he may have been unfaithful, but because he may have experienced something we didn't. I yearned for a passionate relationship, but he would not allow it—indeed, he killed it right from the time we were courting even. Duty! Appearance! Form! Those were his passion."

She sat for a moment, her fingers over her mouth as if barring more words from coming out. Then she said, "You know, Mark, he wrote about her once. He called her his angel Anna. 'If we had a daughter,' he said, 'I would want her to be exactly like her.' Oh, Mark, I feel so betrayed."

A stranger was emerging and replacing his mother along with a new and startling view of his father. She had opened the conversation by expressing how fortunate he was to have experienced Mollie in his life. How different, he asked himself, was Mollie from his Mother? What did she mean exactly by passion? Mollie had given up her music to be with him. Had they grown older together would she have become like his mother, and he more like his father? Had she done so, would he ever have questioned that fact? He wondered if Mollie would have felt what his mother was now expressing. Mildred's compressed lips were almost colourless. In his entire life, he had never seen her angry.

"What exactly was missing in your life, mother? You've always seemed so content."

"ME! I was missing. Now, I'll tell you the truth. I hated the Church—being the wife of the Church."

"Did you ever discuss this with father?"

"No. He would have been incapable of understanding. That's why I am finding this fling he had, or whatever it was, so difficult to take. I am ashamed to talk this way with you. I don't want you to think less of your father—he wouldn't deserve that, Mark. So please, let's put this behind us."

She put her hands to her face and pressed them tightly. Then standing, she pushed her chair back so violently it banged against the cupboards. She snatched up the letter and the photograph and tore them to shreds shouting, "DAMN HIM! DAMN HIM!"

Mark retrieved the overturned chair and gently urged her to sit down.

"I'm sorry. I didn't know you were so unhappy, Mother."

"Mark, dear, I wasn't unhappy, exactly. Just, just—oh, unfulfilled. That was not entirely your father's fault. He was a wonderful man. People loved him but they saw only one side of him.

"The real Sam was encased in a shell. His experiences overseas cracked open that shell. Others can survive that. Your poor father couldn't. He withered and died inside while pretending to be strong. Now he isn't with us anymore and I can't help him. I'll miss him."

She bent down to gather the scattered the pieces of Anna's letter, and broke down again.

"Poor Mark, this must be so distressing for you. I should have been quiet. You, my dear, have been cracked open, too. But you'll survive and take new root."

When she was a bit more settled, he said, "I'm very concerned as to what you're going to do. Do you feel up to talking about that?"

"I know dear, it's something we can't avoid. I've absolutely no idea about what to do. I have a war widow's pension and a pittance from the Church, and several hundred in savings from a small inheritance. We did have an insurance policy, but most of that went to pay for the funeral. I'm fifty-two."

Mark decided to tell her about the Pendleton's offer. He told her of his visit, of the room, and the type of work Arthur wanted her to do. She was flabbergasted.

"Oh Mark, don't you think there might be a lack of propriety in that?"

"How would it be inappropriate? The Pendleton's are good people running a respectable business. You have just finished telling me that your life has been stifled and moulded by appropriate appearances. Let me ask you this. Is it something you would like to do?"

"Oh yes, dear. But I'll have to think about it some—perhaps it's a bit too sudden."

"Well of course, think about it. But for what it's worth, I think it's a good idea. The Pendleton's obviously see it as a good opportunity for them. You're not married to the Church any longer. You must look out for yourself. The church would have you go to Knox Lodge, then forget about you. Arthur said to take as much time as you need."

Mildred stood up and looked around the kitchen.

"I suppose I'd better soon get busy and start packing things up here. They want us out by the end of the month, and there's all your father's papers and things to go through and his things at the church."

"I'll look after that, Mother.

Twenty-two

More Revelations

Mark stood in his father's study trying to focus his mind before clearing it out. Before the conversation with his mother he would have performed the task as a filial duty; but now, his feelings were so mixed the task seemed daunting. The spicy odour of his father's tobacco clung so strongly, he half expected him to be sitting there. Before discarding his rack of pipes, he picked up one and studied the teeth marks on the bite. Then resigning himself, he tossed all the smoking paraphernalia into the box he had brought for rubbish.

He sat in his Father's big chair, and felt how the back had moulded itself to his body over the years. Where should I start? He asked himself. It's just too arduous a job to read through his papers today and try to decide what should be kept or dumped. I'll start by packing the books.

After the third box, he found a slim folder hidden behind the volumes of *Calvin's Institutes*. Mark opened it and saw written in his father's neat backhand, *Confession, Meditations and Prayers*. Each entry was preceded by a Biblical quote.

Flee also youthful lusts: but follow righteousness, faith, charity peace, with them that call on the Lord out of a pure heart.

2 Timothy 3:22

I have nothing in me because I have spilt it shamelessly into a gutter. I have trampled the pearl of Christ Jesus and gorged myself. My heart is empty. I am sick and finished. I cry now and whine and plead like the cringing dog that I am. I do not even have the sincerity to repent, but merely want out of this unpleasantness like a man wanting a cure for a drunken hangover. I have eaten at the trough of sin, swilling and gorging. It is the way of the glutton. Gluttony kills off caring. You know, God, I am cajoling you. I did not fall into temptations but pursued them. I abhor this separation from you. I am an old fool, who has done too much of everything that is wrong. At bottom, my sin is not caring. I have a shadow on my soul as a tubercular has a shadow on his lung. Forgive my sloth and heal me—let me not lie in this limbo of separation from you.

Mark was appalled at the extent of his father's agony. Page followed page of self-degradation. The same pattern of guilt ran throughout of how he was taking advantage of a poor girl who was drinking and distraught, of a woman destroyed by war and his weakness at not being able to stop himself.

Mark was so overcome with rage he wanted to tear the entire study apart, and rip and smash its facade of righteousness to splinters and shreds. He knew he should be commiserative, but his anger obliterated compassion.

An old group picture of three generations of Kerr's performing the laying-on-of-hands ceremony at Sam's Ordination looked out at him. There was also a picture of Mark's Ordination, with Sam performing the same ritual as the grandfathers had for him.

All of us have been cultivated for a life of propriety, he thought. Did those other high priests of Calvinism, his grandfather and great-grandfather also fall from grace and eventually die the agony of the damned? Did the cast-iron shell of respectability kill them also?

A wave of weariness washed over him. He lay his head on his arms and over his father's manuscript. I didn't cheat on the woman

I loved, he thought, but she and our son would be alive if it hadn't been for me. The thought stabbed at his heart. Just as he had been groomed to correctness, he realized his Father had been moulded in the same way. Some of his anger evaporated, and he felt a twinge of compassion. Then rage arose in him again, and he attacked the frigid rectitude that held them all by slamming the ordination pictures in the trash box so hard it smashed the glass.

Twenty-three

Capt. Sam Kerr, Padre

Since his return from the war, Sam Kerr involved himself heavily with the negotiations between the Presbyterians, the Methodists, and the Congregationalists in their plan to join together as one huge united church in Canada. He truly believed it was an important step for the country, for if union went through it would not only unite over a million Canadians but it would provide a spiritual unity in the life of the hundreds of communities, small towns, and cities separated in distance by the vastness of the country. Just as the railroad had linked Canada physically, the union of the churches would do so spiritually. He envisioned it as the great ecumenical move of the century.

His sermons on the subject were buoyant with optimism.

"Think, think of a Canada building itself on Christian principles—we would feed our hungry, use our great resources in a decent and humane fashion, resist war and promote –peace—what a prosperous and loving nation we could be...."

The truth was Sam focused on the national vision of Christ, because his personal vision had grown dim. Even though he talked of his absolute faith in the great unknown plan of God, Sam Kerr was a man drowning in personal despair. He was a man whose sense of reality was split, because he was no longer the man everybody thought him to be. Two events in his life had shattered his belief in the fitness of things: the war, and a brief but drastic love affair he had with a nursing sister. It was after this affair he started writing his *Confessions, Meditations and Prayers*.

The effect of the carnage and destruction gnawed away at him. He had seen and heard too many awful things: too many confessions from the lips of dying soldiers. He had prayed with at least three men executed for cowardice by their own comrades. Sick boys they were, their minds and souls destroyed by the muck and bangs and blood of too much war. He dreaded those sad letters he had to write to anguished loved ones. He forcibly denied his doubts about a personal and loving God as he was confronted more and more with evidence of a great impersonal one.

In the last months of the war he developed a bleeding ulcer. After he haemorrhaged and collapsed, he was moved to a convalescent hospital for officers in the south of France. It was in an eighteenth century chateau with magnificent grounds. Bird song, woods, flowers and immaculate lawns replaced shelling, sudden death and muck. It was in this hospital that he met Anna, the nursing sister. She had a tender way of fussing when plumping his pillows, and the attention she gave him was a salve to his depleted body. In an attempt to nourish his soul, he read aloud to himself from the Psalms. One day while he was reading aloud in his mellifluous *basso profundo* voice, she came into the room. He stopped, but she pleaded with him to go on. She often hummed Wesleyans hymns; and one day while giving him a back rub, she recited Psalm 121.

I will lift up mine eyes unto the hills,
from whence cometh my help.
My help cometh from the Lord,
which made heaven and earth.
He will not suffer thy foot to be moved:
He that keepeth thee will not slumber.

Sam was moved. Her soft voice and tender touch released him, and he wept silently into his pillow. She leaned close to his ear and whispered, "There, there, just let it go."

Later that afternoon when she came in with his medication, he said to her, "You're a bit of an angel, Sister. You're devout, aren't you?"

She smiled and he noticed she had three dimples—one at each corner of her mouth and one on her cheek. Her lips turned up at the ends giving her a pixie look.

"Well to be honest Capt. Kerr, I'm not really. But I do love the old hymns and –scripture—especially the Psalms that you read so beautifully. I was raised on them. My dad was a Methodist minister. But no, I'm not devout. Now open up please and swallow."

She popped in a large tablet from the edge of a spoon and handed him a glass of water. It amused him the way she managed to close the door behind herself while carrying a full tray of medicines. First she went through the door, then reaching back with her shapely leg she hooked her foot around the edge of the door and pulled it after her. Her leaning forward with the tray while her leg was thrust out behind emphasized her back and thigh within her skirt. He called the action her little ballet. His time became a waiting period for her to re-enter his room. In a letter to Mildred, he told her about the wonderful care he was receiving and his good recovery and mentioned, "…the angel Anna, who sang hymns and recited scripture so beautifully. If we'd had a daughter, I imagine she would have been just like her."

One night the clatter of thunder overhead awakened him. In a moment of semi-sleep he thought he was at the Front again, and he couldn't get back to sleep. He decided to slip down to the solarium and watch the storm while smoking a forbidden pipe. As he entered a slash of lightning lit the room; and there in its blue glare was *his Anna* in the arms of a young medical officer, kissing. Devastated, he quickly left in case he was noticed.

For the rest of the night he lay awake confused and jealous and berating himself for feeling so. When she made her rounds, he feigned sleep, his heart beating in his throat. All the next day he felt sad and down. He waited for her to come on duty. When another nurse told him it was her day off he was plagued with fantasies of her being with the medical officer. He forced himself to think rationally; but in the end, to his consternation, he was forced to admit he had fallen in love with her.

As a man who felt himself in control of so many other people's lives, his home, himself and his learning, this emotional stew was new and disconcerting. He was a man who lived successfully in the image of how he perceived others perceiving him, and he wished he was home in the normal comfort and safety of Mildred and his congregation again; yet, his growing obsession with Anna contradicted this. A few days later, she came in with the medical officer. During his examination he said, "Sister, slip down the Padre's pyjama bottoms. Turn on your side, please, Padre, and draw up your knees. Glove and lube, please Sister."

Anna, understanding Sam's embarrassment, gave him one of her dimply smiles of encouragement; but being so basically exposed, he felt degraded. His mortification intensified when he caught a look pass between her and the doctor: a look of intimacy, a look of sharing that ran beneath their formality. His humiliation was complete. The doctor straightened up, pulled off his glove and dropped it into a white enamel kidney dish held by Anna. She then deftly wiped Sam's bottom and pulled the bedclothes back over him.

"Well, Padre," the Doctor said. "You seem to be coming along fine. I can feel no tumours, bumps or polyps in there. I think after a couple more weeks of rest, I'll write an order recommending we send you home."

"Am I that weakened, Doctor?"

"Not at all. But you've done your bit, and this debacle's coming to an end. Why risk your health all over again? If I discharge you fit for duty they'll only send you to the Front—and that could set you bleeding again. Time to go home to the family and heal properly. Good day, Padre."

Anna pushed her little cart after him, but before she left the room she whispered, "I'll be back in a while. There's something I want to speak to you about."

The intimacy he detected between Anna and the medical officer irritated him. He pondered what it might be that Anna wanted to talk to him about. Then the thought struck him that perhaps she wanted to marry the medical officer and that she wanted him to perform the ceremony. Good, he told himself, I'll go home and put this damned silliness behind me. Drop it over the side of the boat on the way. He felt somewhat composed, and he took up the novel he was reading; but his longing for her to return kept drifting in and out of his mind making it difficult for him to concentrate. Eventually, much to his relief, she came in, shut the door behind her and sat on the edge of the bed.

"May I speak candidly with you?"

"Of course."

He smiled and settled himself into his listening posture, head slightly to one side, eyebrows raised.

"It has to do with Dr. Rogers."

Small uncomfortable waves of lightness floated over his heart. I was right, he thought. She wants to marry him. He nodded encouragingly for her to go on.

"Well the truth is he won't leave me alone."

This wasn't what he expected.

"Won't leave you alone?"

"He tries to kiss me at every opportunity."

"And you resent him?"

"Well not exactly resent him. I did reciprocate once about a year ago, but I consider that as over. We were together just behind the lines in a field hospital. There had been a particularly bad shelling. You know how dreadful that can be."

Sam knew indeed. He had seen doctors and nurses almost dropping on their feet from exhaustion trying to repair an unending flow of men torn to shreds. His mind flashed back to one night when he himself held together the severed aorta of a dying soldier who was waiting along with thirty or so other horribly wounded men to be taken into the tent theatre.

"He's had it Padre," a Medical Corps sergeant said to him. "Let 'im go and help me with this one here; he's got a chance."

Sam let go and a stream of hot blood ejaculated from the hole in the man's body and hit Sam in the face. He recalled the stench and the hot sticky feel of it.

Anna's voice broke in.

"We had been working furiously for hours and hours—we lost more than we could –save—it had been like that for a week. Replacement staff came in and we were given a pass. We went to a little village; you know one of those close to the Front that have somehow escaped shelling. We were quartered at an inn—well, I'm afraid we got terribly drunk and euphoric, and we fell into bed."

Sam's heart thumped.

She continued, "But it was just that once. When I was transferred here he was the Medical Officer in charge. Well he won't leave me alone. He's a wonderful doctor—has a family in England—I don't want to make a fuss—can't very well can I? He's going home next month and he's putting the pressure on me something awful. Would you have a talk with him?"

Sam's emotions and mind clashed: the moralist in him was troubled at her indiscretion, the clergyman wanted to place it in God's hands and forgive, but the man was jealous, hurt and unreasonably angry. However, he was professional enough to at least maintain his facade of objectivity; so he listened and said nothing until he collected himself. He felt the intimacy of what she had shared with him entitled him to drop the formalities of titles.

"Anna, my dear—may I call you Anna?"

"Of course."

"This is a very delicate matter, Anna. What is it you would like me to say to the Major?"

"Oh just tell him I told you I want him to leave me alone."

"I see—well, ah dear me—please let me think about it a bit. But what about you? How do you feel about yourself?"

"Do you mean do I feel ruined? A fallen woman? Should I ask God's forgiveness? No. I don't feel any of those things. I have seen too much obscene carnage to put my lovemaking down to sin. Let me tell you something, dear Sam—I'll call you Sam—if my body could have taken a moment of agony away from some of the men who died in front of me, I would have felt less helpless and more humane."

She laughed out a bit hysterically.

"Let's not go into my morals please. I feel perfectly moral, Sam. I'll ask you now, will you be my friend and help me? If you don't want to get involved, we'll just leave it at that."

"I'll do what I can, Anna."

"Thank you, dear Sam. Will I make the arrangements for you to see him?"

"Very well. I'll convey your message."

Later that afternoon, she came back with an orderly.

"Well you can get dressed now, Padre. The orderly here has brought you a nice blue uniform to try on."

When the orderly left she said, "Well, you are to be up and about. The doctor wants you to take nice walks about the grounds and to have your meals in the Mess Hall. By the way, he'll see you after breakfast at 8:30 hours –all right Sam?"

He enjoyed the luxury of being fully dressed and out of pyjamas, and having the familiar feel of his clerical collar again. Up to now he had been out of his room only few times, and even then just as far as the solarium where he had seen the Medical Officer kissing Anna. He decided to go there now and try to think through this whole emotional business into which he had been uncomfortably thrust, then he would have a walk around to see what he could see.

The solarium had various exotic plants and a few small palm trees growing in it. There were also several white cane armchairs and tables with glass tops; the afternoon sunshine streamed in through the glass walls and roof. In a wheel chair sat a young man with a blanket wrapped around his knees. He was staring out to the green lawns where men, dressed in blues, strolled. Some of them walked in pairs, and not a few of them had missing limbs. Sam noticed that the right sleeve of the young man's dressing gown was empty, the cuff safety-pinned to the shoulder. He was not aware of Sam's presence, or if he was he was not acknowledging it.

"Lovely lawns," Sam said.

"Are they?"

At a closer look he saw that the clear blue eyes of the man neither moved nor blinked. He was sightless.

"Yes they are," Sam said gently. "Would you like me to describe them to you?"

The blind man's jaw muscles tightened. "Yes, and after that you can go out and shake hands with everybody for me too. Bugger Off."

There was no unpleasantness, no terseness or anger in his voice. Sam could not tell if he was making a grim joke, or if he really wanted to be alone. He decided to gamble on the joke.

"I'd be happy to but some of them have no arms."

The man chuckled.

"Touché. How about lighting me a smoke? I haven't learned to do that yet." He fished out a cigarette case with his left arm and handed it to Sam, "Have one yourself."

"Thank you, no. I'm a pipe smoker. My bleeding ulcer won't let me–orders, but I do sneak a puff now and again."

He put the lit cigarette between the blind man's lips which he noticed were quite bluish.

"Thanks. I'm Tom Reardon, Irish Fusiliers. You a Yank or a Canadian?"

"Canadian. How are you Tom? I'm Sam Kerr, Chaplin with the Montreal Regiment."

Tom laughed, "I suppose one advantage of being blind is that you can tell a Padre to bugger off without blinking an eye. Well do I call you Father or Reverend?"

"You can call me Sam. My son calls me father."

"Well, Sam, there's many a priest with a son he doesn't let on about. You're not one of those, now, are you?"

Sam laughed.

"Well if I were you don't suppose I'd tell you?"

"Look Sam, if you promise not to mention God to me, or preach to me, I'll treat you like an ordinary human being."

They bantered back and forth like that until Anna came in. She stood in front of Tom and put her hands on his cheeks and in a scolding voice said to him, "Major Reardon, why are you smoking? You know how very, very dangerous that is for you. You're scheduled for the theatre tomorrow morning, I've a good mind to send you right back to the Front. By rights you should not be out of bed, but we let you soft soap us into getting up for and hour and all you wanted was to sneak a smoke."

Tom laughed.

"Anna, you're the original bloody shrew. Marry me and I'll tame you."

"Come on now, I've had enough cheek from you for one day." She started to wheel him out, but he stopped her saying that he wanted a word alone with the Padre.

"Oh alright but only if he promises to tell me the lurid details of whatever you confess to him. I'll be right outside the door."

"What can I do for you, Tom?"

"Has she gone?"

"Yes."

"Alright then, look after this for me 'til we meet again."

He handed Sam his cigarette case. Sam chuckled and slipped the case into his pocket.

"Nothing else?"

"Nothing else, Sam, good luck."

He was about to say *God Bless* but said instead, "Yes, Good luck, Tom."

He felt affection for the young man who was only about seven years older than Mark. His rank was very high for his age, and he was clever with natural good humour. He wished to know more about him.

Sam enjoyed having the freedom to walk throughout the hospital at will. His clerical collar, he hoped, would be an invitation to anyone who might like to talk to him. Screams coming from a ward, marked, *Strictly off Limits to all except Qualified Personnel*, drew him over. An orderly sitting at a desk stood to attention.

"Stand easy." Sam smiled, "May I walk around?"

"Certainly, Padre, I'll accompany you."

They strolled past beds in which men lay curled up like frightened children. Many of them whimpered and cringed and babbled unintelligible noises. Others stood like statues, eyes staring and seemingly oblivious to all around them. One distinguished looking man with clipped gray hair and a military moustache sat on the edge of his cot masturbating and laughing.

The orderly scolded him.

"Captain, you know you're not to do that. Stop it at once, sir."

The incongruity of the formality of the orderly's address and the scolding made the man's plight even more pitiful. He broke into tears as he was being put back into bed. The orderly looked apologetically at Sam.

"They just can't leave the bloody Front, Padre, or else the Front won't leave them. Better off if they'd bought it out there."

Even though he had the uneasy feeling he agreed with the orderly, Sam said, "That's not for us to judge."

Before leaving he went to the crying man in the bed and placed his hand on his shoulder and said a silent prayer for him and the rest of his stricken comrades in that worst of all possible wards. Suddenly a bell rang, and a chorus of frightened howls went up.

"What's that bell, Corporeal?"

"It's the bell summoning those able to attend the Mess Hall. We go through this three times a day for breakfast, lunch and dinner. I've requested it be stopped, Padre. It reminds our chaps of the gas attack alarms at the Front. Do you think you could do something, sir?"

"Yes, I'll talk to someone."

Outside, he met Anna on her way to dine. As they walked together, she said, "I see you have been making a tour?"

"Yes. Tell me a little about Tom Reardon."

"Well, he has shrapnel lodged in his spine, and one lung is punctured. There are bits and pieces throughout the rest of his body; but worst of all, he has a piece dangerously close to his heart. Tomorrow they'll put him under and see if they can clear the heart area. It's touch and go, really, and unless we are very, very lucky we'll lose him."

"Does he know?

"Oh yes."

"Has he seen a priest? I assume he's Catholic?"

"He refuses to see one—claims he's a devout atheist. He was a lecturer in Classics at Trinity. Told the poor priest he likes Zeus better than Jehovah and that Jesus was a Hebrew posthumously converted to a Greek by St. Paul."

"Do you think he might like a visit from me?"

"I don't know, Sam. Would you like me to ask him?"

"Yes please."

"Alright, you go into dinner, and I'll go and ask him now and let you know."

The mess hall was in the opulent banquet hall of the chateau. Huge crystal festooned chandeliers hung from a ceiling ornate with gilt trim and painted with various bare-breasted Greek goddesses and nymphs. It was not difficult to imagine men and women from the past in their powdered wigs and silk finery dining and dancing here. Mirrors and murals covered the walls. Now it was populated by wounded warriors in their nondescript blue flannels.

The mess sergeant in gleaming whites came forward and seated him according to his rank and then asked him if he would pronounce the blessing. The buzz of conversation faded to silence as Sam stood and looked over the room filled with fellow officers all in various stages of disrepair and healing. He quietly asked the blessing and sat down; another officer toasted the king, and the noisy chatter started up again as the meal began.

Anna returned.

"Tom said that he wouldn't mind a visit before lights out. He was being smart, of course. You can stay as long as you need to, but be careful not to tire him. He loves to talk when he gets going. Oh, just use your good sense, Sam."

She touched his hand under the table, and a small surge of elation rose in him. He was pleased that she thought he had good sense.

Tom's room was quite dim in the fading light of day. He sat in bed propped up on his pillows. Sam announced himself before entering and Tom turned his head in his direction.

"Oh, it's the holy man from Canada, come on in Sam and close the door after you and we'll have a smoke."

"I'll come in Tom, but there will be no smoke. I have strict orders."

"Ah, Anna the shrew has got to you. Come on in anyway and pull up a chair."

"It's a bit dark in here, do you mind if I turn up the light?"

"It's bloody dark in here. Suit yourself, Sam; it makes no difference to me." Tom said without rancour. As Sam turned up the little bedside gas lamp he noticed two volumes of *The Iliad* and *The Odyssey* in Greek. He picked one up and said for openers, "I'd have a difficult time reading these. The best I can do is the New Testament Greek."

"Oh you found the blind bard—I dare say you could struggle through it. If I could muddle through the fables of Jesus, you could manage Homer. Open *The Iliad* at Book Six, line 405—you follow, I'll recite."

Sam listened as Tom spoke in the beautiful cadences of the ancient Greek telling of Andromache's farewell to her husband Hector before he leaves to battle Achilles, of her pleading with him not to leave her and their baby son, of her lamentations and premonition of his death, of Hector's helmet frightening the baby, and of his removing it so that he can hold the baby and kiss him.

'...he set his child again in the arms of his beloved wife, who took him back again to her fragrant bosom smiling in her tears; and her husband saw and took pity on her, and stroked her with his hand, and called her by her name, 'Poor Andromache! Why does your heart sorrow so much for me? No man is going to hurl me to Hades, unless it is fated, but as for fate, I think no man has yet escaped it once it has taken its first form, neither brave man or coward.' "

Tom lay back on the pillows his face full of weariness.

"How many poor buggers have played out that scene, since it was written, Sam?" After a pause he added quietly, "Fate has taken its first form for me."

"Have you got a wife and family, Tom?"

"Well now, that's another story, but I want you to hear it. I have another man's wife and she has my son—he thinks the baby's his though. Good enough. He's a better father than I'd ever make. A good man. He was my mentor and friend, Pauline's his wife. She and I were smitten the first time we set eyes on each other, and we've been secret lovers for a few years. When she fell pregnant I decided to go off to war. I never saw the child and a good thing too. Oh we had our soldier's farewell—not as glamorous as Hector's but believe me all the grief was in it. She sent me a photo of the baby and letters—of course I couldn't write back. Look in that drawer Sam, will you. And take out that tin box and open it."

The tin box held several letters and a couple of photographs: one of a baby and the other of a very plain young woman with spectacles.

"I don't want them lying around here after tomorrow. Will you take them and get rid of them for me, Sam? And the cigarette case, she gave that to me, so you might as well get rid of that too."

Sam was saddened. He wanted to pray, but resisted.

"Is there anything else you would like me to do? Try to make contact and give her a message?"

"No need to. I have her here with me and I'm with her—it's all understood." He reached out his good hand into the darkness and Sam took it.

"Goodbye, Sam and thank you. Why don't you take the Homer—I can't read the damn things anyway and maybe you can improve your Greek."

"Thank you, Tom, I will, but I won't say goodbye, just good night. I'll be thinking about you."

Unknown to both of them, Anna had slipped quietly into the room and stood back in the shadows. When Sam turned to go, she held her finger to her lips indicating to him not to acknowledge her presence.

The next morning, she told him Tom Reardon had died. They agreed to meet later for a stroll over the grounds before dinner. In the meantime, he had to meet the Medical Officer to tell him of Anna's wishes.

The doctor's greeting was cordial.

"Good morning, Padre, glad to see you looking well. Looking forward to going home? Have you any specific questions about your condition?"

He ran all his questions together indicating that he really didn't have much time. Sam came right to the point.

"Doctor, I am here on behalf of Sister Lytton. She told me of your advances towards her, and she has asked me to convey to you that she would prefer it if you left her alone. I'm sorry."

The doctor was about to retort something, but checked himself. He swivelled his chair around towards the window. After a moment, with his back still to Sam, he said, "Tell her I won't bother her."

He remained facing the window until he heard Sam say, "Thank you—good morning, Doctor."

Just as he was leaving the room, the medical officer said over his shoulder, "By the way Padre, I would be more concerned about your heart, if I were you, than your ulcers."

Sam wanted to pursue the remark, but the medical officer picked up his pen and began writing.

Twenty-four

Sam Kerr: Coming Unstuck

Tom Reardon's death brought to the surface a turmoil of conflicting thoughts. Several years ago he would have had little to say to Tom Reardon. He would have found his iconoclasm self centered and arrogant, and his morals reprehensible, and he would have classified him as a corruptor under the guise of an intellectual humanist. Sam would have put down Tom's affair with his mentor's wife, to self indulgent lust; and her deception about the fatherhood of the baby, the result of a deep moral flaw–decent womanhood simply did not do what the mother of Tom's Reardon's child did.

But then, Sam thought, had I met Tom several years ago, he would have been in full health, and not blinded and broken; and I comfortably surrounded by my parishioners and I would have been guided by the iron principles of Calvin. I would have thanked God for my sound faith.

But since meeting Anna, Sam was now faced with the question of whether his own morals were wanting. He asked himself, am I glad Tom left behind a son? *Yes.* Now it seemed absolutely right and good that Tom has a son; God forgive me, but it somehow makes Tom's senseless death less futile.

As he sat there in his hospital room listening to the yells of anguish that occasionally reverberated throughout the halls, Sam had to admit to himself that a great deal of his own moral code was in fact, nothing more than conventional respectability.

Respectability! The word drew with it a whole montage of images from his past. A memory surfaced of Mildred, his perfect wife and mother of their son, of how she frightened him with her passion one summer afternoon a short time before their marriage.

Both their families were vacationing on Lac St. Joseph. He and Mildred had taken a canoe paddle around the lake. They planned to go to a little island where they would be joined by the others later for a picnic. It was a hot day filled with the scent of spruce gum, juniper berries, and the whining of tree toads. On the trip over she lay languidly back in the canoe. It seemed that the very heat of the sun came at him through her eyes. He was so overcome with lust he could hardly speak for the huskiness in his throat. When they pulled ashore he immediately walked around picking up kindling for the cooking. He struggled to force down the passion that was taking over his mind. She followed him, silently. He dared not look around at her.

In a tiny clearing all dappled with sunshine and leafy shadows, she stood in front of him holding out her arms. He was perplexed. She went to him, kissed him full on the mouth and rubbed her breasts hard into his chest and pressed her pelvis rhythmically against his. It overwhelmed and frightened him. Mildred, always so shy and timid, at best permitted him to hold her hand and give a warm little kiss on the mouth. The depth of passion and the brightness in her eyes frightened him. He pushed her away from him, and scolded her, "No respectable girl does that!"

She ran from him crying.

Poor Mildred, he thought. After that, she was always respectable. They undressed separately or in the dark, and their sex was perfunctory preceded or followed by prayers.

He thought of the rectitude pervading his congregations. But, not only my congregation, he thought; but how righteous did I feel when I blessed the colours, the drums and a shipment of new guns and gun carriages on a regimental parade amidst the splendour of full dress and polished brass, all in the fullness of military respectability. When I was at the Front those guns blowing men to bits did not seem very blessed. And what about that young soldier tied to a wheel of a gun carriage, his back stretched exposed waiting for a flogging—field punishment for expressing fear in the face of the enemy? Where was the blessing in that? he asked himself. The next day at a trench church parade, the young fellow lay on his stomach on a stretcher, and sang hymns and prayed with both the officer who had sentenced him and the man who had flogged him. A few days later they all died in a shelling.

Drunken officers, drunken nurses, drunken soldiers, prostitutes, fights, rapes, racketeers, politicians, war mongers, blood, filth, terror—the young German prisoners just as bewildered, broken and frightened as their captors. What had Tom done wrong? He had loved and produced a child. Was that not what God made him for?

Sam concluded that the wrongness of it was something determined by respectability. In the very brief time I spent with Tom Reardon, Tom discounted me as a man of God, but he touched me as a man.

Sam was going through the painful business of discounting many of the things he had once stood for; while at the same time, he struggled with the possibility of what he might become.

He lay back and looked at Tom's tin box. His hands shook. He wondered what words were written on the faintly scented paper. Suddenly it was important to know what the letters said. He sat up, picked one from the box and unfolded it. The last page was on the top, he read the farewell paragraph,

Our child is God's gift. I know you will scoff at me, my darling, but I truly feel like all those women in the bible—Sarah, Hannah, and Elizabeth—God made fertile. Don't you see, darling, God always touches a barren place whether it be the womb, the mind, or a situation arid for the want of love, and flowers it. I love you my precious Tom, and our love has blossomed. May Christ's peace be with you...."

Sam read no further. The words struck a chord in him. He looked at the photograph of the plain young woman who apparently had such a deep sense of herself. He understood the level at which she and Tom loved each other. It had nothing to do with contracts, social acceptance, or respectability—it was beyond all these things. Now Tom was alive in the baby and in the heart of its mother. He was filled with sadness for Tom and all the other species of Toms in the world. Who knows when a life is fulfilled or unfulfilled? While praying for forgiveness and guidance he lay back exhausted and wept. Sleep fell heavily upon him until Anna wakened him with a touch of her fingers on his cheek.

They walked along the bank of a swift-flowing stream that meandered through the estate on its way to join a larger river flowing down to the sea. At a little stone bridge, Sam took out the tin box from his pocket and gave it to her to hold. First he tore into shreds the picture of the young woman, then of the baby followed by the faintly rose-scented letters. The little pieces of paper fell on the water like petals.

As Anna looked into the stream at the torn faces on the photographs and watched the ink run on the bits of paper, she thought that these scraps and scribbles were what the lives of men and women she had known thus far amounted to. Before Sam tore them, the letters and photographs were nothing more than a sad, desperate attempt by already broken people to have a semblance of wholeness–a wholeness that came through the love they had. Perhaps it is the most one can expect; wholeness that comes with feelings of love pulsed in the moment. She thought of the slums where her father had preached virtue and love to a people who lived in squalor, and of how this monstrous war had torn to pieces their loved ones.

A few drops from a shower pitted the surface of the stream. She looked at Sam whose face was a pale mask, its sockets empty with grief. Or was it futility? The drops fell heavier making a pitter-pat sound on the leaves.

Sam was feeling absolutely nothing. It was as if his brain and heart had thickened to numbness. It is difficult to say whether Anna recognized the black hole into which she had seen so many men sink, or if she mistook his tragic look as the result of great sensitivity to human suffering.

She searched deeply into his eyes. The only woman who had looked at him so intently before was Mildred that day when they were young. He felt her hand on his fingers tightening and he sensed her fully. She reached forward and kissed him, her lips on his. The rest of her body followed and she held herself against him very tightly. He could not respond until her soft warm tongue slid into his mouth. Not even his wife had ever kissed him like that. His arms went tightly around her and he met her in full passionate response. On the way back they walked in silence through the rain with their eyes down on the wet grass.

That night he was in turmoil as his longing for her warred with his guilt; but it was a guilt that was in his head and it was no match for the longing consuming him. Sometime, what seemed like hours after lights-out, he drifted into a shallow sleep from which he was later awakened. Anna had slipped into his room. He lay in complacent silence as she caressed and kissed him continuously. Not a word was exchanged between them except that just before she left she whispered in his ear, "I love you, Sam."

He was troubled not only by her passion, but also by the realization that she was quite tipsy. In his morning prayers he asked for forgiveness and berated his weakness and stupidity, but at the same time he was suffused with a deeper satisfaction that intensified his longing to see her. He strove to rise above this. He consulted St. Paul on the subject who was relentless in his condemnation of fornication. Sam took some moral comfort in the fact that he did not actually have full sexual intercourse with Anna, but he suffered a mixture of distress and exhilaration about the fact that it was probably inevitable because they both wanted it. He prayed for strength and wisdom while lusting fancifully. Sam was a man no longer in one piece.

Before going to breakfast, he prayed again for guidance. When he had finished, he had firmly made up his mind to speak to Anna and tell her that what had started between them must not continue. Committed to this decision, he made his way to the dining room feeling more in control.

A few days previously, there had been a big push at the Front. The death toll and casualties were so enormous that a decision was made to change the status of the convalescent hospital for officers to active treatment for all ranks. An order came down announcing that those patients determined well enough would be discharged.

All day squads of soldiers erected tents, latrines and field-kitchens, transforming the beautiful grounds into an immense field hospital. Inside the chateau, operating rooms were set up, and the dining hall was turned into a massive ward. Every space possible was utilized.

Sam was ordered to report to the Surgeon Brigadier. He was a rotund little man with a weary, phlegmatic face and voice. He should have been retired from active duty several years ago. Sam received a cursory greeting.

"Oh Padre I'm putting you back on partial duty. I am going to need you here for the next while. I imagine we'll have a large dead and many almost dead. I'll assign a clerk to assist you—you can keep your room which will double up as an office or God knows what else. Oh and by way, your the official designation is partial active duty, but you'll be pretty well full tilt, I imagine. You understand?"

The "understand" was the Brigadier's way of saying have you any questions, but it also implied that he would be stupid if he did.

"Yes Brigadier, I understand." To which Sam was dismissed with a curt, "Good Chap."

The casualty loads were so heavy that all personnel had to work hours without proper rest. He made rounds in the mornings, and performed burial services over mass graves in the afternoons. Throughout the night he attended the bedside of the dying.

In the course of the day he saw a great deal of Anna, and frequently worked side by side with her. Mostly he admired her dedication and compassion, but at times she disgusted him as when he saw her filch a hip flask from a dying soldier. When he rebuked her, she turned on him and snapped, "Oh for Christ's sake, Sam, he won't need it. I do. Mumble your prayers over him and leave me alone."

Anna was breaking down. She would sit with him in his room afraid to leave. Late one evening he had just slumped exhausted on his cot when a tap came to the door. "It's open," he called. It was Anna, tears streaming down her face and sobbing convulsively.

"You are wonderful, Sam—you give so much to those poor boys and to me."

He sat up and put his arm around her and she collapsed into him. "Hold me tightly, Sam. Tightly, please."

Anxious in case someone might come in, he removed her arms and locked the door. When he returned to the cot she flung herself at him again, holding onto him like a frightened child. He tried to talk and comfort her, but she kissed his face and mouth again and again. She was drunk. When he tried to free himself, she sat astride his knees holding on to him tightly, her kisses becoming longer and more passionate until he responded. She unsnapped her bib and opened her tunic, grabbed his hand and plunged it inside to her breast. Then unbuttoning his fly she manoeuvred her bloomers down and positioned herself until he was inside her.

He fell back on the cot, depleted. Waves of disgust followed his subsiding passion. He wanted to get up but she held onto him tightly, pleading with him not to move, "Wait, wait, darling, wait and be still, my dearest Sam."

After that she visited him as often as she could. Each time it was easier for him, but when alone, he was miserable with guilt. He prayed for strength to stop, but he was unable to. Usually, she had been drinking; and that, along with his lust inflamed his self revulsion. As the war moved closer, the night sky flashed and rumbled with gunfire. One night Sam was awakened by an orderly banging on his door.

"Padre. Quickly sir! Come to the solarium."

He threw on his robe and rushed down the corridor past the wounded lying on makeshift stretchers. In the solarium, a small group of nurses surrounded Anna who was crouched behind a chair, screeching. The matron was snapping at her telling her to stop disgracing herself, but Anna shrieked obscenities back at her.

Sam coaxed her, "Come Anna, it's Sam. There, there come now."

She let him lead her back to his room where he held her until the matron and a doctor arrived and took her away. Later he was called to the Nursing Sisters' Quarters. Anna, chalk white, lay on her cot. He held her hand and uttered a short prayer. The Staff Sister said to him, "I'll leave you with her, Padre; she wants to talk to you in private. Try not to stay too long."

Anna smiled at him, "I'm afraid I went a bit over the top, Sam. They're sending me home."

He surreptitiously lifted her hand and kissed it, whispering, "I love you, Anna. I'm sorry."

"I love you, Sam, and I'm not sorry."

He wanted to talk about them both, about how wrong he had been in becoming her lover, but she looked so strained and white and terribly tired, he just slipped away from her bedside.

In the next few days, long lists of casualties were given to him to separate the names of the dead from the living. When a soldier died, he drew a red line through his name and marked a cross beside it. As the lists grew longer the number of crosses increased. Each time he drew a red line he felt as if he personally deleted the soldier from life. Sam's condition rapidly deteriorated. His ulcer was bleeding again and he was ordered to bed. The Medical Officer informed him he was being sent home, and that his heart was not a hundred percent. Anna, in her broken state, left before him. Sam blamed himself for her condition. By the time he boarded a ship for home, he, too, was empty and broken.

Mark was disgusted at the self-degradation and self pity in his father's *Confessions*. He was angry at his father's betrayal of his mother. His weakness and hypocrisy had prevented him from reaching out to her, the one person who might have truly helped him. His inability to trust her generosity might have been his real act of betrayal, for it constituted a lack of trust in her love. Mother will never set eyes on this slop, he told himself. He slipped the folder under his sweater and took it down to the basement to burn it. In the furnace, the flames consumed his father's demented words page by page.

When there was nothing but ashes, Mark raked them over until only a few feeble sparks remained; and as he watched these go out, he made up his mind that the neat bundles of his father's sermons would be burned as well.

Twenty-five

Breakthrough

Mark had an hour to spare before his appointment with Philip Dixon. He strolled into a small park with huge elms and sat on a bench. Incoherent thoughts about his father, his mother, and the Pendletons buzzed around in his mind. A squirrel with its quick sporadic movements tentatively zigzagged over to him. Two lovers sauntered by, and behind him the sounds of various instruments and a soprano singing scales mingled in discord from the open windows of a music conservatory.

It might be nice for his mother to have Sally Pendleton's company, he thought. Sally is a rare sort—no shrinking violet. She seems to have a strong sense of herself just like poor Mollie had. He wished Mollie and his mother had known each other better. They liked each other instantly when they met at their wedding in Edinburgh. Mollie had said about Mildred, "Your mother has a true heart, Mark." And Mildred said about Mollie, "She's a rare jewel, Mark, I'm sure you'll make each other very happy."

His mother's revelations about her feelings towards his father; and his father's guilty ramblings in his journal had left him so perplexed that anger and compassion were confused. A wave of rage swept over him, and he exclaimed loudly, "Shit and damn it to hell." The squirrel scurried back up the tree.

Of course it was not new for Mark to be in turmoil when he

entered Philip's office, and several times he had left, vowing never to return. After a few pleasantries, Philip started probing.

"I know you've lost your wife and baby and you are shattered, but what is causing you to be shattered in your particular way?"

"I don't understand you Philip, you and your damned mazes and nightmares, or whatever. You turn everything a person feels and thinks into something else—like they're fooling themselves or something. What do you mean, 'shattered in my particular way'? Do you think I choose the way I feel about Mollie or anybody else?"

Philip said nothing for a moment.

"Anybody else? Do you mean your father, your mother…?"

Mark shouted, "Do you think I choose the way I feel about Mollie and the baby being dead?"

Philip remained silent. Mark glared, his face white, and his fists clenched. Then Philip said, "They died in an influenza outbreak, didn't they?"

Somehow the phrase tore into Mark's mind.

"Not much damned choice," he snarled.

Philip knew he was plucking away at newly formed scar tissue. He persisted with calculated coolness, "Were there many who died in your parish?"

He felt a slight shift in his mind, a nudge to his memory.

"How many people died, Mark?"

"I think about six or seven."

"Think now. Isn't that a lot of dead for such a small community?"

Mark was confused. His mind worked to find an excuse for something, but for what, he was not sure. His mind went back to the terrible storms, the pallid faces on the pillows, and the sour stink of sickness.

Philip's voice intruded, "Who died first, the baby or Mollie?"

The terrible scene came back to him. He answered, huskily, "The baby."

"I would like you to tell me about that, Mark. Take your time."

"Well, there was a dreadful storm blowing. Many people were sick. I'd been getting around seeing them as best I could. We were all worried and frightened in case the Spanish influenza had come back. All my time was spent trying to get visits in. The baby was quite well—except he had the sniffles and was off his food a bit. Mollie was worried in case he was getting the influenza. Anyway, we put it down to teething in the end.

"After supper, Freddy Fenlon, a neighbour, came banging at the door. His wife was in terrible shape, he said, and she wanted to see me."

Mark stopped. He was having difficulty talking.

"I disliked Fenlon intensely. I remember before she got sick she called in to see me. She was in tears. She told me how her seventeen year old daughter, Janice, had left home pregnant.

"'Do you know the father?' I asked her. Poor Heska. She completely broke down. 'Reverend Kerr' she said. 'There's nothing anyone can do about that so there's no sense talkin' anymore about it. Nobody knows about Janice—though goodness knows the tongues were waggin'. Anyway, Janice left for Boston and I haven't heard from her since. She was supposed to be going to an aunt of mine there, but she never turned up. What a lovely child she was. The teachers in our little school used to remark about how smart she was. When she left, the heart went out of me."

"I wrote a letter to the Boston Police but never heard back."

Mark went silent as he thought about Heska. Philip's voice broke in.

"Yes Mark. A neighbour–Freddy Fenlon's wife–you were telling me he called because his wife was very sick. But just before that you told me that you and Mollie were worried about the baby but assumed he was just teething."

"Yes, yes I'm sorry. I let my mind wander a bit. Yes. Freddy and I battled the storm. He stopped every so often to take a swig of rum. It took us almost an hour to make several hundred yards through drifting snow to the house. Both of us were soaked to the skin and freezing.

"I went straight up to the bedroom. Heska was dying. She wanted Freddy to leave. He was drunk and belligerent and refused.

"The poor woman was in despair. I turned on him and told him his dying wife had something to tell me in private, and if he was man at all he would leave. He swore at me and threatened to throw me out bodily. I was so angry at him it was all I could do not to smash his drunken face. In the end I pleaded with him and he left.

"Poor Heska, her eyes weren't focusing. Her hand felt hot and papery. I told her that Freddy had left. Her voice was weak. I had to put my ear very close to her lips to grasp what she was saying. Her breath was foul.

"'Revered Kerr, if you ever get a chance, tell Janice I love her and ask her to forgive me for not doin' enough.' Her breathing was hard, and her throat rattled. 'Pray for me. Ask God to forgive me.'

"I muttered something about God forgiving us even before we ask Him.

"Her eyes closed tight. I was anxious to get Freddy before she died. I went downstairs and waited in front of the fire watching the flames draw the steam from my wet clothing. I just wanted to be home with Mollie and the baby. Freddy came down and told me that she'd gone. It was about four in the morning by the time I got back to the Manse. All the lamps were still burning."

Mark stopped talking. Philip let him be for a moment, then said, "Go on, Mark. The lamps were still burning. Yes?"

He looked away from Philip and continued, "I found Mollie collapsed on the bed holding the baby. He was dead. She was feverish and breathing with those horrible quick rasping shallow breaths.

"So many things were running through my mind at once. I knew I had to take the baby away from her. I tried but she held on to him tighter.

"I said, 'Mollie, darling, let me take him and change him,' or something like that. But she said, 'No, Mark, he needs me now.'

"I didn't know if she realized. Perhaps she did. Eventually, I was able to get him away from her. I wrapped his little body in the blanket from his cradle and took him downstairs out to the back porch. Then I ran back up the stairs.

"For three days she fluctuated between clarity and rambling, asking for the baby, talking to her parents and her brothers. I don't know how I held on. People came to the door asking me to visit their sick—but I sent them away telling them that the baby was dead and Mollie was dying. A few women came and helped me manage. They took the baby away and when Mollie died they took her away too.

"The storms never let up. In order to carry on, I literally froze my heart and brain. I know I made calls, but I have little or no memory of them. Spring came and with it the burials. I broke. The only thing that got me through was whisky. I drank until they sent me home to my parents."

"How did the Mackinnon's take the news of the deaths—I mean how did they respond to you?"

Mark related the terse cable from Mollie's mother and her rejection of him.

"It must have been devastating news, Mark, losing two sons and then their Mollie. Do you think they blamed you?"

"What the hell do you think?" Mark snapped back. "I took her to that Godforsaken place, didn't I?"

"Why did you do that, Mark?"

"Because I wanted her with me."

"And Mollie, did she love you?"

Mark refused to answer. Philip was relentless.

"She gave up a promising music career. She left her parents and home—parents for whom she was the only one left—parents she fretted and worried about. She must have loved you very much to do all that, Mark."

"Yes, and look how I repaid her," he said, breaking down again.

"What killed them, Mark?"

"The bloody influenza!" Mark shouted. "And I brought it home to them."

"Did you have it?"

"No. I wish to God I did."

"You said that you had to bend very close to Heska's face and you even said her breath was foul. Did you have to get that close to many people you visited?"

"Yes. I can still smell them."

"Then the chances of you giving the influenza to Mollie and the baby are minuscule. Did Mollie attend the sick?"

"Yes."

"Don't you see, Mark, in your nightmare of the man in the chair—the one who terrified you in case he turned around to look at you? That man was you. You were afraid to face yourself. You saw yourself as the instrument of death, and as the killer of Mollie and the baby. But it wasn't you. The disease killed them. The disease was transmitted by direct contact with someone who had it–a cough in the face, sputum, sweat, or excrement."

"But why? Why her...?"

"And not you?" Philip interjected. "For the same reason doctors and nurses who are immersed in disease escape being infected less than others. *Immunity.* My God Mark, if that weren't so, ministers like you and the medical profession would wipe out much of the population. What you got, Mark, is the dreadful disease of guilt and believe me that can be as destructive as any virulent germ. It's a slow and painful killer."

It was on the tip of Mark's tongue to say "It certainly killed my father", but he thought better of it.

Twenty-six

An Afternoon in the Woods

The leaves of a few maples had turned yellow and red, which was a sure hint summer was coming to an end. Mark's last session with Philip had stirred much up in him, and he was unsure of his feelings. He was given to sudden releases of tension, not crying jags exactly, but involuntary silent belly laughs. He was concerned he would have one while he was with Sally Pendleton.

They drove to the woods in silence, each thinking about the other. Sally knew it would be easier if she spoke, but she wanted to keep pressure on Mark by remaining silent. She thought that if she did not speak, he would be forced to think about her. Instead, he just felt trapped and irritated. The drive along the river road through small, picturesque farming communities seemed interminable.

"Where exactly are we going?" he asked.

"To a ravine woods further along the river."

Eventually, she turned the little truck off the main road and bumped along a rough lane leading to the edge of a wood. He carried a knapsack with their lunch; she carried a canvas bag lined with damp moss for specimens. As she searched and snipped shoots of ivy, she explained them to him. He feigned interest out of politeness. When they were down by the riverbank, Sally suggested they eat lunch.

It was a lovely place with trees and bushes overhanging the water. She chose a spot under a great willow tree. Out by a rock in the river, a column of flies hatched, and every now and then a trout jumped leaving a circle of rippling rings. Mark opened a bottle of wine, and asked her if she missed England. She gave him one of her long looks before answering.

"I did terribly for a while. But it was not England so much as for someone I left behind there. He is one of the reasons, but not the whole reason we left. I'll tell you about it."

He poured them another cup of wine. She sipped, looking at him over the cup.

"I have a son. He's still over there. Oh, he's well provided and cared for. His father died at the end of the war. His widow is bringing up my baby as her own."

She drained the wine and held out the cup for more. Mark poured.

"You see my father was the head gardener on the estate of a very old family, as was his father before him and his before him. The son took me when I was seventeen, and after that I couldn't deny him. We carried on for a couple of years. On his last leave I conceived. He was killed shortly after. The cat was out of the bag then. I told Father everything and he confronted his lordship who in turn told Robert's widow. She knew about us—a fling with the gardener's girl, she called it. She herself was barren, so the Earl, not wanting to waste the family blood, made arrangements to raise the baby. Father and I came to Canada shortly after I bore him. Simple as that. I get an enormous curiosity about the baby now and then when the maternal thing catches hold of me. But if the truth be known, I miss Robert's loving more than his baby. I never even think about him much now, the baby I mean. So you see, Mark, in a way, we have some things in common, at least."

He was about to protest but held back. How could his loss of Mollie and his baby be compared with hers? She gave him a strange look with her wide eyes then reached over, stroked his face and said, "Poor, Mark. You are very confused, aren't you?"

She was smiling at him. Her eyes were deep and luminous. She brought her face closer and whispered, "Kiss me."

She lifted his hand and brushed her lips along his fingers, licking them lightly with the tip of her tongue. When their mouths touched, hers was open and wet. He let himself go, kiss for kiss, as she lay back on the grass, pumping her body against him, urging him through the kisses. Suddenly he found it difficult to breathe. He tried to get free of her, but she clung tighter. When she felt him holding back she was more aggressive.

"Come Mark. Mollie wouldn't mind," she panted.

At Mollie's name he sprang back pushing her roughly away from him. The look on her face appalled him. Her face was quite twisted now, and her eyes jaundiced and dull as stone.

"You unnatural idiot! I could show you things your little Scottish wifey could never have dreamed of," she said, slapping him sharply across the face.

Mark, agitated, muttered, "I'm sorry, Sally. You see, I...."

She sprang to her feet and ran away from him along the riverbank.

He didn't follow her. Suddenly, she threw back her head and let out a long shriek that resounded through the woods. He didn't know what to do, yet felt he should do something. He went to her. She turned on him.

"Why don't you take me, damn you!" she hissed at him and pummelled him with her fists. He grabbed her wrists, but she effectively wrestled him to the ground. Then, to his horror, she held the lobe of his ear in her teeth and grabbed his penis. She hissed, through clenched teeth, "Come, you bastard, I want you inside me!"

He was scared to move in case she bit through. So he lay still. In a moment she stood up and laughed contemptuously, "Let's go back, you fool!"

Neither of them exchanged a word, and when they pulled into the nursery, she left without a goodbye. Mark was convinced he had spent the day with a madwoman. Of course what had transpired precluded any possibility of his mother going to the Pendleton's.

At home, two letters awaited him. One was from the Synod asking him to leave for Prince Edward Island as soon as possible. He felt well enough, but he wanted to discuss it with Philip first. The other letter was from Janice Fenlon.

Janice's letter had been redirected from Prince Edward Island. She told him that the Boston police had contacted her. Inside, was enclosed a page for her mother, which she invited Mark to read and deliver.

> Dear Mother,
> I am sorry for not keeping in touch with you. Much has happened to me but most of it good. I would love to see you again. Perhaps you and the Reverend Kerr can arrange something. Please don't tell Dad you heard from me.
> I only want to see you.
> Love, Janice.

She also gave a Boston phone number, and signed herself Mrs. Janice O'Neill. Mark realized that if he was her only contact she wouldn't know of Heska's death. He phoned her. When the call eventually got through, Mark told her as gently as he could over a crackling line that her mother had died. The silence at the other end was so long he thought he had lost contact. When she did come back on he promised he'd write her more details.

He discussed with Philip Dixon about the Church wanting him to return to the Island.

"You can't run away from death by running away from the place where it happened," Philip said. "Most people have no choice but to live on where their loved ones left them. It is all a matter of accepting the fact that they're gone and treasuring the best they gave you while they lived. You've reached the most important part of experiencing the death of a loved one, getting on with your life. The alternative is to negate everything and die with them.

"Now, I want you to listen to me very carefully. You're feeling better than when you first came to see me, but that doesn't mean you are, for the want of a better word, 'cured'. There is no cure in the sense of a broken bone knitting–a broken heart and spirit are quite different. You will not get over Mollie, the loss of your child, or the shock of everything; but I'm confident you will cope. However, you must be brave and vigilant at the same time. You're not given to excesses—it's not in your character. If you feel yourself moving in an excessive direction you must try to think it through. If you can't, that's where I come in."

Mark interrupted him, "What exactly do you mean by excesses?"

"Chronic drinking, being swept away by overpowering emotions, using sex to forget or overcome pain, or conversely, total sexual abstinence for fear of desecrating Mollie's memory. You're a healthy young male, after all. Avoid using work as an anaesthetic. Just look into yourself at the end of the day. You'll increase in strength day by day if you can cope day by day. This is survival Mark. Oh, and the most dangerous excess of all is to let Mollie permeate your every thought and action. That would not be a good way to honour the life of a good woman. The sooner you get involved with some productive work the better. By all means go back to the Island."

At dinner he said, "Mother, the Synod wants me to go back to Prince Edward Island immediately. I think I will. Why don't you come with me? It'll be a change, and it will give you a chance to think about what you really want to do. You could stay in the manse with me and help me out a bit. I'm apprehensive about going back there, and it would be good to have your company. If you decided you wanted to come back here at any time, it would simply be a matter of getting on the train."

Mildred was delighted and agreed immediately.

"You'll like the Island." he continued. "It's a gardener's paradise. Jacques Cartier, when he first saw it, called it the 'Garden of the Gulf.'"

"You make the arrangements, dear, and I'll write a letter to Arthur Pendleton."

But had he known what was transpiring in New Skye, perhaps he might have had second thoughts.

PART THREE

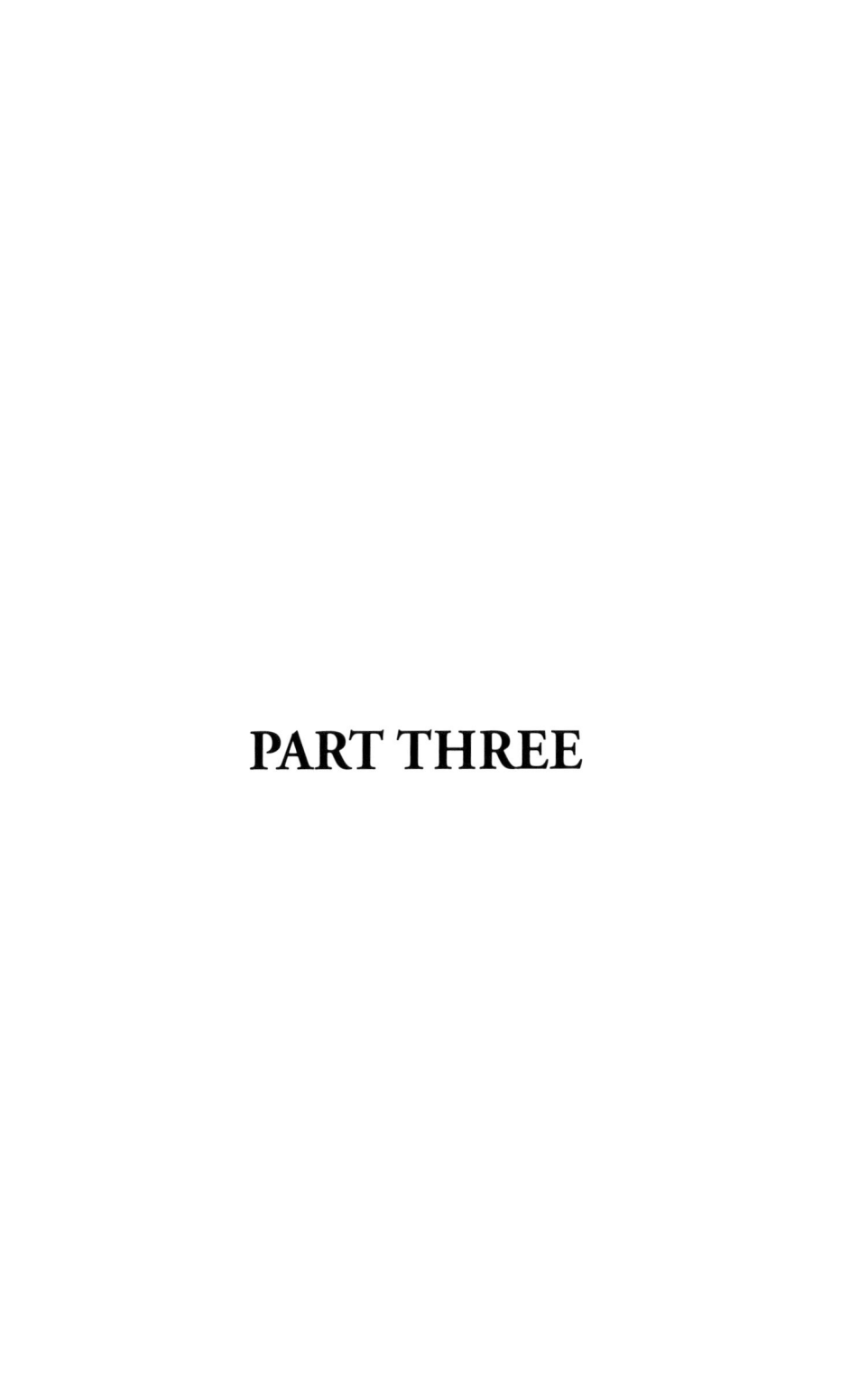

Twenty-seven

Return to the Island

When Myra Swanson heard Mark was returning, she forecast a dark future for Christianity in New Skye. Angus MacLeod stomped out of a meeting of Elders shaking his fist and shouting that they'd rue the day they let Satan's seed back in; but the bulk of the people were glad to have him back. A deputation from the Session of Elders met Mark and his mother at the station and brought them back to the manse in a new Model T. car that was bought for him to help him with his ministry.

At the door he was overcome with anxiety for a moment, and he felt an urge to turn around and go straight back to Montreal; but his mother seeing his troubled look took his arm and insisted he show her around. Everything was spotless. Mollie's and the baby's clothes had been removed as he had asked, and the women had filled the larder with freshly baked bread, pies, milk, eggs, vegetables and meat. Having Mildred with him was a great boon. She watched the late afternoon sunset from the parlour window as it shimmered through the spruce trees and cast a reddish-gold over a thick field of clover. Long after everything else went dark, the myriad of purple flowers still held the golden light.

At supper, she said, "I'm captivated, Mark. This place feels just right–so idyllic, so beautiful. It is exactly the place for one to recover a sense of well being."

"I hope so, Mother."

Immediately, she felt her remark might be gauche and added quickly, "Forgive me Mark, I was thinking of myself, but I honestly believe it'll be best that you've come back here in the long run."

He recalled Philip's remark about not everybody having the luxury of leaving the place where loved ones died.

"We just have to get on with it, Mother. I'm glad you're here with me. I think I'll turn in, now."

In his bedroom he suppressed any desire to indulge himself in memories; eventually, he fell into an uneasy sleep. Several hours later he was brought fully awake by loud banging on the front door.

Twenty-eight

Things Astir

After Sarah Ewart had gotten Charlie out to the barn to do the morning chores, and Ruth had fallen asleep on the parlour sofa, she turned again to prayer. Dear God, help me and give me the strength to do whatever I have to do. Freddy's lyin' down there on the dune. What if he's not dead? What if a neighbour finds him? Somebody has to be told. She could hear Charlie singing away in the barn as he worked. Then it came to her. The Reverend Kerr is due back. Dear God, please let him be in the Manse. He's the one we need to help us right now. She summoned all her strength and hitched up the horse and wagon.

When Mark finally answered the door, he was shocked by Sarah's appearance: caked blood on her dress, and her face swollen and bruised.

"Please, Reverend Kerr, you must hurry and help us."

"Of course, Sarah."

After scribbling a note to his mother, he hastily dressed and joined her on the wagon.

"We've terrible trouble, Reverend Kerr. Charlie killed Freddy Fenlon. Charlie's not the same as when you knew him before. He's went strange, and Ruthie isn't herself either. Oh Reverend Kerr, we're finished. It's terrible. We've been on our knees prayin' an' then I remembered you were due back. Thank God you're here. I'm sure the Lord sent you. You're the only one who can tell us what to do."

The noise of the horse's hooves and the rattle of the wheels over the ruts in the hard clay road made it difficult for Mark to grasp everything. Before they went into the house, Sarah said, "If Charlie talks at all, Reverend Kerr, he mightn't make much sense."

Charlie was still in the barn, but Ruth was awake. When she saw Mark and Sarah through the kitchen window, she ran upstairs and cringed behind the bedroom door with her head between her knees. Every bone in Sarah's body burned and her head was bursting. Climbing the stairs to deal with Ruth was excruciating.

"Ruthie, we're in desperate trouble. Don't you give up! You can't be a good-for-nothin' now. You must help me or else we won't be able to help Charlie. The Minister'll tell us what to do. The Lord wants us to put our trust in Him through the Minister. Get up, Ruth, now, and go out to the barn and bring Charlie in."

"Yes Sarah, Reverend Mark, yes, he's the Lord's angel and my Prince."

"Go on now, Ruth and bring poor Charlie in."

Sarah told Mark again of the terrible events: the rape, the beating, and the shooting. When Charlie and Ruth came in they stood mournfully holding onto each other's hands like children.

"We have to tell the police. We shouldn't delay any longer," Mark said.

Nothing much registered with Charlie. Ruth whimpered, and Sarah said, "Yes. Would you do it please Reverend Kerr?"

He cranked the number for the local exchange. He knew by the time he got connected to the police in Charlottetown, people would be listening in and word would spread along the road. He heard a cough precede the operator.

"New Skye exchange."

"This is the Reverend Mark Kerr."

"Good morning, Reverend Kerr. Welcome back. What has you up so early this morning' now?"

"This is an emergency, Clarence. Please connect me with the Mounties."

"The Mounties now? Right away, Reverend Kerr. Just you hang on now, sir."

The hum on the line increased as more phones were lifted to listen in. A faint voice answered, "R.C.M.P. Charlottetown detachment."

"This is the Reverend Mark Kerr. A man's been shot on the Ewart property, in New Skye. Bring a doctor, please."

"Will you remain there until we get there, Reverend Kerr?"

"Yes."

The community was alive with anticipation. The main road from town was watched for extra traffic; and when an unusually large cloud of red dust raised by the police vehicles was sighted, the men left their morning chores to converge at the Ewart gate.

They pestered the constable posted there for news. Many knew him by name; but Donald, who was a distant relative, was unofficially deputized to ask the questions.

"What the hell's goin' on, Malcolm?"

"Now you fellas just stay back an' let us do our job."

"Ask him if they had a fire, Donald?"

"Lord Jesus they didn't have a fire because we'd a seen the smoke," Donald snapped. He turned to the policeman, "It's somethin' wrong wi' the Ewart girls, Malcolm, aren't it?"

"Never you mind, now, Donald" the police man said aloud. Then in a whisper added, "I can't reveal the details, but it's pretty bad. Not a word now, Donald."

Back in the house while the doctor examined Sarah and Ruth, Mark gave his statement to the Inspector. A detail was sent down to the shore to search the area and secure it against intruders, and another constable was sent over to guard Betty Logan's house. When the crowd at the end of the driveway saw the constable crossing the road and walking up the Logan lane, their curiosity intensified.

"There you see?" a man said. "Maybe little Charlie killed Betty Logan an' the policeman's goin' over to check on the body."

"No, no.! I bet Charlie killed Betty an' most likely Freddy Fenlon too!" argued another.

"Not at all. I think Charlie did them *all* in—Betty, Freddy, Sarah and Ruth, then he hung hisself in the barn with the harness reins. Sure wasn't he as odd as hell?"

"No, no, Donald," another man said, taking the wind out of his sails, "I seen Sarah goin' by with the Reverend Kerr a while ago. Imagine? An' him an' his mother hardly havin' a minute to settle in, like. What'll she think of us?"

After the doctor completed his examination, he and the Inspector went into conference.

"Sarah's injuries could be serious. She's taken quite a beating, and I want her admitted to the hospital for tests and observation."

"Can I question her first, doctor?"

"Better not. She's in shock and needs immediate attention. Maybe tomorrow you can."

"Very well, then. We'll take her in with us in the van. We'll make her comfortable. It'll be faster."

The doctor agreed.

"Corporal, get Charlie in here."

"Excuse me, Inspector," Mark said, "Charlie and his sister Ruth are not quite themselves. They're confused. May I go and get Charlie for you? I assure you he's not in the least dangerous."

The Inspector thought for a moment.

"Very well, Reverend, thank you."

Sarah was lying down with a blanket over her, and Charlie and Ruth were still holding hands.

"Charlie, would you come with me please? The Inspector would like to have a word with you."

Charlie looked at Ruth. She held onto him tighter.

"Please Ruth, tell him to come with me. I'll look after him. The Inspector's a nice man and means him no harm. You stay here and look after Sarah."

She took Mark's smile as a secret message of love, and she let go of Charlie's hand.

"It's all right, dear. You go with the Reverend Kerr."

"Take a seat, Charlie"

Charlie remained standing, head lowered. He wanted to go to his own dark corner. A flash of annoyance at being disobeyed passed over the Inspector's face.

"I'm Inspector Kenneth Rutter, of the Prince Edward Island Detachment of the Royal Canadian Mounted Police. Are you Charles Ewart?"

"Answer the Inspector, Charlie. It's okay," Mark said.

"Yes."

"And this is your place of residence?"

"No, I live here."

"Now, why don't you tell me what happened between you and Freddy Fenlon."

"Poor Freddy went back an' I put him down."

The Inspector took a breath.

"Went back where, Charlie?"

"Freddy the wolf entereth the pen by the back door and ravisheth the flock."

The corporal who was taking down the statement looked to his chief for guidance. The Inspector snapped, "Goddamn it Corporal, just write down everything he says. I beg your pardon Reverend."

Then turning back to Charlie he asked, "Charles Ewart, did you kill Freddy Fenlon?"

"Yes, put him down with two shots. Have to bury him. Granddaddy's dead."

The Inspector, alarmed in case Charlie was alluding to another murder, said, "Whose….who's granddaddy?"

"The Granddaddy fern–the one all the grannies kept alive an' Betty too. Now he's dead and the dune's on fire an' that's the end of the Island."

The corporal shrugged his shoulders and scribbled Charlie's gibberish.

"Where's the gun?"

"Out in the porch."

The Inspector nodded to the Corporal who went out and got the gun and set it on the table.

"Is that your gun, Charlie?"

"Yes, that's her."

"Did you shoot Freddy Fenlon with it?"

"Yes."

"Anybody else?"

"Pepper."

"Pepper? Who's Pepper?"

"The dog."

While the Inspector was trying to glean some semblance of logic from Charlie's answers, a Sergeant returned from the shore.

"Can I speak to you, sir?" he said, motioning with his head. The Inspector followed him outside.

"Did you find a body?"

"We found it all right. The stomach and the top of the head's blown away. It looks like whoever done it tried to burn him. We found the body lying on top of the fire an' these two empty shells and this kerosene can with Ewart's name scratched on it. There's footsteps goin' down the dune and around the fire and goin' back up again. One man's tracks, it looks like."

They came back into the kitchen, and showed Charlie the can and the cartridges.

"Are these yours?"

"Yes. Two shots."

"Stand up."

The Inspector carefully examined the blood and other bits of tissue that had splattered Charlie's trousers and boots and dictated a description of each detail to the corporal.

"Charlie, I want you to go and take your clothes off–boots, socks and underwear, everything and give them to the corporal. We're going into town, so why don't you put on your good clothes, eh?" He turned to Mark and said, "Would you go up with Charlie and the Corporal, please, Reverend, and maybe pack a change of clothes for him."

When they came back down Charlie was in his good suit. Mark remembered him dressed like that when he used to sing with Mollie in the choir, only now he didn't have his tie and starched collar on. The corporal had his barn clothes tied up in a sheet.

"Now, Charlie," the Inspector said. "I'm going to read you something. If you understand it, I'll want you to sign it. But only if you understand. Okay?"

Clearing his throat, he read, "I, Charles Ewart of New Skye, Prince Edward Island, admit to shooting Freddy Fenlon of New Skye, Prince Edward Island, on the night of August 31st, 1924, with a twelve gauge shotgun. I swear that this statement is true."

After some more explaining, they got Charlie to sign. Then the Inspector put his hand on his arm.

"Charles Ewart, I am arresting you by your own admission for the murder of Freddy Fenlon. You will be taken into custody where you will be detained until you appear before a magistrate of the Criminal Court of Prince Edward Island. At that time formal charges will be brought against you. Have you anything else to say?"

"I'm hungry."

Everybody laughed.

"All right Corporal pour Charlie a cup of tea and give him a slice or two of bread."

Relieved, Charlie went to his own chair in the corner. While he was drinking his tea, Mark persuaded the Inspector not to handcuff him. It was agreed that Ruth would go with Sarah and stay with her in the hospital. Rutter reluctantly agreed to getting Ruth's statement later in order not to hold up Sarah's admission to the hospital. He also agreed that Mark could drive in the van with them.

They carried Sarah out to the police van while Ruth whimpered. Charlie fussed about needing to finish his chores and to bury Freddy. As they drove past the neighbours at the gate, some of them pounded the side of the van making a booming noise inside. Jesus sang in Charlie's head about the little sparrow falling so that Old Feardy would not be in the van too.

As the police continued their investigation around the murder site, a flotilla of dories filled with neighbours gathered off-shore. Colonel Wittigar's man was among them.

Twenty-nine

Betty Logan's Arrest

Betty Logan heard the rumble and whine of the police cars. She went out into the yard and saw the crowd around the entrance of the Ewart driveway. A large policeman was striding towards her house. Frightened, she ran back in, barred the door and hid well down behind the Granddaddy fern. The window darkened as he peered in. She crouched lower, trying to get under the fern fronds, but he saw her and tapped on the glass.

"Come on now, Mrs. Logan, open up. Nobody's goin' to do anything to you."

She opened the door a cautious crack.

"There's trouble at the Ewart's. Your name's linked to it, so I'll ask you to stay in the house 'til the Inspector gets here. I'm goin' to stand right here to keep an eye on things. You can shut the door."

Her mind raced. Did I kill Freddy with the little German knife? Maybe I should go up and hide it. She thought about the money he threw at her in the attic and relived the terrible event.

No, I can't go back up there again, she thought. Did Charlie go and see Freddy about him hurtin' me? Maybe Freddy killed Charlie. If Jack was alive, he would a killed Freddy for sure and maybe me too. She wanted to fly out into the yard but instead went to the Granddaddy fern and looked down into him. The green world calmed her and brought Charlie closer.

"Oh Charlie, my little love, love, love. Jack hates us an' we were so happy," she sobbed into the fern.

As the summer had passed, Charlie's visits to the house were more frequent. Charlie trusted Betty, and he grew to love her. They played like children in a world of fantasy when she led him through the enchanted paths of the fern.

"Now Charlie, I'm walking through the fern-wood an' I find you hurt. You're out Charlie, nearly dead–an' I find you. Now you lie down an' close your eyes."

Charlie lay down, eyes closed tightly.

"Let me see where you're hurt now, sir?" she said, gently unbuttoning his shirt. "Here's the wound in your poor heart."

She tenderly traced the area of his heart with her fingertip, and then kissed down along his body until she brought him to orgasm. He shivered in ecstasy, but apart from putting his hand lightly on her breast, he hardly touched her. She held him close while he slumbered.

One afternoon, just before he arrived, she was mist-spraying the fern. Droplets of water on the fronds held the sunlight streaming through the window, turning them into a myriad of tiny rainbows. Transfixed, she gazed in wonder at the bejewelled fern. Desire flooded her. Light-headed with passion, she ran upstairs and hastily removed her undergarments until she wore only a light cotton dress. When Charlie arrived, his child-like passivity aroused her even more.

He felt her warm, silken skin, and she his. She sat astride him, caressing herself. Then to her surprise his strong arms turned her over and she was under him. Arching his back, he plunged deeply into her. She entwined her legs around his and with her heels on his buttocks, she pumped him into her again and again until at last she lay back floating in ecstasy. Both were drenched in sweat and sweetness. They held each other until they drifted into sublime sleep.

She took Charlie through this ritual at least once a week. They copulated in spontaneous innocence and absolutely free from shame.

A few weeks before Freddy had raped her, Betty was convinced she was pregnant, and the belief she was carrying Charlie's child made the rape even more odious and horrible.

Louder banging brought her out of her reverie. She stood frozen in terror beside the fern. She peeked out the window and saw the Inspector step back off the porch to look up at the house. He saw her and pointed to the door for her to open it.

The Inspector and the Corporal sat with Betty around the kitchen table.

"I understand that Freddy Fenlon paid you a visit yesterday afternoon, Mrs. Logan. Is that true?"

Shame kept her from looking at them.

"Yes."

"What time was that?"

"About three o'clock."

"Will you tell us what happened?"

She didn't answer.

"Mrs. Logan, I have been told that you were beaten and raped. I need you to tell me exactly what happened. I know that won't be easy for you, but I have to know."

"What's goin' on, sir?"

The Inspector and the Corporal looked at one another.

"You mean you don't know?"

"No I don't sir."

"Freddy Fenlon's dead, and I'm investigating his murder. So you have to tell me everything you know."

"Who done it?"

"That doesn't matter, now. Tell me about Freddy Fenlon's visit yesterday afternoon."

Betty, slowly at first, told everything. Then the men went outside. She watched them through the window as they talked and periodically consulted the Corporal's note pad. When they came in again the Inspector asked her to take them up to the attic; they saw the bloodstains and the knife and money lying around the floor.

"Is that the knife?"

"Yes, sir."

"Corporal, count the money, put it in a bag and tag it along with the knife. Have another good look around. If you see anything, call me."

He ushered Betty back downstairs to the kitchen, and said, "Mrs. Logan, Freddy Fenlon was shot, but that may not have been what killed him— the cause of death still has to be determined officially. Until then, I am going to have to arrest you on suspicion of murder."

There was no doubt in the Inspector's mind that little Charlie was his man, but he had to allow for all possibilities. He felt sorry for Betty and decided he would take her to hospital and have her examined. The Ewart women would be there under guard, and she may as well join them and be comfortable. The Corporal came back and reported he had found nothing else. As they were heading past the crowd of neighbourhood men, somebody yelled out, "Cockteaser!"

Thirty

Sinister Activity

When Myron, Bubble and Squeak slipped back into Myron's house after throwing Freddy's body on the fire, Wittigar was eating a feed of bacon and eggs.

"There's a strong smell of kerosene off you guys. Get rid of it. Besides it's ruining my breakfast. You sure you saw to everything?"

Myron, while pulling off his coveralls, said, "Yes, an' we smoothed the sand over with juniper brush so that it looks like only one man's footprints just the way you told us. Nora, throw them coveralls over the clothesline, then make more breakfast for me and the boys."

"No Myron, go and burn the coveralls first. You boys go with him," Wittigar said.

He took out his wallet and pressed several notes into Nora's hand. She loved the feel of the money.

"Get something pretty. Maybe I'll arrange a special time just for you and me later on. You make a man a lovely breakfast. Not a word, now," he whispered into her ear.

Then gently pushing her away he walked sedately out of the house and joined the boys burning their coveralls in the open shed where Myron cooked his pig-swill. Wittigar made them go over the details of what they did to Freddy's body several more times.

"It was some friggin' mess," Myron said. "He was wearin' a money belt. We took it off. No sense burnin' money like that...."

"Where is it?"

"Outside in a bag."

"Get it!"

The Colonel looked at Freddy's blood-soaked money belt. Part of the pouch was torn by the shot. Freddy's name was tooled into the thick leather. Wittigar was furious.

"You two slip back down there as fast as hell's blazes and hide that belt in Charlie's tool shed an' keep your damn fingers off the money. An' make sure nobody sees you. Myron, you stay here."

After they left, he said, "You did a good job Myron, but not a word, now. Fenlon must never be linked to us. The Mounties are going to be out here in droves later on. Can you keep Nora quiet?"

A gust of wind down-draughted the chimney, blowing out a bellow of oily smoke. Wittigar coughed and walked out of the shed. Myron followed, assuring him he could keep Nora quiet.

"Look Myron, I'm going to give you a little bonus. Now listen carefully. Show it to Nora and the two of you go over to Halifax for a second honeymoon—you know what I mean?"

Myron sniggered. "B'jesus Colonel, we're not over the first one yet."

The Colonel laughed and gave Myron a wad of notes. "Now I want you two to go right away until the cops have come an' gone. Understand?"

"Well Colonel, it won't be easy just up and leavin' like that. Aunt Myra needs me at the mill."

"Tell her you have to go on business for Lionel Buell. It'll be all right. You go and tell your beautiful bride to get ready. Show her the money. Oh and be sure to tell her I said thanks for the grand breakfast. Okay go on. I'll wait here for the boys."

His Aunt Myra wasn't very well pleased when he told her he had to leave for Halifax right away.

"How could you, Myron? You know how right busy we are?"

"Wittigar said to tell you it's urgent business for Lionel, Aunt Myra."

Her whole demeanour changed.

"Well you'd better get goin' then. Here, take this and you an' Nora enjoy yourselves."

She gave him fifty dollars along with a list of things to do for her. Her response was so generous, he wondered if she and the Colonel were tied up in some way.

Later in the day, Lionel Buell played a game of snooker with Nicholson Fraser at an exclusive Charlottetown club frequented by politicians and businessmen. As he chalked his cue, he said quietly to Nicholson, "It's important that the right people meet with Wittigar at the Abbey tomorrow night. Get them together as soon as you can."

Nicholson realized at once there was an emergency, or else Buell would never have used the predetermined code: *the right people*.

He looked at Lionel, then said, "Hold on a minute and I'll get us a drink."

When he came back, he said, "Tell Wittigar it's on. Eight o'clock for supper at the Abbey."

The Abbey was a small red brick hotel situated on a Charlottetown side street. Many clandestine meetings had taken place there over the eighty-five years of its existence. It was a well-known fact that almost any kind of commerce might be carried on there, and it was a favourite of skippers when they docked at the wharf. Though often alluded to, the nature of its business dealings was never openly discussed. Yet the hotel was regarded as respectable because so many respectable people frequented it, but as one wit remarked, "The Abbey doesn't exist, because so many blind eyes have been turned to it."

The first to arrive was Harry Pilchard, a high-ranking judge. Wittigar greeted him and noticed he was tipsy as usual.

"We have a serious problem, Harry. Drink?"

"Scotch. It better be serious, Walter, to call us together like this."

Soon the others arrived: Nicholson Fraser the politician, Stuart Hoyt, a prominent businessman and Peter McCormack, a top public servant. After they settled themselves with drinks, dinner was ordered and they got down to business. The Pup waited in a side room with Buell, should either of them be needed.

During the first course of heaps of roast wild goose, mashed potatoes and turnips, Wittigar reported on the possible consequences of the Fenlon shooting.

"Since that judicial inquiry in Ottawa on smuggling, the Goddamn temperance lobby is pushing hard for something to be done about the Trade."

He poured himself a drink and continued, "If any connection's made between the Trade and Fenlon's murder, they'll be down here in droves from Ottawa and go through us like a dose of salts."

The civil servant asked, "Well, apart from Fenlon being there to signal the shipment is there any other connection with us? Why did that Ewart fella shoot him anyway?"

"There's no other connection, not directly anyway, but if a connection's made that'll be enough to do it. Buell's from that area and we have investment arrangements with his cousin Myra Swanson out there. He says that the locals believe there was some sort of love triangle between Fenlon, Little Charlie and Jack Logan's widow. Logan used to be our runner along with Fenlon."

"Charlie Ewart's a bit of a head case an' his sisters are on the funny side, too. Anyway the word is that it's likely Ewart was jealous of Fenlon and it ended up the way it did."

The judge, quite drunk by now, mumbled a question more to himself than to the others, "*Insanely* jealous?"

His Worship's drinking was legend around the Island, and many tales were told of him being transported in a state of alcoholic collapse to his home in the middle of the night. As a judge, however, he had the reputation of being one of the best legal minds in the country, and Island pride swelled when he was appointed to head a judicial inquiry in Ottawa into the shipping of blighted potatoes; but those on the inside, knew the inquiry was a sham, and that the judge was really going away to dry out. Whittigar hated him and wished he would die in his sleep. As far as he was concerned, Pilchard had long outlived his usefulness.

"What are you thinking about, Harry?"

"Well Walter," the Judge slurred. "To shoot somebody in the stomach and then blow his head off is either the act of a crazed person or a cold-hearted person. But many a crime of passion is committed in jealousy; though why the hell anybody would think any woman's worth it beats me. But then to deliberately light a fire, douse the body with kerosene and try to burn the evidence—now, that sounds like *calculated* cold bloody murder–motivation? Sexual jealousy."

"But that may not be the only motivation, Harry. Could it be robbery as well? It's just possible they might find Fenlon's money belt hid around Charlie's place."

The Judge didn't answer. It was a favourite trick of his to feign oblivion so that he couldn't be accused of hearing things he shouldn't have.

McCormack asked, "How many of our people know?"

"Probably seven," Wittigar answered.

"That's seven too many. Now I've got another idea."

Everyone acknowledged he was the smartest among them, so he got full attention.

"We throw out a decoy—something that'll keep the Mounties and the crowd up in Ottawa happy. It'll cost us plenty, but it'll be worth it. We tip off the Mounties that there are railway cars headed for Boston hiding a substantial load of liquor. We'll let them know after the train's well on its way over the border."

They argued about it until they finally agreed.

Before the night was over, Charlie Ewart's fate was sealed; and perhaps that of Freeman Mullaly, a potato warehouseman and shipper.

Thirty-one

Stephenson and McQuaid

The police took Charlie straight to the Charlottetown jail. Ruth held onto him until Mark persuaded her to let go.

"Sarah has gone to hospital, and it's very important that you be with her. I'll go with Charlie and look after him. I'll come and see you later."

Only two of the little jail's fifteen cells held prisoners. One was the town drunk who lived there practically on a permanent basis; the other was in for stealing newborn calves from the fields. When Charlie arrived, both of them were mopping the floors. The place reeked of carbolic acid and lime. Athol Mutch, the Warden and head guard, stimulated by the momentous occasion of having a murderer in his jail, gave them an exuberant welcome. But the Mountie reminded him that although Charlie was arrested on a charge of murder, he was merely being detained until a judge would set or deny bail. He also cautioned him that on no account was he to speak to newspaper reporters, or allow them in to take pictures. He also suggested that the Reverend be allowed to stick around to help get Charlie settled. Before leaving he said quietly to Mark that it would be a good idea to get Charlie a lawyer, but Mark had already decided to visit his friends Pius McQuaid and Albert Stephenson.

After seeing Charlie settled, he walked along the dusty Charlottetown back streets towards the center of town. Hunger and a splitting headache drew him in the direction of the delicious smell of bacon and eggs wafting out from a small restaurant. As he ate, he thought of how he would deal with all the problems that had crashed in on him since early morning.

Welcome to my first day back on the Island, he said to himself. Janice Fenlon would have to be contacted about her father. Sarah and Ruth would have to be visited, not to mention Betty. His poor mother, so enraptured with the Island on her first day would now have to awaken to news of mayhem and murder. Oh well, he was sure some of the New Skye women would call on her and make her feel at home.

He looked at the other people in the restaurant: strong, hardworking farmers who had just come into town by train–a cautious undemonstrative people who considered it wise not to reveal too much of themselves. Mark wondered what dark undercurrents in their lives might suddenly erupt and change everything they lived and worked for. Their communities bore optimistic names like New Glasgow, New Haven, New Annan, New Dominion and New Perth—all with their share of Freddys, Charlies, Sarahs and Ruths. But apart from the geographical location, New Skye, he mused, was no different from Old Skye. People lived and hoped for the same things; and generally, whatever it was that might destroy them was common to all of them.

A paper boy came in, calling out, "SHOOTIN' AT NEW SKYE! SHOOTIN' AT NEW SKYE."

Mark bought a paper and read it while he finished his breakfast, then he made his way to see Pius and Albert.

The firm *Stephenson and McQuaid* was something of an anomaly on Prince Edward Island: Albert Stephenson being from Scots Presbyterian stock and Pius McQuaid, an Irish Roman Catholic.

Their partnership, at first, created a stir. The Bishop had a "serious word" with Pius about "mixing oil and water."

"But is it not possible for two Christians to serve the public together?" Pius asked.

"It is not always conducive, my son."

"Then, Your Excellency, is it not time you and I tried to change that?"

Pius was dismissed with a blessing and a warning that he must never desert his own kind. The following week, however, their first small legal contract came in from the Roman Catholic University.

On the other side, Albert was questioned by the Presbyterians.

"Albert, do you think you are setting a good example to the bright lads coming behind you?" he was asked.

"I do."

"How's that?"

"I'm doing what I was taught—sharing knowledge and Christian principles with another human being. Both Pius and I are acting out of good conscience, and judging from the work coming in from the Catholic diocese, we're on the right track."

A small contract was sent from the Protestant college and things grew from there.

As Mark strolled on his way to the lawyer's office, he recalled the first time he met Pius and what a boon it was for Mollie. Pius, a trained violinist, could just as easily have followed a career in music. At a party, he and Mollie astounded everyone with their playing. She was pregnant with little Bobby at the time, and when they returned home, she lay on top of the bed stroking her belly and rhapsodizing about how she and Pius could get together after the baby was born and start a music society on the Island.

"Oh Mark, who knows where it might lead? He told me of other talented musicians here. There's a woman in town who was trained in opera in Vienna and New York! Imagine! And there's a man whose wife's a gifted organist. He actually broadcasts musicales over the wireless from his living room! Who would have thought of such a thing here?"

Poor Mollie, she had such dreams and hopes for bringing music alive on the Island by searching out its "treasures of talent." He remembered how she referred to poor little Charlie Ewart.

"What a voice he has, Mark! He's a wee treasure of talent."

Now poor Charlie was languishing in jail for murder.

Pius and Albert greeted him warmly. When Mark explained why he was there both lawyers looked at one another.

Pius said, "We don't get many murders on the Island, but when we do they're dandies, like this one. Rape, love and intrigue all wrapped up in one!"

Albert chuckled, "And who knows? Maybe a bit of rum-runnin' thrown in. Well it sounds like your kind of thing, Pius. You're always complainin' about how borin' it is around here. But seriously now, Mark, a case like this will be very expensive. Have they any money do you know?"

"Can't say for sure."

"If rum runners are involved that'll open up another whole can of worms—everybody and his dog's into that. They think it's a bit of a lark, but they just don't realize how far the smugglin' business stretches and to what lengths the crooks involved in it will go. I've a cousin in Boston well placed in the U.S. Treasury who told me that a network stretches from the East coast to Montreal, Detroit and Chicago right down to Florida and that it involves some very influential families and politicians," Albert said. After a moment he asked Pius, "What do you think about a retainer of two hundred to start with?"

Mark was aghast but said nothing. Pius nodded.

"I guess. But first I think we should get down to the jail and interview Charlie Ewart. Then register ourselves as Ewart's defence and get his confession from the Attorney General and anything else that's pertinent. The judge will probably schedule a hearing for tomorrow or the next day.

"Mark, do you think Charlie's insane?"

"I don't know about insane, but I'd say he's not right. Neither is his sister, Ruth. Sarah's the one to deal with. I guess she'll have to be the one to retain you. Yes, see her first."

"I'd better get busy."

He went to the phone. The Attorney's General office informed Pius they would be bringing a charge of premeditated murder against Charlie.

Before Mark left the lawyers' office, he called Janice Fenlon in Boston and told her of her father's death and some of the circumstances surrounding it.

"Reverend Kerr," she said. "I'm goin' up to the Island, but first I need to contact a lawyer. Do you know of one?"

"Well, as a matter of fact, I am calling you now from the law office of Stephenson and McQuaid. I'd recommend them."

Thirty-two

Pius

Pius McQuaid had flaming red hair that stood up like a frozen wave. Red eyebrows and lashes made his bright eyes even bluer. He was a tall young man with pale delicate skin. He blushed easily, and his generous mouth moved to a grin giving him a cheeky, boyish look.

One of his law professors had told him that a face that lit up like his could be a decided disadvantage to a lawyer, because it telegraphed what he might be thinking or feeling. His blushes and smiles, however, disarmed and confused his opponents, for they never expected him to be clever.

As he strode through the hospital he drew smiles from the nurses. One whispered to another as he passed, "Oh I just love that Pius McQuaid. He's so fresh and clean he looks like his mother hung him out with the washing on the clothesline to air."

The policeman at the door greeted him, "Good day to you, Pius. Go on in she's waitin' for you."

Sarah was propped up on pillows; Ruth was sitting in a chair with her head down.

"Thanks for comin' in, Mr. McQuaid," Sarah said.

Pius felt sorry for the two sisters. He had two maiden aunts living up the western part of the Island: strong women who could endure the onslaught of day to day hardship; but if something like this hit them, they'd be devastated and extremely vulnerable. His face went red.

"I'm sorry you've run into all this trouble, Miss Ewart. I'm sure you don't deserve it at all. Now what I'd like first is for you to tell me exactly what happened. If you want to stop for a rest or anything, or to ask a question you just go right ahead. I might stop you to ask you a question now and then."

Sarah was mortified at the thought that she might have to reveal intimate details, but she knew she had no choice if she wanted to help Charlie.

"What do you know already, Mr. McQuaid?"

"Well only bits of this and that. I'd rather you just tell me everything and that'll give me a good clear picture."

"My brother Charlie killed Freddy Fenlon. Shot him."

She told the rest of the story in a rambling fashion. Pius listened patiently. When she was finished he asked her, "What time did you go over to Mrs. Betty Logan's to look for Charlie?"

"Well he usually finished his chores by half past four, and that day he hadn't even started. I waited a while but the sun was startin' to go down."

"Did Charlie always do Mrs. Logan's barn work about the same time?"

"It depends on what has to be taken care of before hand. But usually he goes over after he's finished the first part of his day. There isn't much to do at her place. On that day he didn't get over 'til around three or after."

"So you think Freddy Fenlon left Mrs. Logan before three?"

He made notes until he had worked out a fairly accurate chronology of the events. During the interview, Ruth held her hands over her ears and rocked back and forth. Neither Pius nor Sarah took any notice of her.

"Miss Ewart, I want to ask you a couple of questions of a delicate nature."

Though she knew beforehand, she dreaded what he might ask her to disclose. She covered her face with her hands and said just loud enough for Pius to hear, "Yes, ask away."

He leaned forward and whispered, "Do you know if Freddy Fenlon and Betty Logan were lovers?"

Sarah shook her head and answered through her hands, "No. There was no goin's on between them two."

"Are you certain now, Miss Ewart?"

"Yes."

"Were there goin's on between Charlie and Betty Logan?"

"Goodness no, no. Charlie was fond of Betty but nothin' like that."

"How can you be so sure, Miss. Ewart?"

"Our Charlie's just like a child when it comes to that, Mr. McQuaid."

"How can you be so sure about Fenlon and Mrs. Logan?"

Sarah didn't answer. Instead she cried, pressing her hands tighter into her face, "Oh dear, Lord. Oh dear, Lord."

After a moment she said, "*I know* he wasn't *her* lover."

Seeing how ashamed and broken she was, Pius understood. The viciousness behind the beating Fenlon gave her was sexual. He believed it true that Fenlon raped the other woman and got money, which he suspected was in some way implicated with rum running. He admired Sarah's strength, but wondered if she had enough left to carry her through the ordeal of Charlie's trial. If she doesn't, he thought, what'll happen to them? He could see from Ruth's fixed stare and the way she was hugging her body she was mentally ill; and Mark had intimated that Charlie Ewart was worse. Sarah's voice broke into his thoughts.

"Mr. McQuaid, will they hang Charlie?"

The directness of the question forced him to think along a path he had no wish to go with her. His mind raced for an answer, and then he came to a conclusion that the only way was to be frank.

"If Charlie is found guilty of murder in the first degree, yes, they might. But if the charge could be reduced to manslaughter, or if a plea of insanity could be entered he could spend a good part, or maybe even the rest of his life in prison, or an institution for the criminally insane."

"Is there a chance he'll get off?"

Sarah's look told him that she was not grasping for hope but that she was truly trying to assess the situation.

"There's always a chance, but at this point I honestly couldn't say how good."

"Will you help us, Mr. McQuaid?"

Pius wanted to say yes. He knew if anyone on the Island was able to help, it would be Albert and him but that the expenses would be substantial. Expert witnesses would have to be brought in, not to mention extra staff. Sarah seemed to understand. Before he had a chance to answer, she asked, "If you *could* help us how much would it cost?"

"Quite a bit I'm afraid. To get us started we would need a retainer of about two hundred and before we're finished it would run to much more than that."

She told him there was enough to cover the retainer and other expenses if needed.

"If we run out, we'll put the farm up for auction and sale. It's finished as a family farm now anyway."

Pius told her that he and Albert would take on their case, and he ended the interview by telling her that he had to go and see Charlie.

Exhausted, she closed her eyes and nodded, yes. As he was leaving she said, "Tell Charlie we're thinkin' about him."

Thirty-three

A Shrine

Inspector Rutter had ordered a thorough search to be made of the Ewart property as soon as Sarah, Ruth and Charlie were taken into town. The Corporal who found Freddy's money belt in Charlie's shed remarked to the Inspector, "It looks like we've got our motive, Sir."

"Maybe," the Inspector answered, examining the blood-soaked belt. "Did you find anything in Fenlon's house?"

"Yes, but I think it'll be worth havin' a look at that yourself, sir."

"Okay. Let's go."

Rutter examined the open hope chest, and the baby's christening clothes along with the other items spread neatly on the floor. Of particular interest was a large family Bible set shrine-like on top of the dresser. A small bunch of withered wild-flowers lay before it, and propped against it was a silver hand-mirror with a note wrapped around its handle neatly tied with a white satin ribbon. The Inspector carefully undid the bow and read:

Love knoweth all things, Love believeth all things, Love hopeth all things, Love never dies.

Til' Death do us part–Sarah.

"Well. It gets more and more interestin'," he said. "If Fenlon was Sarah's lover we have another possible motive as well as theft. I know you know your job, Corporal, but for God's sake document everything twice and then check it again before you gather it up for the Crime Lab."

Thirty-four

Sorting Details

Pius and Albert went over the material. After they made lists of details. Pius said, "See Albert? Charlie's signed confession, and Mark's account of what Sarah had told him don't vary at all from what Sarah told me at the hospital."

"Right, but as far as I can see, a lot is going to hinge on the answer to the following questions: Who lit the fire, Charlie or Freddy? Did Charlie try to burn Freddy's body? Did Charlie take the money-belt?"

"You're right. The prosecution's goin' to conclude on a motivation based on either jealousy, revenge, robbery or all three. Revenge, robbery and the planned disposal of the body, of course, points to premeditation; but I have a sneakin' suspicion there's more to it, Albert. Why don't we go down and see Charlie?"

At the jail, Athol Mutch greeted them as dignitaries on important business.

"Good day gentlemen. You're here to talk to Charlie Ewart, aren't you?"

"Yes we are, Athol."

"Well now he's an odd little fella. Poor little bugger, all he does is sit and sing to himself." He touched his temple with his forefinger. "But you wouldn't think he'd squash a louse. But then I seen fellas in the war as mild as milk kill like demons. C'mon, now, an' I'll take you down to him."

Charlie sat against the wall curled up with his head on his knees.

"There's a couple' a nice fellows here to talk to you, Charlie," Athol said.

Charlie didn't budge. Pius politely dismissed the warden and sat down on the edge of the cot.

"Charlie, I'm Pius McQuaid and this is Albert Stephenson. We're lawyers. Sarah and Ruth sent us to look after you. I've just been to see them and they said to tell you not to worry about anything and that you should talk to us and tell us what we want to know."

Charlie lifted his head, looked at them then lowered it back down again.

"I hear Freddy went back and you had to put him down?" Pius said.

"Yes, with two shots," he mumbled into his knees.

"I never knew you burnt anything you had to put down—thought you just buried it?"

Charlie raised his head and looked as if he just remembered something.

"I have to bury Freddy."

The lawyers looked at one another. Pius continued, "Well, if you were going to bury him, Charlie, why did you try to burn him?"

Charlie looked confused then jabbered about the end of the Island. After a moment, Albert asked, "Was the dune on fire when you shot Freddy?"

"Yes, I smelt it on the way down. The sparks was flyin' up. When I seen Freddy standin' beside it, I knew Granddaddy was dead. The angel lights was dancin' on the water."

"Angel lights?"

"Yes."

"You like Betty, don't you Charlie?" Pius asked.

"Yes."

"Did Betty like Freddy? Was she his girlfriend?"

Both lawyers watched Charlie's eyes and body for a reaction or a trace of anger, but there was none. Pius asked the question again. Charlie shrugged his shoulders and mumbled that he didn't know.

"How did you feel when Freddy hurt Betty and Sarah and Ruth?"

He didn't react.

"Tell us now, what did you do when you saw Freddy's money belt?"

Charlie got up and lay down on the cot with his face to the wall and said over his shoulder, "When can I go home? I have to bury Freddy an' do the chores."

"I don't know, Charlie. But don't you worry about Freddy and the chores. We'll see all that's looked after. We're goin' now Charlie, but somebody'll be back soon," Pius said.

As they were going back down the corridor they could hear him singing.

Athol Mutch met them.

"Your office called boys. There's a Mrs. Betty Logan in the hospital an' you're to go an' see her as soon as possible. Betty Logan? That wouldn't be Jack Logan's wife out in New Skye, now would it?"

"That's confidential. You're doing a great job looking after Charlie, Athol. You keep protectin' him from nosy people now, will you?" Pius said as they left.

On the way to the hospital they went back over the interview with Charlie.

"Well I think the motive of jealousy and robbery's out. I don't think Charlie lit the fire, which means that Freddy or somebody else must have. And judging from all his talk about having to bury Freddy, I don't think he tried to burn the body, Pius."

"Yes and all that talk about granddaddy and the dunes on fire might not make much sense to you and me, but it does to Charlie."

"Yes, all that apocalyptic stuff about the end of the Island, and angel lights dancin' on the water, remember?"

"Strange all right, but we'll have to get to the bottom of it."

The same policeman guarding Sarah and Ruth was also guarding Betty Logan. He ushered them into her room.

"We're sure they'll be dropping the charges against you very shortly, Mrs. Logan. But in the meantime it's important for us to know some things if we're to help Charlie," Pius said.

"I'll tell you everything I know."

"You claim Fenlon raped you?"

"Yes, he did."

"Now tell us, Betty. Had you ever been intimate with him before?"

"My land no! I couldn't stand him. He tried to kiss me once when he was over waitin' for my husband."

"So you an' Fenlon were never lovers?"

"Dear God, no."

"Think hard now, Mrs. Logan. Did you say, or do anything that might have encouraged him?"

Betty listlessly recounted how Freddy pulled her hair and lay on top of her.

"I told him we should make ourselves more comfortable after we looked for the money, but it was only to get him off me."

She then told them about the attic and the finding of the money and the rape.

"Did you put up a struggle, Betty?"

"He ripped my clothes off an' I stabbed his arm."

They paused a second, then Pius asked, "Could you tell us anything about your husband's connection with Freddy Fenlon?"

"Well, now and then they would go away in a truck an' not come back until the next mornin'. I don't know where he got the money for one of them trucks he was always cryin' poor mouth. I never really knew what they were up to. When Freddy come over to the house that day lookin' for the money, he said somethin' about him an' Jack havin' dealings, an' when Freddy was goin' at me, he said Jack was a rum-runnin' crook. I know we were never without liquor in the house."

"Now, Charlie Ewart helped you with your chores. Right?"

"Yes."

"What sort of a relationship did you have with him?"

She turned her head into the pillow.

"Will you tell me this then?" Pius said after a moment. "Charlie said something about Granddaddy being dead an' the dunes catching fire and the end of the Island. He said you told him that. Can you throw a bit of light on that for us?"

Betty came out of the pillow and looked at Pius for a second then told them about the Granddaddy Fern. Pius and Albert nodded to each other. It was starting to make sense.

"Thank you Mrs. Logan. What you told us will be very helpful. We understand now some of the things Charlie was tryin' to say to us."

"Mrs. Logan, it's very important that you tell nobody what you told us. If the police question you again tell them that your lawyers instructed you they were to be present to advise you. No matter how hard they try, you mustn't say anything. You understand?"

"Yes. I won't say anything. Thanks for comin' in."

On the way out, Albert suggested to Pius that it might be a good idea if they spoke to Betty's doctor just in case there were no signs of rape.

"Do you think she's lyin' Albert?

"No, but the Prosecution will certainly check it out."

They found the doctor and he told them that certain bruising and abrasions pointed to rape, but not conclusively so. What he didn't mention was that Betty Logan might be about six weeks pregnant.

The pathologist's report confirmed that Freddy's death was due to massive trauma caused by gunshot wounds to the abdomen and the head. The next day the charge of attempted murder was dropped against Betty, and several days later she was released from hospital along with Sarah and Ruth. Bail was denied Charlie, and an order went out to poll a jury. Chief Justice Harold Pilchard was named as the presiding judge.

Thirty-five

Ruth

One morning Mildred looked out the window and saw Ruth Ewart standing in the garden. Moved by her dishevelled appearance she went out and spoke to her.

"Hello my dear you're Ruth Ewart aren't you? I'm Mrs. Kerr. I'm glad you're home from hospital. How's your sister? I've just wet the teapot. Come in and have a cup."

Ruth smiled and lowered her head. Mildred gently took her arm and led her into the house. To Mildred's surprise she went straight upstairs.

In Ruth's mind she was returning to her love-home, as she called it. During Mark's absence she visited the empty house often to feel his presence there. At home, while washing clothes or baking bread, she lost herself in daydreams during which Mark looked deeply into her eyes and told her that he could not have survived his wife's death without her. At other times she fantasised he was ill, and she washed him tenderly and dried his feet just as Mary Magdalene had dried her Lord's feet with her hair. She would bring him nourishing food and feed him while a grateful Mark smiled weakly, his blue eyes filled with gratitude. Sometimes, in the velvet darkness and warmth of her bed she would tell herself that she would do anything for Mark. Her heart palpitated and waves of warmth flooded her body as she caressed herself. Her hands were

Mark's hands, and her tongue moving lightly over her lips, Mark's tongue. So real was it that the next morning she would avoid Sarah in case she suspected her secret tryst. Once while dusting in Mark's room she stripped naked and lay in his empty bed convinced that he was having exactly the same experiences at that exact time in Montreal. He asked for her hand in marriage, but she told him tearfully that she could never be his wife because of her promise to her dying parents.

Mildred stood for some time waiting for Ruth to come downstairs. Finally curiosity got the better of her, and she went up to see what was going on. To her amazement, Ruth, naked, was getting into Mark's bed.

"Don't you think you should go home to Sarah, dear?"

"Whither thou goest, will I go."

Mildred recognized the famous words spoken by the Biblical Ruth to Naomi her mother-in-law. She gathered up Ruth's clothing and said, "I will go, then, to thy house. Will you show me the way?"

Ruth got out of the bed and Mildred helped her dress. Both women walked arm and arm down the dusty road. At the porch door Mildred held back, but Ruth gently pulled her inside.

"Sarah dear?" she called out. "Sarah? I have a surprise for you."

Sarah called back from the parlour, "What is it? I'm in here."

Ruth, full of little girl mischief held her finger up to her lips. Mildred let her lead her into the parlour. Sarah lay on the sofa, drunk, with a wet cloth over her eyes. Mildred removed her hand from Ruth's and quickly slipped out before Sarah saw her.

That evening at supper she told Mark about it. He shook his head.

"Well, things are getting worse, Mother. Poor Ruth, when I first met her she was so reticent. Charlie, Ruth and Sarah. I just don't know what's going to happen to them."

"Mark, first of all, you will have to do something about Ruth. I'm afraid for her if she gets worse."

"What do you suggest?"

"Do they have any other relations?"

"I'll look into it."

In addition to the sad news of Ruth and Sarah, Mark was also preoccupied with a letter he received from Janice O'Neill nee Fenlon:

> Dear Rev. Kerr,
> I am coming to the Island to meet with Stevenson and McQuaid. When I finish with them, I will catch the train out to New Skye. I would be very grateful if you would meet me at the New Skye station.
> Janice

Thirty-six

Helper

Acting on Wittigar's instructions, Myra Swanson called on Sarah and Ruth the day they got home from hospital and offered her nephew Myron to help them out.

"Now, now, it's the least we can do as neighbours," she insisted, when Sarah protested. "We're not that busy at the mill and Myron might as well be down here lending a helping hand. An' what about Charlie, the poor dear thing, how's he doin'?"

Sarah resigned herself to the fact that she did need help.

"Thank you Myra, a pair of extra hands would come in handy."

As it turned out, Myron virtually had the run of the place. His orders were to fill in the pit under the fox pens as soon as possible. Why do I have to do all the Joe-jobs? He whined. Why should I have to break my back shovelin' that Jesely mess in? But when he found the army ammunition box and the canvas bag filled with money, his whining turned to sheer joy.

He sat down on a board to try to think it through. Is all this Fenlon's stash? He asked himself. How could it be that I never earned money like that? I bet Fenlon swiped it–skimmed it off some way. But who'll ever know just how much is hid here? Fenlon's dead so there's no way he's ever goin' tell them.

Convinced he would never be found out, Myron clutched his find, and set off like a jackrabbit across the back fields for home. In the dusty recesses of his hayloft, illuminated only by a shaft of afternoon sunlight streaming through a gable opening, he counted twenties, fifties and hundreds, his heart racing.

When he was finished, fear took over, and he had doubts about keeping all of it. Yet if I had *some* of that, the wife an' me could go on a long trip out west on the train. In the end, he decided to take a bit more than half for himself and to give the rest to Lionel to give to Wittigar. Who knows, he thought, the Colonel might tell me to keep it all anyway—at least I bet he'll give me something as a reward. While he was hiding the money he was keeping for himself, his wife called from the yard.

"You up there, Myron?"

"Yeah. What?"

"Lionel's here lookin' for you."

Panic struck him and not able to think of anything else, he shouted, "Send him up darlin'. I've something to show him."

He heard Lionel puffing as he climbed the loft ladder. When he reached the top, he took in Myron's guilty look and guessed he was hiding something.

"Hi ya Lionel. Guess what I've got to show you?"

"I don't know Myron. What have you got to show me?"

Myron showed Buell the money he'd set aside to give to the Colonel.

"Good on ye, Myron," Buell said. "That's what we didn't want the Mounties findin'." He searched Myron's face, then asked, "How much did you cabbage for yourself?"

It was the question Myron was dreading; and even though he had prepared his mind for it, he couldn't manage a smooth answer. He swallowed as he tried to keep his eyes from shifting. Then with forced bravado, he said, "What do you take me for, Lionel?"

Buell laughed. "I don't know what I take you for Myron, but that's not what I asked you, now, was it? What I asked you was how much did you cabbage? Come on now, it's only natural." He smiled encouragingly. "You held back a little bit didn't you?"

Myron relieved by Lionel's understanding and friendliness laughed ingratiatingly.

"Well just a little bit, like, Lionel."

The change in Buell was instant. He snapped, "Well show it to me, *now*, Goddamn it!"

Myron hesitated. Buell pushed him and said, "Who do you want to deal with, me or Wittigar? Now show me the rest of the Goddamn money an' I'll say nothin' about it to *them*."

When Myron uncovered his hiding place, Lionel said, "Just a little bit, eh? You're right stupid, Myron. Don't ever try to cross Wittigar. You're lucky I'm the one that caught you. Jesus, if Wittigar'd caught you, you'd have found yourself on a slab next to Freddy Fenlon."

With that he peeled off a couple of hundred dollars and threw them at him.

"Don't you splash that around. Where'd you find it?"

"In the pit, Lionel."

"An' I suppose you were in such a hurry to bring it home to hide it, you left the open pit exposed? Now you get right back down there an' fill that pit in or you'll find yourself buried in it. Go on."

When Lionel left with the money to give to Wittigar, he pocketed a hefty wad of it for himself. Myron headed back down to the unfilled pit just as fast as he had left it, and he didn't stop shovelling until it was filled in. Drenched in sweat, he made his way to the Ewart barn to help out with the afternoon milking.

While milking a large Holstein, he watched Sarah's unsteady movements and flushed face as she forked fresh straw into the stalls. She caught him looking at her, and said, "You're not goin' to get much done lookin' at me, Myron."

He quickly pressed his head back into the side of a cow's warm belly but continued to watch her out of the corner of his eye. As he pumped squirts of milk into the bucket between his legs, the cat and her kittens sat nearby waiting for a drop to spill. Sarah, carrying a load of straw in front of her didn't see them and stepped on one of the kittens. It screeched, and she lost her balance and fell with a painful thud against the barn wall. As he jumped up to help her, Myron knocked over the milk-bucket. She reeked of rum. Seeing the tipped bucket she pushed him away and made a murderous rush at the cat and her kittens as they lapped up the spilt milk.

Later while he was swilling the pigs, he noticed Ruth talking to herself. She was smiling and patting her hair. He crept close enough to hear her say, "My dearest, dearest Mark."

Exhausted, he made his way home, but tired as he was he decided pay his Aunt Myra a visit. He loved to stir her up with a bit of gossip. She settled him with a cup of tea with a dollop of rum in it and a plate of cookies.

"Well, Myron, how's things down at the Ewart's? Are them two managin' all right, poor things?"

He liked to play Myra like a trout, so he stirred his tea and nibbled on a cookie and when that was finished he started munching another.

"Them's nice cookies. What did you ask me, Aunt Myra?"

"I asked you how the girls was doin'."

"Things is just fine, Aunt Myra."

"Yes an' what about the girls?"

Myron, in no hurry to answer, licked the chocolate off yet another cookie.

"Oh, they're doin' just great, Aunt Myra. Just great." But after a frown, he added, " I guess."

She leaned forward, patted his hand affectionately and said, "Myron, dear, are you protectin' them? You're so closed-mouth and strong—just like your father."

He, relishing the attention and flattery, smiled modestly. She continued, "Well I know you're good hearted—maybe to a fault, dear. Your poor father was like that, too. But if there's any way Sarah and Ruthie needs help we have to know about it, like, to give it." She tousled his hair and added, "Bless you."

Myron licked the paper of the cigarette he was rolling.

"Well Aunt Myra it's hard for me to say, and I know you mean well, but if I tell you, now, I don't want it comin' back at me from somebody else's mouth?"

"My land, dear, may the tongue be ripped out of my head if I speak a word of it to anybody."

He took a long drag and let the smoke come slowly out of his nose and mouth at the same time. Then as if making up his mind to trust her, he slapped his knee and said, "Right, then."

She sat down in front of him with her face very close. He lowered his voice and said, "I think it's sad."

Myra almost exploded with impatience as he kept her waiting.

"Well Sarah was so loaded she could hardly stand. She tripped on a kitten an' killed it."

"Drunk was she, Myron?"

"As a lord, Aunt Myra."

"Her poor mother must be turnin' in her grave, my, my. An' what about Ruthie?"

Myron held out his teacup for more rum. Myra poured.

"Well you're not goin' to believe this. I heard this kinda sweet talkin' you know? So I looked where the voice was comin' from an' there was Ruth talkin' to herself an' sayin' somebody's name over an' over again."

"Did you catch whose it was?"

"Well it sounded like Clark or something."

"There's nobody by that name round here. Clark? You sure?"

"Well she was moanin' it like–Mar Mar."

Myra's face flushed and her eyes burned bright.

"Mark! Was it Mark, Myron?

"Yes, Aunt Myra. That's it, it was Mark. It was like she was talkin' to a lover."

Myra made him go over some of the details again. He was delighted; his Aunt Myra was hooked, so he embellished. "Honestly, Aunt Myra, them two's as crazy as bedbugs, 'specially Ruthie. I'm ashamed to repeat this to you, but all the time she was talkin' she ran her hands up and down herself, like, an' moanin', '*Oh Mark, Mark my love, come to me soon*'."

Malice rose full tide in Myra's breast.

Thirty-seven

More Voyeurism

Just as Mark drove into the Ewart's yard, Sarah was coming out of the barn dressed in a man's shirt and trousers tucked into rubber boots.

"Look at me, Reverend Kerr, I must look a sight in these old clothes."

"Please don't concern yourself, Sarah. I just want to have a word with you about Ruth. Do you mind?"

"No. She's inside. Maybe it would be better if we talked out here for a bit. Ruthie's not doin' very well, Reverend Kerr."

"My mother is very concerned about her, too Sarah."

"Your mother, Reverend Kerr? What's your mother concerned about?"

"Well Ruth visited the Manse yesterday. She went upstairs to my room. Mother was waiting to give her a cup of tea; and when she didn't come down, Mother went upstairs. She found Ruth in my bed without her clothes on. I'm sorry Sarah."

Her face blanched, and she put her hand to her mouth to stifle a cry. She stumbled forward as if she was going to faint. Mark steadied her.

"Just take a minute to gather yourself, Sarah."

"I'm right distracted, Reverend Kerr. She's getting' worse. I don't know where to turn."

"Have you any other family?"

"Yes, we've family on the other side of the Island. Our parent's people, but we're not close. Since our troubles started the only thing we heard from them was a letter telling us how ashamed they were. We wouldn't ask them for nothin'."

"Maybe Dr. McAlister could suggest something? Would you like me to ask him?"

"Maybe Reverend Kerr–let me think about it."

Mark then told her about Janice's visit to the Island.

"Janice Fenlon? My land, none of us thought we'd ever hear from her again. Ruthie and her was real close. We all were. Why don't you come in for a cup of tea, Reverend? It might do Ruth good to hear about Janice. The two of them were the smartest in the school, but Janice was smarter than everybody. Poor Janice, she was so pretty as well, an' Ruthie, too. Now look at her."

When they went in, Sarah told Ruth to set out the cups and saucers for tea.

"Good morning, Ruth. I've news of an old friend of yours, Janice Fenlon. She's coming for a visit," Mark said.

Wonderful, Ruth thought. As girls they used to talk about how each would be the other's bridesmaid. She was sure that Mark had arranged Janice's visit for that purpose. She was convinced that Mark was going to propose to her.

"Mark, dear, that's wonderful news. Isn't it Sarah? We'll make plans an' Charlie will come home for the weddin', an' we'll all be together."

"Stop your nonsense, Ruthie. Reverend Kerr doesn't want to be hearing that stuff, now."

Ruth stood. Her eyes blazed.

"Don't you think you'll spoil it, Sarah. *You'll not interfere.*"

"Sit down, Ruthie, you're being foolish!"

Ruth flung a teacup against the wall then ran out of the room crying. She called down from the top of the stairs, "Come up, Mark and pay no heed to her."

"I'm sorry Ruth, I have to go now." Then in a low voice, he asked Sarah, "Will you be all right?"

"Yes. Maybe you should have a word with the doctor. I'll walk a ways with you Reverend Kerr."

As they were walking along the lane, she broke down, again.

"We don't deserve this torment, Charlie, Ruthie an' me. Why should we suffer because of what other people done? Other people commit sin an' the innocent pay for it." She was thinking of the Ewart stain. "I'm sorry, Reverend Kerr, but Charlie, Ruthie's an' me is bein' punished for other people's sins. Charlie's not right an' they'll hang him."

She wept so bitterly, Mark put his arm around her shoulder. Ruth was watching them from her bedroom window. Sarah's leadin' him on, she told herself. When she saw Mark put his arm around Sarah, she flew into a frenzy.

Meanwhile, Myron Swanson had looked out the barn window when he heard Mark's car coming in. He saw Sarah and him talking in the yard before they went into the house. Sensing something was up, he kept watching and wanting to know more about what was going on. Just as he was about to give up his vigilance, Ruth suddenly burst out of the house stark naked and screeching. The beauty of Ruth's body surprised him. Delighted, he watched her run, her breasts bouncing.

Myron was the type who believed that seeing a woman naked gave him the right of possession. Mark and Sarah turned at the shriek and saw Ruth's white body rushing towards them. She flew at Sarah's head scratching and pulling her hair. Myron ran out of the barn to where they were struggling and grabbed Ruth around the waist trying to pull her and Sarah apart. She collapsed on the grass with Myron on top of her. Mark pushed him off. Sarah helped Ruth to her feet and the sisters walked back to the house while Myron watched them, ogling Ruth's bare backside.

"You and I'd better have a talk," Mark said.

"Sure, Reverend Kerr."

He took out his tobacco pouch and papers and rolled himself a cigarette.

"If you're a man at all, Myron, what you saw here today won't go any further."

Myron scratched a match with his thumbnail, and deliberately drew in a few deep puffs before answering.

"What's goin' on Reverend?"

"You know Ruth and Sarah are having a bad time of it. Now it would be very unkind if you told anyone what you saw today —even your wife. Forget about it. Do you think you're big enough to do that?"

Myron stood grinning with his feet astride.

"I won't say anything, Reverend, but how can I forget about what I saw, eh?"

His cocky attitude concerned Mark. Normally, Myron would have been deferential. Shouting, screaming and wailing came from the house. Mark ran in. When he came back out to the door and called to Myron, "You'd better go on home."

That afternoon Myron feasted his Aunt Myra on the details of what had happened.

"An' can you imagine, Aunt Myra? That Reverend Kerr had the cheek to tell me not to tell you, or my own wife even. Who does he think he is anyway?"

"Myron now, the Minister's right. You haven't to say a word to anybody. That wouldn't be nice. We brought you up better than that."

That night Sarah drank herself senseless, but before passing into oblivion, she flung the Ewart family portraits against the wall, and smashed them.

Thirty-eight

Janice

Pius and Albert met Janice at the train in Charlottetown. After they briefed her on legal affairs regarding her family's property, she took the train out to New Skye. One of her best childhood memories was making this journey once a week with her mother to the farmers' market in Charlottetown and home again. There was always a drunken fiddler who played while people toe-tapped and sang, but it was on this same train she left home for Boston fifteen years ago. That was the saddest day of her life.

The station at New Skye was really nothing more than a shack beside the tracks with a gravel path to the road. As Janice stepped down onto the box put there by the conductor, she lifted the hem of her skirt showing a shapely leg and ankle. She was a striking woman with pretty eyes more amethyst than blue, and she was dressed in the latest Boston fashion: a trim two-piece suit of moss green with a silver fox-fur collar. Three long strings of pearls dangled from her neck and her hat was a matching green with a peacock feather, and a curved brim that slouched down over one side of her face. To those watching she was like a fashion model in Eaton's catalogue. As she walked by, a whiff of expensive perfume trailed after her.

Mark had intended to take Janice to the manse for tea, but she asked him if he wouldn't mind driving out to the shore first. As soon as they got there, she took off her shoes and silk stockings. When she lifted her skirt to unsnap the stockings and roll them down her leg, Mark turned his head away.

Except for a gentle swell, the sea was calm and clear. Strands of ginger-brown kelp floated upwards from the rocks on the bottom.

"Seaweed must be the cleanest of all God's plants. I remember as a child how I loved to pop the bubbles."

Janice stood at the water's edge and closed her eyes, the mild breeze gently lifting her auburn hair. When she opened them again, Mark thought how perfectly they matched the sea.

"Let's stroll for a minute, Reverend Kerr. Do you mind?"

As they walked along in silence, she allowed the spent waves to lap over her bare feet.

"I know it broke her heart not knowing where I was, Mother, I mean." They walked along in silence a little further, then she asked, "Did she tell you what happened?"

"Only that your father–how did she put it? Yes. That he broke your heart. The night she died she prayed that you would forgive her. There were no details."

"I was pregnant. I'd never been anywhere but here. I was so young. Mother made me go away. I was to go to an old aunt in Boston. When I got on that train I tried to make myself invisible. I just wanted it to keep going and never stop. I can't begin to tell you the terror I felt being on that train alone.

"Two nuns came on: an old one and a young one not much older than myself. The old one looked big and strange and seemed buried in folds of black cloth. Her eyes lit on me and she headed straight for me. The young one followed. The old nun smiled and lifted her beads and started prayin'.

"I made to get up, but her hand reached out and grabbed mine. She smiled again and I stayed put. I remember she pulled out a big white hanky and gave her nose a good blow.

"'What's your name, child?' says she.

"She had the gentlest voice, but I wouldn't tell her.

"'My name is Sister Monica and this is Sister Philomena. Are you a little Protestant girl?'

"When I told her I was, she said. 'Protestant children are afraid of nuns, aren't they? Did they ever tell you we steal babies from their mothers and bring them up as Catholics?'

"I'd heard stories about nuns having babies to priests an' drownin' them at birth, but I didn't say that to her. In fact I didn't say a word. She told me that I didn't need to be afraid of her. Then she whispered to me, 'I know you're afraid of something more terrible than the likes of me.'

"She seemed to know exactly what my trouble was an' she got it out of me that I was going to Boston, but I lied about going to my aunt.

"'Boston's a wicked place,' she said, 'an' no place for a young girl the likes of yourself.'

"She told me she lived in a place that looked after girls like me, and if I let her, she'd take care of me. Before the trip was over I trusted her completely. I lied though and told her my name was Allison. Allison was a name I always wished they'd called me. Anyway, I went with her to the convent and gave birth. I never saw the baby. They told me it was with Jesus.

"I met plenty of other wayward girls as they called us. Their stories were all different, but with the same sad endings. We scrubbed, laundered and prayed in that place from mornin' 'til night. We prayed for forgiveness for our sin of concupiscence."

Mark interjected, "Your sin of *concupiscence*?"

Janice's face hardened. "Oh, yes. They told us constantly that we got into trouble because of our seductive nature, an' that we must learn to subdue the Serpent in us or else he'll use us to ruin others and ourselves. They were always at me to become a Catholic. So to get a bit of peace and extra privilege, I converted. They trained us as domestics, telling us that the only other thing open to us was the streets. But many of them poor girls in the convent had already been used as prostitutes an' some as young as thirteen.

"The rich used the convent as a quarry for maids and skivvies. They paid a 'donation' then made the girls work like slaves for little more than room and board, an' on top of that they treated us like charity cases. More often than not we were used us as playthings. I know I was."

They had walked quite far, and the sea was changing colors in the late afternoon sun.

"I suppose we'd better be gettin' back. I hope you didn't mind listenin' about me. I told you all that because you talked to my mother when she was on her deathbed. You tried to find me. I feel you're a link with her, and that in some way if I talk with you I won't have lost her completely," Janice said.

After a few more steps she asked, "What about you, do you have a family?"

"No."

Janice stood for another moment looking out to the deepening colours of the sea. Then they started back, but after a few yards she began talking again.

"A couple with a new mansion on the outskirts of Old Southey took me in. They were Famine Irish stock. He got rich from politics an' shipping an' God knows what else. The Missus was sickly. She'd been delicate all her life and couldn't carry her children full term. They were in their fifties when I went there.

"One night he came into my little attic room. He was a big man and he just put his hand over my mouth and lay on top of me. I couldn't move or was too scared to move—whatever. Anyway I knew the drill an' lay there. When he was done, he put a roll of notes in my hand and told me I had two choices: to say nothing and do all right for myself, or go back to the convent branded as a failure and a thief.

"He grew attached to me so I decided to use him. He loaded me with money and presents an' moved me out of their house an' set me up in a nice little place of my own. I quickly learned a trick or two on how to make money.

"When the Missus died, a hoard of Irish mothers descended on him with their daughters. I was well known among them by this time, an' they hated me. I decided to go for marriage myself, for I knew if one of them harpies got him that would be the end of me. So I took up with another man just to make him jealous. It worked. He went wild an' had the poor fellow beat up. I threatened I'd have nothing more to do with him. He pleaded. I kept him on the hook for a while, then told him marriage or nothin'. He married me. When he died I got all his money to add to my own. That's my fairy-tale life after leaving the Island,"

Mark glanced at her on the drive back. Her face betrayed no emotion as she recalled the names of people as they passed by their farms. But when they turned into the Ewart laneway her jaw tightened.

"Would you mind stoppin' by that tree a minute?"

She got out and stood under a huge Scotch pine overlooking the pasture towards her old home. When she returned her eyes were red. Mark didn't question her.

"I used to come home from school and hide behind that tree to watch to see if my father was around. If mother was there I'd go home. If I couldn't tell, I'd run down to the Ewart's and stay there until I was sure it was safe."

Ruth, Sarah and Janice stood like statues taking each other in. Sarah was astounded at the woman before her. Janice's finery and beauty reinforced their own plight, and she felt ashamed. Janice was appalled at the state of her old friends. Sarah looked old, bruised and haggard; Ruth was unkempt and dirty. Then suddenly as if unfrozen, they embraced each other. In that moment, they shared the brokenness of their lives and the joy at seeing each other again.

Mark said, "Well ladies, you have a lot of catching up to do, so I'll leave you. I'll be at the manse if you need me. I have a meeting in town tomorrow, so I'd better go and prepare for it. Glad to have met you Mrs. O'Neil. Sarah. Ruth."

Janice held out her hand.

"Thank you Reverend Kerr for today and everything you've done for me. I'll be ever grateful. I have to go into town tomorrow. Can I go in with you?"

"Of course, I'll pick you up about nine-thirty."

Janice smiled and fixed him with her pretty eyes, and he was glad he'd be seeing her again so soon.

That night Sarah told Janice that she had been her father's lover, and of how she had committed herself to him body and soul. She spared no details of how he had raped and beaten Betty, and of the beating he gave her and Ruth, and the subsequent shooting of him by Charlie. Then Janice told her story, and the painful revelations suffered by both of them had the salving effect of bonding them deeper.

Early next morning, Janice strolled down to the dune where Charlie had killed her father. The rising sun turned the sea blood red and streaked the sky in fiery hues. She stared at the blackened ring of ashes remaining from the fire, but she felt no pity.

From there, she walked back up to the empty house where she was born and had grown up. Methodically, she went from room to room. Her mother's clothes were still hanging in the closet alongside her Father's. It probably never even occurred to him to move them, she thought. She peered into the hope chest and saw her christening robe, bootees and bonnet. Her mother used to show them to her and delight her by telling her what a beautiful baby she was. Janice, overcome, sat on the bed and said aloud, "Mother, Mother what can I do? If there was only somethin' I could do. There's no need to ask my forgiveness, Mother dear. My own bitterness made me neglect you."

She looked out the window across the fields where she played as a child. Her eyes rested on the distant roof of the Logan house. It had been a long time since Janice had made up her mind that tears were a waste of time; but now she wept for the irrevocable losses in all their lives. As she sat there weeping it slowly became apparent that there was something she could do. She'd help the Ewart's and Betty Logan all she could. I have the means, and I swear I'll make amends.

Before leaving, she looked into her old bedroom. The ticking was removed from the bed where pain and terror had been forced into her. It was still the same wallpaper, mauve with pink roses. She recalled how she forced herself to count every rose while she was pinned down hardly able to breathe with that dreadful, stinking hand over her mouth.

Then she slammed the door shut, entombing the terrible memories."

When Mark called for Janice the next morning, she asked him if he would take her to visit her mother's grave. Mildred was there putting fresh flowers on Mollie's and little Bobby's grave. Mark introduced them.

"Mother, I'd like you to meet Mrs. Janice O'Neil from Boston. Mrs. O'Neil, this is my Mother, Mildred Kerr."

"How do you do, Mrs. Kerr,"

They shook hands and Janice moved to her family plot. Heska's grave was overgrown with weeds. The least he could have done was keep it tidy, she said to herself. Oh well, he neglected Mother when she was living so why would it be any different after she died?

For the second time that morning she wept. Mildred came over.

"Was she close to you, my dear?"

"She was my Mother."

"Well, I'll work on it and make it look a bit more decent. Would you mind if I did that?"

The kindness in Mildred's voice and manner made her feel less angry. The two women talked quietly together while Mark went back to the car and waited. It was the first time he'd visited the graveyard since the day of the burial, and it comforted him that his mother was tending their grave.

"Are you all right?" he asked Janice when she joined him.

"Yes, thank you, Reverend Kerr. Please let's be on our way."

They drove in silence for a while. Then she said, "Your mother told me you lost your wife and baby. It must have been terrible for you. I'm sorry."

"Yes."

"Your mother's lovely. Full of goodness." After a pause she added, "And I think you are, too."

They drove in silence for a little distance.

"How do you think things will turn out, Reverend Kerr?"

"I'm just not sure, Mrs. O'Neil...."

"Please, call me Janice. May I call you Mark?"

"Yes. There are so many sinister factors, Janice. I just don't know. I have to see Ruth and Sarah through Charlie's trial. After my meeting in town this morning, I'm going to see Dr. McAlister to talk with him about Ruth."

"Yes, poor Ruthie. She's got it into her head that you came back to the Island to be with her. Do you know that Mark?"

"Has Sarah told you much about her?"

"Yes, that she's lost her mind. She told me about what happened the other day—about her taking her clothes off."

"Perhaps she'll have to be institutionalized."

Janice was appalled at the idea.

"No. Listen. It occurred to me that if Sarah agrees, I'll take Ruth back to Boston with me. I'm well placed there and could see she gets help. I haven't thought it through yet, but that's what I think I'd like to do. What do you think?"

"She'll certainly have to stay around until the trial's over. She might even be called to the stand. But, yes, I think that would relieve Sarah's mind."

"I intend to stay here until all that trial business is over anyway. How long do you think it'll take?"

The thought passed through Mark's mind that he was pleased Janice would not be going back right away—a thought he immediately suppressed.

"I've no idea how long it'll take. Pius might have some idea."

"Listen, Pius and Albert are meetin' me for lunch at the Abby, why don't you come too?"

"Well, I intended to drop in and see Charlie at the jail."

"Why don't you come to the hotel for lunch and go to the jail after? I'll go with you if they'll let me in."

On the rest of the trip they discussed the details of the case. She was particularly intrigued by the story of the Granddaddy fern. Before getting out, she searched his face for a moment as if trying to read him, then said, "Thank you Mark. I'll be lookin' for you at twelve-thirty at the Abby."

"I'll be there."

He warned himself not to become attracted even though he knew it was already happening, and the thought made him feel uneasy.

Thirty-nine

Friendships

Janice watched Mark drive off. So reserved, she thought, yet there is a depth and a warmth about him. I like him, but damaged goods the likes of me is not for the likes of him.

Albert Stephenson greeted her at the office.

"Pius is over at the courthouse selecting jurors, Mrs. O'Neill, so I'll handle things this morning. He'll meet us for dinner."

"I've asked the Reverend Kerr to join us. Is that okay?"

"Sure. Well, we've searched the title to the New Skye property. It's clear and in order. Your father purchased it from the late Charles Ewart for a nominal fee; and as you're the sole heir, it should go to you unless it's contested. We'll give notice to that fact, and if there is no response we'll re-register it in your name"

After signing several documents, Janice said, "Now there are some other things I'd like you to arrange. I would like to make an offer to buy the Ewart and the Logan properties. I want the offers to be generous with the sellers havin' the option of stayin' on in the houses for as long as they want. No dickerin'."

"I'll need to know a precise amount, Mrs. O'Neill. What about stock and machinery?"

"Just find out the market value of the property an' up it enough to cover everything."

"Okay, I'll draw something up," he said, scribbling away. "May I ask why you're doing this?"

"Personal reasons, Mr. Stephenson. How long do you think Charlie's trial will last?"

"Hard to say. Maybe a month to six weeks."

"Do you think you could find me a comfortable furnished house in a quiet area of town to rent? I want it big enough so that Sarah, Ruth and Betty Logan can stay there when the trial starts."

"I think we can manage that. Anything else?"

"No. I want to have a walk around before going to the hotel."

"All right, Mrs. O'Neill. I'll get started on this."

Janice strolled along Great George Street to the rectangle of city shops known as "Dizzy Block". People in from the country walked around it meeting their friends while in town to do their shopping. Her mother always warned her to stay on Dizzy Block and not to go down the side streets, because of the drunk men hanging around the livery stables. Familiar landmarks seemed to close the distance of her having been away so long. Many of the merchants names were the same, but what had seemed like huge shops before, were now much smaller. The entire city seemed dwarfed after Boston. Is it because Boston is such a large city, she asked herself, or is it because I've experienced so much more?

A huge fern set in the middle of a display in a flower shop window caught her eye. She recalled what Mark had told her about Betty's granddaddy fern and how Charlie was troubled about it. She went in. The florist, a tall thin man with half-moon glasses took in her fine clothes.

"Good mornin', what can I do for you today?"

"I'd like to buy that fern in the window."

"I'm afraid that's not for sale. It's the wife's. We just have it for decoration."

"Well if it *was* for sale, how much would you want?"

The man looked at her over his glasses, "I don't rightly know, now. She's been on the go for a long time that fern. If I sold it, the wife would have my hide."

"Yes. But if you *were* sellin' it?"

"Well, now, I think about three dollars for the fern an' about a buck-fifty for the pot."

Janice expressed surprise, and clicked her tongue disapprovingly.

"*Four-fifty?*"

"She's special, that fern. Been in the wife's family since the Ark."

"I'll tell you what. You make me up a nice bunch of mixed flowers, anyway. About two or three dollars worth and send them over to the Abby Hotel to my suite."

Delighted at the enormity of the sale he assured her he would make her up a beautiful bunch. When he'd written down her name, Janice opened her purse and took out a roll of notes. She fixed him with her pretty eyes and smiled. He smiled back.

"Look, throw in the fern and pot an' we'll make it eight even"

"I wish the wife was here."

"How about ten, then?"

"Done. Abby Hotel."

"No. Send the fern to the jail for one o'clock."

"The jail?"

"Yes. I'm goin' in for a while, so send it care of me. It'll brighten up my cell."

The man laughed, "That's a good one. I'll send the flowers and the fern God help me, over to the Abby for one o'clock."

"No. The flowers to the Abby right away and the fern to the jail for one o'clock. Serious, now."

With that she turned and walked out of the store. The man, bewildered, came out and stared after her.

On his way over to the Abby Hotel, Mark stopped at Albert and Pius's office to find out how the preparation of Charlie's defence was going.

"It doesn't look very good for him unless we can prove he's insane, or was insane at the time of the shooting. Albert and I are looking for the best expert witness we can find to examine him."

Mark thought for a moment.

"Do you mean an alienist?"

"Yes."

"I've got just the man for you. A Dr. Philip Dixon in Montreal."

He told them about Philip and how he had helped him.

"Do you know anything about his training, Mark—you know universities?" Albert asked.

"Yes. I saw his certificates on the wall. His medical degree is from McGill. He studied neurology at Oxford, and he did his psychiatry at Duke University. He lectures at McGill now."

"Do you think you could get him on the phone and introduce me to him. I'd like to talk to him?" Pius asked.

"I can try."

Philip came on the line.

"Mark. Is everything all right?"

"Yes, thank you Dr. Dixon. I'm not having a relapse...."

"Glad to hear that, Mark."

"I am calling on professional business, though. One of my parishioners is on trial for murder. There is some question as to his mental competency. My friend Pius McQuaid is handling his defence. He needs an expert witness, and I recommended you. He's waiting at my elbow to speak to you. Okay?"

"Certainly, put him on."

When Pius came back, he said, "Exactly the right man. I explained what happened and the way Charlie behaves. He was interested and said he'll come down."

When they all met at Janice's hotel suite, a table was set for lunch on a gleaming damask tablecloth. Albert Stevenson laid out the offers to buy.

"This is the Ewart offer, Mrs. O'Neil. It's a very generous amount. If you'll just sign here, and here and down here. Perhaps you would witness it, Mark?"

Mark's eyes met Janice's and they smiled.

"Yes, I'll be happy to witness."

When all the offers were approved, Janice pressed an electric bell to signal that they were ready for lunch. In a moment a trolley was wheeled in bearing an ample dinner of soup, roast beef and choices of meat pies and cold-cuts.

"My goodness. I haven't seen so much food since I used to do a days work in the fields. Anyway, Mrs. O'Neil, it warms a bachelor's heart to behold it–not to mention what it does to an empty stomach," Pius said.

"With that cheeky boyish look about you, I don't think you'll be a bachelor for long, Pius. You don't mind if I call you Pius? In fact, why don't we all go on a first name basis? If we stay so stuffy we're liable to have indigestion."

They all laughed and took their places.

While Janice was serving the main course, she said, "When I was about twelve there was a man who came to build an extension to the Ewart barn. L.R, they called him, but Old Charlie and dad used to call him the half-breed."

"Yes, Janice. That would have been L.R. Arsenault," Pius said.

"I remember he was a big man. He came in on horseback with two big boxes slung on each side. He pitched a tent at the back of the barn and lived there until the job was finished."

"That's L.R. all right. Two fingers missin' on his left hand. He's a legend. Did you ever meet him, Mark?"

Mark shook his head.

"We were told not to go near him," Janice said. "He never talked, just worked. Ruthie an' me were awful curious about him, an' one day while he was up on the roof we snuck into his tent. One of the boxes was filled with tools an' the other was filled with books an' had a change of clothes in it. He'd seen us go in an' came down from the roof. We were terrified. But he just smiled an' told us we'd get into trouble with our parents.

"I can see him yet, sittin' up on his horse, never lookin' back. He's the mystery man in my life. So you know him, Pius?'

"Yes. He grew up in our area. My father told me his grandfather brought him up. He's Métis, an' the story goes that his father was mixed up in the Riel rebellion out west and was killed. In fact that's what LR stands for, Louis Riel. But as you said, everybody just calls him 'LR'. He's a sober, hard workin' man. He travels all over the Island alone, and though they badmouth him about being a halfbreed, they respect him because he's the best at what he does, and he's honest."

Janice was silent for a minute then asked, "Do you know how to get in touch with him? I've a special job I'd like him to do."

"I think so, Janice. He's friendly with an uncle of mine."

"Do you think you could get him to come out to Ewart's to see me as soon as possible. I'll be there tomorrow."

When the lawyers learned Janice was going to visit Charlie at the jail, a look passed between them.

Albert said, "I'll go down with you and Mark an' talk to Athol. But under no circumstances are you to discuss the case, now."

"All I want to do is take him a present and then tell Sarah, Ruth and Betty Logan that he's okay."

Albert was able to get her in. Janice asked Athol if anything had come for her from the florist.

"No nothin'. But you know I'm worried about Charlie, Missus. We can't get him to go out in the yard, or to look after himself like, an' he's not eatin'. It's not like he's locked in. We don't lock the door on him."

Charlie lay on his cot with his arm over his eyes. He had lost weight, and his usually ruddy face was now pale. The slop bucket lid lay on the floor and the cell smelled foul. Janice picked up the lid and put it back on the bucket. Mark greeted him and handed him a brown paper parcel of clothes, soap, candy and cookies.

"Hello Charlie, I've brought an old friend to see you. Remember Janice Fenlon?"

Charlie drew his knees up and stared with dull eyes at Janice. She smiled at him and said, "Remember me, Charlie, dear? We used to play together, you, me and Ruthie."

He put his head down. She sat on the cot beside him and gently touched his hair.

"Charlie, darlin' you need a haircut. Who cuts your hair for you?"

"Sarah."

"If the Reverend Kerr can get a pair of scissors for me, I'll cut it for you. Would you like that?"

He nodded and Janice motioned in the direction of the door with her head to Mark. When he came back he was carrying the fern and the scissors. She signalled to him to put the fern outside the door.

"There now, Charlie, you sit up an' turn this way."

She took a comb out of her bag and wet it under the water-tap and began combing out his hair. Charlie responded like a little boy. As she combed and snipped she asked him, "What was that little hymn we used to sing with your mother, Charlie? You know the one about God lovin' the little bird?"

Charlie began to sing, *God Sees the Little Sparrow Fall*, and as Janice combed and cut she hummed it along with him.

"There now, Charlie, you're handsome. But do you know what would make you feel awful good an' make you smell nice too? A bath. You take off your clothes and I'll give you one."

Without waiting for an answer, she was pulling off his shirt, and instructing Mark at the same time to hurry and fill his wash bucket. She stripped him naked and lathered him from head to foot, washing him thoroughly. Charlie stood passively squinching his eyes closed to keep the soap out.

"There, Reverend Kerr, doesn't Charlie look much better?" she said when she'd dressed him in his clean shirt and trousers.

"Now Charlie, I have a surprise for you. Close your eyes." She nodded to Mark to get the fern.

"All right, open them."

Charlie's eyes went as wide as saucers when he saw the fern.

"But Granddaddy's dead!"

"Yes," said she, "but this is the Grandma, an' as long as you keep her alive everything's goin' to be okay. Now here's what you have to do. You have to water her every day. And I want you to take her out into the yard an' walk her around in the sun. That way she'll stay healthy. Will you promise me an' Reverend Kerr you'll do that?"

Charlie promised he would.

Athol was amazed at the change in Charlie. Janice said, "Mr. Mutch, Charlie's goin' to take the fern out every day for a walk around the yard. You don't mind do you?"

Before she left she kissed Charlie good bye, and told him how proud Sarah and Ruth would be of him and that he'd be seeing them soon.

Before they left the jail, Janice said to Athol, "Mr. Mutch, we're right happy Charlie's in here at a time when you're in charge. I'm goin' to leave a little somethin', a kind of fund, like, for the prisoners in case they have any little needs. I see up on Kent Street, there's a fellow makin' an' sellin' them new radio wireless sets. I'd like to donate one for the staff room. Good day to you, and God bless you, Mr. Mutch."

As they drove back to New Skye the setting sun was suffusing everything in various hues of red. A gentle breeze from the sea blew the ripe grain in a continuous undulation of gold, pink and green. Farm children drove the family cows from the pasture fields to the barn for milking. Janice and Mark were uncomfortably silent.

"You were wonderful with Charlie today, Janice."

Mark was not given to flattering, so sincerity rang in his words.

"Oh, I was going to ask you if you wouldn't mind being with me when I offer to buy the place from Sarah and Ruthie."

"Yes, if you think I can help. Now about Sarah. I don't know if you're aware of it, Janice, but she drinks quite a bit."

"Yes. For a time in my life, I did too, until I caught on that instead of killin' pain, I was sinkin' deeper into it."

Mark wanted to say 'me too' but didn't. "Will you come with me to talk to Betty Logan, too? I haven't seen her yet. To tell you the truth, I don't remember her much. What about her?"

"Well I've talked to her a few times. She's very withdrawn—frightened and alone. The gossip about her in the community isn't very nice."

"Myra Swanson, I bet?"

"Well probably, yes. Anyhow, Betty's had a hard time of it. Lost her husband in the winter influenza. Apparently she got close to Charlie this summer. I believe he used to help her out. I just don't know what the outcome will be for Betty Logan, but yes I'll go with you to see her."

As they pulled into the Ewart yard they were greeted by screams and obscenities resonating off the buildings. Sarah and Myron Swanson were yelling at one another. Ruth stood against the barn wailing.

"You get out of here an' don't come on this property again you good for nothin' shit," Sarah shouted.

Myron yelled back, "Yous weren't sayin' that when I was slavin' to help you out. What would you done without me? Between you swillin' rum an' that loony over there runnin' around without a stitch on talkin' to herself about the minister, an' that other loony shootin' people...."

Mark leapt from the car and pushed him. Myron pushed back. When Janice saw Mark drawing back his arm to hit him, she put herself in between them. Myron's face was white and had the vicious look of a cornered rat. Janice said to him, "You go on home. Don't say another word, d'ye hear? Just go."

He looked malevolently from one to the other. Mark's body was poised. Both men glared at each other. Finally Myron broke the impasse by giving the barn door a heavy-booted kick, splintering one of its boards. Mark stiffened and Myron backed away, his fists clenched. When he reached the corner of the barn, he called out to Janice, "What about you Lady Muck from Boston? We all know about you."

Mark lunged and threw him to the ground, punching him. Myron wriggled free, blood pouring out his nose.

"Some minister you are. When your wife was livin' the both of yous hardly drew a sober breath."

With a bellow Mark made for him again, but Myron disappeared round the barn hurling more obscenities into the air. Sarah led Ruth into the house. Janice held Mark.

"He's not worth it, dear."

She continued holding him until she felt his body relax. She pecked him on the cheek and whispered, "You go home now Mark, and come back after supper."

"No!"

Still in a rage, he went into the house after Sarah and Ruth determined to find out what happened. Ruth was lying on the sofa with a blanket over her.

"The dirty pig had her on the straw tryin' to get her drawers off," Sarah told them. "Lucky I came in. I walloped him a good one with the fork handle. He's no better than an animal."

"Sarah I'm going. I'll be back later," Mark said.

He headed directly up to Myra Swanson's store. She was in back eating her supper.

"I want to talk to you, Myra," he called.

She came out wiping her hands on her apron. Myron had already told her what happened down at the Ewart's and she was ready to do battle.

"Listen Myra, you keep your nephew away from the Ewart's. I know you sent him down."

"I've nothin' to say to the likes of you," Myra snapped back. "He was down there out of a kindness to a neighbour and little thanks he getting' for it. An' as for you, so-called Minister, you're goin' to pay for your behaviour. Minister's aren't supposed to be goin' around hittin' people an' other things."

"Did Myron tell you he tried to interfere with Ruth Ewart?" Mark said.

Myra glared back at him.

"He told me she led him on. She runs about the place naked. Men's not the cause of half the trouble, it's women leadin' them on. You should know all about that."

Mark's stomach knotted. He moved closer.

"You better watch what you say, Myra. Now I'm warning you, you lay off the Ewart's, and keep that nephew away from me. He insulted my wife's memory."

As Mark was leaving, Myra called, "I don't know why you're so thick with the Ewarts' an' why that Janice is so thick with them after them murderin' her poor father."

When he got home he picked over his food thinking about Janice, Myron and the Ewarts. The phone rang. It was Hammond Rutherford.

"Reverend Kerr, I've just been informed that you struck a man. Is that true?"

"Yes, but not nearly hard enough," Mark answered and hung up.

Later on when he arrived back at the Ewarts', Ruth was in bed asleep. He joined Sarah and Janice at the kitchen table. After they talked about Myron briefly, Janice said, "Sarah, I asked Reverend Kerr to come down to discuss somethin.' All right?"

"Sure, Janice. But first, did you happen to see Dr. McAllister, Reverend Kerr?" Sarah said.

"Yes, Sarah, this morning. I discussed Ruth with him, and he said it's not likely she'll get better."

She sat motionless, then asked, "Will she get dangerous?"

"I asked him that. He said somebody might report her to the police if she undresses in public, and if they certify her and put her away you'll have no control over where they put her. As far as being dangerous is concerned, the greatest danger is to herself. After the incident with Myron today you can see why."

"I just don't know what to do," Sarah sighed.

Janice leaned closer to her and said, "Sarah, listen careful now. Ruth'll have the best of care and protection we can manage. I have a big house in Boston an' lots of help. There's some wonderful doctors in Boston."

"Poor Charlie'll never get out. If they don't hang him, they'll put him away just like they'll do with Ruthie. An' even if he did get off do you think he could come back here? He's finished an' so's this place–we all are. I know it in my heart."

"Sarah, I've got somethin' to show you."

Janice took the offers to purchase out of her bag and set them before her. Sarah wearily looked at the papers.

"What's them Janice?"

"It's an offer by me to purchase your place. Will you go over it with Sarah, Reverend Kerr?"

Mark read out the essential parts, then she got up and said, "I'll go upstairs and look in on Ruthie for a minute."

When she came back she smelled of rum. Pointing to the offer, she said, "That's away more than this place is worth. An' the offer to help Ruthie, an' all. Well it would be too hard for me to take that kind of charity."

Janice said nothing.

"She doesn't mean to give charity, Sarah. Janice has personal reasons besides wanting to help out two old friends," Mark said.

Sarah shook her head and still said nothing.

"Sarah, you, Ruthie and Charlie are the closest thing I have to a family. My mother loved you. You provided a home for us an' work for my father. He hurt all of you as well as me an' my mother. When I was over in the house this mornin' I got a very strong feelin' that this is what Mother would want."

"I'll think about it Janice, though God knows what there is to think about. This place is nothin' now, nothin' at all," Sarah said.

Betty Logan had never really fitted into New Skye. Jack had brought her from another community known for its poorer farms and families, and most of New Skye considered he had married beneath himself. Since the shooting, the neighbours gave her a bad time, and Betty withdrew more and more.

As Janice and Mark approached the Logan house they saw the window curtain part slightly then close again. Even though she knew they were not hostile, she was reluctant to let them in. When she did she kept her head down.

Finally Janice said, "Look Betty, I'll come to the point. My

Father hurt you very badly. I know what happened. I'd no love for him. He ruined me when I was a young girl. He gave my mother a miserable life, and I want to make amends."

Betty shook her head, then turning to Mark, she asked how Charlie was doing.

"In good spirits, thanks to Janice. He was glad to see her. He trusts Janice and so do Sarah and Ruth. You should too."

Betty warmed a little. They talked about the farm and how she was managing.

"I don't know what's goin' to happen. None of the neighbours' talk to me, an' the lawyers told me I'm goin' to have to go into town for the trial. Does that mean they'll arrest me again?" Betty asked.

"Pius McQuaid an' Albert Stephenson will look after you Betty."

"They came in to see me when I was in the hospital. They're nice men."

"Well you do what they tell you, an' you'll be all right. You take no notice of the neighbours. You did nothin' wrong. The harm was done to you. Have you anybody on the Island?"

"No Janice, the closest one I have is a sister up in Toronto. She's a widow, too. Has three little ones. She wants me to go up there to her."

"Why don't you when all this is finished?"

"Well she has a hard enough time keepin' things together. He left her nothin'."

Janice looked at Mark and brought out the offer to purchase. They both explained it to Betty in detail until she understood.

"You're an angel, Janice, that's what you are. I'll be able to leave here an' go to my sister an' help her out, too. Oh poor little Charlie. I hope you're prayin' for him Reverend Kerr. I do all the time."

Before they left, Janice told her about her house in town and that she wanted her to stay there while the trial was on. The fact that Janice and Mark had shared in making Betty feel better added to their growing closeness.

The sky was filled with clusters of large bright stars, and the night enveloped them in its warm, velvety darkness. The attraction between them was so strong, he took her in his arms to kiss her, but she gently put her fingers to his lips and whispered, "We'd better not start."

That night Mark lay awake for a long time thinking about her and wondering if she meant they'd better not start anything at that moment, or never.

In the meantime, another call had come through from Hammond Rutherford, informing him that an investigation was being launched into the complaint brought against him for inappropriate behaviour.

Forty

L. R.

The next morning Janice, Ruth and Sarah were met in the yard by a tall man on horseback. Janice knew immediately that it was L.R. Arsenault. Without dismounting, he asked, "One of you the woman from Boston?"

"I'm Janice O'Neill. You're Mr. Arsenault? Did Pius McQuaid get in touch with you?"

He nodded and dismounted.

"What's this about, Janice?" Sarah asked

"It's okay Sarah, I've some business to discuss with Mr. Arsenault. I'd like to talk to him alone. Will you come with me please, Mr. Arsenault?"

They went down to her old house where they talked for about half an hour. When L.R. left, the three women watched him ride away.

"Is him comin' here anything to do with what you were talkin' about last night, about buying this place?"

"No Sarah, it's somethin' personal."

During a recent discussion with her cousin Lionel about their upcoming tractor dealership and a need for more land, Myra Swanson brought up the fact that the Ewart place was finished as a family farm and that Jack Logan's few acres might also be up for grabs.

"If a fella played his cards right," she said. "He could get them places for a song. Not only that, but they're just across the road from each other."

"Then keep an eye on things and find out what you can," Lionel told her. After he left, she called Myron in for a talk.

"How's your poor nose, darlin'?"

"All right, Aunt Myra. A fella isn't safe havin' the likes of that crowd for neighbours, not to mention the likes of that fella' Kerr for a minister."

"I know. They're a scourge. You know, Myron, I think they should know how the community feels about them."

"What do you mean?"

"Well darlin', Betty Logan's no better than a whore. Sarah's a rummy. Ruth's a looney-bin and Charlie's a murderer who should be strung up. I think they need a message sent to them, don't you?"

"I do, Aunt Myra, but what can I do about it?"

"I don't know either, dear. Good people are always at a loss aren't they? Anyway, I've some grain needs baggin'. Will you see to it? Oh an' by the way, I was goin' over the inventory and found we're about five cans of white paint over-stocked. It's lying out there. Why don't you take them for yourself an' maybe you can trim things up a bit."

While Ruth, Sarah and Betty were in town staying at Janice's rented house, somebody painted *Whore* on Betty's front door; and on the side of the Ewart barn, they painted: *Whores, Loonies and Murderers Out of New Skye!* There was also a crude stick-figure cartoon of a man hanging from a gallows with *Hang Charlie,* scrawled beneath it.

When the women came back out from town and saw it, Sarah was mortified.

"Do you think that's the way our neighbours really think about us? Me, Ruth and Charlie was born and raised here."

"Some of them might dear, and I'm sure if you thought about it you could guess who. But no, most of the neighbours wouldn't think like that."

"Janice, I've thought about your offer to buy this place. Maybe I'm ready to sell now. I don't really want to move, but I just haven't the strength to deal with this kind of thing."

When Albert Stephenson was attending to the signing of the papers and the transfer of the properties with Janice, she told him about another matter she wished attended to.

"Albert, I want to get the word out that I'll lend money to New Skye farmers. How do we do that?"

He was mystified.

"Why would you want to do the likes of that, Janice? Most of them are deep in debt to the feed mills and the farm machinery dealers, and they hold notes on their farms, not to mention the banks. An' you know who owns the feed mill in New Skye."

"Exactly. I want to pull the teeth out of that one."

"We'll give notice and put the word around that you're doing it. Then arrange for them to come in. But why should they want to borrow money from you?"

"Cut the interest to half of what they're paying now."

"That'll do it, Janice. When do you want it done?"

"Right away. Don't waste any time. Now if you find cheatin' or skulduggery goin' on with people, let me know."

Albert was thoughtful, then he said, "Now listen Janice, you have to be very careful. Could you please tell me a bit more about why you're doing this?"

She told him about Myron Swanson trying to molest Ruth, and about Mark hitting him, and about the graffiti on the buildings.

"Myra's tryin' to ruin Mark and they'll stop at nothin' to destroy anybody associated with him. Even the Church is gettin' after him. "

"We could take Myron to court," Albert suggested.

"No. Albert. The Ewarts have too much to handle as it is. Do it my way, an' do it so as it'll be legal. An' Albert, could you get L.R. to come and see me again as soon as he can?"

In a couple of days it was arranged that L.R. would meet her at the Ewart's place. She took him around the barn and showed him the writing.

"That'll be hard to rub off. Better if you painted over it."

"Will you do it, Mr. Arsenault?"

He looked down at her with his impassive face, "You don't own the place."

"Yes I do, now. Will you paint the barn?"

"Yes."

"An' Mr. Arsenault, there's somethin' else I wish you'd do for me. There'll be nobody livin' in the Ewart's house or the Logan's across the road for a while. Would you look after things while they're away? You can move into whatever house you want to an' make yourself comfortable."

"Wait a minute," he said.

She watched him stroll over to his horse. He stood beside the animal stroking its neck. Janice wondered if he was talking to it. Then after lifting his head up to the sky, he strolled back to her.

"The Logan place."

She was curious as to why he choose that one over the Ewarts'. He waited her out. In the end she asked him, "Why the Logan's?"

"A lot of years ago, I wanted to buy that place. Had enough money saved to do it. It was just what I was lookin' for. But the sale was blocked because I'm a half-breed. I found out the store people up the road was behind it. I went to old man Swanson and asked him why. I knew why, but I wanted him to say it. He spat on the ground an' said, 'Because you're half a drunken Indian and half a stupid Frenchman, an' you're a bunch of good for nothin' traitors.'"

"Mr. Arsenault, I own that place too. Betty Logan'll be leavin' it. How would you like to live there all the time and manage it an' this place for me?"

"Yes, I'd like that, but I don't want to do farmin'—somethin' else."

"What?"

"Well my grandfather taught me how to dry seeds. I want to grow an' dry seed —vegetable seeds, flowers, grains, an' ship them. The Island doesn't give a long growin' time, but she sure can produce good seeds."

"You grow all the seeds you want."

He looked at her.

"What's your name?"

"You know my name."

"I was told your name. I want you to tell me."

"Janice O'Neill."

What Janice did not know was that L.R. didn't use a person's name for fear he attached a dignity to them they didn't deserve. He was showing his respect when he said, "All right, Janice, you call me Louis."

He gave her a number where she could reach him. Before he left she asked him did he talk to his horse. He gave a quiet laugh.

"I'd rather talk to my horse than most of the people I meet."

As she watched him mount and ride off, Janice knew that legal papers or contracts were unnecessary when dealing with LR.

Forty-one

Growing Closer

That afternoon Janice asked Mark to go for a walk along the shore. Little sandpipers ran ahead of them pecking in the wet sand at the water's edge. She stopped and said, "Mark you are the most wonderful man I've ever met and will ever hope to meet. I think I am falling in love with you."

His heart skipped a beat, for he was strongly attracted to her. He kissed her. She held on for a heady moment, and then broke away.

"What's wrong Janice?"

"Oh nothing, my dear, nothing, it's lovely, but it's me you see. I am not right for you. Let's sit up there and talk."

They climbed a large dune and sat on a beached log lying in a hollow. Around them the grasses swept back by the sea wind hissed softly.

"Now, let me say what I want to say. Mark, you think of what I am. I was raped and given a baby by my own father. I was raped again by O'Neill. Then I deliberately prostituted myself to him to control him. I slept with another man only to make O'Neill jealous enough to marry me. I hated those three men in my life. As well as that, I was into other money makin' things I'm not proud of. I come back to the place where all that started and find dignity in you. But Mark, dear, I am too damaged and used for you, too rough for a man like you."

He put his arm around her.

"Janice, after my wife and baby died, I wanted to die too. I loved Mollie so much the thought of another woman just wasn't possible. I've lain awake nights trying to figure out how it is that you're changing that. You're striking, beautiful, but it's not just that. It's something between us that brings me alive again. Something that cuts across your pas —and dear Lord, Janice what are you but someone who's been terribly wronged? Charlie, Sarah, Ruth, Betty have all been wronged, but you're making it better for them. What I've seen you do here is not the action of one who is damaged beyond repair. You have a sense of fairness and too much goodness and love in you, Janice."

They kissed for a long time.

"Mark," she whispered. "I want to make love with you but I can't. I'm scared of what I'll feel like after. But just hold me."

"We'll give it time. We'll give it time, Janice."

He had understanding and a strength she had never known in a man. For his part, he knew his education and so-called refinement made her uneasy, insecure, perhaps. Why? He concluded that the difference between them lay in how they would appear to others. As they walked back, she asked, "What are you thinking about?"

"Let me ask you something, Janice. Supposing we were a married couple, how do you think our differences in background would affect us?"

"Oh I don't know. Perhaps you might become bored with me. Perhaps I might let you down by saying the wrong thing in company. Supposing somebody found out about my past? How would you cope with that? How do you think your mother would feel? Let me ask you; were you and Mollie happy together?"

"Yes."

"What was *her* growin' up like? Was it very different from mine?"

"Very. She was the daughter of an Edinburgh Fine Arts Professor. Her mother was a talented artist, and she, herself, a talented pianist. Cultured people."

"There you see; how could I ever be like that?"

"You can't, Janice, because you're you. Anyhow, we seldom talked about art, or music or theology."

"What did you do then?"

Mark mused, as he thought about their brief life together.

"We often talked nonsense. We had fun. We made love continuously, and we spoiled each other rotten."

He thought about the passionless life of his own parents.

"Janice, the time Mollie and I had together was so short. Though she seldom complained, I know she missed her music, her parents and Edinburgh. Another form of death was taking over."

"How do you mean, Mark?"

"The death of the transplanted."

She looked at him askance. Frustrated, she said, "You see what I mean? Even the way you talk is different. I don't understand 'the death of the transplanted'"

"Mollie pulled up her roots and was replanted here, but the soil wasn't rich enough. Did you know that Pius is a talented violinist? One night he and Mollie got going together at a party. They played Beethoven and Mozart. I noticed radiance in Mollie I had forgotten about—a radiance that drew me to her in the first place. I suppose it's a bit like a cut flower. At first you don't notice the colour fading from the petals. It still gives out scent. Then one day you look and it's brown and withered. Transplanted death is a bit like that."

"Did Mollie complain about living here?"

"Not really. I did most of the complaining. Mollie use to say, 'Look Mark the only difference between a wee Island like this and Edinburgh is that the people here have to put up with each other more. In Edinburgh, people can hide in their own class, nook and cranny, with each group believing it's better than the other; but what they're really hiding from is the same old twistedness that runs through all of us. On a wee Island like this, people are *forced* to join together, and in doing that they reinforce their own mediocrity. Apart from that they're lovely people. "

Janice didn't understand everything he was saying, but she loved the fact that he spoke to her as if she did. It was the longest she'd heard him talk.

"She must have been very smart, your Mollie."

"Yes she was, Janice, like you. I think if my Mollie had been in your shoes today, she would do exactly what you are doing for Ruth and Sarah, Betty and Charlie."

She hugged his arm and looked up at him. Her eyes were swimming. The love pouring out from her was overpowering. She whispered, "Let's go back up to the dune, darlin'."

They settled themselves in the curvaceous saddle of the dune. Mark took off his coat and spread it over the sand; and there, hidden among the sea grasses, they lay down.

Still, deep inside him was a nagging feeling that he was not doing the right thing. She responded fully to his kisses. Both felt the rise of passion, but she also had to force back feelings of apprehension. She clung to him, and he made up his mind to let the full tide of passion carry him. He undid her bodice and kissed the swell of her breast. But at that moment a gigantic heron which had just taken flight from the marsh behind them, flapped its huge wings darkly over them. The suddenness of it flying so low startled her, and all her apprehensions arose replacing her passion. She pushed him away. The moment was lost for him too. He sat up and looked away from her. She lay for an abject moment. Then she tried to encourage him back, but their hearts were not in it. Instead he cradled her, feeling a distressing mixture of frustration and tenderness as well as a disloyalty to Mollie.

After a moment she said, "I'm sorry, Mark. I want you so much. I've never wanted anyone like I want you."

"I guess we're not ready yet."

And there on that long, deserted beach they sat holding each other against the chill of the darkening day.

Forty-two

The Trial

The night before his trial, Charlie was moved to a cell in the Courthouse basement. He made such a fuss about having to leave his fern behind, Athol told him to take it. He slept little and awoke next morning to a whole clamour of new voices. He was distraught and agitated. Athol brought him a breakfast and did his best to calm him.

"Now you get that into you Charlie an' then I'm goin' to bring you a present."

After Charlie ate and was settled a bit, Athol brought him a new suit and shirt. A few minutes later a local barber arrived.

"Charlie, this here's Jimmy McIsaac, the barber. Pius sent him over to give you a shave, an' your sister Sarah sent you these nice new clothes. You let Jimmy sweeten you up now, an' when you get dressed you'll look as slick as a mouse."

He had grown quite fatherly towards Charlie and ardently protected him from sightseers. Once a newspaper reporter put a ladder against the tall prison wall and tried to talk to Charlie as he walked around the yard with his fern. Athol enraged ran around the outside, grabbed the ladder and threatened to push it off the wall, reporter and all. A group of women from New Skye got together and knitted socks and baked a batch of cookies and a pie. They had been friends of Charlie's mother and had known him since he was a baby. They pleaded with Athol to let them deliver their presents personally.

"Just leave your stuff with me an' I'll see he gets it. Then go about your business, ladies."

"We come all the way down here to bring that poor creature a little comfort."

Athol stuck out his barrel chest and pushed them out the door, shouting, "Well yous can get yourselves all the way back. I'll do all the lookin' after he needs."

Rumours flew. Some said that Athol was a brute and sympathy for Charlie grew; but running counter to that was an equally strong opinion that Charlie was a cold blooded monster and the sooner they hanged him the better. Myra Swanson said that he brought terrible shame upon New Skye and turned it into a den of iniquity. Every day hate mail and pies were delivered to the jail.

On trial day crowds flocked into town. The ground around the squat Victorian courthouse was black with people. Inside, every seat was taken and excited chatter reverberated from the walls and ceiling of the courtroom.

When they brought Charlie in, the room went quiet. Then somebody bellowed, "Bloody murderer. Hang him!"

Two Mounties sprang forward, grabbed the man who shouted and scuffled with him until they got him outside. The crowd and the tension terrified Charlie. Old Feardy was everywhere. He struggled with the policemen to get back out through the door. Pius seeing they were getting rough sprang forward from behind his table.

"All right boys, take her easy, now."

He held Charlie's sleeve and whispered to him, "Charlie, look over there. See? There's Sarah, an' Ruthie, Betty an' Janice and Reverend Kerr."

Charlie looked over and they waved to him. Pius said, "You just stay with the policemen, now, we'll all be right here close to you."

The women stood up encouraging him with smiles. Ruth wanted to go to him, but Mark held her back. Sarah called over to him, "You stay put Charlie, that's a good boy."

Charlie's appearance appalled the women. He was pale and thin, and his suit looked too big for him. A piece of white paper was stuck to his cheek where the barber had nicked him. Betty wept. Some of the crowd snickered, but mostly it was orderly.

The morning sun streaming in through the long windows illuminated the gold leaf on the large Royal Coat of Arms hanging on the canopy over the judge's chair. On the wall behind were two large oval pictures of King George V and Queen Mary. Charlie recognized them from a biscuit tin they had at home. He loved that biscuit tin. The lid had a picture of George and Mary with a battleship between them in full steam, its guns bristling and ready for action. His father told him it was a dreadnought, the pride of the Royal Navy. He liked Mary's long neck and her choker of pearls, and her wispy hair and blue eyes looked like his mother's. The familiar faces of the King and Queen diverted his attention from the noisy surroundings and calmed him somewhat, but he wondered where the battleship was.

"All rise! His Lordship, Harold E. Pilchard, presiding in the case of the Province of Prince Edward Island versus Charles Ewart. All rise!"

The call and the sudden rumble of feet startled Charlie. One of the policeman nudged him to stand up. The judge took his seat and there was another rumble as everybody sat down. Charlie sat too, but the policeman tugged him up again. A few people laughed. Pilchard glowered at them.

"Let me tell you right now: outbursts, talking or laughter will not be tolerated. Is that understood?"

He arranged his glasses and glanced over his papers, then fixed his watery eyes on Charlie. Charlie kept his head down. He didn't like the black-gowned man with his pale, bejowelled face. He thought he looked a bit like a turkey with his wattles; but he reminded him, also, of the old minister who used to roar about the fires of hell.

Pilchard adjusted his glasses and looked at Charlie again.

"Are you Charles Ewart?"

Charlie, with more prompting answered, "Yes."

"Charles Ewart, you have been charged with murder in the first degree in the slaying of Frederick Fenlon. How do you plead?"

Pius answered, "The Defence wishes to enter a plea of Not Guilty By Reason of Insanity, your Worship."

"Is the Crown ready to proceed?"

Emerson Duncan, the Crown Prosecutor, a rotund little man with bushy black eyebrows and a shiny bald head fringed with white hair, stood and bowed graciously.

"Yes, if it pleases the Court, the Crown is ready to present its case against Charles Ewart and show that he is guilty of murder in the first degree. The Prosecution calls as its first witness, Inspector Kenneth Rutter."

The Inspector walked briskly to the stand. Pius accepted him as a qualified witness.

"Will you please tell the court the circumstances leading to your investigation of the death of Frederick Fenlon."

Rutter read from his report in a matter-of-fact voice. The spectators strained forward to hear him.

"On the morning of September the first, 1924, we were informed that there had been a shooting at New Skye and a man was killed."

Emerson interrupted him, "Who informed you?"

"The Reverend Mark Kerr."

"Is the Reverend Kerr present in the courtroom?"

"Yes."

"Will you point him out, please?"

Rutter pointed to Mark. The spectators strained to see, and the jury turned in unison to look at him.

"Please continue Inspector."

"We were met at the Ewart residence by Reverend Kerr who provided a signed statement as to what he believed happened."

Emerson picked up Mark's statement from his table.

"Is this the Reverend Kerr's statement?"

"Yes."

"Read it to the court, please."

After reading it, the Inspector continued his testimony about finding the body.

"Sergeant Smedly along with Constables Williams, Greer and Robbins found the victim's body on the shore west of the Ewart property. It was lying over the remains of a fire with gunshot wounds to the lower abdomen and head. The remains were badly burned. Charles Ewart was questioned."

"Where?"

"In the Ewart kitchen and in the presence of the Reverend Kerr. Mr. Ewart admitted to shooting Frederick Fenlon. He signed his confession in the presence of Reverend Kerr and Corporal Kingsley, the recording officer."

Emerson dramatically held up Charlie's confession.

"Is this Mr. Ewart's confession?"

"Yes."

"Is Mr. Ewart present in the court?" The Inspector pointed to Charlie and said, "Yes. He's the defendant in the dock."

He then read out Charlie's garbled confession as requested. Snickering and mumbling rose from the spectators. The judge banged them into silence with his gavel and told the Inspector to continue.

"When the murder weapon was located, I asked the Defendant if it was his shotgun. He affirmed that it was. I asked him if he used it to shoot Frederick Fenlon, and he answered, 'Yes, used two shots.'"

"Can this weapon be entered as material evidence?"

"Yes the Exhibits Officer has it."

A large Mountie brought the gun forward. Emerson took it and held it up to the Jury, then asked that it be admitted."

The Inspector continued, "Mr. Ewart was charged and taken into custody. His bloodstained clothing was forwarded to the Federal Crime Laboratory in Halifax. A thorough search of the property revealed additional material evidence. A money belt containing a substantial amount of money was found in Mr. Ewart's tool shed. A kerosene can with Ewart's name scratched into it was found at the murder site. These were forwarded to the Crime Laboratory as well."

The spectators couldn't fathom the fact that Charlie's whole demeanour was so contrary to the heinous deed the Inspector said he committed.

Emerson, aware of the impact on the Court, thanked the Inspector and reported to the judge that he had no further questions. His Lordship's head was splitting, and he was getting the shakes. He asked Pius if he wished to cross examine the witness, hoping at the same time he'd decline.

"Yes, My Lord."

Pius strode over to the stand, his face flaming red. People smiled and nudged each other.

"How did you establish where the shooting occurred?"

"From the defendant's statement."

"He also said that the dune was on fire, did he not? Please read his statement again referring to that point."

"'Granddaddy's dead, the dune's on fire an' that's the end of the Island.'"

Charlie, who had been sitting with his elbows on the railing of the dock, sat up and called out, "Betty, Grandma's alive."

The courtroom broke out in spontaneous laughter. Pilchard banged his gavel, shouting, "Enough! Enough!"

Pius was pleased. Charlie's outburst would help reinforce his plea. When there was silence again, he continued, "Granddaddy's dead, the Dune's on fire, that's the end of the Island? What do you think he meant by that Inspector?"

"I don't know."

"Did you try to find out?"

The inspector frowned and after thinking a moment, answered, "Not really, no."

"You didn't know what he was talking about?"

"No."

"Yet you were taking a statement you didn't understand from a man who had admitted to shooting another man. I suggest, Inspector, that you didn't bother to ascertain what Mr. Ewart meant, because you concluded that Mr. Ewart was not normal in his head?"

Emerson was on his feet shouting,

"Objection. My lord, my friend is leading the witness and dealing in supposition. Inspector Rutter can not be expected to comment on the state of the defendant's mind."

Judge Pilchard said, "Sustained. Strike the Defence's question. You needn't answer that, Inspector."

Pius let things settle for a moment, then asked casually, "Well then, it seems Mr. Ewart wasn't making sense?"

"Objection, My Lord!"

The spectators were delighted.

Pilchard called Pius over to the bench. He looked down at him with his jaundiced and red-rimmed eyes and said in a low voice full of strain, "You're pushin' it, McQuaid. How much longer are you goin' to question the Inspector?"

Pius, guessing his Lordship was badly in need of a drink, whispered, "If your Lordship could indulge me for just a few moments longer?"

"Alright, make it snappy an' no tricks."

Pius went back to the Inspector and lifted up the police report, then faced the jury to make sure they'd catch every word.

"Now you state that Mr. Ewart said he shot Frederick Fenlon because, and I quote, 'Poor Freddy went back 'an I put him down. Freddy the wolf entereth the pen by the back door and ravisheth the flock'"

He paused for a moment before turning on the Inspector.

"How did you interpret that?"

"Well at first it went through my mind that he meant he went back to the dune."

Pius interrupted, "Ah, that was the sand dune that was on fire, right?"

"Yes—I mean no."

A ripple of laughter ran through the spectators, but Pilchard was in such pain he ignored it. He was about to go after Pius but decided if he kept quiet it would take less time for him to finish.

Pius continued, "Did you believe the dune was actually on fire?"

"No."

"Do you think Charlie believed the dune was on fire?"

"No—he meant the fire *on* the dune!"

"But you said you didn't know what Charlie meant?"

Pius's questions were rapid fire, but the Inspector quickly composed himself.

"We had it explained what *going back* meant and what the defendant meant by the wolf and the sheep door."

"Well what does it mean, then?"

"Well when a tame dog, say, reverts to being wild they say it's gone back—I suppose Mr. Ewart meant that he thought the victim was like a wild beast."

Pius moved a little closer to the jury and fixed it with his bright blue eyes.

"Or, that Charlie Ewart literally and absolutely believed that Freddy Fenlon *was a wild beast*? Is that the thinking of a normal mind, Inspector?"

The Inspector snapped back, "I am not qualified to judge."

"I have no further questions at this time, your Lordship."

Pilchard was about to adjourn, but before he got the words out, Emerson called Mark Kerr to the stand and the Clerk swore him in.

"Reverend Kerr, you were present when the Inspector questioned Charles Ewart, the defendant?"

"Yes."

"Did you observe any undue pressure or coercion of any kind being brought to bear on the defendant to make him sign his statement?"

"No."

"In your opinion was the police interview conducted in a humane, reasonable and professional fashion?"

"Yes."

"Thank you, Reverend. No more questions, your Lordship."

Pius was on his feet, "If it pleases your Lordship, I wish to cross-examine the Reverend Kerr."

His Lordship answered with painful resignation, "Very well."

"Reverend Kerr, you have testified that Inspector Rutter questioned the defendant in a humane and reasonable manner."

"Yes."

"Now what about the defendant. Would you say he *acted* in a reasonable state of mind?"

"I don't understand. Do you mean was his reason intact?"

"Exactly."

"No."

Emerson objected that Pius was leading the witness. The judge growled at Pius.

"I hope you are going to make a point."

"I am, your Lordship"

"Overruled, continue."

"Earlier the Inspector admitted he did not understand some of the Defendants answers to his questions. Do you think the Defendant always understood the Inspector's questions?"

"No. He was quite confused in his mind."

"Thank you, Reverend Kerr. No more questions, my Lord."

The judge banged his gavel and quickly announced, "Court adjourned until two o'clock p.m. Stand down Reverend."

Pilchard left the courtroom so quickly he was out before the spectators were fully on their feet.

In the lawyers' chambers, Pius found a telegram from Philip Dixon stating that he would arrive on the Island on the weekend. As it happened Emerson was also in the Chambers.

"Emerson, could we discuss the calling of expert witnesses testifying to Charlie's mental competence? No doubt you intend to call one?"

"Sure Pius. I'm calling Dr. Machum from the Asylum, and you?"

"A Dr. Philip Dixon from Montreal."

"Would you agree to a request for an adjournment to give us time to prepare the doctors and swap papers?"

"Yes. We'd better. Let's go and see Pilchard."

As soon as he had got to his chamber, his worship poured a tumbler of scotch, sat on his toilet, and gulped.

"Piles and piss-ups," he muttered to himself. "What's the good of it all anyway?"

However, by the time Pius and Emerson Duncan came in to see him, he was in a better mood.

"Come in boys. What do you want?"

Both lawyers stated the need for an adjournment to organize examinations and affidavits from expert medical witnesses. Pilchard agreed, but stated he had a personal distaste for allowing alienists spouting their mumbo-jumbo in his court. He thought to himself that the only thing those birds prove is that they don't know what the hell they are talking about. He had turned testy again and virtually threw them out.

Pius dropped into his own office and phoned Philip Dixon.

"Hello, Dr. Dixon. I got your wire and I'm very pleased you're coming down."

"I hope I can be of help to you and your client Mr. McQuaid. I'd like to combine my work there with a bit of a vacation. How's the trout fishing on the Island?"

"The best, doctor. We'll arrange a place for you to stay, and of course we'll meet you at the train."

Albert Stephenson didn't join Pius in the court for the afternoon session because he had to see the farmers who had responded to Janice's advertisement inviting them to apply for loans. When he returned after lunch, the waiting room was filled with them. Albert explained the terms Janice was offering, and it didn't take them long to see the advantage of consolidating and paying off their current debts at such a low rate of interest.

One man asked, "I'd like to know, Albert, what's in it for Janice?"

"That's her personal business."

"Well, anyway, it'll be good to get out of Myra's clutches, for as long as we owe her we're forced to buy seed, machinery an' get the millwork done at her place at her prices. Now this gives a fella the chance to shop around."

Albert knew that Myra Swanson had a lot of power over the people of New Skye, but he didn't realize the extent of it. When the bank got word of what was going on, they restricted her credit.

Forty-three

The Crown's Strategy

It was the Crown's strategy to create a picture of Charlie as a monster, a man completely without morals who clearly intended to kill his victim and dispose of his remains by burning them. In addition to that, Emerson wanted to convey the idea that he had added robbery to his crime. After having he Exhibits Officer produce Freddy's money-belt and Charlie's kerosene can. He called the corporal who found them to the stand. Emerson ostentatiously studied the tag on the money-belt and read out, "Money-belt presumed to be that of murder victim, Frederick Fenlon.

"Corporal, is this the belt found by you and which is now entered as material evidence?" Emerson asked.

"Yes."

Emerson showed Freddy's bloodstained money-belt to the jury, making sure each had a good look at it. The spectators strained to get a look at it. Emerson paused before continuing.

"Here, gentlemen, you can see where the belt was shattered by shot. These are the stains of Freddy Fenlon's blood and tissue. We know it is the victim's belt for several reasons which will become clear when we hear the Corporal's testimony."

He turned, and dramatically held up the belt.

"Where did you find this belt, Corporal?"

"I found it in the accused's shed behind a tool chest."

"Did you associate this belt with the crime?"

"Yes."

"Why?"

"Because of the fresh blood and tissue on it and the gunshot damage and because of the victim's name tooled into the leather. The Crime Lab report states that the blood on the belt matches that of the victim."

"And what did you conclude upon finding it?"

"That it was taken from the victim's body and hid in the shed."

"Now have you other material evidence?"

"Yes. We found a kerosene can."

"Where?"

"A few feet from the body."

Emerson showed the can.

"Is this the can in question?"

"Yes."

"Do you associate this can with the crime?"

"Yes."

"How?"

"Well the can has the name *Ewart* scratched into the side of it, an'.... "

Emerson intensified the interest in the court room by stopping him and pausing dramatically before he spoke again.

 "Just a minute please, Corporal. We need to be absolutely sure. Spell the name scratched on to it."

"E-W-A-R-T."

"Now apart from the fact that the can was found a few feet from the body, in what other way did you associate it with the crime?"

"The victim's body was doused in kerosene, and later we asked the defendant if it belonged to him and he said that it did."

Emerson showed the can to the jury, and said, "You see, gentlemen, the name Ewart scratched clearly? Thank you, Corporal. I have no further questions at this time my Lord."

There was a rumble of voices, and somebody behind Sarah said, "That's it. Charlie's had it now."

Mark squeezed Sarah's arm reassuringly. The Judge asked Pius if he wished to cross-examine. Pius strolled leisurely forward smiling and shaking his head incredulously.

"If it pleases your Lordship, yes indeed. My Lord and Gentlemen of the jury, the Defence fully accepts the fact that the money belt belonged to Freddy Fenlon, and that the kerosene can is the property of the defendant. The Defence has read the Crime Lab reports and also accepts that the blood on the belt, and the pieces of skin and intestine are those of the victim's. Yes, and that the belt and the can were found where the Corporal testified it was, and that the belt was taken from the victim's body. We accept all that. But what concerns the Defence, however, is that the wrong impression may...."

The Judge cut in.

"Mr. McQuaid, will you refrain from making a speech. You'll have an opportunity to do that in your summation. If you wish to cross-examine the witness then get on with it. I don't like grandstanding."

"I'm sorry my Lord, I didn't think my learned friend had left me any room to grandstand."

The spectators laughed. Pilchard banged his gavel. Pius then turned to the corporal.

"Do you think the defendant, Charlie Ewart, removed the money belt from the victim's body?"

"In my opinion he did."

"You *conjecture* that he did?"

The policeman not knowing the meaning of conjecture looked puzzled. Pius knew that most of the jury would not know the meaning either. He rephrased his question.

"As a professional, you *guessed,* you *deduced* that he took the belt from the body?"

"Yes."

"But can you say beyond a reasonable doubt that the defendant *did remove* the belt from the victim's body?"

"No, but I...."

"Thank you—no 'buts' please. Can you say for certain?"

"No."

"Then you must agree that it's possible someone else could have removed the belt?"

"Yes, but not likely."

A murmur went round the courthouse. When it died down, Pius continued, "*Not likely*? A man is on trial for his life here. This evidence looks factual, but it is circumstantial. You'd better be certain of your facts, Corporal. Could someone else have moved the belt yes or no?"

"Yes."

"In your opinion did Charles Ewart hide the money belt in his tool shed."

"In my opinion, yes."

"Can you say for absolute certain that he did?"

"No."

"Then is it possible that someone else could have hidden it in Charlie Ewart's tool shed?"

"Yes, I suppose, but...."

"Now. Is it possible that someone else beside Charlie Ewart could have taken the can from Charlie Ewart's tool shed and placed it close to the victim's body?"

"Yes, I suppose."

"You suppose? It's not your job to suppose in a court of law but to deal in facts. Is it possible that someone else, a third party, took that can and placed it close to the victim's body?"

"Yes."

"Now my Lord I'd like to draw attention to the Crime Lab report on Charles Ewart's clothing. It mentions that the blood matched the victim's. It mentions that the sand on Charlie Ewart's trousers and boots matches samples taken from the dune where the body was found, but nowhere, *no where* does it mention that there were traces of kerosene on the defendant's clothing."

"Question the witness, Mr. McQuaid."

"Very well my Lord. In view of the absence of kerosene on the defendant's clothing is it possible that someone else, a third party or parties, could have doused the victim's body?"

"Yes."

"No further questions, my Lord."

Emerson realizing that Pius had taken the wind out of his sails decided to play down greed as a motive and concentrate on jealously and love. He called Sarah to the stand. Pius had warned her beforehand of the strong possibility that the prosecution would question her about her relationship with Freddy. So when her name was called she reeled. Now, she thought, the last bit of respectability we have will be took from us.

As she walked towards the stand, Charlie called to her and reached towards her over the dock only to be pulled back by the policeman beside him. Sarah smiled at him.

Emerson began gently.

"Miss Ewart what was your association with Freddy Fenlon?"

"He was our hired man."

"Nothing more?"

"He was also a long time neighbour and a friend."

"Mr. Fenlon was a widower, I believe?"

"Yes he lost his wife to the influenza this past winter."

"Did you become his lover?

It had come. The dreaded question. Sarah shut out everything around her: the jury of men, the crowded courtroom and the man questioning her. She allowed only enough space in her mind for his words and for the reply that formed in her mind.

"Yes."

The courtroom gasped. Emerson waited for silence.

"Tell the court what happened just prior to the shooting."

"Freddy beat me up."

"Did you yourself attack him?"

"Yes."

"Why did you do that Miss Ewart?"

Sarah refused to answer. Emerson waited then said, "I suggest you attacked him in a fit of jealousy."

Sarah remained silent. The judge glared at Emerson and said to him,

"Mr. Duncan is all this germane? Why are you pursuing this line of questioning?"

"My Lord, the Crown believes that the circumstances leading up to the shooting are germane, and that the charge of murder in the first degree can be the substantiated. Events just prior to the murder have a bearing on Charles Ewart's decision to kill Frederick Fenlon."

"All right continue.'

"Miss Ewart, just prior to attacking Freddy Fenlon had you visited Mrs. Betty Logan?"

"Yes."

"Why?"

"Charlie was late coming home to do the chores and I went over to get him."

A ripple of laughter and a buzz of comment went through the court.

"And what did you find there, Miss Ewart?"

"Betty was sittin' there with the clothes half tore off her and bleedin'."

"What had happened?"

"She told me Freddy Fenlon interfered with her."

Loud talking arose from the spectators. Betty was sobbing. Pilchard banged and roared for silence. When the noise died down, Charlie was singing, and the policeman was telling him to shut up.

His Lordship announced to the court, "I am going to halt proceedings until this courtroom is cleared of spectators. I will hear the rest of this testimony *in camera*. Only subpoenaed witnesses and the jury may remain. The Policemen flung open the doors and herded the protesting spectators outside. Charlie continued singing. Through it all Sarah sat immobile. When the courtroom was finally cleared, the judge asked Sarah if she would like a break.

"No. Just a drink of water."

Emerson continued, "Miss Ewart, to the best of your knowledge was your brother Charles, Mrs. Logan's lover?"

"No. Charlie's not like that."

"Yet when he was late coming home to do his chores you knew exactly where to find him?"

"Charlie did Betty's chores for her. When he was late I felt somethin' was wrong an' went over. Our cows was bellowin'. You can set your clock by Charlie."

"Charlie's a good farmer?"

Sarah, pleased to be able to say something good about her brother, answered, "One of the best."

Emerson said, "My Lord, I have no further questions at this time."

Pilchard asked Pius, "Do you wish to cross examine the witness?

Pius declined.

"My Lord, the Prosecution wishes to call the Provincial Pathologist, Dr. William Townsend, to the stand."

The pathologist a dour, thin man read his report in a monotone voice.

"I examined the body at eight o'clock p.m., on September the first. The body was extensively burned in the anterior region of the torso. There was also extensive tissue trauma in both the abdominal area and the cerebrum caused by gunshot. The wound sustained by the brain was most likely the actual cause of death. The victim also sustained a wound from a sharp instrument to the right forearm, and on the right cheek there were four claw marks probably caused by human finger nails."

The doctor droned on giving details of the weight of lead shot taken from the body and the depth and length of the nail scratches to the face. Emerson, seeing the jury's attention waning, interrupted periodically to ask for clarification in layman's language. When the doctor was finished, Emerson called Sarah back to the stand.

"Did you claw those scratches on Freddy's Fenlon's face?"

"I suppose."

"Because you were furious with jealousy?"

"No, because he was such a brute."

"What happened next?'

"He beat me and kicked me and he nearly strangled my sister, Ruth to death when she tried to pull him off me."

"What did your brother Charlie say or do when he found out?"

"Nothin'. He just said he had to finish up."

"What do you think he meant?"

"He had to finish up in the barn."

"But in fact he didn't go to the barn. I suggest he went and got his shotgun to finish off Frederick Fenlon?"

"I don't know what he did then."

Pius objected on the principle of conjecture.

Sarah broke down. Emerson dismissed her, and the judge adjourned the proceedings until the psychiatric experts could prepare their affidavits.

That evening the papers put out a special edition with large headlines reading: POSSIBLE THIRD PARTY INVOLVED IN FENLON MURDER! and CHARLIE'S SISTER ADMITS TO BEING MURDERED MAN'S LOVER!

Forty-four

Experts

Philip arrived on one of those balmy days towards the end of September when everything on the Island seems suspended in a haze rising up from the red earth. Flocks of hungry gulls swooped down on freshly turned soil as farmers followed their ploughs. Pius lost no time getting to the point.

"Dr. Dixon, we need you to see Charlie Ewart as soon as possible. The judge has given us a short adjournment. The Prosecution's having him examined by the doctor who heads the mental institution here. Charlie's only hope is to have him certified, or at least make him eligible for a plea for leniency. If we don't get him admitted to an institution, it could mean the gallows or life imprisonment."

Philip spent the next few days examining Charlie, Ruth and Sarah. Sarah told him about the Ewart family secret. He later told Pius that most likely insanity ran in the Ewart family.

"Both Charlie and Ruth have a *dementia praecox*. The disease is progressive. It'll be a problem determining just how advanced Charlie was at the time of the shooting. But apart from this, he seems to be suffering from a chronic form of anxiety compounded by some other degenerative brain and personality disorder. One that makes him appear simple minded."

"How does each affliction affect him? Do they affect him the same way, or differently?" Pius asked.

"The dementia is characterized by hallucinations. For example, Jesus sings in his head. Fear, which he calls Old Feardy is in the form of an amorphous monster. The only thing that holds Old Feardy in check is Jesus. Now in this we see the anxiety and the *dementia praecox* working together–one sets off the other."

Pius stopped him. He got his notepad and said, "I truly have to understand this so that I can ask the right questions when you're on the stand. We Prince Edward Islanders hate to appear stupid. We have a whole code of behaviour just to avoid it."

Philip laughed, "You don't have a monopoly on that one, Pius. You're no smarter than the rest of the human race."

"Now, let me see if I got this, doctor. Charlie has three things wrong with him: one, he has a *dementia praecox*; two, he's filled with morbid anxiety; and three, he has something else in his brain that is degenerative and which also affects his personality. Did I get that right?"

"Yes. I can't put a name on the last thing, because I haven't had enough time with him. The *dementia praecox* is probably inherited. The anxiety he has learned from childhood; it is a life experience. The third one may be inherited, or else it's some kind of brain injury either congenital or from an accident. I can't say for sure."

Pius scribbled on his pad, and then said, "You'd better explain the *dementia praecox* a little bit more."

"Well it's a psychosis—madness— that usually starts to show itself in late adolescence. The youngster will withdraw. People might think he's very shy; but, in fact, he's melancholic and delusional–he hallucinates. It's hard to detect at the start because it's quite normal for young people to be shy and moony and have fantasies, but the difference lies in the fact that the normal young person knows the difference between the fantasy and reality. The psychotic person does not.

"The other degenerative thing, or a combination of all three, makes him susceptible to suggestion—particularly to someone he is fond of and trusts. This is the part that makes him seem simple-minded. In my opinion, Charlie has probably deteriorated quite a bit."

"Do you mean when Betty Fenlon told Charlie that when her granddaddy fern dies the sand dunes will catch fire and that'll be the end of the Island, he would take that literally?"

"Yes, but not only that, he could become fixated on it. Ruth has the same problem. She's fixated on Mark and has deluded herself into thinking that he's her heaven-sent lover. In her case she's so obsessed she undresses compulsively to reciprocate the love she imagines Mark has for her."

Pius made more notes and pondered them for a while.

"Now Charlie repeats over and over again that he used two shots, and he follows that with 'ammunition's not cheap you know.' He keeps insisting that Freddy went back and that's why he had to shoot him. What do you make of that Doctor?"

"It most likely comes from a past experience coupled with a strong suggestion. And, of course, fear underlies everything. I would be willing to bet there's some sort of a link with a past, traumatic childhood experience."

"If what you say is true, Doctor, the sooner we find that link the better. Do you think you can do it?"

"Well, I don't think there's time to draw it out of Charlie, and if we did we might not be able to trust its accuracy. The only hope lies in Sarah knowing something."

"Let's go then."

When they got to Janice's house they took Sarah into the parlour. Pius explained to her what Philip had told him. She had a great deal of difficulty understanding it.

Philip said, "Sarah, let's try this. I will ask you questions about Charlie's childhood and you try to answer them as best you can."

"I'll do anything if it'll help Charlie, sir."

"All right. Now do you remember if Charlie had a particular fear when he was a child?"

"He was scared of all kinds of things, but most of all he was terrified of Father. We all were. There was one terrible time when Father made him go into the mare's stall and pull out her dead foal. She was wild and she kicked Charlie."

"In the head?"

"Yes, I think so. He certainly had an awful bruise on his poor little head. Father was very harsh with Charlie. He made him bury the foal an' him only a little boy. Mother was beside herself."

"Why did the mare go wild? Do horses go back?"

"Father slaughtered a pig. The smell of the blood made the mare slip her foal she was carrying, and she went crazy. But she was all right in a couple of days."

She thought for a moment, then said, "Oh my dear God. *Went back!* Charlie had a little dog that went back an' it killed the hens. Charlie had to shoot him. Oh the poor little dear, he was so upset. I found him up on his bed cryin', heartbroken, an' he told me about havin' to shoot Pepper because he went back. Kept cryin' over an' over again, 'Pepper went back. Pepper turned wolf. Oh my God, doctor, the day Freddy beat me an' Ruthie we called Freddy a wild beast an' Ruthie said 'If you had a dog like that you'd shoot him.' You don't think...."

"I don't know, Sarah, it's possible. Can we go down an' see Charlie, Pius?"

Athol let them in saying that it was a good thing the Judge gave him a bit of a break from the trial.

"He's been under a right strain It made him some moody if he could be any moodier than he was before."

Philip said, "Charlie, tell me about Pepper."

"Pepper went back. Had to shoot him. Two shots instead of one an' ammunition's not cheap you know."

"You should have used only one shot Charlie?"
"Yes."
"Who told you that?"
"Father."
"Did he make you shoot Pepper?"
"No, Freddy."
"And Freddy went back too just like Pepper, eh?"
"Yes. Used two shots."

When they were back in his office, Pius poured a couple of drinks and said, "That was a brilliant piece of work. Imagine a person being linked like that to an event in the past. Now I can plan a more subtle defence. Thanks. Here's to you, Philip."

Philip smiled and tipped his glass to Pius in acknowledgment. After a sip, he said, "Yes Pius, but think how dangerous a person like Charlie is. All it takes is for him to make a connection to that past event, and we have a killer on the loose."

During his meeting with Emerson Duncan, Roger Machum declared that while Charlie was mentally abnormal he was not insane.

"There is no doubt," he said, "Charlie's suffering from a mental disorder but he's not totally irrational."

"What exactly does that mean, now?" Emerson asked.

"Well his mental illness is sub-clinical, meaning he knows the difference between right and wrong, between reality and unreality. He's physically sound, but mentally he's simple but not severely so. Charlie's able to count, read and run a farm."

"What about all that gibberish he talks about goin' back, an' using two shots, you know, the fern an' all?"

"He might be faking. True Charlie has certain eccentricities of behavior, but he could well be embellishing for effect."

"It's probably a stupid question, Dr. Machum, but why would he do that?"

"Not so stupid, Emerson. You see that's part of his being somewhat feeble minded. He's not trying to fox you all into thinking he's a madman, but he's doing it more to cover up his guilty feelings. I believe he sees himself as being a bad boy and he's scared of being punished. Guilt can make even the stupidest of us very cunning. I think he's faking in that sense."

When both doctors read each other's affidavits, Machum remarked, "Hmm typical. The Duke School of lookin' for things that aren't there." While Philip said of Machum's, "Simplistic drivel."

Forty-five

Mildred and L.R.

Not all the farmers accepted Janice's loan, but every time one did and paid off Myra, she lost power. She knew Janice was behind it.

"That whore and that excuse for a man of God!" she raged to Myron. "Where do they think they get off tormentin' a decent woman tryin' to make a livin'?"

If one of the farmers whose debt she lost came into the store she glared at him with her bulging malachite eyes and banged his purchase down on the counter. The farmers relished her annoyance and tried to goad her into making conversation, but she refused to speak to them. To make matters worse for her, Albert had discovered that a large tractor and farm machinery manufacturer was in the process of negotiating a dealership with her. Lionel Buell was putting money into the venture as a silent partner, and Myron was to be sent away for training to manage it. Albert reported this to Janice. Without hesitation she said, "Put in a counter bid. Can we go out to see L.R?"

When they arrived at New Skye she came right to the point.

"Louis, how would you like to be my partner in the tractor and machinery business? I'll put in the money an' you manage it. You take forty cents off the dollar after expenses? In a couple of years we'll look at the deal again."

"I thought you said I could start a seed business here."

"What's wrong with doin' both? The Swanson's up the road have a store, a grain-seed business, a mill, an' unless I beat them out of their bid to get this tractor dealership, they'll be doin' that too,"

"You biddin' against them, Janice?"

"Only if you're interested, Louis."

He laughed and said, "Sure, why not. But you're goin' to have to get me some help."

"You look around. I'm sure we have a chance of gettin' the dealership. You only have to say the word an' I'll go for it."

"Go for it, then."

While they sat there talking over details, Janice was surprised to see Mark's mother walk in carrying a pie. She noticed how L.R.'s face brightened. Mildred was slightly flustered when she saw them and said, "I'm sorry, Louis, I didn't know you had company."

"Not to worry, Mildred," he said, "This here's Janice O'Neill and her lawyer, Albert Stephenson."

"Janice and I have met. How are you dear? How do you do Mr. Stephenson? Mark has told me about you and Pius."

L.R. had become acquainted with Mildred when he called to the manse to see Mark. They liked each other and talked about plants and flowers. She had shown him the Bobby Rose and told him the story behind it.

He said to her, "You know, he mightn't make it through a winter here. That's the worst about the Island, summer's too short an' the winter's too hard and long. She's in the way of everything that blows in from the ocean an it sticks to her like snow on a fence post. It kills things."

She thought about Mollie and the baby and how it nearly killed Mark's spirit. One thing led to another; and over a cup of tea, he told her about his grandfather teaching him how to preserve herbs and seeds and about his plans to grow and export them. Since then they met often. She liked his quiet manner, and they were both comfortable with each other.

One evening he said, "Mildred, I'm a bit troubled. I'm a half-breed, an' the people around here might talk bad about you visitin' a half-breed man."

She smiled and said, "Louis, you might be a half-breed, but that doesn't make you half a man. You're my friend. I spent my life living in a situation where appearances were all important. When that changed I vowed I'd never to do it again."

Another evening he had asked her if she would be interested in going into the seed business with him, and after spending a sleepless night mulling it over she ran out of reasons why she shouldn't. Now in front of Janice and Albert in Betty Logan's kitchen, L.R., said, "Janice, Mildred's interested in the seed business. I have asked her to come in with me. That suit you?"

"That's a great idea, Louis. It'll give you a bit more time to look after the other business too."

Mildred had noticed how much happier Mark was since Janice had come into the picture. As she and Albert were leaving, Mildred whispered to her that Mark was home in the Manse. Janice, in turn asked Albert if he minded going back alone. "I think I'll stay out here at the Ewarts,"

There was a bit of chill in the air, so she lit a fire in the parlour before phoning Mark.

"Hi, there. I'm at the Ewarts. It would be some nice to see you."

He was soon on the doorstep. Janice put her arms around him and kissed him. The only light in the parlour was from the fire. She threw a rug in front of it and sat down. He joined her. They were ready to make love. They luxuriated in the feel, taste and smell of each other. They slumbered, awakened and made love again. Later, she said to him, "I wonder what's down the road for us."

"I don't know Janice. I don't count on the future anymore."
An atom of fear rose in her.

Forty-six

Machum on the Stand

After a week, the public was readmitted to court. Emerson Duncan called Dr. Machum who testified that Charlie while abnormal, simple-minded perhaps, was not insane. Emerson bowed to the judge.

"My Lord, the Prosecution rests."

"Thank you, Mr. Duncan. Mr. McQuaid do you wish to question Dr. Machum?"

"Yes Your Worship."

Pius took his time. Dr. Machum by virtue of his position was a man who made most Islanders apprehensive. Having a family member under his care was something people felt ashamed of. He was referred to derisively as the doctor in charge of the "bug house"–a dark building hidden away in the woods. The derision, however, was only a way of dealing with an unspoken dread of ending up there. Emerson had been deferential, now everyone waited to see how Pius would handle him.

"Doctor, is it your opinion that the defendant knew what he was doing when he shot Freddy Fenlon?"

"Yes."

"Given that may be true, can you say he knew *why* he was doing it?"

"I don't know what you mean exactly?"

"Well is it possible he acted under a compulsion?"

"I don't think so, no."

The jury looked mystified.

Pius explained, "When we farmers talk about crop rotation and fallow fields, people from the city might have *an idea* of what we mean, but they don't understand the meaning of those terms in exactly the way we do. When a couple of you psychiatrist fellas get together and talk about *compulsion* you have an exact meaning, right?"

"I suppose."

"Will you please explain what *you* mean when you use the word 'compulsion', Doctor?"

"It's an irresistible urge to perform an irrational act."

"Meaning they can't help themselves, like?"

"They can't help the urge."

"And if the urge is powerful enough they can't stop themselves—so powerful in fact they don't even stop to think about the act even though they might know the act is wrong. How would you describe the state of that person's mind?"

"They would have a mental illness."

The judge who was feeling uncomfortable at this line of questioning, snapped at Pius, "Mr. McQuaid this is a court of law, not a classroom. The doctor is here to give expert opinion not to teach us about psychiatry."

"Begging your Lordship's pardon, but is not a court of law a place for us to judge the fitness of our fellow human being's behaviour, and before we can justly do that must we not take advantage of whatever knowledge will shed light on that behaviour?"

"Don't presume to teach me about what a court of law is or is not. Is that clear? Get on with it."

"Begging your Lordship's pardon. There is no way I can presume to teach your Lordship anything."

Pilchard wanted to tick him off but was afraid if he did, he might draw attention to the fact that Pius was being sarcastic when most in the court might not have realized he was. The judge waved his hand impatiently for him to continue. Pius's jibe, however, did not entirely go unnoticed, and light laughter rippled through the spectators.

He continued, "So doctor, they would have a mental illness? Could compulsions of that magnitude drive people to commit heinous acts?

"Yes they could."

"Might they be suffering from extreme fear?"

"They could."

"Might they hear voices?"

"Yes, if they are insane."

"Might a person's illness have been caused by brain damage at birth or through an accident later in life?

"Yes."

"Is it possible that Charlie Ewart might be such a person? A person who can carry out his day to day God given tasks but then suddenly something triggers a memory and a compulsion takes over?

"I don't think so in his case."

"I am not asking you what you think is his case, doctor, I'm asking you if it's possible?

"Well you see...."

"Please answer my question, Doctor. Is it possible?"

"Yes, it might."

"Doctor. Did you examine Charlie Ewart for the possibility of him suffering from a *dementia praecox*?"

"No."

"No?"

Pius was incredulous. He turned to the judge and in a voice laced with contempt said, "No more questions from *this* expert witness, my Lord."

The jury looked mystified as did most of the spectators. The court was adjourned until the following Tuesday when Pius would present the case for the defence.

Forty-seven

Myra's Nemesis

"You get out here, Lionel, right away," Myra yelled into the phone.

Lionel poured a splash of rum into his coffee and tried to figure out what might be bothering her. Had the Mounties been out to look at the books? If they ever compared the cash flow with the actual business accounts of the store and the feed-mill, that could spell trouble. Well I can trust Myra not to cave-in, he told himself. Did they take Myron away for questioning? That would certainly upset her, she hovered over him like a mother buzzard. If they did take Myron, that could be dangerous, because the little weasel would spill his guts under pressure. No use callin' Wittigar until I find out what it's all about, he concluded. Well I suppose I'd better head out and see her.

When he arrived she closed and locked the store door. He had never seen her so livid.

"What's up, Myra?"

She threw a telegram at him.

"Read that!"

It was from the tractor and farm equipment manufacturer telling her that her bid for the dealership had been turned down in favour of another bidder.

"Do you know who it is?" Lionel asked.

"I've a damn good idea. That Janice Fenlon, that's who."
"How can you find out for sure?"
"Easy. I'll ask her."
She called town and got connected.
"Is this Janice Fenlon?"
"This is Janice O'Neill. Who's this?" Janice asked knowing full well who it was.
"Myra Swanson. I wanna ask you somethin'. You goin' into the tractor business now?"
"That's right, Myra."
"Well, may you roast in hell for a whorin' bitch!"
"Don't bite that tongue Myra in case you poison yourself," Janice said.

Myra crashed the phone down, her huge bosom heaving and her face mottled purple with anger. Lionel pulled out a hip flask and poured her a drink.

"Sit down Myra. You're not gonna get anywhere throwin' your weight around. Here take a swig. It'll settle you. We'll talk."

She gulped down the whiskey.

"Now Myra, we're gonna really miss out on somethin' good if we don't get that dealership. More an' more tractors is comin' on the Island an' we'll be gettin' in on the ground floor."

"What are you, Lionel, deaf, blind and dumb? We have lost it to that slut."

"Now, now, Myra, there's a nicer way to catch flies besides shit. Try a bit of honey."

Myra grunted at him and poured herself another drink.

"Lionel that one's bought up a lot of my debts. I'm losin' my trade, an' now she's pulled this one."

Lionel thought a moment, then asked, "Why's she doin' that Myra? You musta rubbed her the wrong way, now. What happened?"

Myra pouted, then said, "Well, Myron went after Ruth Ewart in the barn, and the minister was down there an' he hit Myron, an' then he come up here shootin' off his mouth an'…."

"An' you bad-mouthed him back, right? Look Myron's stupid. Is he worth losin' a good deal for? She's outsmarted you an' she's got the money and obviously the brains to do it. Now what else did you do?"

"I put in a complaint about Kerr."

"Well he's a friend of hers an' she's gonna do you in, Myra. I don't wanna lose this tractor deal. It could be worth thousands down the road an' you have the perfect setup for it. Now listen to me. You get her back on the phone an' tell her you're sorry an' ask her if you can come and talk with her tomorrow. She's just doin' it to spite you. Why the hell does she want a tractor dealership an' her livin' a way down there in Boston? She might be glad to get out of it. Or worse still, she might sell it to somebody else. There's plenty that'll buy into it. Be nice Myra an' be prepared to make her a good offer."

Myra finished Lionel's hip flask and went to the phone.

"Janice? This is Myra Swanson again. Look dear, I'm sorry."

"For what?"

"For not makin' you more welcome. I was just sittin' here thinkin' I've known you since you were a little girl. You're a right smart one Janice."

"What do you want, Myra?"

"To meet me for a little talk, like."

"What will we talk about?"

"Why don't we wait an' discuss it tomorrow, dear."

"Now or never."

"Well not on the phone. You know how everybody listens in?"

"I don't mind. They're all my friends. I'm gonna hang up if you don't state your business."

"Well it's about *the thing,* you know?"

"All right I know what you're talkin' about. What about it?"
"Well I'd be willin' to work out a good deal with you for it."
Janice's silence seemed an eternity to Myra.
"Listen Myra, I'll tell you what. You write a couple of letters. One to the Church tellin' them you withdraw your complaint against the Reverend Kerr an' that you made a mistake, an' another to the Reverend Kerr apologizing to him. Put a copy of that letter in the one to the Church. Now you send them letters to me by hand for first thing in the mornin' an I'll see they're delivered. You do that an' when I get them, I give you my word there'll be a good chance I'll back out from the you know what."
"Are you sure, now Janice?"
"Look Myra, what choice do you have?"
Myra snapped into the phone, "Alright then. I'll do it."
"Thank you, Myra. By eight o'clock in the mornin'. An' Myra?"
"What?"
"I forgive you."
"What for?"
"For anything nasty I'm sure you've said about me."
When Myra told Lionel, he said, "There now, good on ye Myra. Get busy. You've letters to write. I'll take them in with me."
The next afternoon, Myra phoned Janice again, "Did you get the letters, Janice?"
"Yes, thank you, Myra. I mailed them out as soon as the post office opened."
"An' did you get in touch with the company?"
"Ah Myra," Janice said, "I wanted to do it but my partner wouldn't hear of it."
"An' who's your damned partner?"
"Mr. L.R. Arsenault. Know him?"
When Janice saw Mark she handed him Myra's letter.
"Here, a little present for you."

Forty-eight

Pius Presents

On the first day of Pius' presentation for the Defence, the courtroom was packed as usual. It was stormy and pouring rain. Excitement was high and the smell of damp wool permeated the courtroom. Water flowed down the long windows distorting the shapes of the trees and houses outside. Thunder rumbled and growled in the distance and lightning played over the sky. As the storm moved closer the courtroom darkened, and fusillades of thunder grew louder until they cracked overhead like cannon. Long veins of lightening preceded each ear-splitting bang, filling the darkened court with garish light. Some of the women screamed and the men let out spontaneous shouts of "O-hoh!"

Pius waited until the elements and the people settled down. Then he strode forward and called as his first witness, Inspector Rutter.

"Inspector Rutter, on the day you arrested Charles Ewart, you made a second arrest in connection with your investigation, true?"

"Yes. Mrs. Betty Logan."

"Under what charge?"

"Suspicion of the murder of Freddy Fenlon."

"What made you suspect her?"

"She admitted to stabbing him in the arm with a knife earlier in the afternoon. So until the actual cause of death could be verified, I was obliged to charge her. She was subsequently released."

"Did she tell you why she stabbed Freddy Fenlon?"

"Yes, she claimed he raped her that afternoon."

Betty lowered her head, feeling the eyes of everyone burn into her.

Pius continued, "I have here Mrs. Logan's statement in which she says that Freddy Fenlon came to her house looking for an old army ammunition box containing money. Has that box been found?"

"No. But some loose money was found in the attic where the alleged rape was supposed to have taken place."

"Did Mrs. Logan show signs of having been in a struggle?"

"Yes. She was badly beaten and we sent her to the hospital under police surveillance after the arrest."

"Do you believe she was raped?"

Emerson jumped to his feet shouting, "Objection, my Lord. We are trying a murder case here not a rape."

Pius responded, "My Lord, I'm attempting to establish that there were other sinister circumstances that took place in Betty Logan's home that could affect the outcome for my client."

The judge knew Pius was trying to implicate the rum-runners. He was going to stop him; however, in the interest of appearing objective at all costs he overruled Emerson's objection, but added, "I caution you Mr. McQuaid, don't wander too far off the track."

Pius bowed and turned back to the Inspector.

"Inspector. What possible reasons could Freddy Fenlon have for beating Mrs. Logan?"

"Well it is alleged he wanted money that belonged to him that Mrs. Logan was keeping from him."

"What money?"

"Mrs. Logan in her statement alleges that Mr. Fenlon and her late husband Jack Logan were rum runners together and that Mr. Fenlon was looking for his share."

Pius paused to let the information sink in. He then told the judge he had no further questions. Emerson declined to cross examine. Pius called Betty Logan. She was agitated and wept continuously.

"Mrs. Logan. Were you and Freddy Fenlon lovers?"

"No. He tried but I hated him. He was drunk when he come over."

"Tell the court what happened on the afternoon of Fenlon's visit to you."

Betty told her story to a shocked but titillated courtroom.

"Mrs. Logan were you aware that your late husband might have been dealing in rum running?"

"No. But I knew there was somethin' goin' on. Freddy Fenlon and him used to go out in a truck and not come home 'til the next mornin'."

"Did you know there was money hidden in the house?"

"No. Jack never told me his business. He was always cryin' poor mouth."

"Was there much money in the box when you found it?"

"Yes. I never seen that much money in my life. It was filled with fifty an' hundred dollar bills."

Pius then questioned her about the fern and got her to relate how she told Charlie that if it ever died the sand dunes would catch fire and that the Island would be finished.

"Why did you tell him that?"

"Oh, it was just an old tale my mother used to tell me when I was a little girl."

Emerson accepted the invitation to cross-examine Betty. He stared hard at her with his deep blue eyes before questioning.

"Mrs. Logan, were you and Charlie Ewart lovers?"

Betty broke down and the judge told her to get a grip on herself.

"Mrs. Logan were you and Charlie Ewart lovers?"

Betty's mind grappled with whether or not to tell the truth. The entire courtroom seemed to press in on her. She was carrying Charlie's baby. Charlie was looking over at her. She longed to tell him.

Emerson's voice cut into her again. "Are you lovers?"

She looked over at Charlie and said quietly, "I love Charlie, he's the sweetest gentlest person."

"Mrs. Logan, *were you lovers?*"

"No!" She almost shouted. Then composing herself said, "No, friends that's all. All we done was talk with me doin' most of the talkin'."

Emerson gave an exaggerated thank you, then asked her, "Was Charlie Ewart the first to see and talk to you after Freddy Fenlon had allegedly raped you?"

"Yes."

"Did you tell him about it?"

"I forget."

"Did you tell him about the money?"

"I forget."

"Mrs. Logan, I suggest that you did, and that Charlie Ewart was angry. And he decided to get back at Freddy Fenlon, and he also decided to get all that money off him."

"Charlie wouldn't do the likes of that, an' it was Sarah I told."

"Yes and she testified how she flew into a jealous rage and attacked Mr. Fenlon."

Pius protested vigorously on the grounds of supposition and leading the witness. Betty was hysterical and the judge ordered her removed until she got control of herself. Emerson said he was finished anyhow. Pius then called Sarah to the stand. He specifically wanted to know the details of Betty Logan's state when she found her, and what Betty had told her about the money and Freddy's remarks about rum running. He gently persuaded Sarah to tell the story in her own words.

Emerson objected, "My Lord, Miss Ewart has already given us these details. It's a matter of record."

Pius said, "My Lord, the Defence knows that. I would ask the Court's indulgence, because I think the context is important."

Pilchard told Sarah to continue.

"When I went into Betty's kitchen, Charlie and her was sittin' in the dark across the table from each other. They weren't talkin' just sittin'. I lit a lamp an' saw the state poor Betty was in. Her dress was all tore off her an' her face was bruised with dried blood on it. I sent Charlie home an' Betty told me what happened to her. She said Freddy took the box with the money, an' he told her the money come from rum runnin'. She said he was drunk."

Pilchard looked down over the spectators and met Colonel Wittigar's hooded eyes. He stood, but before he turned to go he fixed the judge with his stare and banged his cane on the end of a row of seats. The whack resounded through the court like a rifle shot making people jump. He bowed to the judge and begged the Court's pardon, then turned and walked out with all eyes following his white suit as it went through the door. It was a clear warning to Pilchard. He glared at Pius and told him to continue.

"When you first saw Charlie with Betty, was he angry?" Pius asked

"No. Charlie never gets mad."

"Where was Freddy when you attacked him?"

"He was in his porch with oilskins on and he was trimmin' a hurricane lantern."

"What did Freddy Fenlon do to you?"

"He put his hand over my face and beat my head against the wall then he kicked me in the stomach and side when I fell. If it wasn't for Ruthie he would have killed me."

"What did Ruthie do?"

"She jumped on him to get him away from me, but he got her by the throat an' dragged her out to the yard an' throttled her 'til she dropped. Ruthie told me when she come to she seen him walkin' away towards the shore carryin' his lantern."

"Now Miss Ewart, this is very important. Was Charlie angry when you told him what happened?"

"No."

"Try to remember exactly what you an' Ruth said then."

Sarah thought hard, knowing she must recall everything accurately. Pius told her to take her time. Then she said, "I said Freddy was just like a wild beast, an' Ruthie said, 'If you had a dog like that you'd shoot him.'"

"Then what happened?"

"Well Charlie said he had to finish up an' left us. I thought he was goin' back to the barn but as it turned out he was goin' for his gun to shoot Freddy."

"How do you know he shot Freddy?"

"When he come back he had the gun an' he told us."

"What exactly did he say?"

"He said poor Freddy went back an' he put him down with two shots."

Pius said he had no more questions.

Emerson declined the invitation to cross-examine, and the judge adjourned the proceedings until the following morning.

The rain was still pouring down when the people were leaving the courthouse. The thunder had passed but it still could be heard rumbling in the distance. Far out on the horizon lightening trickled down from an inky blue sky onto a rough dark sea.

Forty-nine

Pius Continues

The next morning the courtroom was flooded with bright sunlight that penetrated the judge's retina, paining him. He found it excruciating just to be alive. The evening before, Colonel Wittigar had visited him.

"What the hell is going on in that Goddamn courtroom, Harry? McQuaid's running rings around you."

Harry Pilchard was a man so far gone in corruption and drink his feelings drifted from practically everything that was meaningful, but a mere vestige of conscience was still lodged in his dying soul, and it tormented him. He was in that stage of drink when his deeper voice told him he was loathsome. He hated Wittigar standing before him smugly smoking a cigar and questioning him. He swallowed a drink of scotch and said, "Why don't you read the Goddamn papers?"

"That's not what I mean, Harry. I mean that our operation's not far enough removed from the picture. Pius McQuaid's raising too many questions, and you're letting him get away with it."

"Who's up there on the bench, you or me? Get the hell out of here, Wittigar, an' leave the courtroom stuff to me."

Wittigar tried to get assurances out of him about the outcome, but Pilchard, overcome with rage threw a full tumbler of scotch in his face. The colonel lifted his cane and setting its point at the center of the judge's chest pushed him back into his chair.

"Listen you drunken fart, you know how this farce has to end. See that it does."

Before he left, he swung his stick at his lordship's bottle smashing it. When Pilchard heard the door bang shut, he got a new bottle and drank from it until he passed out.

As Pius strode forward, the sun playing on his red hair, Pilchard wished he had adjourned the court for another day. Noticing the judge's discomfort, Pius said in a deliberately loud voice, "I wish to call the defendant Charles Ewart, your Lordship." Then going closer to the bench said in a low voice "Do you mind if I have a quiet word with him first just to help him settle into it?"

Pilchard closed his eyes and shook his head and motioned with a weary hand for him to go ahead. When Charlie saw Pius walking towards him beaming, he stood up and leaned over the rail of the dock. Pius spoke softly to him, pointing to the jury.

"Now Charlie all those people over there in the jury want to hear about why and how you put poor Freddy down. It's important for them to know. So when I tell you to, you tell them, and if you get stuck I'll help you. All right?"

Charlie nodded.

"Charlie," Pius began. "Would you please tell us if Pepper was a bad dog?"

The judge squinted at Pius and wagged a warning finger at him. Pius hearing a mild ripple from the spectators knew he was getting the focus and attention he wanted.

"My Lord, I know the question may sound somewhat strange, but believe me it is germane."

"What has Pepper being a good or bad dog got to do with anything. I will tolerate you Mr. McQuaid to a point, but let me caution you, that point has almost been reached."

Pius bowed, and addressing the Court in general, said, "My Lord, thank you for the Court's indulgence, but I intend to show there is a direct link between a dog called Pepper and the death of Frederick Fenlon."

There was restrained laughter and a shuffling of feet from the spectators. If Emerson Duncan had a flaw it was that he couldn't resist making a bad joke. He called out, "My Lord the Crown received no notice of this dog, does my learned friend intend to call it to the stand?"

The courtroom burst into laughter. His Lordship banged them to silence again, and growled, "Mr. McQuaid, you see what your foolery is doing? This is not a circus."

Pius slowly positioned himself and answered in a voice clear and loud enough so that not a single word was missed.

"My Lord, believe me I *am* deadly serious. My client may lose his life. I am well aware that in this courtroom is practiced the finest and fairest system of justice ever produced by mankind– *British Common Law*. It is a system your Lordship and I are both honoured to serve. Your Lordship is quite correct. It is not a circus, nor is it a cruel Roman court. My learned friend saw fit to make a joke, not I. A man is on trial for his life."

The courtroom went so silent the only thing to be heard was the rustling of the artists' paper as they sketched Pius and Charlie, the Judge and Emerson Duncan. Pius' allusion to the Roman court touched Pilchard's remaining vestige of conscience. He wanted to attack Pius but knew he dare not. Instead he called the two councillors to the bench.

Leaning over, he spoke behind his hand, "McQuaid, you cut out the preaching and histrionics and you, Duncan, one more bad joke out of you and I'll cite you for contempt."

Both men bowed to the bench. Emerson returned to his seat berating himself for being stupid, and Pius walked back to Charlie, conscious that he had the court's undivided attention. He repeated his question, "Charlie, would you please tell the court if Pepper was a bad dog?"

Charlie looked off into the distance and said in his simple way, "No. Poor Pepper went back, like."

"And what did you do?"

"I put him down like Freddy told me. Freddy tied Pepper while I got the gun."

"You shot Pepper?"

"Yes with two shots an' ammunition's not cheap."

"Were you mad at Pepper?"

"No. Sad. He turned wolf an' entereth the fold."

"What did Freddy Fenlon do?"

"He went back an' entereth the fold."

"Were you angry at Freddy?"

"No. I put him down. Used two shots."

"What did you do with Pepper's body?"

"Buried him. I have to bury Freddy."

"Charlie, did you light a fire on the dune?"

"No. The dune caught fire because Granddaddy died an' that's the end of the Island."

"When you found Freddy at the shore was the fire already burning?"

"Yes."

"And what else did you see down there on the shore?"

"Angel lights dancin' on the water."

Pius brought over the money belt. He held it up to Charlie.

"Charlie do you know whose belt this is?"

"Freddy's.'

"Did you take it off his body?"

"No."

"Did you throw kerosene over Freddy's body and try to burn it?"

"No. I have to bury him."

"Charlie. Do you know where an army ammunition box full of money is?"

Charlie looked puzzled.

"No. What box?"

"It doesn't matter Charlie."

Pius, turned and nodded to Albert who then lifted a large object wrapped loosely in brown paper. He uncovered it. It was Betty's fern, it's fronds wilted and brown. Charlie recognized the brass pot. He called out,

"Granddaddy's dead. But Grandma's alive so it's all right now, Betty."

Pius turned to the Judge and said, "My Lord, I know all this sounds bizarre to the court, but it makes perfect sense to the defendant. Will the Court indulge hearing a short explanation?"

Pilchard, though he was intrigued, knew that an explanation could lead to a further implication of the rum running operation.

"No Mr. McQuaid. Let the testimony stand on its own. You will have ample opportunity for that in your summation. To do so now could be construed as leading your witness to a conclusion."

The jury looked disappointed. Pius, however, was not concerned, for he knew Philip Dixon's testimony would provide the explanation and would be given more weight because of the delay. He thanked Charlie and told the court he had no further questions. Emerson accepted his option to cross-examine. He moved to the dock with Machum's affidavit in his hand.

"My Lord, I would like to refer back to Dr. Machum's affidavit."

He then turned to Charlie and said, "Now, Mr. Ewart, you have regaled us with your stories about Pepper your dog, the Granddaddy fern, the dunes catching fire and angel lights on the water, but none of it has absolutely anything to do with the facts of this case. The first fact being by your own admission you shot Freddy Fenlon twice with a twelve-gauge shotgun and killed him.

Other facts are Freddy Fenlon's money belt was removed and found hidden in your tool shed, and Freddy Fenlon's body was doused in kerosene and burned. I suggest, Mr. Ewart, that as Dr. Machum has stated in his sworn affidavit and under oath here in this courtroom, that you are a cunning fellow."

Pius objected, "My Lord, my friend is not questioning the defendant but is making a speech characterizing him."

The judge still upset at Emerson's bad joke sustained the objection.

"The Crown will confine itself to questions."

Emerson was at a loss.

"All right then, the facts. Did you kill Freddy Fenlon?"

"Yes."

The judge interrupted, "Mr. Emerson, the defendant has already admitted to all that. Unless you have some new facts to bring to light I'll ask him to stand down."

"My Lord that is true, the defendant has admitted to the killing. He has recognized the money belt taken from the body, but...."

"That's enough Mr. Emerson. Have you any further questions?"

"No my Lord."

Pius called Philip Dixon. After he was sworn in, his credentials cited and approved by the Crown, Pius commenced.

"Dr. Dixon, I have here your affidavit the substance of which states that in your opinion Charles Ewart could be suffering from three mental disorders which seem to be acting in concert with each other. Did I interpret your findings accurately?"

"Well yes, to a point, perhaps. When you say they act in concert with each other—that can be misleading. It would be more accurate to say they are reactive or causal."

Pius noticing some of the jury frowning, quickly asked, "You mean they get each other going, like?"

"Yes."

"Now, Doctor let me see if I can follow what you say about these diseases. The first one you mention is called *dementia praecox*. You say that this is a progressive disease. Does that mean a person who has it doesn't get better?"

"They get worse."

"So. A person say with this disease last year might be worse this year? What way does it effect a person?"

"They hallucinate. They are withdrawn."

"Hallucinate? Meaning they can hear voices or see things that aren't there? And they could be thought of as extremely shy and quiet or unsociable?"

"Yes."

"Does it run in families?"

"Very definitely. But it usually doesn't show itself until adolescence."

"How do you psychiatrists define it?"

"As a psychosis."

"As madness, insanity?"

"Yes."

Pius painstakingly took Philip through his affidavit, teaching the jury without them realizing it. His apparent intense interest and his seeming desire to learn carried them with him. He had Philip explain how a suggestion could trigger off Charlie's memory of his dog Pepper and create a compulsive drive to kill Freddy. He explained that Charlie's childlike nature would be unlikely to make him want to kill out of sexual jealousy or to rob, even. Pius could tell the jury was absolutely fascinated, as were the press and the rest of the spectators in the courtroom. Only his Lordship Harold Pilchard sat with apparent disinterest. After taking Philip through his explanations, Pius asked, "How then can a person like Charlie be a killer?"

Philip paused before answering.

"Yes he can be a killer all right but an innocent one."

"An innocent killer. How so?"

"He's as innocent as any eleven year old doing what a good boy does. Doing what he's told."

"Doctor Dixon. Charlie mentioned seeing angel lights dancing on the water. Would these have been hallucinations?'

"Yes and no. He might have seen real lights on the water, but because of his state of mind interpret them as angel lights."

"Like the lights of boats, for example."

At this Pilchard said, "Mr. McQuaid. All this is supposition and opinion in the extreme, and I cannot allow you to continue this psychiatry lecture any longer. Please wind up your examination of the witness if you have no more actual facts to go on."

Pius said, "I have no further questions for Dr. Dixon and at this point the defence rests."

"Does the Prosecution wish to cross-examine?"

Duncan stood and smiling said, "Thank you your Lordship, no. Your Lordship's remark regarding opinion and supposition in the extreme just about says it all as far as the Crown is concerned."

The court adjourned for the day. That evening the papers contained sketches of Pius and a full transcription of his speech about British justice. There was a sketch of Pius holding up the dead fern and Charlie forlornly gazing at it. Philip Dixon's testimony was reprinted almost verbatim. One editorial was headlined, IS RUM RUNNING INVOLVED IN THE FENLON MURDER? Interest in the trial reached a new plateau. Sympathy for Charlie was widespread while Freddy Fenlon emerged as a villain, a mystery man and a rum runner. Sketches of Sarah and Betty represented them as distressed and tragic figures.

The next morning people travelled from all over the Island to try to get into the trial. Hundreds milled around the courthouse. Ministers led groups in prayer, and youths and boys climbed the trees outside the courthouse windows to catch a glimpse of Charlie.

When the court assembled, the judge invited the Crown to make its summation.

Emerson bowed to the bench and then with pointed seriousness addressed the jury. He looked at each one in turn, then began.

"Gentlemen, you have the difficult and painful task of deciding the guilt or innocence of Charles Ewart. Difficult, because Charles Ewart is not a habitual criminal but has been a decent hard working Island farmer all his life. However, he has taken the life of another human being. He shot Freddy Fenlon to death—in cold blood. He claims that Freddy Fenlon went back, became like a wild animal and that's why he killed him. Well, gentlemen, maybe the same could be said for Charlie Ewart, himself, that maybe he went back.

"But we can't deal in *maybes* here, we must look at the bare facts in the clear light of the law. The law must always be safeguarded against sentimentality or else the innocent will not be protected, and justice will not be served.

"Charles Ewart is charged with murder in the first degree. You have heard the testimony and have seen the material evidence—you have also heard it from the defendant himself. *I killed Freddy Fenlon with two shots.*

"On the afternoon of the day of the murder, Charles Ewart found the woman—who declared her love for him in this very courtroom—found her in a dreadful state—clothes torn, bruised and bleeding, allegedly raped by Freddy Fenlon. Shortly before finishing up his barn work that evening, he discovers that, that same man has savagely beaten both his sisters!

"Now, did he fly into an angry passion? No. In the first instance he went quietly home and attended his chores. In the second instance when his sisters whom he loved, were beaten, did he fly into a rage? No. He said simply, 'I have to finish.' Finish what? We know now he meant to finish off Freddy Fenlon.

"No wild rage. No great show of passion. He coolly made up his mind to shoot Freddy Fenlon. So, he calmly got his twelve gauge, loaded it with a shell in each barrel—*two shots*—and tracked him down. 'I should have used only one shot' he said. He shot him first in the stomach. When he saw he was not dead, he calmly pointed the gun at his victim's head and blew the top of it away.

"He planned to shoot him in the head in the first place. But don't forget, Freddy Fenlon was facing his killer—all the wounds show that. Charlie aimed, Freddy moved forward. The first shot did not go where it was calculated to go. So a second shot was necessary. Charles Ewart knew exactly what he was doing every measured step of the way before and after the murder–no anger, no outrage, no blind passion. The killing was planned–premeditated.

"Was Charlie Ewart insane? Is he insane? The distinguished Dr. Dixon, from Montreal, testified that he was insane all his life. Yet he grew up like any normal boy. Went to school. Learned farming at his father's hand. Ran that farm successfully after his father's death. Sang in the church choir. Is a gifted singer. Attracted the love of a normal woman. He can read, write and calculate. Like all good farmers he knew the value of a hard-earned dollar.

"The money belt was on the body at the time of the shooting—crime lab evidence proved that. Yet that money belt was removed from the body and found hidden in Charlie Ewart's tool shed–*a fact.*

"The defence has raised the possibility of a third party involvement—very far-fetched. His kerosene can—clearly marked with his name scratched into it - was found beside the fire upon which Freddy Fenlon's body was found. The police testified there was no evidence of other footprints—nothing pointing to the presence of a third party, or parties. *Facts* not phantoms. *Facts* that stand out clearly over talk about sand dunes catching fire, dead ferns, and angel lights.

"Dr. Machum, our own resident psychiatrist, and head of our insane asylum has stated that while Charles Ewart might have certain abnormalities—meaning he might be a bit odd, he is not insane, but that he has cunning.

"Gentlemen, the Crown has clearly laid the facts before you. It is your duty to consider those facts in a clear reasonable manner so that our cherished law that says *Thou shalt not kill* is protected. If you do your duty, you will return a verdict of Guilty of murder in the first degree—premeditated murder. Thank you."

Emerson Duncan bowed gracefully both to the jury and to the bench. Justice Pilchard invited the Defence to give its summation. Pius moved slowly, his blue eyes bright with intensity. He resisted smiling giving his face a look of deep concern. Before speaking he shook his head sadly.

"My Lord. Gentlemen of the jury. My learned friend is quite correct when he states that the Law must be preserved to serve and protect the innocent. But let us not forget that the law was born, not out of harshness, but out of mercy. It seeks not only to protect innocent people, but the *ideal* of innocence itself.

"Freddy Fenlon is dead—so we will never know for sure why he was on that sand dune. That is where Charlie Ewart found him and shot him. What was he doing there? We will never know for certain.

"We do know that he did wreak terrible violence on the persons of Betty Logan, Sarah Ewart and Ruth Ewart. There is factual evidence that a struggle did take place in the attic of Betty Logan's home where Betty Logan was violated. Fenlon's blood was found on the floor and on Betty Logan's clothing. Money was found scattered about, proving that money matters were involved. The ammunition box supposedly containing the rest of the money has not been found. A substantial amount of money was found in Freddy Fenlon's money belt—a very large amount for a hired man. Perhaps someday it will come to light just where that money came from. But in the here and now we cannot know for certain.

"We can only guess that Freddy Fenlon after beating Ruth and Sarah made his way down to the shore and lit a fire on the dune. Why? Perhaps it was to signal boats on the water, the lights of which appeared to Charlie Ewart in his state of mind as angel lights dancing on the water.

"The truth hidden from us in the present may surface later. What is cloudy now may be pristine clear in the future. As the Bible says, we see through a glass darkly at first. We may find out that men in boats were being signalled from shore. They heard the shots—saw even, what happened—and then put ashore, took Freddy Fenlon's money belt, covered up their tracks, then hid that money belt in Charlie Ewart's tool shed. But we cannot tell for sure, *now*. Nor can we say for sure *now*, that Charlie Ewart took that money belt, or that Charlie Ewart lit that fire. There are no facts to substantiate that he did or did not.

"My Learned Friend accuses me of being far fetched, but given the short time he left his sisters, got his gun, walked to the shore, shot Freddy Fenlon and returned to his sisters, I doubt if he had time to gather wood for the fire, remove the money belt, douse the body with kerosene and drag it onto the fire. That seems far fetched to me.

"No traces of kerosene were found on Charlie's clothing. And the gun. Where was the gun found? Not in his tool shed, but in the porch of his house where he simply left it against the wall. Does it not seem likely that he would have hid his gun in the tool shed, too, had he gone directly back there to hide the money belt and kerosene can? I think it unlikely that Charlie Ewart lit that fire and stole and hid that money belt. There is too much doubt, too much *reasonable doubt* for it to be taken seriously.

"I go into all this detail because the Crown has attempted to plant in your minds the idea that Charlie deliberately and cunningly tried to burn the body to get rid of it, and that he greedily stole the money, therefore characterizing him as a cold-hearted, and premeditating murderer. Because of the substantial doubt surrounding the circumstances, I beg you to remove *that* thought from your minds if it is in there at all."

Pius let his words sink in, then he pointed to Charlie who was leaning forward resting his chin on his arms on the rail of the dock. His eyes were closed. He was not sleeping, but musing in his head.

Pius continued, "The Crown has tried to make a case of Charlie Ewart being a normal boy who learned his lessons at school, and became a good farmer and so on. But I tell you, Charlie was not a normal boy—he only appeared to be so, for hidden deeply within him was his disease, his insanity—a disease lurking deeply in his mind waiting to reveal itself at that time of change when a boy becomes a man.

"In addition, Charlie Ewart had an abnormally harsh and difficult childhood. He lived in constant fear of his father who beat and bullied him. In one instance he was forced to go into the stall of a frantic mare who had slipped her foal and was made to drag that foal out. She kicked him and he sustained a possible brain injury. Charlie was a boy of eleven years! Charlie Ewart was not a normal boy or man; and through no fault of his own, the condition of his mind kept getting worse.

"Charlie Ewart is not innocent of the death of Freddy Fenlon, *but he did act in innocence.* In the confused and compulsive state of his mind Charlie did what he believed was his painful duty. The deranged state of his mind caused him to reason that Freddy Fenlon was no longer a man but a wild animal.

"Charlie Ewart is innocent of premeditated murder, and if he is found to be guilty of such, our ancient and venerable system of justice will not be served. I ask you gentlemen, in the interest of all that is humane and compassionate to return a verdict of *not guilty by reason of insanity.*"

Justice Pilchard shuffled his papers briefly, made a few quick notes then charged the jury.

"Gentlemen, you have heard the evidence both for and against the accused. Now it is your solemn duty to retire and consider the facts which have been put before you. I charge you that whatever your conclusions, you must arrive at your verdict so that no reasonable doubt remains. Therefore, it is the facts, and only the facts of the case with which you must deal to enable you to reach your decision.

"Let me remind you that Frederick Fenlon's way of life or deeds are not on trial here. Frederick Fenlon is the victim. It is the defendant Charles Ewart who is on trial for murder. The only way we must consider the victim is from the point of view that his life was wilfully taken. It is not our business here to pass judgment on the victim. The accused stands before you. You must assess the facts and answer the question, *did he wilfully take the life of Frederick Fenlon?*

"You have heard references made to rum runners and the possible involvement of a third party or parties. These must not enter into your deliberations, for their existence has merely been guessed at.

"You have heard the testimonies of two learned doctors, Dr. Roger Machum and that of Dr. Philip Dixon. These learned doctors have expressed rational opinions as to the state of the accused's mind at the time of the murder. Yet brilliant and learned as they are they disagree substantially with each other. Therefore, we must conclude that two rational opinions, which contradict each other about the state of a man's mind, do not, and cannot accurately tell the state of a man's mind. Therefore, you cannot treat these opinions as fact. They are inconclusive and cancel each other out.

"You must ask yourselves: *Did the accused kill Frederick Fenlon?* If you conclude that he did so, you must ask yourselves: *Did he know that he was doing it, and if that is what he intentionally set out to do?

"You must retire now to deliberate in a secret place provided for you. You must not under any circumstances discuss this case with anyone other that your fellow jurors. You will be kept under lock and key until you have reached a unanimous decision. At such time you will be returned to this courtroom where your foreman will deliver your verdict. Food and other essentials of life will be taken to you.

"Councillors and officers of the court please remain within a reasonable distance of the courthouse and before you go tell the Clerk how and where you may be reached. This court now stands adjourned until such time as the jury reaches its verdict."

People go about their daily business from sun-up to sun-down thinking the circumstances of their own lives are unique. However, the Charlie Ewart case took them beyond themselves. Charlie's name was on everybody's lips. Newspaper boys were relieved of their bundles as soon as they appeared on the streets. Every aspect of the case was covered–there was even speculation about Colonel Wittigar's dramatic exit from the court. One journalist wrote:

A distinguished Charlottetown citizen, Colonel Walter Wittigar, angrily exited the courtroom banging his cane against a seat. The Colonel, however, acted with gentlemanly decorum when he apologised to Judge Harold Pilchard.

It is believed that Colonel Wittigar feels that the Ewart family is being put through unnecessary tribulation with this trial. When asked why he walked out, the Colonel answered, tersely, "It should have been over and done with before this."

Another newspaper which tended to agree with the Prosecution's point of view that Charlie is a "cunning faker." It reported Wittigar's angry exit as exasperation for wasting the taxpayers money on something that was a foregone conclusion. Readers who held similar or opposing points of view hotly debated them.

Fifty

Mullaly's Operation

There was one person, however, who knew the real reason behind Colonel Wittigar's angry exit from the court–Alicia Bernard. Alicia had an intimate knowledge of the rum-running operation through her late boss and lover, Freeman Mullaly. When it surfaced that rum-running might be involved in the Fenlon murder, she took an active interest in the trial.

Mullaly had owned a lucrative potato warehouse and shipping operation that also doubled as the Island's main storage and distribution point for the smuggling trade. He lived in a large house in an out of the way place where he often entertained mainland guests, associates of Wittikar and his cronies.

Freeman's charm lay in his warmth and affection for people, and he was regarded by the younger set on the Island as a hero of fun and devilment. He was intelligent, good humoured and openly contemptuous of organized religion and the moralizing rectitude of "respectable people."

After the meeting at the Abby Hotel by the "Right People", word came down that there was to be one last shipment to Boston, and that the authorities would be tipped off about it, thus enabling the Federal authorities in the United States to make a sizable seizure and the Mounties in Canada to make a few arrests. The heat would be taken off the overall smuggling operation on the Island as well as along the east coast of the States. The objective was to create the illusion that the operation on the Island had been smashed, and an Islander, of course, would have to be charged. Hoyt negotiated with Freeman; and for a good price, he agreed to be the sacrificial lamb.

The bust, when it took place, was a combined operation of the Mounties and the FBI. A freight train *en route* to Boston was stopped, and dozens of FBI agents with the help of railroad workers unloaded tons of potatoes before eventually finding cases of liquor hidden beneath them. At the same time, Royal Canadian Mounted Police constables were raiding Mullaly's barn on the Island. The night they called with their warrant to search and seize, a party was in full swing.

"Away you go, boys." Freeman laughed. "Head down to the middle warehouse an' you'll probably get lucky."

The corporal leading the raid called him outside, and grabbed him by the shirt and said, "Listen Mullaly, don't you play the gobshite with me. You'd better enjoy that little soiree yer havin', for it's not goin' to last too long."

He told one of the constables to wait in Mullaly's house and not to let him out of his sight. A girl was dancing on a table. The Mountie told Freeman to get her down.

"Why?" Freeman asked. "Is it was a crime to dance, now?"

"No," the Mountie answered, "but it is to have booze an' women dancin' with their tits hangin' out."

"Well," Freeman answered. "It's all for medicinal purposes. We're all sufferin' from the cold and bein' down in the dumps "

Everybody laughed, including the Mountie. Freeman shouted, "Okay, everybody. Take your medicine, now. One, two, three, down the hatch. Come into the kitchen, Constable, I've got somethin' to show you."

He opened a cupboard and showed the Mountie shelves lined with scotch, rum, gin and rye. Then he poured out a healthy drink of scotch and left it on the counter.

"Isn't it a shame all this good stuff's goin' down the drain? Ah well, excuse me for a minute, I want to tell the boys to take the girls home."

When he came back the tumbler was empty. The Corporal came in and arrested Freeman. Three days later he was arraigned for trial. He pleaded guilty, his trial date was set and he was let out on bail. A week later, the day before the trial, he arranged to have a party to end all parties. People came from near and far—neighbours, people from town—anybody who wanted to drop in was welcome. Fiddle music, singing, dancing and laughter echoed over the fields throughout the night.

The next day when Freeman didn't show up for court the judge issued a bench warrant for his arrest. When the police went out to look for him, they heard wailing coming from the barn. They found Freeman's body hanging from a beam, and a woman desperately trying to lift him to take the strain off his neck. A blackened steel drum close to the body contained the charred remains of notebooks, ledgers and various bills of lading. A thorough search of the house resulted in more liquor being found along with a stash of banknotes.

The headlines were dramatic: *Rum Running Trade Smashed! Ring Leader Kills Himself.* The coroner's report stated that Freeman Joseph Mullaly took his own life while the balance of his mind was disturbed. For a few days, the case of Freeman Mullaly even eclipsed the news items on Charlie Ewart, but people who knew Freeman could not believe that he would do such a thing.

"Nobody loved life more than Freeman," they said. "Wild, yes, but he'd give you the shirt off his back."

The official view was that Freeman hanged himself and the case was officially closed; but in the mind of Alicia Bernard, it was far from closed. Alicia loved Freeman. Of all the women he knew, she was his favourite, and he trusted her more than anyone else in the world. Alicia, who knew she could never have Freeman as her one and only, contented herself by helping him with his books, and sharing his bed whenever he was available.

She was thoroughly acquainted with the rum running operation though none of its inner circle knew she was. They saw her mainly as one of Freeman's whores. The love she had for Freeman was matched by a passionate hate of Colonel Walter Wittigar, who relentlessly pursued her.

As she became more acquainted with Charlie's case she was moved by pity for the Ewarts and Betty Logan. In her mind, the victim Charlie merged with the victim Freeman. She knew that Pilchard's presence on the bench would probably spell Charlie's doom. Her pity for the Ewart's fuelled her anger and hate for Wittigar. She agonized as to whether or not she should go and see Pius, but in the end decided against doing that in favour of another plan for avenging Freeman's death.

Fifty-one

The Verdict

Five hours after the jury was out, Pius and Emerson were called back. The city was taut with expectation. As the jury slowly filed back into the courtroom, Sarah's entire being was concentrated in prayer. The jurors looked strained and tired but otherwise revealed nothing.

Pilchard turned his dissipated face towards the twelve men.

"Gentlemen have you reached your verdict?"

The foreman arose and answered, "We have."

"What is your verdict?"

"We the jury find the accused guilty as charged, but we also put forward a plea for mercy."

Sarah sat immobile. In her very depths she knew this would happen, but now that it had come to pass a hollow weariness consumed her. She had missed Charlie terribly, but she was convinced that both Charlie and Ruth were gone from her forever. She let acceptance of their separation become acceptance of the fact that everything that had befallen her family was punishment from God.

Charlie sensed the tension in the courtroom, and Old Feardy came up to him in waves. He could hardly breathe. Pilchard took the paper from the Clerk and said, "Will the prisoner rise."

The policemen gently urged Charlie to his feet. Pilchard looked at him, and pronounced sentence.

"Charles Ewart you have been found guilty of murder in the first degree by a jury of your peers. A plea for leniency has been added, but for such a heinous crime of killing a fellow human being in a cold and premeditated fashion, the full measure of the law must be brought to bear. Do you have anything to say before sentencing?"

Betty screamed and shouted, "Charlie I love you." Charlie responded by singing a prolonged high-pitched note. Cries of, "Shame! Shame! came from the spectators. The Mounties moved quickly bringing order.

The Court was hushed as His Lordship lifted and placed a small black skullcap with ear lugs on his head. The solemnity of the moment, however, was broken by a spontaneous laugh that was quickly and scornfully hushed by others. It was no doubt a nervous reaction, and a laugh released by Pilchard looking so ridiculous in the curious cap. He ignored the disturbance and continued, "Charles Ewart, I sentence you to death for the murder of Frederick Fenlon. At an appointed time, you shall be taken to a place of execution where you will be hanged by the neck until you are dead. May the Lord have mercy upon your soul."

The tension and silence in the court was almost unbearable. Mark stood up and walked before the judge and said in a strong clear voice, "May the Lord have mercy on *your soul*."

Pilchard briefly met Mark's eyes before he hastily left the courtroom.

Fifty-two

Wittigar's Visitor

That evening Colonel Wittigar, along with Bubble and Squeak, headed back to his large Victorian house on a fashionable street in Charlottetown. Except for the fact that either Bubble or Squeak slept overnight in a tiny room at the back of the house, he lived alone. The Pup had a key to let himself in each morning so that he and the Colonel could have breakfast together and prepare the business of the day.

When they reached the gate, Wittigar held up his hand. The old swing seat on the porch was squeaking rhythmically. The henchmen hid in the shrubbery in front of the porch. The Colonel continued along the pathway, holding his walking stick poised as a weapon. A woman's voice spoke from the shadows.

"Hello, Walter."

He recognized Alicia Bernard's sultry voice with its trace of Quebec. Holding his ground he waited until she stepped out of the shadows.

"What's the matter, Walter? You afraid of me?"

She was wearing a long fur coat that reached almost to her ankles. Stepping back on one foot the coat fell away revealing her leg bare to the thigh.

"How about a drink?"

"Sure," he said, briskly walking past her. "Come inside."

Before going through the door he said to Bubble and Squeak, "You two make yourselves scarce. Just check up on the place periodically, and whoever's on duty tonight slip in quietly through the back door in about three hours time."

Bubble gave a wink of complicity, but the Colonel ignored him and shut the door in his face. Inside, he looked at her hard, then holding out his hand, asked, "Can I take your coat?"

"Not yet, Walter, dear."

He took off his own and motioned her into a large parlour.

"What would you like? Scotch? Gin?" He asked, pouring himself a tumblerful of scotch from a cut-glass decanter.

"Gin."

"Are you here because you've had a change of heart, Alicia, or to cause me trouble?"

She answered him by dropping a shoulder of her fur coat.

"Both. Walter, I'm loyal to one man at a time. I've always found you fascinating. Also, it may interest you to know that I know everything about Freeman's dealings. I need a new boss, now."

The Colonel downed another drink. He stood over her, looking at her with his hooded eyes.

"Show me your credentials."

She lay back on the sofa, letting her coat fall open, revealing she was completely naked. He didn't react but barked at her, "Stand up!"

She did so, slipping her arms out of the sleeves. He looked her up and down, then walked behind her appraising her. She felt his cold hand sliding between her buttocks.

Fighting revulsion, she uttered, "*J'aime ca. Oh, J'aime ca!*"

He spun her around and pushed her back onto the sofa. To her surprise he remained standing, his sallow cheeks flushed.

"What can you do for me?"

"Anything. All you have to do is tell me. What'll be my pay?"
"That depends on how well you perform. Follow me."

She slipped back into the fur coat and followed his straight back up a polished oak staircase while grasping the handle of a knife in her pocket. In his large bedroom, he disappeared into an adjoining bathroom.

"You wait there," he called.

She heard the heavy plunge of water running into a bathtub. Alicia was frightened, but her hate and desire for revenge steeled her. She was determined to play out the game until the opportunity arose to kill him.

To help compose herself she took in his large brass bed. On the wall opposite was a portrait of a genteel looking woman with an engraved brass plate saying, Eliza Wittigar. Alicia assumed it was his mother. The room stank from a mixture of mothballs, perfume and wax. His voice called out, "Leave your coat and come in here."

In panic she wondered if she should run. If she left her coat she would have to abandon her weapon. What if he was going to drown her?

"Do you hear me? Come in here!"

Gulping down her fear, she decided to obey but was determined to fight for her life. She placed her coat over the end of the bed and went in. The place was filled with steam saturated with oily perfume. He was dressed in a maroon, silk dressing gown with black silk piping along its edges. He pointed to the tub.

"Get in. I want to wash Mullaly's stink off you."

Mentally, she offered up a prayer, *"Ah doux Seigneur aide moi."*

He took hold of her wrist, saying, "Don't sit. Stand."

She complied, still praying. He commenced lathering a large sponge and washing her front and back. At last, he made her get out and with surprising tenderness dried her with a large towel.

"Go and sit on the bed, Alicia."

She thanked God she was within reach of the knife again. He joined her, carrying a large black lacquer box with a reproduction of Michelangelo's David on the lid.

"Now here we have a fine box of tricks."

Inside the box was a cover of red velvet, and under it was a neat array of several replicas of penises in wax. Also in their own compartments were four silken ropes neatly folded and tied in hangman's nooses. There were also several bottles of oils.

Mullaly's words came back to her after she complained to him about the Colonel pestering her.

"Wittigar's an old pervert who just likes power. He'd like you better if you were a boy, I bet."

The Colonel took off his gown and stood before her. His huge blue-headed member lay slack over an uneven, elongated scrotum. Across the full width of his belly an old scar ran.

With an alacrity that took her completely by surprise, Wittigar grabbed her wrists and forced her arms back over her head and lay on top of her on the bed, his slack genitalia dangling between her legs. He began licking her face and neck on down her body until he reached her breast. He took her nipple between his teeth and bit hard. She shrieked as a sharp needle of pain seared through her. He held on savagely until she almost fainted. Then standing up, he let out a loud raucous laugh. She sat up, holding herself. Anger took over and she rushed at him, pummelling into him. He laughed harder, grappling with her until he had her on the floor.

Holding her, he hissed through his teeth, "Ease up you little French whore. Now that you're angry, I'll let you tie me up and you can give it back to me."

Realizing his game, she stopped struggling. He got up from her and lay spread-eagled on the bed, shivering in anticipation of what might come.

"Bind me. You can punish me for being a naughty boy and biting your little titty. Then you can use your imagination with my box of tricks. There will be a nice present for you."

Alicia, trembling and burning with pain, realized her opportunity had come. She was ice-cold with hate. She went to the box and lifted up one of the ropes and dangled the hangman's noose in front of him. Wittigar laughed and said, "Poor old Freeman. Eh?"

She slipped the noose over his wrist and tied the other end to the brass bed end, then did the same with his other wrist and ankles.

"Close your eyes, *Cherie*," she said.

She drew the knife out of her coat pocket and held it before his face. It was one of those little curved ones, sharp as a razor, used for cutting twine. The Colonel opened his eyes and saw the knife slowly waving in front of him like a snake about to strike. Alicia eyes glittered. She turned the handle towards him, saying, "Look at the name burned into it, *Freeman*! Now you know whose knife this was."

Seized with terror, he struggled to free his wrists and ankles.

"*Porchon*! You had him killed."

She reached over and pinched his nostrils hard between her finger and thumb. When he opened his mouth to gasp for air, she rammed one of the wax penises into it, forcing it into his throat until he gagged. He writhed, choking. Then climbing on top of him she sat on his thighs, and placing a heel under each armpit, she held the knife against him and said, "I would castrate you, but you're already dead there."

He tried to bounce her off him, but she reached forward and tightly squeezed his testicles. He tried to yell out, but the wax gag and pain immobilized him. His eyes pleaded for mercy.

"Shut up!" she hissed. "Shut up and watch!"

Perspiration glistened on his body and chalk-white face. He tried to look down, straining to see what she was doing.

"This knife of Freeman's has a point like a sharp needle. I am going to place it at the edge of your belly-scar and if you move it will sink in, slow."

Wittigar felt the point of the knife against his scar. He felt it prick at the tissue. He lay deathly still, his temples throbbing violently.

"Why shouldn't I slit you open and spill whatever's in there?"

She took out the wax penis far enough to allow him to speak.

"Alicia, I'll give you money. Right now. As much as you want."

"Where is it?"

She jabbed the dreadful point into the scar a little, drawing blood. He screamed, "I'll tell you! I'll tell you!"

She climbed off. He was gulping for breath. She still held the knife point on his scar. He managed to tell her through sobs and gulps where to find the money. It was hidden in a false panel in the wall of his clothes closet. When she came back she took the pillow from under his head, removed the case and stuffed it full of money. Then leaning over him, she jammed the pillow over his face and lay on it. He threshed wildly, moaning horribly. Suddenly, his right arm and leg went quite and still, his left limbs still threshing. His bowels went slack and the room filled with his stink.

She got off him and removed the pillow. Wittigar's face was scarlet, a vein at his temple stood out like a tiny, wriggling worm, his eyes horrible to see. He dribbled bile. His right side was completely lifeless as if half of him had died. He tried to speak, but only sounds blubbered from him. She realized he had a stroke. She herself was wet with perspiration. Putting the knife back into her pocket she went into the bathroom and doused her face with cold water. When she returned, she said to him, "Now I don't have to kill you, you bastard. I just leave you here in your own shit."

Alicia picked up the pillowcase full of money and left the house and the Colonel weeping the silent tears of the stricken.

Bubble and Squeak were sitting on the veranda swing having a smoke and drinking from a flask. They made to get up, but she said, "Sit still boys. The Colonel is sleeping like a baby. Before I left he told me to tell you if I saw you not to disturb him."

Squeak said, "What 'ya got in the bag, Alicia?"

"A little present for being a good girl."

"You must have had some good time in there, Alicia?" Bubbles quipped.

"He's some man, that Colonel," she said over her shoulder as she disappeared into the darkness.

It was her intention to leave for Montreal immediately and send the Mounties a letter telling all she knew about the rum-running trade and naming all who were involved.

Fifty-three

Parting

On the day Charlie was sentenced, Mark drove Janice, Sarah, Ruth and Betty back out to New Skye. Barely a word was spoken during the journey. When they arrived at the Ewart's, Janice asked Mark to stay with her. She said, "Let's walk over and see Louis."

Dusk had settled and a light frost glittered. In the west there was a mere glimmer of the remaining day.

"You know I'm leaving as soon as possible," she said. "What about us?"

For days now he had been trying to come to grips with the thought of her leaving. Yet he knew he couldn't plan a future with her. Mollie's death was just too fresh; and though he felt no disloyalty to Mollie's memory for having made love to Janice, he was not ready to make a commitment. Yet, he did not want Janice to leave. His mother had talked to him about her one evening.

"She's a wonderful woman, Mark. You know she's in love with you, don't you?"

"Yes Mother and I am very attached to her in a way I never believed I would be to anyone again."

"Are you in love with her, Mark?"

"My feelings tell me I am, but my mind resists the idea."

"Have you told her that?"

"Not in so many words."

"Then my dear, Mark, do so in plain words. It's my guess she will tell you to go with your mind. That's what I'd advise you to do."

Mark sat silent for a while.

"There's something else, Mother. I am thinking seriously of leaving the church."

"What will you do?"

"I'm not sure. But what concerns me most is what are you going to do?"

"Well, Mark let me tell you, I'd like to stay here. In fact, I will stay here and work with Louis."

"No doubt you've thought it all through, but some people might give you a rough time."

"Yes, Mark, I've thought it through. I know I've always got you. Now kiss me and go and see Janice."

Standing with Janice in his arms and feeling the warmth of her against him, he had to answer her question. He decided to take his mother's advice.

"Janice, all my feelings tell me to hold on to you. I hate the thought of your leaving, and I don't want to let you go...."

"But your Mollie's holdin' you back, right? I understand, darlin'. It's just too soon." She held him tighter and whispered, "But I hope to God we don't lose touch."

They kissed then walked a little further. He told her about wanting to leave the church and that he was thinking of going back to Montreal or abroad to study.

"One of the stumbling blocks is mother, but she wants to stay here and work with Louis for at least a year. But where would she live, how would she manage? She has a very small pension."

Janice smiled.

"I wouldn't be surprised she has all that worked out. Anyway, I'll hire her as a partner to Louis. Mark, have you thought of Harvard, or some place like it. I'll be right there in Boston."

"I'll think about it very hard, Janice," he said, kissing her again.

Louis stepped out of the dusk and greeted them.

"Janice, the Mounties brought these to the other house." He gave her the hand mirror with Sarah's note tied to it. Janice's heart tripped when she saw it. She wouldn't touch it.

"Take it down and put it in, too. I want you to do it tonight, Louis."

"Everything's set."

Mark was puzzled but asked no questions.

"Mark, Louis is goin' to do somethin' for me. Will you stay with me?"

"Yes, Janice."

She turned to Louis. "It's dark now. May as well start."

They went back down to the Fenlon house. Louis went inside then came out after a few minutes. As they stood against the large tree across from the house, Janice shivered. Mark held her closer. She said, "I'm not cold. Something just walked over my grave."

At that moment flames lit the upstairs and were soon licking their way along the roof. Louis went inside briefly and came out again. Glass splintered and Mark could see the upstairs crashing into the room below followed by wood cracking and more splintering glass. A shower of sparks spiralled into the air as more flaming structure dropped inward from above. Something exploded heightening the intensity of the flames. Mark realized Janice was trying to purify herself. He said to her, "Why don't we walk away, now?"

"No. I want to stay 'til there's nothin' left but ashes. Nothin'."

Her eyes reflected the flames consuming the house. The fury of the fire seemed to match the fury of her anger creating a sense of equilibrium.

Louis strode over to Mark and Janice and said, "Now any minute that roof's gonna cave in, then the walls. I've rigged her like that—everything right into the cellar. You'd better go back a bit farther just in case."

They moved further away. The roof moaned as its spine twisted and cracked. Louis, silhouetted by the flames, pushed against a gable with a long pole. Another crack resounded as another beam broke. The gable collapsed and Louis ran backwards out of the avalanching sparks. He charged and attacked each flaming wall with his pole until the entire house was transformed to a bizarre assortment of flaming beams piled and leaning against each other in a pyramid of twists and angles. He then pumped water over the inferno sending up great hissing clouds of steam, reducing the brightness of the flames to a glow. Janice called him over.

"How much longer will it take 'til it's ashes?"

"'Til mornin'. I'm goin' to stay here the rest of the night. Why don't you go an' wait at the Logan place an' come back in the mornin'? Once the neighbours know there's a fire they'll be down here in droves. "

"Will you stay with me, Mark?"

"Yes. But let's look in on Sarah and Ruth."

Sarah lay in a drunken sleep with Ruth beside her, but Betty was awake sitting at the kitchen table. Mark and Janice brought the smell of smoke into the house with them.

"Thank you Janice for everything you done for us. I'll be leavin' the Island tomorrow. I want to be as far away as possible when Charlie goes. Will you be with him when it happens Reverend Kerr?"

"Yes, Betty, I won't leave him."

"Oh, thank God for that. Why did they have to do this to him? I love him an' I would have looked after him the rest of his life."

She wept.

"Betty, always remember, because of you, Charlie had a warmth and love he would never have known," Mark said.

Janice urged her to her feet

"Come Betty dear, I'll go upstairs with you."

She led her up and lay down on the bed cradling her and gently stroking her hair. In the dark of the room, Betty told her about the baby. Somehow the sharing of her secret and Janice's closeness lifted some of the weight off her heart. Janice whispered, "Betty, I'll go now. I want to be alone with Mark."

Janice and Mark lay together for the last time. They spoke little, but held each other as if trying to infuse each other with the love they shared so that it wouldn't leave after they parted. In the morning they went back to the burnt house.

She walked around the cellar now filled with charred remains, her face as ashen as the debris. Her foot kicked a round metal object. Curious, she picked it up and saw a copper armband burned blue. There was engraving on it filled in with ash. She spat on it and rubbed it clean with her finger until the inscription *Lord Vulcan, Eater of Fire* was legible. She pondered a moment, then tossed it into the scorched and blackened remains of what was once her home.

Fifty-four

Farewell

    Charlie was scheduled to hang at 3:00 AM. All week long the carpenters constructed a gallows, their sawing and hammering reverberating off the tall yard-walls of the jail. What followed then was a series of dreadful mechanical clanks as an engineer and his helper dropped bags filled with sand tied to a rope through a trapdoor. Athol was distressed.
    During a tea break he said, "You'd think you fellas would have all this worked out. It's not right him havin' to listen to that damned sound all day long. How'd you think he feels listenin' to that?"
    The engineer before answering stirred sugar and milk into his tea.
    "It's different every time, Athol. If we don't get it exact, it's the difference between him being choked or snapped."
    "What do you mean?"
    "If the weight and the length of the drop isn't exact you might have to do it twice. But if it's right, once is enough. It snaps his neck on the first go."
    Athol walked over to the window and looked out at the gallows. He could see the sand bag hanging as still as a builder's plumb line under the staging.
    "The poor little bugger shouldn't be goin' through this at all."

"Not our business. C'mon we'll finish up an' get the hell out of this place," the engineer said to his helper. They downed their tea and left.

Although the inevitability of death permeated the little jail and lay oppressively on the hearts of everyone, Charlie seemed oblivious. He wanted to take his fern out for a walk around the yard and got quite upset when Athol wouldn't let him.

"Not now, Charlie, not now, son. There's things goin' on out there. Later you can do it."

Mark came in about midnight. Around the tall walls crowds were gathering. All week long they, too, had heard the carpenters banging the gallows together; and though they couldn't see anything, they felt a strange inner excitement at being that close to it.

In Athol's office, several officials, including the doctor, sat glumly making small talk. Athol said to Mark in a distraught voice, "I'll take you right down to him, Reverend."

As they passed by a small room in the corridor, Mark noticed a tall dark man sitting smoking a pipe.

"You know you're not to be seen," Athol said to him. "You keep that door closed 'til we come for you."

He quickly pulled the door shut, and whispered to Mark, "I wouldn't want his job."

Charlie was humming quietly. Mark sat opposite him. After a moment, he said, "Your fern looks great, Charlie. You really looked after her. Would you say a prayer with me? I'll start by thanking God for something and then it is your turn to say thanks for a blessing."

Charlie nodded. Mark began, "I thank God for my friend, Charlie, who is such a good man."

Charlie hesitated a moment, then looking at his fern, said, "Thank God for the Granny Fern an' Betty."

"Yes thank God for Betty, and for Sarah, Ruthie and Janice who love you very much, Charlie."

They continued through a litany of "thanks" until they heard muffled words and footsteps coming down the corridor.

Mark ended softly with, "Thank God for your baby, Charlie, that Betty's going to have."

Charlie looked intently into Mark's face. And for a moment it seemed a smile of understanding illuminated his eyes. There was a knock at the door.

The sky was clear and heavy with stars and the first frosts glittered on the hardening earth. Hardly a sound was heard from the dark crowd around the wall as if it were a sacrilege to speak above a whisper. Somewhere inside the wall the sound of a door opened. The crowd, drawn into oneness by the intensity of their listening, became even more silent. Then the sweetness of Charlie's singing rose and all faces looked up.

Jesus, lover of my soul
let me to thy bosom fly,

The belief had been spread that it was twelve steps from the door to the gallows, and then twelve steps up to the platform. Some silently counted as if tracing Charlie's last walk; while others, recognizing the old hymn, sang softly along with him.

Hide me, O my Saviour, hide,
'til the storm of life has passed....

The singing became strangely muffled, barely audible and the word was passed round: "They've put the hood over his head."

More joined in with the singing,

Cover my defenceless head
with the shadow of thy wing....

Other's hushed them. The singing inside had definitely stopped. The strained silence was broken by a mechanical clunk echoing off the tall walls. After a moment all quietly dispersed.

Mark drove back to New Skye with Charlie's fern beside him. He was numb and cold. As daylight increased it filtered through banks of soft clouds gathering in the east. When he arrived he went directly into the church. Memories filled the emptiness of its little sanctuary—Mollie earnestly playing the organ, Charlie's rich voice and the assortment of neighbours in their Sunday best crowding the pews.

He turned to the windows of Jesus. He looked at Jesus walking on the sea holding out his hand to a drowning and frightened Peter whose face was almost covered by the waves. He saw his father's face in Peter's. Poor father, you couldn't reach out to my mother and those who loved you, and you sank. So many faces have gone under those formidable waves. And there was Jesus carrying the lost lamb home on his shoulder. Below were written the words, *Raise the fallen, cheer the faint, heal the sick, and lead the blind.* He thought of Charlie and placed the Granny fern on the organ.

As Mark left the little church, the first flurries of snow were swirling, reducing the distant spruce trees to black twists and smudges. He thought of Mollie and the baby and that terrible journey of hopelessness he had traveled. He thought of Janice and wished she were still here. The falling snow was now blanketing the fields and graves in the cemetery turning the red earth to white. He turned up his collar and walked into the thick flakes, dreading the onset of winter.

THE END

About the Author

Tom Crothers received a Prince Edward Island Heritage Award for *Out of Thin Air: a history of early radio*, which he co-authored with Betty Large. His short story, *The Eleventh*, was placed in the winning circle of *The Edmonton Journal Short Story Competition*. He has published in various Canadian Magazines. *Sandfires* is his second novel. Tom was born in Ireland and educated mainly in Canada. Ireland and Canada share a large part of Tom's psyche and his work tends to reflect this. He lives in Toronto.